THE

SCARLET CRUISER

OR,

THE WOLF OF THE WAVE.

A MATCHLESS ROMANCE OF MARITIME LIFE.

BY THE AUTHOR OF

" The Crimson Corsair; or, the Queen of the Pirates," " The Sultan
of the Sea; or the Buccaneers of the Blue," etc., etc.

PROFUSELY ILLUSTRATED.

"Sail on, oh, SCARLET CRUISER! sink or keep
Thy independence on the fathomless deep!
Bays, gulfs and oceans, all shall be,
Till the foe perishes, a field for thee!"
Wordsworth.

LONDON:
WILLIAMS & Co., 11, BLACK HORSE COURT, FLEET STREET.
NEW YORK:
WILLIAMS & SON, NASSAU STREET.

THE SCARLET CRUISER;
OR,
THE WOLF OF THE WAVE.

THE NIGHT ATTACK.

CHAPTER I.

THE TRADER'S PERILS—DEALING DESTRUCTION—THE AVALANCHE OF DEATH—LEAPING FOR LIFE—THE LAST MAN.

OUR story opens in a small romantic bay, on the south side of Cuba, about forty leagues from Havana, land-locked by curving shores and numerous rocky islets, that extend nearly across the mouth.

The bay at its broadest part is not more than half a league, and in length about a league.

It is a secluded spot.

No town is seen upon its shores, and only here and there a ruined hut, put up in the season by some hunter.

The shores are wild and wooded.

Not a breath stirs the air.

The sea is as calm and shining as a looking-glass.

1

On the beach, in the shade, were some twenty men.

They were stripped to the waist, and busy, under the eyes of a couple of officers, in scraping turtle shells and packing fruit and bark.

They were the crew of that round-headed, high-sterned, short masted brig, anchored in the bay.

The air was so clear that you could read her name from the shore.

Under her cabin windows, cut out in old-fashioned letters was—

"THE HONEST TRADER. London."

* * * * * *

About an hour's easy sail from this bay, in a creek or small stream that entered the land to some distance, were two other vessels.

Their yards had been set a-peak, so that they were close to the wooded shore, the braces and lifts being almost entangled with the boughs.

One of the vessels was a schooner.

She was a Spaniard by build as by her yellow flag, sprinkled with castles, lions, and lilies.

The other was a far finer and larger craft.

She was a brig, but her length abaft the main-mast permitted a third mast to be shipped, when a trade wind required it.

She had no cabins on deck, nor any house except a mere box, for the caboose—all was flush.

Her greatest breadth of beam was abreast the foremast, and there she spread out about thirty feet, perhaps more.

Forward, she lessened until her cut-water was as sharp as a woodman's wedge at the water's edge, though her bow flared out above until it spread spoon-like at the wale, insuring her the quality of a dry boat in a heavy sea.

Aft, her lines narrowed, until at her stern she was as sharp as she was forward.

She lay low in the water, shewing depth, and, of course, stability.

She only had the white French flag at her gaff, and a pennon trailing from her mainmast ball, with the name—

"THE NEEDLE (*Aiguille*)."

That suited her fine lines and thin yet strong appearance.

The shores of the creek smelt most foully with the cargo which both the vessels were taking aboard, as fast as their respective crews could bear them.

These were hides, salted down and sun dried, from horses' to smaller skins, as of iguanos and water rats.

Some log-wood, mahogany and dye-wood, in blocks and bundles, were also going off to the ships.

The captains were seated on a log together, in a hut, overlooking the workmen.

"Senor Dicque Chiquitos," said one of them. "I'm not the man to stay here for five hours more."

"The man he was" was one with a bullet-shaped head; a pair of small gray eyes, so keen and sharp in their expression that they seemed to look right into and through the object of their gaze.

His form was tall and lean.

Yet he was muscular—all bone and muscle—no flesh—no fat.

His features were prominent; his nose, long and of the hawk-bill order.

Heavy, bushy eyebrows, and a long chin, as well as high cheekbones, made his face "a picture in its way."

One word will reveal his character.

His ship the "Needle," had been the dispatch boat from Brest to the Mediterranean ports.

He was only lieutenant then, this Loys de Goupille, but he waited till his superiors and a good part of the crew had landed for a week's diversion on the Island of Corsica.

That night, he persuaded the watch, they slipped cables, and, short handed as they were, ran past Gibraltar and out to sea.

He gave her a new name and a coat of paint, and boldly went into the West Indian trade.

"Why, Senor Loys," said the Spaniard, "on account of the Indians?"

"Yes."

The Frenchman darted a searching look at the other.

"We have almost everything under hatches," said he, "and the Indians promise to bring more hides in a few days."

"But I shan't wait for them, and I don't like to go to St. Thomas unless I have my schooner full to the rim of the hatchway."

"My idea, Senor Dicque!" cried the Frenchman, taking the other by the hand. "What do you say if we should find enough and plenty to spare of picked hides, well baled, woods and fruit——"

"Ah! on shore?"

"Better—in a vessel, alongside which we may lay, and dip out of her at ease."

"Ah!"

The Spaniard was thinking.

"It is piracy," said he, rather faintly. "It's a hanging matter——"

"Not to touch an enemy's ship."

"Aha!"

"It is an Englishman."

"Spain is not at war with Great Britain."

"That may be. But didn't your own governor of Cuba say that the trade should repel at all hazards the encroachments of outsiders? I can show you the order."

The Spaniard suffered himself to be overruled.

"I fear the Englishman is well armed," said the Frenchman, as he and the other captain went down to their boats.

The other commander was pretty sure of that.

His colleague would not have given him any part in the action, unless he had feared that he would have come out at the wrong end if he tried it single handed.

The necessary commands were speedily issued.

Before half on hour, the two vessels were slowly warped down the creek.

As soon as the open was reached, they trimmed ship, and kept just off the shore, clearing for action as they went.

* * * * *

In the meantime this is what had happened to the Englishman.

Soon after the schooner and her companion had got under sail, a party of the "Honest Trader's" crew, who had been hunting, came down from the highlands.

"Well, Bill Bowse," cried one of them, sitting down on a bale of skins, and tossing a bunch of gay-coloured birds upon the sand, "how're you getting along?"

"Have the stuff stowed away by to-morrow night, Derrick," responded a short, thick set sailor, who was knotting the cords round a roll of fragrant bark.

"Where's Frank Rogers?"

"How should we know, Derrick. The young chap went away with you."

Derrick, a Hollander, instantly jumped up on his feet.

"Mein Gott, hasn't he come afore this. Why we lost him on the mountains, and thought he must have runned down to you. Ain't that so, Ned and Tom?"

"Of course."

"We ain't seen anything of him," replied Bill Bowse.

"We don't want to lose that boy," said the Dutchman.

"In course not," cried Bowse, sharpening his knife. "There's good stuff in him—he can eat biscuit as hard as an iron-bound block, that shows what a admiral he'll make, if he lives long enough!"

This foundation for prophecy completely silenced the doubts any of the rest might have had, either the loaders or the hunters.

"There's only one thing I can do," said the Hollander.

"Do it, then," rejoined Bowse, giving a kick to the bale that tumbled it down the sand. "Especially if it concern the lad."

Derrick proceeded slowly towards a shelter of green boughs, which protected the master of the "Honest Trader" from a sun a little too broiling for a native of Chelsea.

"Captain Beckets," said he, "I report my ten hunters all safe; you can see the birdses and beastesses down yonder."

"I saw 'em as ye came," returned the old man, smoking calmly.

"Only, captain," went on the Dutchman slowly, "that boy that's always laughing—Frank—he's not come yet, hein?"

The captain rose to his feet quickly.

"Look'ee here, you blundering, thick-headed, Dutch son of a canal maker's tribe," he broke out wildly, "do you go for to say that you've let the red skinned thieves snatch up that young chap in the woods!"

The Hollander, his eyes wide open, said never a word.

"The Lord forgive you!" went on the master. "Why that lad's a treasure. He can reckon up four figgers afore I can say two and one is five! Bless your soul, I'll choke you with your own long ears, you beggar! I love that lad better'n my own son, if I had one!"

"Thank you, captain!" cried a voice lightly.

The new comer, in the same trousers and woolen shirt as the rest, with a red handkerchief twisted in his long black hair, looked handsome as a statue given life.

He was of good height and well made, slender, yet with hard muscles and steel-like tendons.

Already, with three years of the sea-farer's life, he could lead the most expert in a race from bowsprit tip to stern ports, from mast head to the slime in the lowermost hold.

Better than all, he was a general favourite with everyone on board.

It was not only from fear of what the captain would do in angry grief that made Derrick greet the youth warmly.

"I thought you was lost mit the woods," said he, enfolding the lad's hand in his large one. "I is glad you was come here, Frank."

"My fault, my fault, Captain Beckets," cried Frank. "I left the party out of a freak, but it led me to make an important discovery——"

"Gold?" exclaimed the Dutchman. "Mein Gott, hear me! I always say that that boy would find a gold mine!"

And he slapped his thigh.

"An Indian village, more like," said the captain, not so enthusiastic. "You young rascal, your freak will bring fifty of the red devils to go shooting arrows at us. I've had a taste of such things."

"No, captain."

The youth lowered his tone.

"You know we thought the coast line free for leagues? Well, I saw from above there——"

He pointed to a rocky peak, high over the woodland.

"I saw, not one, but two vessels, following the land, inside the reefs and sure to pass our bay——"

"The devil you did!"

"They slipped out of some land-locked bay or mouth of a river, for if I had been a minute sooner, I would not have spied them at all."

"What are they?"

"One's European—French or Italian in rig—she's as low in the water as a water-logged tree-trunk. That's the brig. T'other's latteen—two-master."

"No flag?"

"Not a show."

"Well, I don't see. There's no war. Only the Indians here, is all I'm afeard of."

"Ah—but, captain," said the young man, earnestly, "don't you remember the warning that the 'Gosnold' gave us when we were twenty days out? She was fresh from here, and said that eyes must be skinned or bodies would!—as the traders called us all interlopers."

"Come now, lad, what would you do?"

Frank looked at the speaker firmly, then glanced at the vessel in the bay.

"I'd hurry everything on board, and clear ship for a fight and a run, I'd never let a picaroon of a Spaniard drag me to St. Thomas or Havana in irons!"

The captain smiled.

"Good boy," said he. "We'll see."

He picked up a broad plaintain leaf in which his tobacco was kept, rolled it up, stuffed all into his pouch, and, still smoking, strolled down on the beaph.

"Anderson!"

That was the first mate.

"Send a sharp-eyed fellow to the top of the rock at the point, and let him have a pistol to fire, if he sees anything on the water."

"Ay, ay! Something new?"

"Yes. Couple of Don Somebodies coming to interfere with an honest trader. I'll teach 'em. I think we've plenty of powder aboard, eh?"

"Oh yes, captain. Enough to scorch them scoundrels' whiskers, never you fear!"

Presently, the last of the goods were embarked, and the boats, towing rafts, made for the brig.

A good deal had to be done.

While part worked the tackle in lading, the rest were rapidly bending on sail, and seeing to rigging, all of which had been neglected during the late busy time they had had.

Then a kedge was taken to the mouth of the bay, so that the brig could be warped up there and lie under the high cliffs on that side.

If the vessels seen by Frank Rogers intended no mischief, they would go by the bay, not seeing the Englishman.

Otherwise, time would show what would happen.

The crew had just gone down to supper.

"Crack!" went a pistol shot.

It was their lookout on the cliff.

A boat was instantly shoved off with a couple of men, to bring him aboard.

His report was to the effect that the two strangers had reduced sail, and lowered each a large boat, filled with armed men, which latter were pulling away towards the inlet.

Not much doubt now.

Frank Rogers had his meals in the cabin, on account of the partiality—affection we may say —that Captain Beckets had for him.

"What do you say to that, my lad?" said the captain. "They are going to attack us."

"Ah! but easy," replied the youth. "Only two boats. That shows that we have a couple of hours yet. They are going to try and surprise us in the dark."

"I shouldn't wonder," exclaimed the master. "Yes, I'll bet a guinea that you are right, Frank."

"I think so too, sir," said Anderson. "They must be loggerheads if they think forty or fifty long-legged, grinning-headed, outlandish pig and orange eaters can take the 'Honest Trader' in daylight. I'm going to finish supper at ease."

And so they did without an interruption.

Darkness came on.

A slight haze all over the land, and seemingly over the sky, caused it to be thicker than is usual in those latitudes.

All seemed to have been subdued by sleep on board the trader.

The light that glimmered from her after windows appeared to burn dreamily.

Not a sound, as she slowly and gently moved up and down on the ripple sweeping into the bay.

At this moment, a man might have been seen at the western outlet, hidden among the trees, and cautiously examining the lay of the English brig.

Having well studied her for half an hour, and seen the last few lights go out in the cabin, he sent up a cry of no great loudness, in imitation of a gull.

Soon after, one of two large boats came in shore, and the man ran up along an oar and leaped into her.

"Well, Mauregard?" said the man in her sternsheets.

"It is well, Sir Captain de Goupille," returned the French sailor. "The lights have all gone out aboard her, and I don't think the watch is kept a bit too strict."

"Very well. Now, my lads," said the Frenchman to his crew, "it is like cutting a cheese— a steady but an easy hand will do it clean. You understand. The cargo to myself and my fellow-labourer. The sailors' goods and all other odds and ends to be diced for?"

"Very well, sir captain," chorussed they.

Goupille made a sign to the Spaniard in the other boat, and that fell into his wake.

All precautions had been taken, such as muffled thole-pins, nothing white or bright about the men's dress, arms covered with a boat cloth, and the lantern that each launch carried shoved under the sternseat, and the slide well on.

Slowly creeping, like a centipede in deadliness of pace and purpose.

The "Needle's" boat rounded the point.

She kept well in under the deep shadow of the bank.

The Spaniard immediately followed.

The very waves that slapped up against the bows seemed to know their bloodthirsty intent.

Along the circle of the bay not a rustle.

The boats' crew held their breath.

Loys de Goupille made a sign.

The Spaniard sheered off into the open.

Thus the boats contemplated taking the doomed craft between them.

Slower, and still more slow, they neared the brig.

The tide had changed, and the "Honest Trader" after leisurely swinging round, was pointing her figure-head of a "gentleman of the day," out of the harbour.

Oars were noiselessly shipped on each of the sea maranders' launches.

Under but slight way, carried by the tide, they parted as if the bow had divided them with its wedge, and glided along, one each side, almost scraping the sides of the doomed ship.

There had not been the least stir on the ship. Even the watch, if any had been set, must have gone to rest.

Loys started up in the stern of his boat.

The men had shipped oars some time since.

All were busy.

One of them was standing, a coil of rope in hand, to throw it up through the main mast chains.

Another distributed the weapons carefully.

The Frenchman waved his hand.

The stroke oarsman had a boat-hook ready.

He drove the iron deep in the planks beside him.

The noise seemed very loud, in the extreme silence.

From the other side of the brig a similar piercing crash resounded.

Loys brandished his sword.

"Up with ye all!" shouted he.

They raised a loud yell.

But before they could leap up to grasp the gunnel low in the waist of the "Honest Trader," they were bound as by a spell.

Like magic, the brig had started from profoundest death into life the most active.

On either side, from heel of the bowsprit to taffrail, seemed to be lined with either man, lantern or weapon.

Where a fierce face did not frown defiance, a cutlass flashed.

Where a candle-end did not gleam, the reflection did, upon barrel of musket or pistol, or head of pike.

And loud as a trumpet, they heard the answering cry, to their too hastily uttered cheer of triumph.

It was the boy Frank who was directly above the Frenchman's launch.

He took the words out of the mouth of his superior, the first mate.

"Stand by all!" cried he, in his sharp voice. "All ready! Let go!"

One of the heaviest trunks of logwood, as

weighty as a cannon, had been lifted up and leaned upon the bulwark.

At this order, a dozen pair of hands raised its inner end, while as many shoulders impelled it.

Thus tilted up, the great mass shot over the wooden wall, and descended, like a bolt from the sky, perpendicularly on the large shallop.

There was no time to avoid it.

The five men that its massive head struck, were felled upon the planks.

It had followed fast, and drove their crushed bodies through the jagged gap that it made.

The victims, still alive, still groaning, were so wedged in the opening by the giving of the broken planks that their mangled forms prevented the enormous trunk piercing altogether the bottom of the boat.

So, the upper end fell forward upon another man, and made the bow sink deeply with this second shock.

The water rushed in furiously.

The shattered launch rocked so much after the blow that the men could hardly retain their feet.

As, in their panic they grasped for support at one another or at the brig's side, a second cry from the young voice that had been a death-signal before, pealed forth—

"Steel and shot, give it 'em all!"

A dozen muskets and pistols spat fire downwards.

That awoke the Frenchmen from their stupor.

Those that had firearms, pulled trigger at the range of faces above them.

The rest sprang upwards, holding on by the slightest projection from the side of the trader.

It was a marvel to see them clinging to a bolt head, a scupper hole, a two-inch ridge line, and, a few, the main-chains themselves.

Steel crossed steel, here and there.

Loys de Goupille, furious as a tiger, had leaped upon the log. He had dropped his sword, and wielded a long boat-hook desperately.

He aimed one furious blow at Anderson, but only tore away a splinter of the gunnel.

A second time, the cursed spike entered a seaman's shoulder.

His howls redoubled Loys' fiendish exertions.

Bearing all his weight on the shaft, he actually dragged the sailor over the bulwark and down on the sinking pinnace.

There he was quickly run through.

The French cheered at this exploit.

Loys let go his hook, picked up a cutlass, and, seeing that he was almost alone in the boat, and that it was nearly level with the blood-stained water, hastened to follow his men in the escalade.

The crew of the "Honest Trader," man and boy, told up to thirty-five.

Each of the launches had held about thirty men.

Their first losses (the Spaniard on the starboard having fared no better than his comrade) left the enemy stronger still in numbers.

The invaders, still kept out of the ship, were nearly all on the bulwark.

If it had not been for the difficulty of their foot hold requiring them to give one hand for support, they might have won the affray long before.

Loys, and half a dozen who were in the main-chains, were thrusting through the rattlins above at their antagonists.

The next party to them were four or five, and they had got footing on the ridge-line that ran round the brig, and, hatchet in hand, were chopping open a port.

Every now and then, an assailant, bleeding and burnt, would make a superhuman effort and mount the gunnel.

But while he stood there, recovering his energies ere he leaped down within, a trio of bullets, fired point blank, or a couple of blades, would pierce him, and the next moment the body would break its back on the fragments of the submerged and wrecked shallop.

Such failures as these maddened the stormers, whose position was indeed precarious, now that retreat was out of the question.

"My sons!" cried Loys.

There was a species of pause among his followers.

"All as one," said he in French. "We live and win, or die!"

His companions repeated the battle-cry enthusiastically.

Moved by the same impulse, they swarmed up.

Each of the little band slew his man or engaged him in deadly combat.

But the rest bid fair to be on the deck at last.

We have said, three or four of those outside, unable to climb up, were battering in a port.

They suddenly saw it open full width.

With his own hands, Frank Rogers had cleared away the aftermost of two carronades amidships.

The smoke had added to the darkness.

By a pistol-flash, or gleaming of steel, one alone knew where to strike.

Frank had supposed that the attack on the porthole signified something important.

So he prepared the gun, and drew the port-bolt quickly.

The men jammed themselves into the square orifice.

They could not see before them as they struggled through.

No resistance was offered, and they expected to be the first on the English deck.

The delay had been no fault of Frank's.

He bore all his weight on the gun, and its breech slowly rose, until the depressed muzzle gaped at the square before it.

Then the boy snatched a pistol from the belt of the seaman next him, felt that there was powder in the pan, and clapped it to the touch-hole.

The report shook the deck, and made all hearts leap around it.

Two men were in the port-hole, and the heads of a second pair entered.

The close discharge of the carronade blew all four to scorched atoms, which rained down upon the wave, too ensanguined to be much dyed by a new shower of blood.

A scream of horror burst from the lips of those who beheld the effects of the shot.

The trader's men were compelled to fall back as far as the hatchway, at the impetus which that sweeping away of existences had given the foe.

The hand to hand contest now began.

No more of muskets or pistols, unless as clubs or bludgeons.

The deck smoked with wadding and blood.

It was strewn with bodies transfixed with pikes, or sword-blades, or writhing in the agonies of wounds.

Above the level of the yard, all was still where the sulphur vapour circled.

From the main top to deck, the whole strife raged.

All were there, and all were so active and so full of change, that it seemed, at times, that the very dead were lifting their shattered hands to claw the fighters that trampled over them.

Loys and a handful made a desperate effort.

Overthrowing all who were in their way, they bounded over the hatch and came to the succour of their fellow-pirates, the Spaniards

This success compelled the crew of the "Honest Trader" to rally.

By mutual agreement, both parties permitted a breathing-spell.

Captain Beckets was wounded in the left arm and side, but was not dead, as the starboard party had fancied on seeing him struck down.

Each, in fear that the other band would have time to clear away a carronade, soon broke the truce, and renewed the struggle.

In the height of it, Loys de Goupille, who had taken a pike now for his weapon, disarmed Beckets, and levelled his spear at his heart, as the old man lay on the deck.

Frank rushed forward.

He was too late.

He saw the savage deliberately accomplish his cruel deed, despite the attempt he made to push aside the pike.

Wounded in several places, helpless, the captain might surely have been spared.

But the Frenchman ran him through remorselessly.

Frank gave a scream of grief.

The old man had been like a father to him.

He was weaponless, and Loys laughed at him, as he left the pike pinning the corpse to the plank, and strode to where he was needed.

Frank was about to rush wildly after him.

He paused.

A sudden fancy checked him.

He rapidly surveyed the scene.

His friends were overmastered.

He picked up two hatchets from under a dead man, and thrust each into his belt.

Unseen, his slender form glided out of the ferocious groups, and then flew swiftly up the ladder till the main cross-trees were reached.

Such was the trampling below, and the shocks of meeting, amid the columns of smoke that mounted to him, that he was confident he would not be heard.

With the hatchet, he cut away right and left.

He seemed to have gone mad, and to be venting a lunatic's rage on the rigging.

But there was meaning in his every act.

He was severing the lifts, the braces, and all appendages to the main-top-sail-yard.

Then he encircled the mast with his legs, crossed them, and, thus seated, hammered away with the hatchets at the hoop ringing the mast and securing the yard.

When he had blunted the edge of the first axe, he flung it down dexterously into the thickest of the enemy.

The long boom, acted on by what air there was stirring, began to sway ominously, almost unfettered as it was.

Frank smiled.

He gave another cut.

The iron, tough and stubborn, began to crack hesitatingly.

The youth could hear the fibres parting.

"No pity for you beggars that don't understand English," muttered he.

He dealt another stroke.

Then, with all his power, he lifted his voice in a warning hallo—

"Friends to the trader!" he cried, "to the forecastle, for your lives!"

His young voice was audible amid the uproar, as the whistle of the wind in a thunderstorm.

Instinctively, Anderson, Bill Bowse, Derrick, and others, flung their streaming and dented weapons into the faces of the foe, and fell back to the fore.

The others, suspecting some trick, ignorant of the language in which the caution had been conveyed, recoiled in the opposite direction.

They receded to their doom!

Stepped into an awful grave!

Ere one could look, either to one side or above, there was one sharp, clear chink of steel on iron.

The axe had severed the last inch of metal.

Frank, seizing the cross-trees convulsively, looked down, awe-stricken by the missile he had launched.

The long spar fell nearly directly down, as soon as the hoop had snapped.

It stretched across the deck.

It landed on the group of Spanish and French, like the rod of a giant, and laid a dozen prostrate and broken in bone.

On touching the deck with such tremendous force, it bounded up a few feet, shivered from ring-bolt to ring-bolt, snapped in two at the centre, and both pieces returned to add more to those it had slain.

The massive timber ground the corpses on the deck, ere settling into quiescence, as if the blood it had made outpour had congealed and glued it into a rest from slaughter.

Of the remaining pirates this weapon of destruction had left three.

One was Captain Loys.

The instant that he—like the others spellbound—could recover, and understand, he took the only possible path for safety.

He bent himself and stole under some of the smoke, along between the cabin-house and the larboard bulwark, and reached the tiller.

One of his men followed him mechanically.

The last one, a Spaniard, was shot down as the "Honest Trader's" crew, having shaken off their consternation at their deliverance, pressed on to see if the spar had left a single soul.

Frank was on the point of descending.

But he caught a glimpse of the two survivors, who were hauling in the slack of the painter to the boat towed behind the trader.

"Not one shall escape!" he muttered.

Quick as thought, he dropped from where he was upon the main yard.

He ran out along it in an instant, and slid down the lee-brace, like a flash of lightning.

Like a bolt from a gun, he fell between the two Frenchmen.

Before either could lift a hand, he had sheathed the knife he had already drawn in the side of the man nearest him.

It was not Loys.

The stricken sailor threw up his arms, turned round, and fell over the taffrail into the water.

Captain Loys knew that if he delayed, even to win victory over the youthful form beside him, he would be lost.

He leaped overboard, so quickly following the dying sailor's plunge that the splash seemed as one.

Frank hesitated not an instant.

He plunged into the blood-stained sea.

As he dived, the first two came up.

Not pausing to dash the water and his long hair from his eyes, the youth struck out for one of them who was battling frantically with the waves.

He fairly leaped at the swimmer, and was as tightly and eagerly clutched by him.

For a space, the two made the water seethe with their repeated turns and twists.

At length, the younger ran one hand inside the other's arms, and got his enemy by the throat.

He put all his might into the pressure.

He felt the strong man thrill in the last throes of an agonising death.

He remembered the old captain receiving the spear thrust, his mute appeal for mercy, and he was as pitiless.

* * * * * * *

A few minutes afterwards, Bill Bowse and Derrick, in the boat, picked up the nearly drowned couple.

They held a lantern up to their faces.

"Oh! it was the boy!" cried the Dutchman. "Mein Gott! I was going to run both of them through mit der boathook."

Frank soon recovered, although nearly suffocated by a dash of brandy that Anderson had poured into his mouth.

The face of his late antagonist, with eyeballs glaring, cold, gleaming with the wet, looked at the youth like a spectre.

"A thousand flames!" exclaimed Frank, staring into the face of the corpse, "this is not the captain!"

It was the sailor that he had stabbed.

He had been strangling a dying man.

Loys de Goupille owed his life to the blindness of revenge.

"Hell and furies!" continued the youth, "whenever I meet that fiend again, and meet him again I will, I'll terribly avenge the old man's death. And as long as a drop of blood be left in these veins I will track him to his doom!"

CHAPTER II.

THE FURY OF CAPTAIN LOYS—THE GUARDA COSTA— THE THREE AGAINST ONE—THE PIERCING OF THE "NEEDLE" — THE CHRISTENING OF THE CRUISER.

WHEN the only man escaped out of the large party that had attacked the "Honest Trader" with every hope of success, had swam ashore, he looked back at the smoke-enveloped brig with deepest hate.

As soon as he had caught breath, he darted into the chapparal, cursing as he went.

It was no easy matter to push through such a thicket, as Captain Loys had to do, to reach his vessel by the nearest way.

In twenty minutes, he found himself on the shore abreast of his vessel and the goletta which lay tranquilly moored.

To his surprise, a third vessel was inside the reef and apparently in communication with his friends.

He ran out on a point of sand and shouted, waving his neck scarf.

In a very short time a boat came from the "Needle" for him.

His men looked rather surprised at seeing their captain in clothes torn to tatters, as well by bullet as by the trees, his face and hands bloody.

He gave no explanations, but in feverish haste used an oar with his own hands to reach the ship the sooner.

His first act was to send an officer to acquaint the Spaniard with the disastrous turn of affairs, and to ask him whether he was ready to help him avenge their fallen comrades.

Then he demanded—

"What's that stranger ? "

"Spaniard," was the answer. "The Guarda Costa el Zephyr."

"The 'Zephyr' coast-guard, eh ? " said Loys. "All the better. Here, Raoul, you can jabber Spanish. Come aboard the 'Zephyr' with me."

Something like an hour was spent in Captain Loys' visits to one craft and the other.

He succeeded without any great trouble in inducing the two Spaniards to combine with him in another attack upon the Englishman, who must have been too severely handled to make much of a resistance this time.

This agreed upon, all the men, except the watches, went to rest against the work cut out for them on the morrow.

The mere handful on the "Honest Trader" had no repose however.

They had their brig to prepare, and, being so shorthanded after the engagement, that was a heavy task for wearied men.

As there could be no smoke without fire, so the boats that had attempted to cut them out proved ships being in the neighbourhood.

The captain's cutter, sent to the mouth of the bay, reported the presence of three hostile sail.

The breeze freshened all night, and was agreeably strong at dawn.

The "Honest Trader" got under her top and mainsail and her fore-staysail, and changed her station to the western side of the inlet.

There she had herself moored by a kedge aft, and her larboard bower down.

So she was shielded by the land on that side, and saved a moiety of her force by only having one half her ports to work.

Young Frank, by an intelligence that the crew had never seen him display to such intensity before, had made himself the master-spirit over them all.

First mate Anderson was a good seaman, but had no inventive powers.

He gladly let the youth propose the acts which his experience approved of.

Old sails were hung up around the outer wale of the forecastle, to serve instead of the boarding netting.

That left the stern quarter and the middle-deck alone to be cared for.

The twenty men were to defend that line.

The port carronades had been shifted to the other side, to be ready in case of accident or uselessness through overheating.

As the sun rose, the lookout on the cliff signalled that the little fleet of the enemy were in motion, and he came running down to the shore to be taken aboard.

"Now for quick work!" said Bill Bowse.

"Yes, Bill, some among us won't chew tobacco the next time old day lantern is hoisted up."

The coastguard vessel, a felucca of three hundred tons, with a long thirty-two and two twenty-six pounders as broadside, a smart sailer too, was leading her companions.

As she was in the regular, or at least the government service, her commander had forced Captain Loys to subside into a secondary place.

He, besides, much against the Frenchman's will, spoke of having a parley with the "Honest Trader."

If the latter would quietly give up the vessel, and all the merchandise, he would let the crew go about their business.

So generous was Don Diego de Haro, captain of the "Zephyr."

But the English were in no humour for talk.

Presently they saw the felucca cross the mouth of the bay, and in the entrance let go her anchor and sails at the same time.

Her broadside slowly swung round, and menaced the "Trader."

"Ned Little," said Anderson, "you can shoot a big gun."

"I always thought so," replied that sailor.

"Take you one shot from the bow gun."

The fellow ran forward with a couple more, one bearing the loggerhead, red hot from the cook's fire.

The goletta and the Frenchman were rounding the point, letting most of their canvas shiver, to deaden headway.

The felucca was clearing the captain's boat to bear him to the "Trader," and have the palaver.

Meanwhile, Ned was at his task.

Although the Guarda Costa sat low in the water, the surface was so smooth that she presented a fair mark.

"Steady, Ned," said one of his comrades, fastening up the portlid, "there's a lot of the beggars all together at the companion way, d'ye mind? What a shot to plump in among 'em!"

It was the group of captain and his officers, in full uniform.

Ned looked along the gun.

"She'll fetch that snaky-looking, homely-rigged garlic-trader somewhere about the main-hatch," said he.

He just touched the gun to improve the aim.

"There!"

One of the men poured a gill of powder on the touch-hole.

Ned took the heated iron from his neighbour and clapped it to the breech.

The gun expelled its messenger, and rolled back in a cloud of smoke.

Instantly Ned ran his head out of the port to see under the smoke the effects of the bullet.

It fell short.

But, striking the water in a cloud of spray, it rose again, with force but little abated, and fulfilled its work.

It crashed through the bulwarks, stove in a water-breaker, shivered all the woodwork over the cook's head in his little house, and, glancing out from the fragments of ironware, ended its gambols by upsetting two men at the very side of Don Diego.

He foamed with fury, and although his ship had not done recovering firmness from the shock of the dropped anchor, cried—

"Fire every piece that will bear! Oh, the thrice accursed jolterhead of a beef-eater."

While he stamped on his gilt and laced three-cocked hat, his men obeyed him.

As they feared to delay and receive their commander's wrath, they let fly the whole tier of guns without so much as an attempt at aim.

Some balls went smashing into the woods, and sent the shivers flying about after the startled birds.

The rest dashed the water up on the "Trader's" side, but did no harm.

Ned had loaded up again.

The felucca, on delivering her fire, careened over, and showed a deep space below her water-line.

As that moment, Ned applied the loggerhead's red end to the gun.

A cheer rang over the "Trader" at the effect of the shot.

It had penetrated into the hull before the felucca had recovered her keel, and she was surely in distress.

In ten minutes her boats taking to the water, and her ugly leaning over, betrayed her speedy doom.

In a quarter of an hour, when a detonation, made by the confined air tearing an outlet through the deck resounded, she rapidly descended, the ripple closing over her.

The hull grounded on the reef, and her two masts, only seen to the block of her mainyard lift, were all that was visible.

In the meantime, her men had rowed, or swam off to the goletta, and were condoled with by their countrymen.

Meanwhile, too, Ned Nittle had been applauded by his friends.

"If you only do as well by the others," remarked Captain Anderson, "the turtles will have houses for the winter."

At this moment, the goletta shook out sail on the foremast, and taking a tack to prevent her being raked, and firing one gun from the bow to cloak her movements in smoke, shot into the bay.

As she coasted the opposite shore to the Englishman, within musket range, she ran her guns out and fired.

The only shots that did damage were some that flitted through the cordage, cutting everything in the way like a knife.

One, a chain shot, glanced from the bow, carrying away a splinter of some size, and then cut the cable on the very edge of the water.

The "Trader" as her carronades exploded, had their aim spoilt by this mischance.

She swung round quickly, the current that played about the inlet being powerful.

The goletta was going about, having to do it almost on their centre, so little room was there for evolutions, and in another five minutes could empty her unused guns.

The "Needle" was taking advantage of the Englishman's reply to the goletta, to enter the harbour.

The beautiful craft, after rounding the point gracefully, darted in past the wrecked Spaniard, blazing away with both her bowchasers alternatively.

Suddenly Captain Loys had an idea.

He waved his hand.

"CHRISTENING THE CRUISER."

"Antoine—Ivan! 'way aloft, all hands, man the fore and main rigging!"

He was obeyed, though the men next moment believed him mad.

"Lay out topsail!"

"Ay, ay!"

"Man topsail halyards and sheets—haul out! Sheet home and hoist topsails'"

That was done.

But why on earth sail should be clapped on within a little bay where there was no room to expend headway, was more than any of the crew could conceive.

"Haul out the spanker, jam the boom hard a-port!"

The "Needle" was flying before the wind, dead aft, rushing into the harbour as into a funnel.

"Cease firing for'ard!" cried Captain Loys.

They passed the word.

In silence, except for the swash of the foam the swift brig cleft, it glided on.

Loys went to the helm himself.

They were nearly a-breast of the "Honest Trader," which, swinging, as said, from the breaking cable, seemed to block up half the bay.

The "Needle" could have passed her, and raked her, if she had been high enough in the water; anyhow she could have smashed away all on the level of her guns.

2.

"Drop the port lids!" cried Loys. "Every man hold on for life! Antoine, clear the fore-deck! 'ware the splinters! scaldings in the bow!"

Then he put all his strength on the tiller, and jammed it hard.

The brig instantly turned her sharp prow upon the "Honest Trader."

The French captain had taken advantage of the roller that she brought into the harbour with her.

The "Needle," lifted out of the water by the rush of every man to the stern, as they saw their commander's purpose, not only struck the English brig amidships, but fell upon her, so to say.

There was a deafening crash.

The Frenchmen were thrown off their feet, and water-breakers, the cook house, battery, and the gun rammers, everything loose, in a word, rolled on the decks.

The long gun on a pivot abaft the foremast was dismounted off its rather high wheels, and plunged on the deck from its pedestal.

An unlucky devil, who had hugged it to keep his own balance, was crushed beneath it.

The carriage, parted from the gun, caught his legs near the knee, and jammed them almost to a jelly.

The blood spirted and trickled down upon the deck in a gathering pool.

He was dead before they could relieve him.

The bowsprit of the "Needle" had pierced the bulwarks of the "Trader" as if made of steel.

Her bow, entering after, bore the wreck down till she could float off.

"Cut everything that holds!" roared Loys, running forward, as soon as the violent rocking had ceased. "Let go the jib and foresail by the run cut, if a line jams. Shove off!"

The "Needle's" stern swung off from the line, and when the sails on the main were hauled round, the wind blew her strongly off.

She floated up the bay, stern first.

Her jib-boom was wrenched and cracked, and her fore top gallant mast shook from the stays, being broken.

But the shock had not started a plank, or opened a seam, showing how clean she had cut.

Alas, it was otherwise with the anvil that that hammer had pounded.

The "Honest Trader" was shattered as if a house had fallen on her side, and she leaked like a sieve.

The "Needle" lowered every strip of canvas, dropped both anchors to bring up shorter, and followed the example of the goletta in firing single guns at the Englishman.

In several of these discharges, ten of the latter's crew were slain or wounded at their guns.

Among the dead were Anderson and three more officers.

Frank Rogers, stripped to the waist, was made to assume command by the remainder.

"What the devil next?" cried Ned Nittle.

A chain-shot from the "Needle" had knocked two ports into one, killed two men, laid Bill Bowse on the broad of his back, and passed through the opposite side.

"I tell you what," said Frank. "Give me your ears, friends."

The dozen men came to him.

All was silent then on the target exposed to so many shots, and giving no replies.

"In a word," said the youth, "I am death to the rich and oppressing! Let's have that beautiful devil of a vessel that's ruined us, or die for it—what say?"

"Agreed!" said the younger men.

"She's out of hand's reach," remarked Bill Bowse.

"And we only count up a dozen," said Ned Nittle.

"Keep me captain," said the youth, "and we can make a bold push for her, anyhow!"

It was strange to see the big bearded men shaking hands with the lad, and swearing to follow him to the last.

They let the two enemies keep up their fire.

The red cross remained flying spite of that.

They cut the cable, and then shook out the topsails.

They were immediately filled out by the breeze that kept rushing in to fill the vacuum caused by the explosions.

A touch to the helm, and the "Honest Trader," tumbling forward, shattered as she was, like a drunken man, bore down upon the goletta.

There was no room, no chance of escape.

As they neared her, the Spaniards saw flames rising from twenty different places in the English craft.

Ned Nittle, and two others, torch in hand, were up aloft, kindling the sails and ropes as they slid down from the vaneball, where their operations had commenced.

The Spaniards shrieked with horror, and some leaped overboard in fearful anticipation.

Presently the fire joined here and there until it formed one mass.

The ship became a mere gigantic wick to the furious flame.

Smoke of tar enwrapped the goletta from water's edge to the tip of her transverse latteen yards.

In five minutes more, the two hulls had joined

Then, except for the shrieks that rose from one of them, each blazed to that degree that none could have told the fire-ship from its victim.

The wind seemed to die away, as if awe-stricken at the crackling pyre.

The melted tar ran upon the waters, calmed them, and turned the surface into a mirror of seething pitch.

The swimmers, with scorched heads and flayed hands, rose in agony to drink in the parching air, were mantled with the fiery oil, until their wreathings on the bed of horror made it equal a pool in hell itself.

In the meantime, Loys de Goupille, somewhat against his will, lowered everything that would float to pick up the wounded.

The score of men he left with the shipkeeper, were busy in pulling the brig up to her anchor.

A shred of flaring sail, an end of burning rope, a patch of fired tar, might give the "Needle" such another fate as consumed the goletta.

The boats engaged in lifting the swimmers out of water and keeping off the heated ground themselves, had occupants too busy in that work to notice anything else.

Frank Rogers and his sworn followers had cleared away the best boat, rolled into it, and shoved off from the fire-ship under cover of the smoke.

They boldly headed inland, in the teeth of the foe, executed a circuit, and shot alongside the low-lying Frenchman, undreamt of, as well as unseen.

It was an easy matter to climb on board.

They did so noiselessly.

They saw every man on the forecastle deck.

They rushed thitherward, firing pistols as they went.

"Single out your man!" cried Frank, levelling his pistol.

The dozen bullets left the muzzle as if sent by the touch of one finger.

The mates were then emptied, and, flinging them down, cutlasses came into use.

Frank cleft and cut like a fiend.

"Captain of a cruiser of my own," muttered he, constantly.

In a few minutes, he saw that he, Bill Bowse, Derrick, Ned Nittle, Tom Tacktackle and three more, every one wounded more or less severely, were the victors, and the only men alive on the deck.

"I'll swear I had that captain under my arm," said Frank, glancing about in the pistol smoke.

"Must have leapt overboard," said the rest.

Loys de Goupille was not among the corpses, and he was not to be seen.

Frank took a look at the whole view comprised from the deck.

The boats of the "Needle," alarmed by the scuffle on their craft, were turning that way.

"Aloft!" cried Frank. "I'll cut both cables myself. Get something out to catch the wind!"

"Ay, ay, my lad!" cried Bill, springing up the mainshrouds, and laying out on the mainyard, where he worked like three.

His example was not thrown away.

The few men did an enormous amount of work in a few minutes.

At the end of that time, Ned Nittle, at the helm, could look up and see main and maintopsail, fore and foretop and foretop gallant drawing splendidly.

Then the maintop gallant was set, and all the studding sails on that mast run out.

The "Needle" leaned over, and begun to hum as she went through the ripple with increasing way.

Two boats, the nearest, had reached her.

Their crews were astounded at the half dozen men who had unfurled what forty of them could not have done quicker.

Their stroke-oarsman stood up as their late vessel came to them.

"Mon Dieu! vat you doo! who name of three thousand million devils—who you be!" cried they.

"Take that, you pollywoos!" cried Bill Bowse.

With his words, he dropped a bag of powder and a red-hot loggerhead into the boat that was challenging.

The explosion only burnt those that it alighted among but several of them rolled overboard in pain and terror.

The other boat, approaching still more nearly, received a huge iron-bound block from Ned Nittle, while Derrick, the Dutchman, hove an eighteen pound shot over the bulwark.

The latter drenched the crew with water, and the block set two or three dancing with the effects on their toes.

The "Needle" passed triumphantly through the mouth of the inlet.

Behind her the flames going up from the double ruin, and the boats dancing in her wake.

Beside her, the Guarda Costa's wreck.

"So it'll be!" cried Frank. "Wherever I and mine go, we'll leave death and destruction behind!"

*   *   *   *   *

Some hours after, the vessel, under such small sail as her incomplete crew commanded, was threading her way gracefully among the isles.

The helm was lashed.

All were assembled around the captain.

Frank was laying down the last leaf of a roll of manuscript that he had read to his companions.

"So you see," said he, "that I was shipped on the old "Trader" to gratify a rich and titled villain. You see, too, that even honest Captain Beckets dared not resist the power of the wealthy. But we, who all of us have experienced equal injustice, declare war against the whole world of such wretches!"

"Ay! War against the whole world!"

"We'll show no mercy to the oppressor!" continued the young man, with flushed face and fiery eyes. "Such have been rulers over the earth too long—after thousands of years, such as we have a right to rebel!"

"War!"

"As long as life is in me," said the youth, "I'll lead you, and be true to you all."

"We to you, Frank!"

There was a pause.

"What will we call this beauty of a prize?" asked Ned Nittle.

"I'll tell you," said the young commander. "Look around!"

The deck was shining with pools and lacework of blood, and dead bodies lay all about.

"What do you see?"

"Blood, and the dead!"

"Look aloft!"

A cannon shot had scattered a man's brains in the foretop, and spattered the foresail like a wine soaked cloth.

A chain shot had cut a man in two on the maintop crosstrees, and the portions fouled in the bars had been drained of the life stream, which trickled down, smearing canvas and cordage to the very deck.

"What do you see?" asked Frank.

"Blood, and the dead," was the reply once more.

"Give me the flag we tore down here?"

Ned unrolled the French flag, white and specked with lilies.

The young commander spread it out on the capstan.

He pressed the gaping wound of a corpse on a gun-carriage, and dipped his fingers into the blood.

"You have seen——we begin the work with red of death and red of fire! The instrument of our vengeance and defence is——"

He scrawled the letters on the white ground.

In one voice, the men cheered, and exclaimed—

"Hurrah! The SCARLET CRUISER!"

CHAPTER III.

THE BEAUTIFUL PRIZE—THE HAUNTER OF THE SHIP
—THE TWO THRUSTS IN THE THROAT—THE
SHADOWS.

As the new named "Scarlet Cruiser" was gliding on her way, the ship was cleared of the remains of the conflict.

Then, well-armed, three or four followed their young leader down below.

They made a strict search, for fear that some of the crew might have concealed themselves.

But there was nothing of the kind.

When in its turn the cabin came, Frank went down alone, a pistol in one hand, his cutlass in the other.

On opening the door, which he did with difficulty, as a stool had been set up against it inside, his weapons fell from his grasp in surprise.

For the seat that ran round the cabin, under the stern windows, was occupied.

It was a young girl.

Her hands covered her face, and they were wet with tears.

Though her features could not be discerned between her fingers, yet the gracefulness of her figure augured a countenance lovely enough to correspond.

Frank approached her softly and touched her arm.

She had heard him approach, and had, with a girl's curiosity, peeped at him through her tears.

When he had pacified her, she told the little she knew, or was willing to avow.

Genifrede de Goupille, daughter of the captain of the late "Needle," had lived in France until her father had run away with his brig.

She had been on the ocean ever since with him.

That was all.

Frank wished to heaven that she had a story to tell thirty times longer than this little.

It was so pleasant to be seated beside her and begging her not to be afraid whenever she stopped after a sentence.

Frank had to acquaint her, in return, with the particulars of the recent fight.

Although he did not believe it himself, he assured Genifrede that her worthy parent must have leaped overboard in the bay and been taken by his own men.

At all events, he had not fallen among the slain, for Frank had sought after him too closely to be ignorant of that.

Whether it was that her sorrow had come to its end, or that the youth's pleasant speech would have consoled a harder-hearted creature than herself, the girl found her eyes dry after a while, and a smile appearing on her lips when she, or the new disposer of her fate, made a laughable blunder in the broken language they were talking.

Her English was not of the best, truth to say.

At last, Frank arose.

With a desire to calm a queer agitation that had crept over him, he diverted himself by over-hauling the lockers and swinging cupboards in the cabin. In one box, that he had to pry the lid of with his cutlass, he found no inconsiderable sum of money.

He turned to Genifrede, who was watching him with interest.

"You can take whatever amount you wish of this," said he, jingling the coin. "I am going to send a boat to St. Thomas when I reach my chosen anchorage. You will then be free to depart."

His tone had a tinge of sadness in it, as if he saw no great occasion for rejoicing in the idea of knowing her for so short a time.

She could only bow gratefully.

The cabin was partly divided athwartship by a line of posts.

This was with a view to strengthen the quarter-deck, on which a long pivot gun had formerly been mounted.

Frank drew the sliding doors from their place.

"Within here," said he, pointing to the after room, "no one enters without your permission. You may sleep in peace, for my men do not quarrel with women!"

But, somehow or other, the young corsair captain was often in the girl's room.

As she never went up on deck, it was, after all, only kind of him to keep her company in her loneliness.

The "Cruiser" arrived at a small and uninhabited island, in the only harbour of which anchor was dropped.

Two sailors, who were old hands in those waters, were chosen to go to St. Thomas, and enrol a score of men of the right stuff.

They were given a couple bags of coin, and told not to spare the dubloons and quadruples, if to secure genuine sea rovers.

As their boat was bumping against the brig's side, Frank, against his will, slowly descended the cabin stairs, and knocked on the sliding doors.

He fancied he heard voices within.

But it must have been an error, for when a sweet voice said "Come in!" only the captain's daughter was there.

And a confusion that flushed her cheeks, was, no doubt, that emotion natural to a young girl at the sight of a handsome fellow who had the power of life and death over her.

"The hour has come to redeem my promise," said he. "The pinnace has its sail up and is only waiting for you. I have made the men swear especial care shall be taken of you."

"I am very thankful," said she. "But I do not want to leave the ship."

This was a reply to startle one.

Her tone was tempting as ever, yet hardly implied a love confession.

Frank tried to read her real thought in her eyes, but they avoided his by studying the carpet on the floor.

Now, he liked the idea of her remaining.

But a women on the ship baptized in blood, and devoted to a crimson course that should leave one battle-ground for another, its lighthouses burning ships, its buoys wrecks — a female, young and lovely, among such men of steel as he would have, could hardly be.

Still, he desired her good opinion too much to tell her what his future life was to be.

But he insisted that she could go to the port, where she might live at her ease until news of her father should reach her.

She smiled mysteriously when he said this, and thus deepened his bewilderment.

"In short," said he, growing annoyed, "how long would you stay my guest?"

"I do not know," replied Genifrede. "In a week, even less, I may be as eager to go as I am now to be permitted to remain."

Frank could make nothing of it.

"At least, you will tell me why you prefer this dreary life to one on shore, where you will be a queen, with that money and your charms?"

She darted one quick glance at him.

His heart beat at the brilliancy of the look.

"I must not go," she said, firmly. "For your sake!"

Frank was amazed at the deep feeling of her accents.

He would have let all his love flow in burning words at this apparent advance on her part.

But as he was stretching out his hand to take hers, he recoiled.

She was shrinking from his forward step.

"For your sake!" repeated she.

"Why? how?"

"I was alone, in your power, and you have acted nobly to me! I may be able to repay you sooner than you dream of! Send away that boat without me."

"I do not understand, but I obey," said the young commander.

In two hours after the sails of the pinnace disappeared in the distance.

The remainder of the crew were given a holiday, after they had filled a few casks of fresh water and gathered some fruit.

The heavy work of altering the brig for her new life of a terrible letter of marque, was put off until the coming of the recruits.

That night, a beautiful one, the men were seated forward on the heel of the bowsprit or leaning against the rail, smoking and chatting.

The sea breeze was coming in, and though they were all too wind-proof to be chilled by it, the sharpness did remind them that their supper would be very acceptable.

One of the set, who had the turn at cook, started for the galley.

Presently a stove pipe emitted a long train of smoke, and after that again, that delectable perfume that comes from a kettle of the mess that has as many names as the materials it may be made of.

The skilled noses of the hungry men could distinguish the blended odours, swept as they were right up to them.

"That's the slice of pork that is going under the lid," said Bill Bowse, pressing his lips together.

"There goes the fish we caught to-day," remarked Ned Nittle, returning from a walk of three steps, and a turn in the direction of the caboose. "Ain't they mild and mellow when they're a-boiling, though!"

"Whew!" said Derrick. "Dunderswousel! dere was a schmell! only *look* at it! shoost like sourekrout, only much nicer!"

"It's the peppermint that we picked on shore. The Ingins use it in their stews of men!" said an old tar, who had been captured by the Caribbeans in years past, and perhaps had tasted of their cookery.

The line of smoke continued to float by.

"It's a stunner," said one.

"With that for sauce," cried Bill Bowse, "a man could stow away a pound of old rope 'twice said!'"

"It's loverly!" said Ned Nittle, biting at a plug of tobacco to keep his mouth from melting with its watering.

All was dark amid ships.

On either side of the galley, however, the red light streamed out of the doorways, and glimmered in the damp planks.

As the hungry seamen kept their eyes on the spot, two or three of them started.

For a shadow had seemed to pass through the light, but swiftly as a storm-driven cloud.

There was a slight clatter of pans in the caboose, the wind bringing the sound as it did the vapour.

"Oh, here comes Jack!" said the sailors in gladsome chorus.

Instantly they sprang to their feet every man of them.

"The devil!"

"I saw Jack come out of the galley this way!"

"By heavens! he melted into the smoke, then!"

The deck was untenanted as ever.

Uneasy, for all had seen the shadowy form, their senses were all on the alert, and directed to the spot.

The smoke rushed through the pipe, and streamed out, increased in volume and density.

It was altered in nature, too.

Before it had an alluring aroma of meat, fish, and sweet-scented herbs.

Now it was gross, sickening, horrifying.

"By jingo! There's blood!" cried Bill Bowse, jumping up from the chain heap he had made his couch.

"Blood, it is!"

"And man's flesh!" said the Carib's captive.

"Nonsense!" said Ned Nittle. "You're a pretty gang to man the 'Scarlet Cruiser,' and don't know the frying-pan when you see it. Jack slapped a steak of that wild hog that we killed this morning ashore on the coals!"

"S'pose you go, Derrick, and help Jack to fetch the kettle here. We've all our knives and I'll do without my spoon, for one," said Bill Bowse.

"Yes. Derrick, go on!"

The poor Dutchman did not relish the task.

However, though he was big enough and fully able to resist, he always gave way, out of his good-nature.

He rolled along, like an animated hogshead, down the forecastle ladder and towards the cook's house.

All was still there.

But as Derrick approached, he was almost choked by the hideous exhalation.

The men forward saw their envoy go up to the caboose slowly and cautiously thrust his head within the doorway.

"Mein Gott in Himmel!"

That was what the Dutchman howled as he fell flat on his back, shaking the deck as if an ox had been dropped from the maintop.

All the crew leaped down on the deck and rushed to the place, whipping out their knives as they ran thither.

"Are you hurt, mate?" cried they.

Derrick flopped about like a whale in his death flurry, and only moaned.

"Old Nick! he was there! Davy Jones! oh, oh!"

Ned Nittle dashed at the door of the caboose, and slid it fairly back.

There was light enough within.

Jack, doubled up in a shapeless heap, was

half resting on the red-hot stove at which he had been cooking.

The flame had run over him, and was smouldering on his clothes.

"Poor Jack!"

One unhooked a lantern by the companion way, and lit it at his pipe.

They dragged the body out on the cool deck, and flung a bucket full of water over it.

But their efforts were in vain.

"Poor devil!" said Bill Bowse, "he must have fallen into the fire!"

"Why didn't he cry out, then?"

"Yes, why didn't he? You're right, Ned."

They examined the corpse, blackened and charred as it was.

In the midst of their scrutiny, Frank came on deck and joined them.

"He was dead before he touched the flames," said Ned.

"Why do you think so?" said the captain.

Ned laid his fingers on the neck of the corpse and indicated a mark on the flesh spared by the fire.

As all shuddered and drew back, Frank bent down, and drew a knife from the ghastly wound.

"Good heavens!" exclaimed he. "It's a thrust in the throat!"

"Thrust in the throat!" repeated a voice.

It seemed like echo, to be in the air.

"Who spoke?" cried Frank.

"Not me, sir!"

"Nor me, no more, and I'm sure my mate didn't."

"Any one aloft there?"

All the little crew were encircling their captain.

"Who's that for'ard?" cried Frank, as there was a slight rattling as of the chains slipping in the tier there.

A loud laugh rang out, full of defiance and triumph.

Some of the men trembled.

Derrick's knees knocked together.

"Dunder!" groaned he. "Der duyvel wast der bloodspiller!"

"Devil or no devil, I'll hang him up at the ball of the foremast for a bloody ensign!"

As Frank said this, he brandished the dripping knife fresh from the gash, and sprang forward, followed by all.

But the forecastle was bare.

They rushed below and plunged the blades into every dark corner.

In vain.

One or two dropped over the bow, but no one was clinging to the chains.

The mist that hung upon the water might, however, have veiled the approach and departure of the mysterious slayer.

That he was an Indian, native of the island, was the only theory that presented itself.

"You must keep watches," said Frank. "We are punished for having been so careless."

"Ay, ay, sir; but I'm going to sleep on deck the rest of this cursed night," replied Ned Nittle.

Come to find out, none would go below in the darkness.

Morning came, without another incident.

With the light, a more minute search was made throughout the craft, but as fruitlessly as before.

When Frank was asked by his guest the cause of the uproar in the evening, he told her.

Genifredo started, then sighed, biting her lips as if to restrain some words that almost were uttered.

"Poor man!" said she.

The sailor's body was sewn up in his hammock and taken ashore.

After the boat's crew had buried him, and piled stones on his grave, they explored the islet.

"Well?" inquired their captain, when they returned.

"Not a blessed footprint 'sides our own,' replied Ned Nittle.

There was no other land in sight.

The thought of the murderer having been one of the crew was idle, for they had been all together at the time.

But the enigma made them all thoughtful, and there was no more of the unrestrained gaiety that had hitherto been theirs.

Frank was gloomier than any of them, and he bent all his mind on discovering the concealed truth.

The day went by, and another night came.

The seamen had determined to spend it on the deck again, their sleeping-place being so full of the unknown terrors engendered by the hovering cloud.

It was sunset.

Derrick had just come down from aloft with Captain Frank's spy-glass.

But there was nothing in sight, and the boat could not be expected before the next day.

The sailors were growing merry again.

The prospect of a joyous company was inspiriting.

"I hope they'll be a jolly lot of buccaneers of the blue," said Bill, coiling his legs up under him as he loaded a big pipe.

"Let them that's gone for 'em alone for picking and choosing," said Ned. "I always suspected that both of them had scuttled silver ships in earlier days."

"All the better," said another. "We want old rascals of the deep to give us lessons. Who wouldn't learn how to empty a gold galleon of Spain to the tune of a border jig?"

"You have all got pipes but me," remarked Ned. "I wish I was in the fashion."

"Well, why ain't you?"

"Cause that clumsy Dutchman broke mine by sitting down on my chest. Lor', whatever took such a lump as him to the sea!" laughed Ned.

Derrick joined in, as he always did.

"I can walk round mit der capstan mit anybody," said he, "or pull mit a brace."

"That's so! but you never went farther aloft than a topmast for fear the spars would break!"

"Good, Ned. I declare to thunder," growled Bill, "that I saw the Dutchman once clearing away the gaff topsail when he looked like an elephant in a cobweb."

"But I'll lend you a pipe, Ned, old boy," said the Carib's prisoner. "It's a short stem, a reg'lar nose-scorcher."

"If it'll burn 'bacco, it'll do prime. Hand it over."

"Oh, it's down below, on the chest of my bunk."

"That's another coloured nigger," said Ned.

"Oh, if you're a-feard to go down the ladder——"

"Not a-feard, you know, but sort of puzzled-like—I can't get that poor Jack out of my head!"

"I'm on the same books, Ned, and I 'spect most of us are. I'll go with you, for I want to get that song of the 'Falmouth Pet' out of my bag."

"Come on, Tom."

So the two descended.

Their mates looked at them disappearing much as if they were bidding farewell to them.

As for Derrick, his round face assumed a rueful expression, much as though he had seen his friends going down the mouth of a volcano.

However, Ned was whistling all the time, and, though deadened, the cheerful sound continued to come up the stairs.

In a few minutes, Ned's face and breast appeared in the opening.

"We did it after all," said he, laughingly. "You ought to have seen me and Tom jump when a big rat rolled off somebody's chest."

"Where's Tom, then?"

"Oh! now, don't try to pull hair over an old tar's eyes," said Ned. "I didn't think he'd go for to hide and play off on me."

"What do you mean?" said Bill Bowse. "Tom ain't here!"

"Word of honour?"

"Honour bright."

"Lord G——"

And Ned dropped down the stairs with the speed of desperation.

The sailors sprang to their feet aghast.

"It wast der duyvel come again!" muttered Derrick.

"Come down, mates!" cried the voice of Ned.

One of them caught up the lantern that they had lit for the convenience of their pipes, and all swarmed down into the forecastle.

They found their comrade kneeling and supporting the motionless form of Tom.

"He went up a-head of me," said Ned, to all their questions. "I thought him among you. I only waited a second. I find him dead!"

"Dead!"

"He couldn't have fallen off the ladder and broken his neck."

"I would have heard that."

"How then——"

"See!"

They lowered the lantern to the body.

A red pool was on the planks, and tracing the ruddy line to its source, they saw it begun in a dagger wound.

"The thrust in the throat!" the awfully strange voice seemed to whisper in their very midst.

Derrick gave a yell of terror, sprang up the ladder, ran along the deck, and, blundering down the cabin stairs, thundered on the doors.

"The thrust mid der throttle again!" repeated Derrick, with pale face and quivering lips.

Frank hurried to the scene of death, and found the report but too true.

"Who was with Tom, you say?" demanded he, laying one hand on the pistol he thrust in his belt.

"Ned."

Frank let his hand fall.

"Ned Nittle, the handiest, truest man about the ship," said he.

"Thank you, sir," said Ned, in a grief stricken voice.

"I could believe any one guilty of the act before you," said Frank. "But I must do what seems right. To the old breadroom with him. When the new hands come, I will have a trial."

"You'll let my hands be free, sir," entreated Ned. "You, see, sir, I loved Tom here—poor lad! and the wretch that robbed him of life can't be no friend of mine! That stands to reason. And if it comes at me, I'd like to have a fair chance in a grapple, you know, sir."

The sailor's tone affected him he appealed to.

"Let him go altogether," said he. "No, Ned, nobody can believe this. I am sure you was not the author of the other crime. Yet the same hand did both!"

Frank was tossed on the sea of doubts.

"Let me see the steel that did it," said he.

Bill picked up the instrument.

Frank started.

It was but a simple dagger, and it was not the stains on it that startled him.

He had seen it before—not long ago—not ten hours since.

"It was not you, Ned—forgive me! Nor any of you, lads!"

"Is it a ghost, as Derrick says?"

"Does Derrick say so?" said the young captain.

"Yaw, cap'en," responded the Dutchman. "I was see something twice't in der hold as look like the duyvel."

"Saw something—what like?"

"Oh, it was gone quicker dan a moment. But it had a face like, Mein Gott! it was der doppel ganger—the very same like dat Frencher captain of dis vessel!"

"A face like that captain's," repeated Frank, as if that confirmed some suspicion he had entertained.

And, full of sadness he went up on deck and to his cabin.

He looked into Genifrede's divided room.

She was there, quietly busied at some woman's work, a piece of embroidery or what not.

She did not know he had opened the door.

But his eyes were not for her that time.

They were fastened on a trophy of weapons on the wall between the windows.

There were pistols, guns, pikes and swords, crossed to form it.

But two of the iron pins which had secured part of the decorations now held nothing.

Two daggers were gone from their places.

Frank drew back, closed the panel, and fell upon a seat.

No doubt could remain now.

That fair and gentle-looking creature resembled her sire too much in features not to be something of his kind in heart.

It was she, to avenge her father, that remained on the ship, although persuaded to go.

It was she who crept out of her retreat, secretly, stealthily, and stabbed the unsuspecting men.

It was she, in a word, that had haunted the ship.

The love that Frank had imagined she experienced for him was merely the deceit of deepest hatred.

"One who could murder with a hand so firm," muttered the young corsair, "is no longer a woman. I will watch her, and if I seize her in the act I'll——I'll strike her dead as I would a dog!"

Hours passed.

Frank, his ear to the bulkheads, listened to the movements of the inmates of the cabin.

Before midnight, the silence therein, broken by merely the soft breathing of Genifrede, shook Frank's belief.

Or, at least, the murderess, happy, content at her double guilt, was enjoying the dreams of those yet to die!

Frank gave up the spying for that night.

He lay down just as he was, a pistol in his hand.

He did not mean to sleep, but to listen.

In the meantime, the monotonous slapping of the water against the bilge, the droning of the sea-breeze in the rigging, sent him off into sleep.

He had a dream.

All was darkness around him, as well as stillness.

In the centre of the gloom, slowly approaching him, was a form.

He knew it was a human being by the glitter of its hateful eyes and the dim white line that the lips, drawn back in blood-thirstiness, revealed of the teeth.

A shining line in one hand was the streak of a dagger—the *third* dagger menacing his throat.

He could not move his armed grasp and fire the pistol to alarm his comrades.

Then, somehow or other, that face was accompanied by one precisely resembling it.

But not so hateful, no, not hateful at all, even affectionate in its glance on him.

This second face was like a sister to the other.

Then a deep whisper said—

"He must not die!"

Still the dagger threatened him.

Again the interfering voice, more firmly than before, repeated—

"He must not die!"

The dagger disappeared then.

And a voice, harsher than the first, growled in his ear—

"Not yet—but, nevertheless he *shall* die by the thrust in the throat!"

All vanished.

Frank woke up, beaded with icy drops.

He struck a light.

He was completely alone in his little cabin.

He clapped his ear to the partition.

The breathing of Genifrede came faintly through the panel.

Perplexed, even distressed, Frank could not lie down again.

The fresh-primed pistol in his hand, he sat at the table, watching the doors right and left of him from midnight till the morning.

CHAPTER IV.

GENIFREDE'S TREASURE—THE MYSTERY REVEALED —THE THRUST IN THE THROAT ONCE MORE.

On the following day three dots were sighted.

At noon they had come alongside.

They proved to be the messenger pinnace and two large shallops, containing three or four-and-thirty men. At St. Thomas, there were th unemployed men of two slavers that had been wrecked on the West Rock Key.

The envoys of Captain Frank had resolved to sin on the right side by engaging a surplus number.

The young captain questioned every one of them, but found that six did not promise to come up to the mark.

He did not offend them, however, by telling them that, but pretended to take them into the company with the others.

Thereupon a whole month passed in the reverse of idleness.

The ship was repainted, and the whole set of the standing rigging changed.

Her colour now was a brilliant scarlet, unflecked except by a golden streamer that ran along her side.

A double suit of sails was prepared, so that the "Cruiser" might easily be disguised.

A spar that would serve as a mast, was kept on deck, ready to be shipped as a mizen-mast on occasion, and make a barque of her.

During this time no repetition of the startling assasinations had disturbed the general repose.

The old crew, with a prudence that Frank applauded, had refrained from talking of them.

But Derrick, in his cups, was not so reserved as when sober.

From him the tale went the rounds, and excited much sensation.

The presence of the female passenger who never came on deck, and who was daughter of the dispossessed captain, caused some grumbling.

Frank heard several such speeches, as the following now and then.

"I say, Marco," observed one of the new hands to a comrade, "this craft will beat anything ever I sailed on."

"She will! or anything ever came into these waters. I only hope we won't have that bloody weight around our neck on the first cruise."

"Oh, you mean that girl that's s'posed to have slipped a knife into two of the old hands 'cause her dad was knocked on the head?"

"Yes. If anybody gets stuck in the hawsepipe while I'm on board, I'll cut cable and run, good service or not."

As was natural, the feeling grew worse, and Bill and Ned had something to tell their young leader every day of their comrade's thoughts.

In the mood that these reports gave him, Frank went down into the cabin one day.

As briefly as he could, he told Genifrede what was muttered among his men.

"I will do all I can," added he, "but I can only offer you my feeble defence. When I am away from you, I doubt, I must confess. But when I am by you, as now, seeing how lovely, amiable, womanly you are, I wonder that I could ever have dreamt you guilty of such thoughts, much more of the execution."

Genifrede laid her hand in the youth's.

"Believe me, I never have shed blood, never wished the death of any one," said she.

"I do believe you. Now, you may do as you will. But I would counsel you to go. I shall have to send some of my men, new hands, who are unsuitable, back to the harbour."

Genifrede seemed to reflect.

"Come to me this evening," said she, "and I will decide."

THE SCARLET CRUISER.

"REACHING HIS ARM DOWN AS FAR AS HE COULD, HE WAS SETTING FIRE TO THE CURTAIN WITH A LIGHTED CANDLE."

"Very well."

When it was dark, Frank returned for the answer.

The girl expressed her willingness to depart.

She would accept of the money that Frank freely gave her.

And she desired another favour.

A large chest was by her feet.

"I would have this go with me," said she.

"Fill it with what you will," said Frank. "Load it with treasure! I shall not stay it, nor will I let its lid be lifted."

"You promise?"

"Sacredly."

"Many thanks."

On the ensuing day, the captain summoned all his men.

He called six from the ranks.

"I find that you six are not the lads for me," said he. "I shan't go into my reasons. You receive in a few minutes five dollars a day for all the time you have been with me, and ten more a piece for a service I wish you to do."

The fellows were cunning enough to hide their disappointment.

"This lady——"

Here Genifrede came on deck, for the first time for many weeks.

"This lady will be taken to St. Thomas by you in the boat I give."

In a short time, the large boat was ready. Genifrede and the half-dozen men in it.

"Four men to bring up that large chest in the cabin."

The box was brought up with difficulty.

They had to clear away a block to lower it into the boat.

Genifrede displayed an anxiety while this was being done that proved her interest in the contents of the case.

"Good-bye," said Frank. "Good fortune to you and your treasure!"

The boat shoved off, and was soon speeding on his journey.

"I didn't catch what she said, Ned," said Frank. "Did you hear?"

"Yes, sir. The lady said that you'd be thankful she was gone with her treasure, as you call that box."

At one moment, Genifrede had begged to remain in the ship for his sake! At the next she said he should be thankful that she had gone.

He shut himself up in the cabin and kept his glass on the boat until it was lost to view.

Then he fell back on the cushions, where he had seen her recline so often, and felt as if the tears were coming to his eyes.

"Farewell!" said he. "It's my heart that you bear along with you!"

*   *   *   *   *

Night on the ocean.

In the moonlit waste, but one speck to cast a shadow.

The boat dismissed from the "Cruiser."

In the stern sheets, the only waking man, steering her for the invisible port.

Her prow was decked over, and in its shadow lay the five other men, wrapped up in boat-cloaks, and their faces covered for fear of the moon's poisonous beams.

Near the helmsman, that large case which Genifrede was slumbering beside.

Her arm, escaped from the shawl that veiled her face, gleamed enticingly white as it embraced this chest.

Noiselessly the steersman moved.

He rose to his feet and glanced around.

Alone on the measureless expanse.

Avarice and murder gleamed from out his fierce eyes.

He cast the end of a line round the tiller and fastened it so that the sail should continue to draw.

The little craft glided on as lightly as if she carried a freight of joy, or loveliness alone such as Genifrede possessed.

Amid the stillness, the bare-footed sailor stole forward like a phantom.

Four times a knife-blade in his grasp flashed upward and downwards upon the sleeping men.

There was a gasp, a groan, a gurgling under each cloaked bundle.

That was all!

Not enough sound to startle the nautilus, whose tail, of all colours, in the moon rays glittered around the boat.

A last time, the murderer lifted his weapon.

"He is my brother," muttered he, "but I will have the treasure alone!"

And he drove the blade deep into the last form of the five.

They had solved the problem between the mystery of earth's sleep and the slumber of Death the Unknown!

Still, without a sound, the quintriple murderer returned to the helm.

A change in the variable wind had threatened to take the boat unawares, and fling the butchered and slaughtered into the sea.

When again the steady breeze had returned, and the helm might be lashed in safety, the slayer let his horrid eyes linger on the girl's recumbent form.

It would have tempted more than he.

"She first?" muttered he, "or the treasure!"

His hand, nervous with avarice, stretched out on the box and clawed at its lid.

The blood was drying on his fingers, and the moisture glistened as if they were five snakes with ruby scales.

"She first!" said he, at length.

What a triumph for the poor girl!

Her beauty had outweighed the treasure.

With that ruddy hand, the shawl was plucked away.

Genifrede sat up, her eyes scarcely open, in bewilderment.

The sailor caught her hands in one of his, and held her down.

"Pretty one!" said he, hoarsely. "One word. Be willing! I know an isle where no whites go! We will share this treasure, we will buy the Indians, and live in joy! What say?"

She hardly understood him, so hurried was his utterance.

"Let me go! Help! help!"

He laughed.

He encircled her waist and drew her shrinking face nearer his parched lips.

"Help! help!"

The cry ran along the glittering waves and startled the gaudy angel-fish that were on the water's edge.

"Help!"

"Fool! the kiss! Silence! there's nobody here but me and Death!"

"Right! Death is here! Your death!" shouted a loud voice.

The brutal sailor had forced the girl close to him, and she felt his breath and the smell of his bloody hand equally horrible on her face.

She had vainly put forth all her strength.

When the stranger's voice had so awfully thundered, both girl and man started.

She with joy, for she knew that voice meant salvation.

He with affright.

The five bodies pierced by his blade lay yet in their mound.

But out of the chest, as out of a tomb or coffin, had risen a tall and frightful form.

Pale with confined air that he had been compelled to breathe, haggard with the emotions of the last month, fired now with the sight before him, Loys de Goupille had never presented a more terrible view.

He dashed the sailor from the girl with one hand, picked up the crusted knife gleaming on the seat, and, holding the seaman down on the seat drove the knife with a mighty *thrust into his throat!*

A flood of the life-stream gushed forth from the severed veins.

Ere they had poured the last remnant of existence out, Loys de Goupille lifted the body in his arm and hurled it over the gunnel.

It splashed on the waves and reddened their silver tips as it rolled sullenly on them.

The remaining bodies followed.

As Genifrede sank on her father's breast, a singular crunching snap gave a check to her effusion at deliverance.

She glanced behind.

In the wake of the boat, the six bodies had floated.

But five were there.

And as she opened her eyes still more widely, one of them vanished as if wiped out by a giant's hand.

Of the four left, three went under like the former.

And a long white streak that slid through the reddened foam gleamed out once more as the last body was drawn from sight.

"Their tombs are the maws of sharks," said Loys. "May all our enemies perish like them!"

And when she sank to rest, tired out, her head on his knees, Loys steered the boat calmly.

And yet, on either hand, the sharks swam steadily.

They waited for a supplementary dish to their banquet!

"Right," said Loys to the fish, as if they understood him. "Be my friends! and you shall have feasting wherever Loys de Goupil goes!"

*   *   *   *   *

A few days after, the image of a man, carved to replace the figure-head of the "Scarlet Cruiser," was pronounced finished by the carpenter.

Frank came forward himself to see the old one removed.

When they struck the first blow of an axe on it, the head of the tool went right through it.

"Mighty rotten wood!" remarked the carpenter.

"No!" cried Frank. "The figure is hollow."

So it was.

And, moreover, crumbs and a blanket and sheet denoted that it had been tenanted.

A communication with the forecastle seemed to exist.

It was clear that anyone in the secret could penetrate the vessel fore and aft without suspicion.

"That was how the captain escaped," said Frank. "I understand the girl's words now. She stayed for my sake, indeed, for she must have held back the hand that could have killed me in my dream. And she departed because the treasure was her father, that she, despite his crimes, can love."

That night, though the hammer was ringing at its work, the open sea lay around the "Scarlet Cruiser."

CHAPTER V.

OUT OF THE PAN INTO THE FIRE—JUSTICE IN ANTIGUA—CAVENDISH SHOVES HIS OAR IN THE CUP OF THE CENTIPEDE—IN THE DEATH AGONY IN THE DEPTHS—THE NAMELESS TERROR.

Loy's whole care was to reach the shore as soon as he could.

He knew well how to raise allies for any enterprise having booty in prospect.

His whole idea was to get back his vessel and avenge the loss.

He took a course by which to avoid St. Thomas.

While his companion slumbered, he worked a scraping off the betraying name on the stern, and washing away the bloody traces of his act, and those of his own victim.

It was at Antigua he landed.

He hastened to dispose of the boat, and with the proceeds, took rooms for Genifrede in the Foreigner's quarter of the town.

She was left most of the time quite to herself, for the Frenchman was deeply buried in his projects.

She had nothing to do but sun herself at the window.

Little amusement was that.

In fact, she was about to give that up in disgust, when her attention was attracted to a person of different appearance to the rest of the passers by.

He came through the miserable street daily, and looked up always at her casement.

She shut it at the hours of his going by, but still his passings were constant, although his features wore a disappointed look.

She made inquiries.

The handsome young man in blue and gold was Lieutenant Lance Cavendish, commanding the little despatch-boat that ran in and out of the islands.

The young officer was often in town, they told Genifrede.

Gradually she found that it wouldn't be very improper for her to be at the casement now and then.

She felt a little glad of having done so, when she perceived a bright look on the lieutenant's countenance thereafter.

But then she had not thought that other eyes than his had found her alluring.

One night, she had retired to rest, lonely as ever.

She was full of thought.

Loys sometimes now was not seen by her for a couple of days.

She was wondering how it was that Captain Frank's image was fading away before that of the young officer, when a violent knocking at the frail door of her house, threatened to have it off its hinges.

She heard the old woman who was landlady go to open it.

Then there was a heavy trampling of feet as half-a-dozen men rushed in.

To her surprise, they came upstairs, and paused at her room door.

A heavy hand banged on the panels.

"Open, in the name of the king!" cried a voice, rough as the raps were loud.

Genifrede huddled on her dress and opened the door, in great tremor.

Two or three of the men on the landing were negroes, who held large lanterns.

The others were Spaniards.

One of them was in a costume which consisted principally of a cocked hat as big as a balloon, and a sash with more gold lace than cloth, and more fringe than lace or cloth.

This important dignitary turned to a man in black, and said—

"Senor Don Leopardo, do you recognise this as the woman?"

The man in black looked at Genifrede for a second, and replied that he knew her well, or he never hoped for salvation.

"Sure?"

"Sure, Senor Don Pinto."

Pinto waved his arm.

Two of the lookers on, who were apparently soldiers by their swords, unceremoniously took the girl by the shoulders, and dragged her out on the landing.

Till now she had been silent, abashed at being in the centre of all the rude gazers, disarranged as she was.

"What do you mean?" said she, indignantly.

"Take her down stairs, Sebastian!" said Senor Pinto.

"Keep your hands off!" cried Genifrede, holding the heavy candlestick threateningly. "By what right do you touch me?"

The soldiers hurried her downstairs.

There was a litter, to which were harnessed two mules, at the door.

The soldiers intimated that she was to get into it.

Still more soldiers were in the street keeping a rabble off, whom the glare of torches had drawn to the spot.

Genifrede held back.

"I won't get into it!" cried she. "I will know why you outrage me. Help, help!"

"Silence!"

"Then tell me why you have seized me?"

"Not seized you—arrested you!"

"But why that, either. Tell me, what have I done?"

Pinto repeated his sign for her to be forced into the litter.

"Help! help!"

She broke away and appealed to the crowd.

"Oh, aid me!" she cried.

But the mob showed no inclination to interfere in her behalf.

Indeed, they laughed as much at her as the soldiers themselves.

Genifrede struggled in vain.

A last time she raised her failing voice.

"Is there no one to aid me! no one to tell my father of this wrong?"

"I will!" cried a voice. "What the deuce are you all about here?"

"English officer," murmured Genifrede, clasping her hands in gratitude.

It was Cavendish.

He stepped up to her, after having pushed through the ring between two of the soldiery, and thrust back one of the guards who had had his hands on the girl.

Pinto gave his moustache a twist.

"Your accent and your manner proclaim you a stranger, young man," said he, grandly. "I overlook this. Go, and keep out of trouble."

The soldiers lifted their eyebrows in marvel at the immense generosity of their chief.

The young Englishman did not exhibit the least symptom of going to fly from the spot.

"English youth," said Pinto, majestically, "do not get between the law and the guilty."

"Get between a goose and a dove," returned Lance Cavendish in the fellow's teeth. "I've heard a little of the goings on in Antigua. Now, in one word, what are you dragging that poor girl away from her home for?"

Leopardo whispered to the soldier.

"I am captain of the governor's guards," said Pinto thereupon, "and that woman has broken the law. She is a confederate of Culchillo, the desperado who passed five thousand reals off on the merchant Devega, of the Warf Royal. Are you answered, English youth?"

Cavendish was afraid that his chivalrous nature had got him into a pickle. He did not know the girl from Eve, and what wonder if she was all the captain said?

He turned towards her, mechanically.

But he did not see her cowering under the weight of guilt.

No, Genifrede was quivering with wounded pride.

"I an ally of robbers?" cried she. "I never even heard those names before. Oh, do not you believe them, sir," continued she.

She took Cavendish by the hand, she seized his sleeve, she wept on his breast, she implored him by every sacred thing not to let this strange abduction be perpetrated.

His blood was fired by her touch. He could not think of weighing his doubts, but resisted the evil contemplated towards her.

But Pinto was as stubborn as he was firm, and the Englishman was sure that he could not rely on the assistance of the crowd.

Pinto laughed triumphantly at seeing him hesitate, and gave the order for the last time.

They forced Genifrede into the litter, while half a dozen, with swords drawn, formed a line against the lieutenant.

The latter had half drawn his sword, but he felt a hand laid on his arm.

It was the man in black, Leopardo.

"Senor is lieutenant commanding the despatch boat," said the Spaniard, in a silky voice. "If he would only go to the palace with the party and hear the examination. The prisoner will have a still fairer chance, if Senor Englishman is there."

As Lance had determined to follow the litter in any event, he took this advice.

So through the unpaved streets, by the light of torches and lanterns, the procession proceeded.

In the centre, the litter, with Genifrede, too proud to weep, searching the crowd for a glimpse of her father, and only feeling less disheartened as she caught sight of the young Englishman.

The soldiers encompassed the vehicle, and a mob of all colours, from white or Indian red to mullatto yellow and negro black, halloo'd, danced, and ran along with them.

The palace was a very large and ancient building.

It had been built long before, when the Spaniards had made the natives do so much labour for them, cementing stones with blood, and laying down lives with their burdens.

Leopardo, who had kept near Cavendish during the march, pointed up to the building as they neared it after leaving the town.

"If Senor Englishman," proposed he, "would like to speak to the governor on behalf of the prisoner, before the case comes on, he may come with me. He may be out of temper at being disturbed at night, and a word from you may set all right."

Lance knew enough of the corruption about

THE SCARLET CRUISER; OR, THE WOLF OF THE WAVE.   21

the public authorities not to be at all embarrassed now.

"I have never seen the governor," remarked he, "but I suppose my uniform will introduce me?"

"I could manage that even better," replied Leopardo, grinning.

"You?"

The rusty black suit, and unwashed face, hardly seemed a fitting passport to the presence of the mighty potentate of Antigua.

"I," returned Leopardo, still grinning.

"Here's a piastre," said Lance, giving the coin, "Let us hurry on ahead and be before those rascals."

The two slipped from the crowd and soon reached the palace.

The guards at the portals made way for Leopardo with an alacrity that augured well for the fulfilment of his promise.

"You have introduced me inside the palace," said Lance, looking back on the procession around the prisoner before he went up the staircase. "Here!"

It was a sort of page who was passing that the lieutenant called.

"Is the governor here?" asked he.

Leopardo exchanged a look with the page.

The latter replied that he did not know.

"He is not in the reception-room at all events," added he, hurrying off.

Leopardo smiled.

"You'd better accept my services again, sir," insinuated he.

Somehow or other, the lieutenant had conceived an aversion to the man.

Still, that was no reason why he should not be served by him.

"I know where the governor is," said Leopardo, seeing he hesitated.

"It is well."

"It will be better if I take you to him, as I can easily."

"For money?"

The other laughed in a repulsive manner.

"Of course. There are few see Senor Pecador without paying anything for it!" said he, emphatically.

Still the lieutenant hesitated.

Just then, a tumult at the gates arose, and the echoes penetrated the palace.

In a few minutes, Genifrede would be before her judge. If he did not appease that judge, he might regret so great an opportunity of proving his love all his life.

He put half-a-dozen more coins in the snakey fingers of the man.

"Lead on," said he.

"You shall see the governor," returned Leopardo, turning off into a side passage from the corridor.

"This is not the usual way!"

"No. It's a private passage, it leads directly to his room."

The lobby extended a considerable way, with several turnings.

Just as Lieutenant Cavendish was growing impatient, the guide stopped, laid his hand on a curtain, and turned.

"His chamber is there."

He pulled a cord, which seemed to be a bell-pull, but the sound on the other side of the door-way was less like a bell than a sharp click, as of some mechanism.

Leopardo made way for the Englishman by standing aside.

"He knows you are there now," said he, letting go the cord. "All is ready for you. Go in."

Lance stepped forward.

He saw a light gleaming through the tapestry, as he drew it aside.

At that moment the light that had glimmered alarmingly, went out.

He hesitated on the door-way.

He felt Leopardo's claw-like fingers laid on his shoulders and pushing him forward.

He let go his sword-hilt, and grasped the curtains with an eager clutch. His feet had found no hold.

The folds yielded, luckily not abruptly, and he hung suspended in a circular hole, whose smooth sides presented no clinging-place whatever.

Then the light above in the room blazed out again.

Leopardo's face, wearing a hideous grin, was on the brink, ten feet above him.

The light flooded the villanous visage with brilliancy.

"I am the governor! Poor fool! why have you come between me and my pleasures?" he asked.

No disguise now! He feared not to boast why the poor Genifrede had been so boldly abducted.

Lance was gathering his energies, for the abrupt fall had greatly shaken him.

"Wretch!" cried he, "you shall answer for this crime!"

"Who will accuse me? Not you. For this is the centipede's cup! Wait till you fall to the bottom, and when the reptiles crawl over you and cling to you, you will know whence the name!"

Involuntarily, Lance tried to look down, but the wall was lost in densest shadow.

Every now and then, in the silence, there was a rustle, a hiss, a spurting of vermin, that resounded far below.

"Villain, I am an officer of His Majesty! Beware that you do no farther with me."

Senor Pecador laughed.

"Peace, little Englishman!" sneered he. "Great as is the power of Britain, it'll never know where you were eaten up by the mildew, body and soul."

Cavendish held his tongue.

He would tire out the arch rascal, and, should he be left to himself, prove that his sailor's skill in climbing had been underrated.

But the fiend above seemed to forestall his thought.

"Oh, no," cried he. "There's no getting out of this cup. You'll clamber up this curtain, eh? I'll leave precious little of it for you."

He went away from the edge of the gap, but only to take up a massive candlestick and it's large lighted taper.

Cavendish, his neck strained with holding his head up, was trying to pierce the gloom beneath, when a hot drop fell on one hand.

He looked up.

The governor, reaching his arm down as far as he could, was smearing the curtain with the melted wax.

If he had not hinted at his design, it would have spoken for itself.

Cavendish nerved himself for the task, and began to climb up, hand over hand.

But Pecador had applied the flame to the waxed cloth.

It blazed up furiously.

Still the lieutenant climbed.

It was a race between him and the flame.

But each puff of the latter severed a thread, and the curtain began to tear.

Still Cavendish persevered, although his hands were actually gripping the smouldering folds.

He put all his energies in one mighty effort and leaped up.

The curtain, completely burnt and torn away, fell half into the pit, up which came smoke and flame.

The lieutenant had got one hand upon the ragged edge of the floor.

But he saw, close to his agonised face, that of the demoniac governor.

The latter lifted the heavy candlestick and brought it down on the hand that supported the suspended body.

The bruised fingers relaxed, and with a scream Cavendish descended into the abyss.

The governor held the light up and strove to gaze downward.

Then came up the sickening crash of the falling body meeting hard ground, and sparks spangling the pall of smoke.

"Winding-sheet over the fool!" said the governor.

He went to one corner, opened a large armoury, and put all his strengh in a lever there.

The platform of stone, matching the floor, turned back into its place, and covered up the centipede's cup, of which to taste was death.

"And now to see my fair captive," said Pecador, smiling.

But at the door he met three men.

"Oh, is that you, Pinto?" queried he. "Is the girl all safe?"

But the three men surrounded him, and two laid their heavy hands on his shoulders.

"What's this?" cried he, loudly.

"Hush, our orders are to take you, alive or dead!" said one man's stern voice.

"Orders, what orders?" cried the astounded governor.

"The captain's, the captain of the 'Scarlet Cruiser!'"

*   *   *   *   *

When Cavendish recovered from the fall he found himself racked with pain.

Not only were there the bruises of the descent, but the mouldering damask had scorched his face, arms and body.

He arose, with aching limbs, and groped about in his prison.

It was a circular wall of stone, damp and cold, leaving him scarcely room to extend his arms.

The floor was a compound of trodden earth, of bones that were doubtless human, and the rags of the curtain.

The fire had had one result of good.

The still lingering smoke had driven and now kept away the poisonous reptiles.

On one side was a snake dead.

In the centre, the lieutenant's feet crunched several small shelly objects, which he believed to be dead millipedes and centipedes

The smoke would fade away by some outlet in time ; and the lieutenant had no food.

If ever, he must escape now.

He repressed the pain that thrilled every nerve in him.

He drew his sword and sought for means of egress.

He intended to climb up first by sticking his dirk and sword in the interstices of the stones, but a discovery altered his idea.

There was a large gap in one place.

It was irregular, only a foot or so wide, by a height of four feet.

"Some former inmate has tried to make his escape," thought he.

He thrust his sword-blade and arm into the loophole and touched nothing beyond.

All was in the dark there as well as in the well-hole.

Suddenly, he started back.

"It was not some one trying to get out of this, but somebody bent on getting in!" exclaimed he.

The gap was wider cut in the thick wall on the other side than in the interior.

"What instrument could it be?" marvelled he.

The hard stone, that his sword could scarcely reach, was indented, ploughed up, grooved deeply by a powerful chisel.

"Good God!" murmured he. "It is like claws and teeth, but, oh, of what a size!"

He shuddered as if something more than the cold was in the blast coming through that orifice.

An unknown terror crept over him, completely mastering him.

The heat of his young blood faded, and he leant against the wall to recover calmness.

Afraid to enlarge that opening, he worked away at the opposite wall, where a stone, already loosened by some poor wretches fruitless labours, invited him.

The day passed.

Hunger tortured him, and then came a torpor, a dullness, which made him reck no more of food, of drink, of life.

He flung down his blunted weapons, he flung himself down on the moistened floor, and waited sullenly for death.

He had covered his eyes with his hands, to deepen the blackness enshrouding him.

He had not heard a strange series of sounds approaching the pit by the passage ending in that curiously torn-open rent.

A breath of air, as if from a grave, with the taint of blood upon it, suddenly made his heart rise.

He took away his hands from his sight.

He rubbed his eyes in terrified amaze.

Two lustrous points glared in that fissure in the solid wall.

He started up.

"Help, at last!" cried he, going thither, half crazed with the unexpected joy. "Oh, heaven be thanked!"

But as he neared the chasm, a growl of immense force, which made his heart leap, resounded hollowly.

And he felt, by the sudden motion in the air, that something like a huge beam had been darted through the gap at him.

He fell away from that danger.

A second time the air moved over his body, driven by that unseen object.

Then there was a snarl of rage, and the whole pit echoed with it.

The shining balls seemed to be eyes fastened on him.

Eyes!

Eyes of those dimensions, and of such devilish ferocity.

He thought he must be going mad.

He shut his eyes, the objects were invisible.

He looked—they were there, more savagely glaring than ever.

Then came a clatter on the stones without, and he heard, besides, the fragments of stones fly under those blows, as if a giant stone cutter was at work.

The thing, only to be guessed at in that gloom, was trying to widen the orifice and reach him.

Why were there so few bones on the floor, when the place had clearly been constructed for more victims than he.

Cavendish shuddered to imagine the key to the mystery.

Perhaps the cause of the disappearance of the mortal remains was there.

A serpent?

Not a serpent with such claws.

It seemed rather as it was, one of those gorgons to be read about, not to exist.

The horror that had enchained him, fell of a sudden at the fear of such a death as that messenger must bring.

Cavendish, pressed against the opposite wall, to be as far as he could from that miasmatic breath. He felt the fear revive him.

An hour ago, he had prayed for death.

Now he panted for another breath.

He caught up the broken piece of his sword, and plied at the stone he had already dislodged.

The unknown workman, too, redoubled his energies, as if conscious of the attempted escape.

On one side, the young man, with a dread that gave him back more strength than starvation and cold had deprived him of, plied the steel at the cement.

He was trying to get out of the grave.

On the other side, the unknown labourer bit, tore, scratched, splintered the granite, till the fragments fell about like hail.

With the agony of that impending death in his heart, the lieutenant worked wildly on.

There was a sound behind him, as if the creature was drawing in breath between its set teeth.

He even fancied that he could discern the indistinct outlines of a hideous head.

A head, to judge by the great balls of blazing eyes, but the head of no imaginable monster, to presume by such a shape.

Cavendish looked round never again. It would have paralysed him.

He caught hold of the rocking stone with both of his bleeding hands.

He wrenched it loose; he seized a second and drew it forth.

The rest came more easily.

He pierced an aperture in the wall.

He widened the hole.

He felt earth beyond.

He scooped at it until the nails were torn off his finger's ends.

Suddenly there was a yielding before him.

There was vacancy beyond,

Some passage, or at least a cave, in the subterraneans of the old building.

At the same time he heard a crash.

The whole of the semicircle, right and left of him for six feet up and four on the floor, was drawn back.

The solid masonry was thrust away like a card, by the mighty grasp of the unknown.

Cavendish plunged head foremost into the opening, and dragged himself on through the narrow tunnel by hands, elbows, and knees.

As he fell on the other side of the well to the same level as the prison he had quitted, his ears seemed to be split by a thunder of disappointment and rage, as the whole of the pit he had quitted appeared to be filled by gigantic wings, arms and body, the frame of the baffled and enraged Destroyer.

CHAPTER IV.

THE DOOM OF THE TRAITOR—LOYS PICKS UP A WAIF—ON THE ROAD TO THE TREASURE—THE FIRST BAR IN THE WAY.

THE "Scarlet Cruiser," had taken a long reach westward from her cruise, and stood towards Antigua.

Under scant sail she tacked about one spot, waiting till her boat came off land.

As the moon was going down the lookout called—

"The signal, sir; boat's coming off."

A pistol shot had been seen to flash on the water.

Before long, the yawl, from which it was fired, came up to the vessel.

The officer of the deck, Ned Nittle (who had been made mate), sent a boy to rouse the captain.

Frank came up on deck just as the yawl disembarked her crew.

The three men who composed it, shoved a man's body up, to be caught by the hands on deck.

Trembling, Governor Pecador was thus unceremoniously placed before Captain Frank.

"All hands on deck," ordered the latter.

The whistle piped forth.

"At the wheel, there! take her aback, and let her come slowly with the wind again. Deaden her headway as much as possible."

The Cruiser hardly seemed to move at all, and her sails shivered against the masts.

She was not the "Needle" of other days.

A gun was at each port, and pikes glittered around the masts.

The numerous crew, weather beaten, sun and storm proof, were fierce-browed and wore a fighting look.

Frank stood up with them all arranged in a half circle before him.

His officers stood beside him on either hand.

The governor, pale as the setting moon, hung his head and stood by the main hatch, afraid to stir.

The deck was lighted up with half a dozen battle-lanterns, but spite of that a cold grey cloud was what the scene was swathed within.

"Stand forward, Tonio!" called out the young captain.

At the sound of the name, the governor started out of his dread torpor.

At the sight of the man who answered the summons, Pecador turned green with affright.

"Alive!" murmured he.

"Silence, prisoner!" said Frank sternly.

"The accusers are alone to speak till the judge's turn comes."

The man, a Spaniard, waited for the command with a cheerful patience that spoke well for Frank's discipline.

"Tell your story," said the boy commander.

"You sent me ashore, captain," said Tonio, "to pay the governor, Señor Don Leobardo Pecador, yonder, the first advance of your thousand piastres."

"For which he bargained to aid the 'Scarlet Cruiser' and all belonging to her, to escape any attempt to take her or injure her friends," said Frank. "Was not that so, Pecador?"

The governor nodded lugubriously.

"He took the money and gave me a quittance," continued the sailor. "Then he asked me to tell where the ship lay. I answered that the 'Scarlet Cruiser' was on the wave a Wolf to the oppressors and the tyrannous rich! Away from her friends and near to her foes."

A murmur of pleasure ran around among the seamen.

"He pressed me to reveal. He offered me a quarter of the money, half of it, all. I laughed at him. Then he threatened me, and I laughed louder than ever. He pretended that he was only joking and, as I fell into his humour, he left me to send for wine. Two stout fellows came in and assaulted me. I killed one. As the other held back, I remembered him as an old messmate, one of the slaver-schooner 'Battle Lantern's' dare-devils, I showed my red shirt with the S. C. of the Cruiser, on it, and he helped me to escape. He is here."

Tonio fell back into the ranks.

In his stead another Spaniard stepped forth.

"My name's Mannelo," said he. "The senor governor hired me for queer jobs a week ago. He called me to settle my friend Tonio, but I twigged him and we made it up between us."

"That will do," said Frank. "You are paid three hundred dollars for that service, Not that the life of even a 'holder' in the Wolf of the Wave is not dearer than that; though, Mannelo, I shall want your services myself."

The man bowed.

"I have a suspicion you know where the governor *kept* his treasure, for his profits by the slave trade have been large."

"I do know, captain."

"That's right. The Cruiser is heiress to all the property of traitors," said Frank.

The governor felt cold perspiration stream through every pore.

Not only was his life at stake, but his hoard.

He was about to speak in desperation, when the young commander silenced him with his own voice.

"Pecador, you have heard that charge. You tried to give death to one of your brethren, for all who swear over the steel to be true to the Cruiser and her cause of the poor and oppressed against the rich, are brothers. Breaking that law is——"

"Death!" cried all, in one voice.

"But I——I——" stammered Pecador.

"Silence. It is impossible to deny it. And now, brothers of the crew, and my officers," said Frank, "let me add more. For that attempt to murder, he merits death. But we are just, and for that we would only give the quick death in return."

Pecador shuddered.

"Only a quick death!"

"That item is far from the sum of his failing towards us," resumed the captain. "I will tell you why he wanted to know the whereabouts of our vessel. Loys de Goupille, the most earnest of our foes, is equipping a craft over on the Blue Key. The governor had entered into the enterprise. They hoped to capture the 'Scarlet Cruiser' with a brig and a hundred and fifty of the yellow miscreants of Antiua!"

The crew laughed derisively.

"We cannot suffer the least attempt to mar our plans of benefitting the down trodden. That vessel shall disappear this night."

"Hooray!"

"Oh! this act of justice first. When it is a deed against us all, all have their say. Pecador, do you deny any of this? Not a word. To the vote. Is he guilty, think you?"

All hands were held up.

"The doom. Death?"

All hands again were raised.

"How. Hanging?"

All except one.

"Bill Bowse, bo's'n," said Frank. "You dissent. Your reason."

The old tar had let his hat drop on the deck. He cleared his mouth and stepped forward.

"Well, d'ye see, captain, I hain't got no particular prejudice ag'in' stringing the rascal up—if you would have it done with his own neck'chief rove through a block. But I've got a deep fondness for the Cruiser a'ready, and I hate to think of spoiling a rope and bending a stud'n'sel-boom with that 'ere chap. That's all, cap'en!"

"Don't hang him! shoot him! sling him over to the sharks!" cried all, overcome by Bill's idea.

"Come to one mind," said Frank.

The men held a consultation.

"All agreed, cap'en," said Bo's'n Bill.

"Well?"

"Maroon him. There's many a lonely island in these seas."

"He shall be marooned. The island he shall be king upon will be narrow as his mind, barren as his heart; he shall groan to lay down his life to the devil, and his body to the winds. For the birds shall refuse it, and the sharks shall not reach it. Such is the traitor's doom!"

*   *   *   *   *

The morning broke greyly over the ocean, smooth except for the everlasting swell.

On their long slopes rode a boat, filled with men.

At the helm was Loys de Goupille.

He was glad at heart.

"These fellows," thought he, as he gazed on the rowers, "complete the equipment of my new craft. We will sail this night on the red track of that accursed 'Wolf of the Wave.'"

He knew every point of his former vessel's sailing, and hoped to win her again by that knowledge.

"That boy to command the brig that I used to lord over," growled he, in rage. "Oh, let me but come face to face with him again. Curse that girl, Genifrede, that I ever let her stay my knife when it was over his breast!"

He was interrupted in his musing by the stroke-oar.

THE SCARLET CRUISER.

"RIGHT! DEATH IS HERE! YOUR DEATH!" SHOUTED A LOUD VOICE.

"Something straight ahead, cap'en!" said he; "can't see for the sun."

Loys shielded his eyes from the rays of the rising orb.

"A stray spar," said he. "It lies in our way; we'll see. Pull away, lads, pull!"

In half an hour they had come up from the object.

Around it the waves were lashed to foam by the furious and ravenous movements of a dozen sharks, snapping at one another, and at the tit-bit just beyond their teeth.

It was a large flag-buoy.

To it was tied a man.

Around his neck was wound the bight of the flag cord, so that, if the fastenings to his hands should break or come undone, he would hang himself by pitching forward.

But, to prevent him killing himself, when the pangs of exposure and the reflected glare to famine and thirst should drive him mad, his legs were secured, so that he should not slip down, and so strangle himself.

At every dip of the buoy the sharks swarmed

4

forward to receive the prey, but ere they could turn to open their maws, the float would right itself, and snatch the victim from their ravenous jaws.

Above the buoy was a cloud of birds, screaming, fluttering, making swoops now and then.

But ever scared by the flaunting of a flag on the pole.

The boat drew near, and the men lay on their oars.

A puff of wind straightened the streamer, till it lay flat as a board.

On a jet black field, in red letters, was the word—

"TRAITOR !"

"He's dead," said one.

But at the sound of the human voice, the bonded figure shuddered, and the breath came hoarsely in a sob between the lips, bleeding, and crusted with the salt, dried from the spray.

"Cut him down," said Loys. "No one can tell what a waif may be worth."

At that moment the bouy dipped.

A young shark, as if knowing that the newcomers were rescuers, launched himself upward to seize the prey.

"Stand aside !" cried Loys.

He rushed to the prow, from seat to seat, and caught up the boathook.

An instant he poised it over the white belly of the fish.

"There !" cried he, darting it harpoonwise, "There's something sweet for your gullets."

The sharks, as the blood spouted out and flavoured the brine, followed the victim, and soon tore him to pieces.

Meanwhile, the suspended man was taken down.

Loys wiped the face of the senseless form with his sleeve.

"By Saint Denis !" cried he, "it's my friend the governor ! Who could have done this, when I saw him ashore yesterday afternoon !"

One of the men turned his blanched face towards him, and mutely levelled a trembling finger at the buoy.

Loys looked.

They had not before noticed that on its side was a name—

The "SCARLET CRUISER."

Loys scanned the horizon eagerly, at this.

The ocean was vacant.

Except straight ahead, where a dark cloud steadily hovered.

"Pull away, lads," said he, on seeing this. "The men have kindled a fire to signal us. Lay down to it with a will ! Spring, while you're about it !"

While the oarsman rowed on lustily, the Frenchman devoted himself to reviving the governor.

Pecador, his brain almost turned by the frightful fate that he had been consigned to, remained long in that state of unconsciousness.

Suddenly an exclamation broke from the bow oar.

"Better look yonder, captain."

Loys started up from bathing Pecador's face.

The pillar of smoke which he had long before descried, indeed came from a fire.

But it was a fire that made him shudder with pain.

"Pull away, men !" cried he, letting the

governor come to life himself, while he grasped the tiller-ropes more seamanly.

In ten minutes, the long boat had come within easy sight of the shore of a long promontory of azure limestone, called the Blue Key.

The sunbeams fell in a bright orange glare all around on shore and wave.

On the water its light was outvied by the ruddy blaze of a large brig on fire, from stem to stern, from royal mast to water's edge.

The hull was a mass of conflagration, the yards and masts and booms rained down the incandescent rags of the fresh-bent sails, unfurling luridly of themselves.

On the sands and rocks, the sun's rays glinted on broken weapons that were still griped in stiffened hands, lopped off from perforated bodies.

Still again, half floating, half held by their weight on the shingle, rocked other corpses, around which the beautiful angel-fish were in schools like a flock of flies about carrion.

When any of these bodies were caught by the reflux and came out into deep water, the sharks speedily rent it into ensanguined tatters.

Loys' boat pushed on.

The canopy of smoke, sparks and tongues of fire overhead, the road obstructed by charred timber and streaks of burning tar.

The boat was run upon the beach.

Loys ran to each man, one after another, but life had been let out of all by pistol, cutlass, or pike.

"Who has done this ruin ?" cried he, in rage. "Will no one speak ?"

"Look !" cried Pecador, who had been dragged out of the boat and dropped on the sand.

He was pointing in the direction of the sun.

All eyes were bent thitherward, like his own.

On the broad face of the orb was defined the full sail of a vessel.

She seemed to be on a holiday, streamer at the fore and main and peak.

But above all, on the main, a large banner spread out, broad as a topsail, in silken glory.

This, blotting out the disc of fire, the strange craft had a wierd and ghastly look.

She seemed not to cleave the blue of the sea with keel, or the azure of the sky with spars, but to float in that crimson radiance.

Loys knew her.

"The Scarlet Cruiser !" cried he, for the second time within the last few hours.

And the sailors with him, and Pecador, glanced on the pall of vapour shrouding the consumed hull, and on the corpses reddening the shore, and shudderingly said—

"The Wolf of the Wave ! "

*   *   *   *   *

While the "Cruiser" had gone to wipe out this antagonist in embryo, her captain was not idle on his part.

The land was to witness an attempt as daring.

Frank took Ned Nittle, Bill Bowse, and another seaman named Jack, with him.

Mannelo accompanied them to act as their guide.

They went round Antigua and pushed into the chapparal of thorns and aguaves in the rear of the governor's palace.

Mannelo led them by secret paths to a cave in the hill side.

The trees, thickly growing all around, kept

them from fear of discovery from the palace distant, beside, as it was.

"Now," said Frank to the guide, "you assure me that this gap, here, leads to an underground passage by which the governor's mansion may be reached."

"Yes. You are sailors, and have a pocket compass. You take your bearings, and there you are."

"And you do not know more about this passage?"

"I don't know anything, sir. Nor anybody else. There's no native of Antigua would go down into the subterraneans."

"Why not? Let's have the whole story, while my men get all their equipment ready."

The sailors were all armed well, and had lengths of rope, &c., so as to be ready for any emergency.

"It's a short tale," replied Mannelo. "Yonder big building was built by the Indians, over whom were the monks, who converted them and civilised them."

"Aha! taught 'em how to hew stones, to build houses for the priests? Go ahead," said Frank.

"Well, this was long ago, at the early settlement. The savages got savage one day——"

"Wanted to build houses for themselves and family?" suggested the young captain.

"I don't know, sir. However, these Indians attacked the monastery, beat back the monks, and chased them through all the chambers."

"And slaughtered them all?" said Frank.

"Not exactly. They did butcher some. But here's the mystery. They drove the priests from hall to room, from room to the last of them. They burst the door in and rushed in, but the holy fathers had vanished!"

"Miracle!" cried Frank,

"Well," said Mannelo, doubtfully, "everybody did say so for about two hundred years. But another tale sprang up then."

"Oh, indeed?"

"Yes. Two Spanish hunters were shooting on the hills here, when a wounded bird fluttered away into this cave. One hunter followed it. He came out of the cavern, told his comrade that he had found a long passage built up——"

"And that's it?" said Frank Rogers, pointing to the black tunnel before them.

"That's it. As I was saying, the two hunters went into the hole, and penetrated to a considerable depth. They managed to get out all right, but dreadfully frightened."

"Well, how?"

"They found the interior of that great hill like a buried house. The monks had built it up in halls, cells, and kitchens, and everything."

"Whew! You don't mean to say that the hunters found the monks fat and lively after two hundred years?" laughed Frank.

Mannelo shook his head.

"No, but the hunters found a great chamber with a floor of skeletons! and what was more horrible, there wasn't one bone left to another!"

"How was that? Did the Indians get down there?"

"Oh no. That's the enigma. The hunters told their story at Antigua. No one would believe them. They got tired of being called liars, and offered to go down again with any party."

"Pleasant invitation!"

"Senor Terribio, nephew of the governor of that day, and half-a-dozen more young gallants, agreed to make the exploration. They came here, followed by half the city. They went down, with plenty of blessed candles and a long rope, that they uncoiled as they went in."

"Stay a minute, my men," called out Frank. "Go on, Mannelo."

"Very little more, sir.

"In about a quarter of an hour the rope was shaken. The party were coming back. Suddenly the people standing here, just like you or I, heard a roar or a yell, or some terrible sound that they had never known before.

"There were brave men there, senor, but the whole crowd shook like so many leaves.

"They hastened to pull in the rope, and half climbing, half dragged, Senor Terribio was got out of the cave.

"He fell down senseless among them all.

"When he came to life, he wouldn't speak a word till he was in the high cathedral of Antigua. Then, pale and trembling, he solemnly, in presence of the altar, declared that he and his companions, while looking at the hall-strewn with dust and bones of men, had beheld, rising out of the ground, the Devil!"

"What?" cried Frank, taken aback.

"The Devil! *Maldita!* the Prince of Evil himself!" replied Mannelo, crossing himself. "The apparition had wings, claws, and teeth! and such teeth and claws! Senor Don Terribio saw his five or six comrades struck down and bitten through like a squirrel champing nuts.

"He had his sword out and made a lunge, but the blade was knocked out of his hand in a minute. He fled to the hole, grasped the rope, and could not tell even how he had been saved. He had heard a direful flutter of monstrous wings behind him, and the last sound in his ears was that inexpressibly appalling shriek of rage, which the people without had also heard."

"Whew!" whistled the young captain again.

"Laugh away," said Mannelo; "I only know that nobody ever went down that gully hole since."

"But Don Terribio, the coward who deserted his friends?"

"No coward, senor. He was a famous soldier in European wars. He never was himself after that day. He had used to be the very devil himself among the gay mulatresses of the South Quarter, but he shunned the world, and for all the interest he took in anything but pious acts, he might as well have been a priest out and out."

"And the friends of his?"

"Never heard of."

"Now, captain," said Ned Nittle, respectfully.

"You won't come along?" inquired Frank.

"No," replied Mannelo. "I don't suppose there's another man on the island who would have come so near as this."

"Well, take care of yourself, then. Goodbye!"

"The saints have you in keeping!"

The men of the "Cruiser" were left to themselves.

"First thing!" said Frank to them. "This may be a more perilous task than I presumed. We will all be equal before danger. We were all messmates aboard the old "Honest Trader." We'll be Jack and Frank, Bill and Ned, now, till we have this bout out."

"If you like, captain," said Bowse.

"There you go again with your captain," laughed the youth. "However, first plunge for me!"

So saying, the speaker scrambled into the cave.

Soon he entered a narrow tunnel, built up strongly, and of a circular shape.

A man had to crawl through it.

This narrowness had evidently been designed for the better defence of the entrance.

After a gentle descent of some thirty feet, Frank found himself in twilight, and in a large cave.

Stones were built up on the sides, but the earth had fallen in here and there.

In a few minutes the sailors were all together.

"Strike a light," said Frank.

Bill produced some dry rope-ravels, and lit it by flashing some powder in a pistol-pan.

The candles they had brought were then lit.

But scarcely had they crossed the first cave and entered a very long corridor, than Frank said—

"Halt! This won't do. Though every one of us carry a candle, there is not light enough with this subterranean so lofty."

He unhooked the flask at his belt, and poured the brandy into a hollow of a flagstone under foot.

"Do the same," said he to the others.

They passed him their gourds or bottles cheerfully.

"We'll have lots to drink," said he, "before long, if this road's right.

He poured out all the liquor.

While so doing, he looked around.

"Ah," said Bill, "I know what you are arter!"

He produced from his capacious pocket a length of rope, from which he cut three yards or so.

This, doubled up and twisted, formed a piece of a couple of feet long and several inches thick, while being almost as stiff as a solid body.

The cut ends and bight of this, Frank also sopped in the brandy.

Then he bound that extremity all around with some sailcloth.

"That will burn for some time," said Ned, approvingly.

"Shall we light it now?" asked Bill, about to apply the candle to it.

"No. Not till we actually need it," answered the captain.

That moment seemed near at hand, for even while the words dropped from his lips, a sound, not made by them, echoed ominously in the corridor.

"Hark!" cried they all.

"Wind," said one.

"More like the whizz of wings," said Frank.

He was right.

CHAPTER VIII.

THE MAN-EATER SEEKS TO DEFEND THE CAVERN— WE MUST KILL, OR BE KILLED—THE UNHEARD-OF CONTEST—THE PTERODACTYLE'S DEATH—UP FROM THE DEPTHS.

THE same thought presented itself to each of the four friends.

The sound was, in truth, precisely like that drumming a pheasant will often make, only inconceivably louder, and hence more frightful.

"Be what that may," said Frank, at once, "this is no place, so slippery and contracted in room, for us to meet it."

With that, lighting the spirituous torch, he strode forward.

His naked sword was in his other hand.

Ned came next, holding ready the pistols.

Then Bill with the candle.

And Jack in the rear.

Rogers had made his men bring straight swords in lieu of cutlasses, as a fairer match for Spanish rapiers.

Against their expectation, not a thing was visible or audible in the corridor, up or down.

"Shall we go back?" asked one.

"Put it to the vote. I'm for going on."

"And I—and I!" said the others in a breath.

"So am I," said Bill, "if it comes to that. Only I likes to be prudent when one don't know what thing of the earth above or depths here below, one may have to face."

To the end of the corridor they went.

To their right was a turning.

They went into it.

After some twenty feet, a little down-sloping, they came to another turn, in the direction of the long corridor, which they had so long been traversing.

This new tunnel stretched along for a good distance, as well as the absence of any other light than their own permitted them to judge.

There was a circular box of masonry in an ample recess.

Frank went over to it with Ned.

"It's a well," cried the young captain.

Boyishly, he dislodged one of the stones of the curb.

The mortar was good, though, and he had to apply force.

The square, heavy piece of stone, toppled inwards, fell into the black mouth.

Rumble, rumble, was the sound, now and anon, as it bounded from side to side.

Fainter and fainter faded away the entombed echoes.

"Deep, I tell you," said Frank.

After a space, which seemed incredibly long to the listeners, a complete cessation of even the most feeble noise told that the stone had reached the end of the lengthy shaft.

"I would not like to have to wait for a drink till the water was hauled up out of there," laughed the youth.

Ned approached the candle to the pit's mouth.

"They once did use it," said he. "You can see marks of a framework at the top here. Ah!"

A rush of air up the orifice had blown out his light.

"Yes," said Bill, suddenly, "Frank seems to have woke up the air."

"Something more too."

As Frank spoke he pushed with all his might at the stone coping.

"Bear a hand, quick!" cried he.

Jack up with his foot, armed with its heavy boot, and dealt the already shaken stone such a kick that a huge mass tumbled off its setting into the hole.

It thundered down the funnel.

It had reached, perhaps, half-way, when it seemed to encounter something.

The collision caused a quite audible shock.

Then a piercing and terrifying shriek of some-thing in agony rang up the mine to chill the listeners to the marrow.

"Mercy! what in the name of heaven's that?" exclaimed they, starting back.

The like of it had never startled any of them before.

The echoes died suddenly away of that horrid scream, being drowned by the louder ones of the fallen stones pounding on the bottom.

Once again that outcry resounded from the core of the gulf, but weaker, much weaker than before.

There was a silence below and above.

Ned mechanically, with a shaking hand, lit his taper at his comrade's flaming link.

A third time the inarticulate accents of the unknown in torment reached the sailor's ears.

It would seem, too, that the torture-wrung cry was heard elsewhere.

For a sort of answering call quite forcibly responded.

Very faintly, but, nevertheless, perceptibly, the whirring sound which had first alarmed the companions uprose.

It ceased; to be followed by a whimper of pleasure, which equally changed into a murmur, that to a growl, and ended with a positively astounding wail.

"It must have been Old Scratch that was hit by the stones, when coming up," said Frank, "and that's young Nick grieving for him."

"It's no jest, sir. I'm older than you, my lad, but I never heard the like of that."

"Nor I neither, Bill."

"Nor I. Nor do I ever want to do so, again," said Jack, griping his sword-hilt convulsively.

However, the cause of their uneasiness was hushed.

All was still down the bowel of the earth.

Jack pushed over some more stones, at a nod from the captain.

They all stood ready, but there was merely the rattle of the missiles.

Nothing more.

"Come on," said Frank, more lightly.

They followed him with readiness.

But hardly had they gone up the turn of the lobby, than Jack, who brought up the rear with owse, turned around, pressed his shoulder, and pointed.

Bill saw what fear-stricken countenance his mate wore, and rightly concluded that the matter now was no laughing one.

The others turned the same.

Supported by two paws, garnished with talons like a bear's or a tiger's, a head of the size of a wolf, or a very large fox, rested on the broken edge of the deep well.

The glare from the flambeau was reflected by its blazing eyes and grinding teeth.

More than its head, its neck and shoulders rose into view.

The friends were appalled already by what they had seen of it.

The hideousness of the monster, so little unveiled yet, was increased, impossible as that seemed, by another head, the eyes of which were shut, and the ears limp and drooping, that was over its shoulder.

"Good God!" ejaculated Rogers.

Except that exclamation, they were all too fascinated to move or speak.

They forgot they had weapons in their hands.

They gazed, that was all they could think of doing.

Up rose the object, black as Sin.

The eyes, ferocious beyond expression, yet swam in grief—a grief so evident and so poignant, that the fiendish visage almost grew human.

Folded up and ribbed, netted and hairy, the unused wings that were attached to the brawny arms or forelegs, and to the other limbs, as they were presently to behold, now appeared.

With an effort the mammoth bat clambered over the circular wall down upon the slabs.

It shook off its load.

For the head, which had increased its aspect by having the appearance of belonging to it, really appertained to another form of the same species, but smaller.

This second one, borne on the back by the other, had been hooked on to its shoulder by its claws.

When shaken off upon the stones, it half spread itself out, ere settling down at full length, an inert mass.

Its body, on the back, which was uppermost, and its head, had the fur scraped off here and there, and were all powdered with lime and stone dust.

Blood speckled its dark skin, and even streaked it in one or two places.

The live animal surveyed the dead one almost tearfully, and then turned its ferocious orbs on the enemy.

It would actually appear as though the being, divining that the death-givers to its mate would be found above, had carried, with infinite trouble, that carcase to confront them.

For a second, the single avenger eyed its little band of foes.

Then, standing up on its hind legs, set far apart, the talons scratching the stony floor, it opened widely the arms.

From wrist to wrist the wings unfolded, and from ankle to ankle.

But by some unaccountable provision of nature, the line of the outer edge did not extend either curved inward, or straight from member to member.

In the middle, that is at its breast-height, a splint of bone so projected that it widened the web.

The whole sweep of the flying membrane, from tip to tip, could not have been less than five yards.

The figure stood, though its legs were wide apart, perhaps as many feet high.

It gnashed its teeth.

It saw the seamen range themselves, with flashing lights and sword-blades, in the entrance of the passage.

Of flight, not one of them dreamed.

Three or four times the monster flapped its wings, taking a step between a double hop and a stride at each time.

Its claws rattled as an accompaniment to the champing of its jaws.

As this beginning of an approach was so slow, the seamen fancied that they would have plenty of time to prepare for it, brief as was the space between.

But, most unexpectedly, uttering an angry scream, surpassing in thrilling and terror-strik-ing intensity any that it had ever split that awful cavernous air with, it flew like lightning forward.

Not expecting this, the four friends were overwhelmed by the gigantic sweeping pinions.

Frank groaned.

He alone had escaped, thanks to the torch which he had happened to hold at that terrible moment.

His sword, thrust at random into the wings of the bat, had fallen from it harmlessly, dashed from his hand.

As he started back, unwounded, but a little bruised, he could see, by the uncertain flickering of his fanned torch, that the beast had enfolded the three of his companions in the compass of that inky mantle.

Horrified, he could not move.

But the hideous jaws, open to let out an awfullly fiendish growl, opened still wider to snap at the victims just under them.

Another moment, and the already half-suffocated men would have surely been bitten to death.

The captain of the "Cruiser," swore a tremendous oath at himself, for his really pardonable pause.

Then he leaped at the animal as fearlessly as if it had been not near so unearthly and horrid.

Dauntlessly he began, vigorously he continued, his efforts to set his friends at liberty.

A dagger in his left hand, the flaming torch in his right, he stabbed and banged away at the head of the monstrous pterodactyle.

It at least could not bite his comrades.

The flambeau, put out by such a series of sounding blows, fell from his hand.

All was darkness—blackness—in the cavern.

All was gloom, but far from silence.

Indescribable was the devilish clamour of the wild beast's growls, spittings, and howls, both of rage and pain, for its head was all scorched.

Forgetting its three captives almost, it clawed at the young champion.

It could see in the dark.

His dagger-strokes at random, missed even so great a target, at times.

It fell upon the youth.

All rolled upon the stones.

"Blung, blung!" went hollowly two pistol shots.

Jack, pressed against the breast of the monster, and squeezed up with his two fellows, had overcome the first confusion, and excited by the pain of suffocation, had pulled the triggers of his brace of fire-arms, even at the risk of killing his friends.

The swords of the others, half strangled as they were, were useless all this time.

Amazed at the explosion, though the two-fold wounds it received only inflamed its rage, the beast, choking, too, with the sulphurous vapour that began to steal up out of its bosom, unfolded its wings.

The three mariners drank greedily of the free air.

For the exuding perspiration of the animal was not excessively fragrant.

The struggle was not concluded.

The monster yelled, snapped at Frank, who parried its bite with a slash of his sword, opened its pinions with a force that rolled Bill off one side and Ned the other, and fell bodily on the captain and Jack.

It bore them to the ground.

Its furious onset would have easily pulled down a horse or a lion.

Ned, while still rolling, encountered something sharp, which scratched his hand.

It was a sword.

He scrambled to his feet.

The eyes of the creature, gloating over the bodies of his fallen friends, shone in the obscurity, perfect beacons.

The sailor marched quickly to it, and with all the force he could put into his arm, he delivered a lunge.

"We must kill or be killed!" cried he.

The well-thrust steel ran along under the lower jaw, pierced the throat, escaped the main vein and the vertebra behind, by a miracle, and bore back the beast to the wall.

Ned pressed on.

The blade entered to the very hilt.

The point met an interstice between two stones of the wall, penetrated the mortar deeply, and there remained.

The creature flapped its wings, torn and broken in places, clawed at the air, howled and battled.

All in vain.

It was pinned to the wall by the blade, no less effectually than a moth is attached to cardboard.

A fragment of the spirit-soaked rags that had helped to form the improvised link, still sparkled in a corner.

Ned ran to it, picked it up, swung it in the air till it flamed, found the candle by its means, and lit it.

What he beheld was certainly not cheering.

The young captain lay across Bill's body, both senseless.

Jack was rising, looking ruefully at the arm of his jacket, torn into strips by the bat's claws, and stained with its blood.

He picked up his knife.

"There's your sword, mate," said Ned, laughingly now.

He pointed to the transfixed thing, which had both ceased making motion and complaint.

"Let it stay," said Jack. "I'd rather it were through him than he loose, and tearing about. Ah!"

And he drew a long breath of relief.

When a few drops of brandy, luckily left, were sprinkled on the faces, and a few more drops put upon the tongues of the two insensible men, they showed signs of life.

In ten minutes all were ready to move on again, or as they might decide.

"Is it quite dead?" asked Frank.

He was examining the apparent corpse.

"Quite, I should say," replied Ned, "I have been watching it."

"It is easy to make sure," remarked Jack.

He had re-charged his pistols.

"I'll blow his ugly head into a thousand bits!" said he, stepping forward.

Ned pulled him back.

"No, no. It is useless to waste powder and ball. He's welcome to the sword, if that's why you would shatter it. Let us be off from here I never felt such a pang in all my born days, as that monster gave me, when I beheld him enclose all I held dear—I mean when you three were all buried under his horrible wiugs."

"A wrap-rascal, I don't fancy," laughed Bill, hoarsely.

"I couldn't use my sword, and how Jack managed to pull a trigger, I don't see."

"I don't know myself," said Jack, "and if our black friend on the wall knows, he don't look as if he could impart much information, now."

"Thanks to you!" said the other three.

They all pressed Jack's hand.

A last look was given to the fiend-like form, motionless as if carved of the stone it was hanging against.

Turning their backs on their conquered antagonist, which they would not have done while he lived, the four, recovered now from any petty injuries they had received, proceeded along the vaulted road.

After a while, it sloped a little, rising a foot in fifty or so.

Then a short turn, a level passage, another turn, and a passage ending in a door.

It was decayed, but still held together.

It could have been beaten down easily.

But the bar and a bolt were inside, on their side, and the key was in the lock.

The latter was of no use, for rust had prevented it ever turning.

Bill battered at the iron plate.

He had it off in a few seconds.

"I don't think much of locks," said Frank, abruptly, as they were passing through.

"No, my lad," returned Bill, "a hand requires pratice more than strength, and aided by a clever head, I don't think but that a man could enter a king's palace easily."

"Or get out of a king's prison," said Jack.

All laughed.

They were mounting a flight of stone steps.

At the top, Frank turned.

"Friends, we are approaching the level of the ground. Let nobody speak. Am I to be leader still?"

All nodded.

At the end of the still vaulted path from the head of the stairs, was another flight.

They ascended.

On the landing, Frank beckoned Bill.

There was a door.

Bill went to work on it, with less noise than before.

"Jack," whispered Frank, "run back to the last door, and report how it looks on this side."

The sailor nodded to imply that he comprehended, and retraced his steps.

Enough light came down to him.

He returned.

"Marks all over it, around the lock and about where the bar-pivot is. They couldn't get through, though," concluded he.

"As I thought," observed Frank. "This door has a lock more than a hundred and fifty years newer than those we have been pushing through. Somebody has tried to come down exploring, but has been stopped by that door."

"It wouldn't check me long," remarked Bill Bowse, chuckling.

"Ah, but it is old now."

Meanwhile, Bill had picked the lock with a dagger point.

He tried the door.

"No bolt," said he, "but a bar."

Frank turned round.

"You see. Somebody, long after the monks buried themselves alive far beneath the sunbeams, found out this way."

Bill had tapped the upper part of the door all over.

At last he smiled.

He fitted a tool, taken from his pockets together, selected a spot in the panel, and went to work drilling a hole.

The others watched his actions tranquilly.

One hole bored, Bill made another a couple o inches above it, on the same line.

He replaced his bitt by a fine saw, by aid of which he cut down from one hole to the other.

That saw he laid aside for one still finer.

When that was in play, the sound was not of severed wood, but of metal biting away metal.

Presently he stopped.

Out of his pocket he drew a fine, but extremely strong, horse-hair line.

He formed a large loop, and introduced it through the slit with a delicate pair of plyers.

He drew it tight, and went on filing again.

At last, he pulled out his saw, put away all his instruments, and pushed on the door with all confidence of its opening.

In fact, it gave way, a little rustily, but with no other resistance.

They looked at the other side.

Half of the sundered bar was hanging by the horse-hair line.

"Pretty," said Frank, as Bowse laid down the piece of iron, and pocketed the twine that had prevented its falling and making a noise.

"Oh, that's nothing," said Bill. "But no more talk, I propose."

After half-a-dozen steps, the road seemed to end.

There was only a slit in the side wall of about the width of a man at the shoulders.

"Steps!" said Frank. "The light!"

He advanced upwards.

The narrow flight, very irregular, with frequent turns, apparently without cause, continued almost endlessly.

Not a window, loophole, or slit, let in light.

There were one or two air-holes, though.

The termination was an iron plate.

The captain examined it by the help of the candle.

The knob in its centre yielded when pressed.

The plate moved on one side.

Frank pushed it as far as it would go.

An opening, square, about five feet high by three wide, was before them. It gave a view, only arm's reach from it, of a stone wall.

The youth looked down.

"Oh!" said he.

He saw a large slab of stone beneath him, and two dogs of ornamental brass.

"It's a fire-place," said he. "We're in a chimney!"

Cautiously, by means of the jutting stones, he descended.

"Come down. No fear of spoiling your clothes, for there hasn't been a fire lit here since we were little boys."

"Sweep ho!" said Jack, following him.

Jack was a funny chap in his way.

The four stood in a high and wide apartment, as rich as grand, but as deserted and dusty as anything else.

"Take a chair, one and all," said Frank, sitting down himself, after dusting a chair. "This is all too lonely for us to fear intrusion. Bill, empty your pockets of the provisions. Let's have our snack. Our late adventure with that child of Davy Jones, who would have eaten us, ought to have sharpened our appetites."

CHAPTER IX.

THE ROOMS WHERE NO LIVING TREAD HAVE THEIR
SHADOWY TENANTS—THE GRISLY HORROR—THE
PHANTOM'S TRAEGDY—THE PALE TERROR.

THE wing of the palace, completely abandoned,
was not likely to be suspected as the refuge of
the adventurers of the " Cruiser."

The only portion in use was where the Governor Pecador had lodged his captive, Genifrede.

The sailors waited till the rest of the day and
night should pass.

They kept quiet, and took by turns the slumber
they were all so much in need of, till morning.

At early dawn, Frank, whose youth made him
uncommonly active, made two discoveries.

He was peeping out through a hole in the
ruined blind, and through the encrusted pane
(which he had to clean) upon the kind of enclosed court or garden that it commanded.

Whom should he see in the dawn's grey
streakings, attended by a stern duenna, but
Genifrede.

If she had looked entrancing in the light of
the cabin of the " Scarlet Cruiser," much more
ravishing was she in the clear pure air.

Graceful as the flowers she bent to pluck,
fresh as the dew that glistened on their blossoms,
lovely as those buds themselves, Frank, with
that transcient, far off glimpse, felt his heart
leap to be thus blessed with another view of
her.

He watched her enter the house.

He saw that the duenna, who appeared to be a
mere attendant, was really a guardian, and that
Genifrede was evidently a prisoner.

He could not imagine how she had come
within this palace.

If he had but suspected that the governor had
thus seized upon her, how he would have
sharpened the punishment he had already inflicted on him.

Suddenly he thought he had guessed it.

Loys was in league with Pecador.

He had probably left his daughter here, to be
in safety while he pursued his revengeful
designs.

Her sorrowful look was thus explained.

At noon he determined that he would try and
see her.

" Let us go find the treasure," said he, then.

The floor they were on was the second over
the ground floor.

The one above had no outlet.

There was no egress to this, except the chimney place, and its secret door connecting with
the staircase in the wall ; the regular stairs to
above and below excepted.

They descended.

The rays of the sun filtering through the
coated panes of the blinded casements above, had
et some light illumine the place.

Here there was none at all.

They had to ignite the wick of what was left
of the extremely useful coil of waxed string.

Its glimmer fell upon the interior of a room,
very magnificently gilded, and enriched with
carvings, on the ceiling, the walls, the cornices,
and round the doors. It had one window. The
curtain was torn down from it, and smoothed
boards replaced it.

They entered the apartment, to which the one
they had just left served as an ante-chamber.

Its windows were also boarded up, but the
heavy curtains, fleecy with woolley dust, still
hung by their brazen but tarnished rings on a
rod of the same spoilt metal.

There was a tall cabinet, a writing-stand, a
praying-desk, a dressing-table, a closet in one
corner, and in another a large bed, over which,
to match its ponderous frame, was the framework of a canopy.

But the curtains, the valance, all the decorations and appendages of the couch, had been
removed.

This stripping of the place impressed the
scene with a still more lonely air.

Why some things were taken, and others, of
equal value, left, was unaccountable.

It would seem as if the workmen had been
interrupted while half through their labours.

" Come on," said Frank.

Wondering, they passed into the next of the
series.

A very grand hall, rather than a room.

At one end, to the seamen's right as they
entered by the side, was the chief object
between the four walls.

Besides it were a long table and many chairs.

Flanked on either side by a window, boarded
up, and the curtains half disengaged, was a
low dais or staging, approached by three broad
steps.

Four iron posts, thin, gilded, rose each at a
corner and ended in the ceiling.

Arranged so as to slide on them, but now
wrenched out of place, and within a few feet
of the stage, resting on the remains of a crushed
chair, was a square, befringed, laced, em-
broidered mass.

Its face, or lower part, was of satin and velvet,
gold and silver, exquisitely worked. This
showed that it must have been up against the
ceiling, a canopy to the kind of throne.

But its body and top was one extremely,
weighty mass of metal, heavy enough to crush
an ox, bone and body.

No marvel that the chair underneath it was
all ruined, stout as it was.

The sailors approached.

" Stay," said Ned, who bore the light.

He pulled back Frank, who preceded him.

He indicated what caused his act.

At their feet, on the carpet, between the head
of the long table and the dais, was a great patch
or dark stain.

On looking closer, it was found to be surrounded by other spots, which continued and
led to the dais.

Its upper flooring was stained still more
plentifully than the carpet.

" Some bloody deed," said Rogers. " By the
style of the chairs I should say whatever did
happen was years ago."

So saying, he went round the head of the long
table and crossed the room.

His friends walked close to him.

Ned Nittle was last.

As the three before him were stepping through
on that side which offered no resistance, the
faithful rearward cast a glance, more from habit
than aught else, over his shoulder.

Whatever he saw, it rooted him to the spot,
except that it made him wheel quite around to
see it better.

Too much affected to speak, he grasped the
arm of Jack convulsively.

The latter, pained as well as startled by the
grip, uttered an exclamation.

THE SCARLET CRUISER.

THE GUARD OVER THE BLOOD-BOUGHT TREASURE.

He very naturally looked round.

"What now, mate?"

The words were frozen on his suddenly-chilled lips.

Like the other, he could look on aghast, that was his utmost power.

On hearing Jack's low cry of surprise, the other two imitated his action.

The magical influence did not spare them.

All four, with bewitched eyes, glared at the room on the threshold of which they were immovably planted.

It was the same, yet different.

The duskiness that had previously been alone lessened by the adventurers' little light, was gone.

Nothing was there to furnish a single gleam, and, for all that, a vague and shifting pallid lustre floated all around.

It was of the nature of the will-o'-the-wisp, or like the moonlight one sees in a dream.

Unnatural was it; unnatural was the new objects it hovered around.

The whole table, each side and the end, was surrounded by seated persons, men and women.

Richly dressed, their faces not unhandsome in shape, yet so unearthly glittered their gold and tinsel, so corpse-like was the violet tint of their countenanes, that only their being immaterial and shadowy made a view of them possible.

Granting them more substantial, no one

human could have let his eyes linger for the sixtieth of a second on them, and not go mad!

There were dishes on the board, but the smoke that rose slowly from the uncovered meats, was like exhalations from a fat church-yard of a hot summer's day.

There was a peacock, cooked in its plumage, and a boar's head garnished and glazed, but the eyes in the long feathers were eyes shining like phosporescent eye balls of fish; and the teeth of the boar were grinning while it rolled its half-baked, discolored orbs on the guests.

None of them had eyes for the detestable regales.

They were all staring—staring with a force and fixedness hard to conceive, at the end of the hall where rose the platform.

To that turned the attention of the living witnesses as well.

They could hardly believe what they beheld.

The fallen canopy was down, and yet its likeness was up, up against the ceiling.

The crushed chair was yet dismembered, and nevertheless there stood, as if unharmed, the very semblance of itself.

And more; a man sat in the counterfeit.

His face and hands were very white, perhaps because his attire was a suit of rich black velvet. His hair and beard were light, but seemed to be of a yellower hue from a species of fire they caught from the reflection of his eyes.

Like lightnings issuing upwards from a tomb—lightnings of hell, not heaven—shone they upon the figures confronting him.

This stood upon that stain of the carpet on which Ned Nittle had prevented Jack from stepping.

It was a female shape.

In a golden-coloured robe trimmed with red, her olive complexion glowed like burnished copper, her jet eyes sparkled like black diamonds, and her raven hair gleamed like a dark blush on Satan's face.

Another visage still, only the head not the body, was visible.

The curtains veiled the rest.

For behind their folds, deep in the cloudy embrasure of one window, appeared to be hidden a man.

That countenance of his, dark like the woman's, and possessing a rude likeness to hers, covered with crisp, black locks, and marked with a ferocious moustache, owned eyes which flared with that changeable brightness of white hot coals.

He watched the woman bow to the man on the seat.

He watched the latter rise, and she extend her hand to accept his.

A dagger gleamed in the grasp of the spy.

There was a shudder of the canopy on high.

Without a sound, which made the ghastly act all the more appalling, down came that loaded mass with the swiftness and the deadliness of a thunderbolt.

The rising man was forced back into his just-quitted seat, and that and him were both together brought to earth, crushed, crushed, crushed—one into splinters of wood, the other into a pulp of flesh!

As this occurred, the man, who had doubtless cut the cord that had upheld the destroying canopy, darted out, and plunged the dagger again and again, quicker than eye could wink, into the bosom of the woman.

The guests at table started up.

A blueish, flickering light streamed on their suddenly bared blades.

This was the picture:—

The fallen square upon what had been a human shape. A woman, with a dozen gashes in her bosom, sinking to the floor. Her triumphant murderer hastily dyeing his poignard, dripping with her heart's blood, in the ruddy current running down the platform steps. The spectral guests in all the attitudes of surprise, horror, and amazement.

But, lifelike as was the play, still there was a mocking air in all the actors, and an unreal veil over all that prevented the living gazers from throwing off their enchantment, and punishing the double assassin as their hearts would have otherwise prompted them to do.

The murderer, dropping his instrument of crime, slowly moved towards them.

Frank, unable to cry out, to lay hand on a weapon, drew back one step on Ned Nittle.

He against Bill, Bill against Jack.

They were outside of the room.

The phantom still came on.

They still drew back.

They saw that the hall was empty and dark again.

Were all that train of grisly figures to follow this single one yet visible?

It alone continued to follow them, or rather chase them.

They recoiled up the room.

It crossed it altogether.

A door opened at a wave of its hand.

With its other it beckoned them.

They could not resist.

They saw only it, not one another.

Turning their face to that awful guide's, one by one they followed.

Frank seemed to have been singled out, for by some mysterious impulse, he could not help taking the lead of the adventure.

How far they went, what they passed through, they did not think of noticing.

All they were aware of was that through darkness they went, only seeing that super-natural avant courier before, always the same in pace, always the same command in his air.

At length he stopping, they halted.

They were in another room, small, and only containing a table, a chair, and a bed.

On the table was a coffer.

It was a metal box, banded with enamelled strips of ornamental gilt.

The key was in the lock.

With a wave of the hand that answered all the ends of speech, the spectre pointed to that box.

Then he called off their attention to himself again.

The murderous light in his repulsive eyes had died away, and altogether the spirit that clothed him was less substantial than before.

As the moon fades before the sun's coming, he—villanous reflex of vengeful assassination—appeared to wane before the approach of something brighter and better than he.

He crossed the room and displayed to them the secret spring of an unsuspected door.

He was gone.

Bill lit the candle on the table.

It shot up a merry flash, and even sparkled cheerily.

Frank flung up the unfastened lid of the coffer.

Only a parchment was inside.

It was hard to read, but by doing so slowly, Frank contrived to give himself and his three hearers an idea of it.

"I, Cosmo di Ponali, am a free citizen of the great and grand Republic of Venice. A Spanish ambassador had in his suite a noble secretary, who wronged my daughter and stole her away. I found her and him in Antigua. I heard he was to occupy the palace, as he was governor. I disguised myself. I offered myself to his steward as a decorator with rare, novel, and pleasing devices. I had my own way in the mansion. What I did you have seen. Scorn ever to wrong a woman. Seek ever to avenge your honor!"

That was the whole.

They were about to comment on it, but their speech was enchained yet.

But not by the same influence of incomparable terror, but by another power, gentler, yet as binding.

They looked up.

Between them and that wall through which the spectre of the vindictive Italian had disappeared, was another visitant, not of this world.

All in white, with a face flooded with a radiance like the placid reflection of a sleeping moonbeam on an unruffled lake, as swiftly graceful as the lilies that unfold their petals on the same smooth brim, this phantom relieved their hearts.

Another fright, and their agony would have been past bearing.

Lovely as was the vision, it revealed another charm by smiling encouragingly on them.

Then she summoned all their attention.

She pointed to the wall beside her.

"Listen!"

She scarcely seemed to have uttered the word, so faintly was it breathed.

She faded away into nothing.

As she vanished, another word had flown from her lips.

"Act!"

For a minute, each as he had been, not a stir did the seamen make.

Then drawing a breath of relief together, they looked at one another.

"Listen and act," repeated Jack, breaking the silence.

"Ah!" said Frank. "And here are some things that will be very useful in the acting part."

He went to the wainscoting, to the part which had attracted his attention.

A trophy of horse-pistols, daggers long and short, and, best of all, four swords hung there.

All of the blades he took down.

Feeling the weight of each, bending them, trying a cut and a thrust, he selected two.

A long and truly formidable rapier he took for himself.

"Giachimo dele' Arti, Milagno."

That was the inscription accompanied with a significant, transfixed heart, graven on the blade.

"Milan make," said the young captain. "I could not have guessed better."

And he handed the other weapon to the sailor who was unarmed.

It was a light and thin cut and thrust sword, elegant, the handle of ivory and gold, and a little steel chain here and there in extremely good taste.

Frank read off the motto it bore.

"'In love and war, push forward'; or, go in and win," added he; "that is better English of it."

"Hark!" said Bill Bowse. "Here's scaldings."

Rogers motioned all to be hushed.

A sound of steps was audible, cautiously marching in the next room.

They all approached the wall.

"We are to 'listen,' remember," said Frank, as he saw the sailor flourishing his new sword.

"And to 'act' too," said the latter.

But he did as he was advised.

A voice arose like one at meeting a person whom he had scarcely dreamt of seeing.

"You!" exclaimed the voice of a man.

"The English lieutenant!" said a female in a tone of surprise.

The first voice was Cavendish's, the other—well Frank Rogers knew it—Genifrede's.

The two young people, after the natural interchange of explanations, would have gone on to say—they alone knew what.

Genifrede could not but be interested in the story of the young officer's horrible imprisonment for her sake, and his narrow escape from the unknown monster.

But other eyes than Rogers' party were upon the couple.

Governor Pecador, saved by the Frenchman, returned to his palace with all haste. Loys accompanied him, burning with eagerness to avenge the destruction of his poisonous plant so abruptly ripped in the bud.

Pecador left Goupille and his men at table below, and came up to the maiden's apartment to hold a conversation with her.

At the sound of voices, he peeped in by a secret loophole.

His amazement was immense.

To see the English officer free at all was incredible, but for him to be sitting beside the captive on friendliest terms, almost made him believe the globe was inside out.

He hastened, as soon as recovered, to carry out the fresh designs that the sight prompted.

Suddenly Cavendish started.

He had heard a noise.

Quick as a flash, he kissed the girl, pushed her gently into a corner, and flung his whole weight against the door.

Well was it he braced himself thus.

For the forces of more than one man were pushing at the other side.

A loud voice, that of Pecador, resounded over a clattering of drawn weapons.

"With a will now, Gargaison and Vedro! It yields! It gives! Now, altogether!"

Crash!

The door flew open.

CHAPTER X.

THE FRIENDS IN NEED—THE DESPERATE CONFLICT—HOW THE GIANT FELL—THE SHOT FROM THE SEVERED HAND—LOYS IS FOILED AGAIN.

Lance's sword was out and dazzled their eyes,

so that the foremost hesitated to cross the threshold.

"I'll kill the first of you who steps foot across that line!" cried the officer.

"Then, I'm the first man!" cried Pecador, "Let's see you kill! Come on, you fellows!"

In they swarmed.

"There's more not far below," continued the governor; "and if you don't deliver your sword immediately, I'll save the gallows the task, and chop your head and arm off!"

"The gallows!" repeated the officer, puzzled, still on guard though.

"The gallows, of course!" said the Spaniard, in answer, as he led on his crowd another step. "We know you for all your innocent air," shouted the voice of Frank, as captain of the 'Scarlet Cruiser'!"

"We know you!" chorussed the gang.

"Your'e crazy, knaves," retorted the officer, lowering the point of his sword.

"So you say!" sneered one.

"I say I am Lance Cavendish, lieutenant of the Royal Navy!"

"Very fine, my prince of pirates, but you are the Cruiser Captain!"

"Sirrah, you lie!"

"You lie, dog!"

The lieutenant turned.

The same glance that told him that Genifrede had suddenly been spirited away from the corner where he had placed her for safety, showed him four men behind him, mysteriously come through the wall.

Had he turned more quickly, he would have seen the secret door gape and emit the four sailors.

He only saw them in the room, as it was.

Against them, too, he hurriedly put himself on guard.

But the first words of their young leader set his fears in that quarter at rest.

"You lie!" said that leader, sword in hand. "Where I am, who but I dare say another is Captain of the 'Wolf of the Wave'!"

"The pirate, by all the devils!" exclaimed the Spaniard, recoiling.

Still the governor had numbers on his side, and determined to try an attack, in which he had so much to gain.

There was Goupille's help coming soon.

Clash! went his rapier on the fine sword of Frank Rogers.

For he was cunning enough to avoid meddling with the elder seamen whose metal he guessed, or with the lieutenant, whom he suspected to be a good swordsman.

The combat was commenced instantly.

All were mingled together.

Here Jack's long Italian rapier described a sweep which defended the breast from three simultaneous thrusts.

There Ned Nittle felt his blade encounter that peculiar yeilding resistance that flesh of a living being offers to a piercing instrument.

In this corner old Bill, his back against the wall, his foot on a dying wretch, whom a slash over the head and ear had so soon brought to the ground, traced zigzags with his trenchant steel.

Pecador and Vedro had driven Frank into another corner.

The room was empty of furniture, save two chairs and an old commode, over to which the young commander retreated.

With a kick, dealt during a breathing spell, Frank flung over the cabinet on its face.

It formed a barrier, and at the same time a pedestal to him.

By mounting on that, he became superior in height to his two antagonists.

He could reach their breasts and their heads.

His two adversaries could only make points at his chest.

Domineering over the whole chamber of battle, drunk with the sparks that flew from the reddened swords, filled with an energy that came from the view of such a scene, the youth felt himself fired with that heroic feeling best expressed in our manly tongue by "to do, or to die!"

"Give in, you young knave!" shouted a new comer.

It was a very tall man, Gargaison by name.

A moment disengaged from Ned by a swaying of the ring around him, he thought he would put the valuable governor under an obligation to him, if he should take the noble youth in the flank.

"Give in, or I'll gut you like a lark."

So tall was he, towering over Pecador, that he was almost as high as the youth on his elevated stand.

Frank's flaming eyes glowed bright with indignation at the coward making the party three to one.

"Dastard! take care!"

He warded off an upward thrust from Pecador, a side cut from Gargaison, and retaliated by drawing an inch or so of his weapon over Vedro's fingers.

"'Ow!" howled the latter, dropping his cutlass.

"Take care?" sneered Gargaison, covering his head to receive a downward sweep before he returned it. "Of what?"

"You are not long for this earth, master six feet of uselessness!" retorted the young captain.

He had risen on tiptoe and moved forward, reckless that Pecador, seizing the chance, prepared to push in at the opening.

With all the strength of which he was capable, the son of the sea swung his sword up, around and down on the tall man's head.

The latter had his hanger up on guard.

The meeting of the metal made a myriad of sparks fly off.

The undermost blade beaten down, lowered its end.

The other following it, drew its point from the temple transversely over the nose and cheek to the jaw.

The big bully dropped his weapon from his disabled hand, and covered his slashed and blood-running features with his ten fingers.

Like a thought, Frank was quick.

As he recovered his sword, he made a little turn that saved his heart from the governor's lunge, and pushed his blade at the tall ruffian's body.

It found the slit between two ribs, and buried itself therein.

The man fell back.

So suddenly, that the dealer of his death, unable to keep his balance, fell forward, the sword's hilt still in his hand, its other end half buried in the dying man.

So was he pinned to the floor.

The youth fell on top of his body, half kneeling.

At the same time Vedro and the governor were moved by a similar thought.

The former picked up his cutlass with his bleeding hand, the other lifted his.

Both of their weapons impended over the prostrate youth.

His foot slipped in the blood of the dying man.

Past ability to rise, or even throw up his unarmed hand to protect himself, Frank believed that his next breath would be the last he was ever to draw.

But he had saved Ned's life in the cavern.

And Nittle ever paid such debts to the full.

He had run the man opposed to him through the shoulder, and almost severed his sword arm with a swift cut.

Douro, the other opponent of his, fought with a loaded bludgeon in lieu of the steel, for in the first encounter with Bill Bowse he had been disarmed.

He was swinging it about his head and aiming at Ned.

The latter felt but too certain that if ever that club dashed against his blade, it would hardly be useful after such a weighty shock.

Hence he avoided any clashing with the cudgel, while he kept the man in play.

Douro was certain to be tired out first, having the heavier instrument to wield.

Thus was the seaman engaged at the important moment when the two swords of Damocles hung over Frank's bent form.

Ned gave an exclamation of pain.

With the sudden and sure spring of a serpent stretching out its coils, his lithe steel glided along the bravo's stick, and slid still further through his left pap into his side.

Douro yelled with agony.

Red bubbles broke on his lips, as he half wheeled round, grasped at the air, and fell on the floor.

Five minutes after, he was cold dead.

Ned whipped out the fatal instrument from the sufficient orifice, and leaped to the spot where his presence was so much required.

Such was the fury in the upward sweep which he gave Vedro's down-coming blow, that the latter's cutlass remained stationary, but quivering all over from tip to haft in his palsied hand.

The next instant an extension of Ned's left arm and clenched fist sent him rolling clean through the threshold of the door.

In vain did Pecador, just warned in time, seek to change his attack on Frank, into a defence of self.

Back over his head, Nittle forced his arm, twisting his wrist till the pain was beyond endurance.

As Pecador swung himself half round to ease the turn of his hand, the mariner flung him from him.

"Think yourself lucky you are let wear out your shoes," said he.

Now, as that shove was applied to the uppermost portion of the Spaniard's body, sending him along, he would have speedily reached the ground head foremost.

But Ned, with a kind of justice, lifted his foot instantly, and applied, lower down on the governor's back, one of those kicks which till then Pecador (who was not utterly ignorant of

such treatment) never had believed in the power of any living thing excepting a horse, to inflict.

The consequence was that, perfectly upright, but not rising his feet, he skimmed along the floor without power to check his flight, met Vedro just rising in the doorway, knocked him down again, and, after executing an admirable summersault, stood on his head for a space in an angle of the next room.

Rogers rose.

"Your'e not my debtor long," said he, giving Ned his hand.

The latter shook it heartily, motioned him to arm himself, and plunged into the still continuing fray:

For all was not over so soon.

The young lieutenant had ranked himself side by side with Bill, and they rivalled one another in defending themselves against double their number.

They were not wounded, though their clothes were ruffled and ripped in places.

But they had marked, though not killed, their man a-piece.

As for the sailor Jack, he had pierced the thigh of one of his brace of opponents, and made him rest himself, half-sitting, against the wall.

As Ned prepared to help whoever should most need him, he saw Bill's cutlass flash out, and one of the pair before him leap in the air to fall immediately.

Nittle then rid him and Lance of the third, by attacking that individual himself.

Freshened by his short respite, the sailor bid fair to make short work of him.

Each had his man now.

Frank was watching Vedro and Pecador outside the door.

As the first named, the breath knocked out of his body, was too weak to rise, he was not very formidable.

The governor, with his position changed from the topsy-turvy to a more natural one, was diving his hand into his bosom, no doubt to staunch some painful wound.

Hence Frank could not take his attention off them.

Well that he did so!

For what should he see but one of the supposed corpses, his face bathed in blood from his split skull, rising on his shattered leg and one hand.

With the other he held a pistol.

His own hate foiled his bloody intent.

For he had ample time to kill the nearest foeman to him, if he had quickly pulled the trigger.

Frank, if winged even, could not have reached him in time.

Almost glued to the spot by horror at such devilish coolness, the youth beheld that dying man, who sought to give death to others, deliberately wait till a pause in the changes of the fighting men should answer his purpose.

It was the hand of Bowse that had stretched him there.

It was Bowse at whom he steadily aimed.

Bill neither saw him nor suspected his wicked purpose.

In two long leaps Frank was over by the man; with one cut he severed the hand, just pressing the trigger, from the extended arm!

It fell, detached in sinew and tendon, flesh,

bone, and skin, from the member, which spouted blood.

With the life in death that has been known to make a stricken-off head blush at an insult, the hand, still grasping the fire-arm, moved, as if some unknown montrosity crawling on the carpet with three of its stiffening fingers.

It was but a spasm.

But the convulvise pressure sufficed.

The trigger was pulled, the hammer, faced with flint, dropped in the pan, and found enough powder unshaken out to spread its sparks.

A ringing report filled the chamber with its sound.

The harmless load, the bullet bounding along the floor, filled it with smoke and a flash of flame.

As the scream of pain still hung upon the lips of the would-be assassin, foiled and punished, the young captain's streaming sword found the way to his black heart.

The smoke circled all through the place, all the more thickly from being so confined.

Still the fight went on.

The four seamen and the man they had befriended, confronted the four surviving men, and drove them back.

At the sound of the pistol shot within, a cry, peculiar, and of the nature of a signal, echoed outside and below.

"Hilli-i-ahoy!" cried Vedro, in reply.

The rush of many feet on the hollow stairs was heard.

Then Pecador, who had not been searching in his bosom for a wound, as Rogers had imagined, hurriedly and with joy tried to scramble upon his feet.

With all the breath he could command, he raised an appealing call.

An answer came.

The sound of feet drew nearer.

"This way, captain! Help, senor Goupille, help!" bellowed he.

He and Vedro scrambled to their feet

The approaching succour inspired the rascals with fresh power.

But it also was a spur to their enemies.

With a fury that their opponents could not begin to meet, the five allies beat down all guards, turned the edges and points from them, and bundled their antagonists out of the door to stumble over Pecador and the other, busy in halloaing the reinforcements on.

"Who burnt powder?" roared Loys' hoarse voice.

He glared around, in the smoke, wrathfully.

"Who burnt powder, I say? Do you want all the servants up! The palace is roused now—and a curse on ye! Where's senor governor? Well, Senor Pecador, what's all this over one man?"

"*One* man," groaned the Spaniard.

He hastened to explain to Goupille all that had occurred.

The latter started in amazement.

"Men of the 'Scarlet Cruiser' here? and their young captain? Plague on it, if I had only known! Where?"

"In there!"

Loys lifted up his voice, while he pounded on the stone floor with the hilt of his sword.

"Tumble up here, quick, all hands!" cried he.

Besides the three or four sailors who had come upstairs with him, more rushed from the dining-hall, and began to swarm up the stairs.

"There's the lopers inside," continued the Frenchman, "that wrecked the craft we were going to have merry cruises on! D'ye hear, fore and aft?"

"Aye, aye, sir!"

"No clapping in bilboes for them, but death!"

"Death!" chorussed all.

The door through which the surviving combatants had been shoved, had been slammed very rudely on them.

In fact, Ned, Jack, and Bowse, had instantly dragged the bureau on which Frank had been mounted, to the door, and propped it against the panels.

Quick as they, Frank and the navy officer flung the now broken pair of chairs against that.

The bodies, not one of which had life, were piled on top of that barricade.

"Heavy, if nothing more," said Rogers. "That will give us a bit of respite."

They heard Goupille growling as he listened to Pecador's quick recital.

"Now," said Loys, "don't stand there gaping at the shut door, you set of curs!" said he to his men around him, who hesitated.

The fact was that the story Pecador had to tell, supported by the bloody and battle-stained look of the remaining sufferers, had prevented the company expressing eagerness to open the entrance.

"Shall I wake you up?" snarled Loys, swinging his sword menacingly.

They still stood motionless.

"Scampia!" cried Loys, to one of them "as the door won't open, up with that steel bar man, heaven's alive—don't you know your craft? Have out a panel with it—it's good as a hand-spike!"

As, really, the lower part of the door was immovable from the weights placed against its the smashing in of the upper was the feasible, plan.

In a trice, Scampia's crow had ripped out the oaken plank.

All of the men drew back their heads from the opening, in full expectation of their curiosity being saluted by a volley of bullets, or a few inches of steel.

"Now then, what do you see, lubbers?" cried Goupille, advancing.

As the chamber was very quiet, that—to those men who had been told that the fighters were within—was only the more sinister.

The Frenchman boldly thrust his head in the burst-through gap.

"You awkward scared crows!" said he, "there's nobody there."

"Nobody!"

How that assurance relieved them all!

Busy as bees, they hammered on the door; and had its fragments down on the pile in a minute or two.

Goupille took hold of Scampia by the waist, and rolled him clean over the heap of bodies, right into the chamber.

"Empty," said he.

But the corpses and the blood stains, the severed hand and the weapons, assured him that Pecador's story had been only too full of truth.

"Vedro!"

They shoved that individual under Goupille's nose, every one being glad that he was not wanted, for they knew that their captain, when he picked out particular birds, generally set them an unpleasantly hard tune to sing.

They were in error for once.

"The rascals have scudded! Run you down as we came; take three men, and keep good watch, or I'll skin 'em."

Vedro—only too glad to get out of the place, where only hard knocks in disagreeable profusion were to be expected—made one jump.

That took him out of the death-chamber.

With three or four more, he was out of the palace into the garden.

Meanwhile, Goupille was stamping about the room in a rage, like a caged lion trying to get out.

They ripped up the carpet.

The blood had soaked through, and dyed the floor.

That is all that was revealed to them.

The ceiling was intact.

They sounded the wall.

"I'll track 'em," said Loys, grinding his teeth in spite. "I'll track 'em every league of their course."

In several places, Scampia's bar tore down a plank or strip of wood.

"Here's the hatchway, I'll wager my head against a dollar," said Scampia, hammering with a pistol-butt on the secret door.

"Down with it, out with it, in with it, away with it!" said Loys. "I only hope they're on t'other side of it."

A furious pounding at the door made the room ring again.

In ten minutes, they had the passage into the Italian's room revealed.

Scampia, bar in hand, led the way.

"No one here," growled he.

CHAPTER IX.

THE NAMELESS ISLET—BLACKBEARD THE ARCH-PIRATE—THE GUARD OVER THE BLOOD-BOUGHT TREASURE.—THE STRUGGLE IN THE CREEK.

"PATIENCE is the best knot, it holds best."

It was old Bill Bowse that said so.

He, and his mates, with the young captain, were on the top of the largest of the little islands, continuing the range of Antigua, and called the "Humps" by sailors.

Rogers had a spy-glass in his hand, and was eagerly scanning the sea which lay around on all sides.

The day had been spent in their successful efforts to escape Loys and the governor's guards.

Genifrede had taken refuge with Lance Cavendish on his vessel.

The flag over it prevented any open attempt to touch her.

But no doubt Pecador was busy with new schemes.

Rogers lowered the glass again.

"The 'Cruiser' 'll touch hereabouts for us perhaps to'ards morning," remarked Ned.

"I'll look again in an hour—the moon will be up, then," returned his commander. "Now, men, take supper."

The sailors fell to eating some bananas that they had picked, and such biscuits as Bowse had left in his bag.

As the moon began to shine forth, all lay down except the captain.

He had volunteered to keep watch for the first hours.

He wanted to be alone.

He went up on the still higher rocks and gave himself up to reveries.

One time he blamed himself for having let Genifrede remain under the escort of the lieutenant.

Then again he was glad that he was not burdened with her care.

He was much puzzled at Loys de Goupille being foremost in an attack in favour of Senor Pecador's designs.

A suspicion that he had felt before recurred.

Despite a resemblance in features that might be only accident, it was not impossible that the young girl was not daughter of the vindictive Frenchman.

He hoped so.

He had a foreshadowing that his hand was more than once yet to cross weapons with the murderer whose destruction he had doomed.

Suddenly, awakening from his musing, which had made him quite forget his watch, he looked up.

The sea was an uneven mirror of silver far and near.

He was about to arouse the sleepers as he descried, with the naked eye, a speck in the distance.

But reflecting that the vessel, if a vessel, would be some time yet sighting them, he forbore spoiling their slumber till he had examined the object with the telescope.

It was not the "Cruiser."

The moon lit on the new-comer's canvass, but they glinted the rays back with a white surface.

The "Cruiser" should have on her war-suit of sails, the blood-hued drapery that mated her tinted hull.

The stranger was a large brigantine, Rogers saw, as the space between her and the islet diminished.

She seemed headed towards that very group, and presently towards that very island.

Yet the young commander had chosen it for the place where his ship was too pick him up, because of its loneliness and barrenness as regarded temptations to passing craft.

The glass told him that her destination was reached at last.

On her decks, white with the moonbeams, men began to run.

Her studding sails and stay-sails, for she had had the light wind on her quarter, had been taken in before.

Now her fore and mainsail were let fall, and the square topsails brailed up.

The anchor was let go, for the look-out saw her stem swing round as the currents fought with the hull, still steadied by the jibs.

But they too were let down by the run, and the strange brigantine rode at anchor, still as if cast of metal and embeddied on a face of melted silver.

Rogers was puzzled.

She was too far off land to have come only to

be moored there, and yet too near the islets to have chosen the spot for a roadstead of any permanency.

A glance of his expert eye told him that the sails were in readiness for a speedy departure.

Even as he saw that, he observed a small skiff launched overboard, and then pushed by the man who had jumped into it, towards the gang-way aft.

After some minutes, this boat was shoved off from the two-master.

Four men were in it.

Two at the stern.

Two pulling the oars.

The small boat came straight for the islet, the steersman heading, without regard for the many eddies and whirls over and around the coral reefs.

As soon as Frank made sure that their destination was his own comrades' refuge, he returned to the latter.

Certain that four men were all the number to be opposed, if necessary, he only intended to awaken one of his companions.

"Two of the "Scarlet Cruiser's" band were equal and over to double their force," thought he.

As he stood by the sleepers, he hesitated which to disturb.

Trusting in their young chief watching over them, the three seamen lay tranquilly.

Rogers stooped down over them, for two had spoken in their repose.

But their words were of little value.

Bill Bowse was muttering:—

"I tell ye our cap'en's no waister! He was born under the gun—a reg'lar spandangalus cap'en, he is!"

The listener laughed at the praise no doubt implied by the tar's queer word.

"A sin to wake him," murmured he.

Ned Nittle was the other dreamer aloud.

He was apparently trying to recollect a song, for his disconnected sentences had something about:—

"Oh, they married the jib to the bowsprit and fore!"

Frank laughed again.

"Oh! I must wake him after *that*," said he.

And, laughingly, he whispered in Ned's ear.

The latter started up instantly.

By this time the boat had neared the outer reef that ran all around the islet, like the rim of a wheel around the hub.

Ned needed no glass to assist his skilled vision.

"Not our'n, sir," said he.

"Certainly not. What's that craft, Ned?"

The mariner looked long and steadily at the stranger, clearly defined in the moonlight.

"Might 'a' been 'riginally English," returned he, "but they've so transmogrified her to make her sharper-looking and faster-going, that the dockmen who first launched her wouldn't swear to her again."

"Suspicious, Ned."

"Yes, cap'en. Too much ' go ' in her for her to be a steady trader."

The young man saw to his pair of pistols.

"I'm going down on the strand to see what those fellows are. Hullo! they're landing at the farther end."

He shut the glass with a snap, and handed it to Ned.

"I'm going down," repeated he. "If you hear a shot or see anything out of the way, wake up Bill and Jack."

"You won't take a man along captain?" asked Ned, anxiously.

"What's the use? It will double the trouble in hanging near them to see what they are after. Then, if we did come to blows, there's enough crew to eat us in yonder craft."

"Yes. You are right, sir. Good luck, I may say."

The sailor cut off a slice of tobacco, and re-placed a "soger" of a quid.

Frank nodded, and carefully descended the rocks.

He had to go through the thicket, and as he could see nothing on his own level, he went by the moonlight's bearings directly towards the boat.

When he arrived on the sands, he was close to it.

Only one man was in the little skiff.

He was bailing it out, and singing in a low voice to himself a verse of that rude rhyme which meant much in those days, when its subject was chief of cut-throats on the Spanish main.

"It was a Blackbeard,
  In good time be it heard,
  That killed many hundreds, and often struck
    stroke!
  With hatchet and rope,
  Old Wick's forlorn hope,
  He led till the sea was dark with hell's
    smoke."

Frank examined the fellow more closely.

He had a villanous phiz, and his seaman's dress was more remarkable for an ugly, but fearful predominance of black than anything else.

His belt, as broad as a horse's girth, was full of long pistols and a knife or two.

As the youth scanned him, unsuspected himself, the sailor finished casting the water from the boat's bottom, and lying down in the stern-sheets, appeared to study the sky, his face up, and his body at full length.

Frank heard him vent half-a-score of oaths in connection with a remark that he felt sleepy, but dared not shut his eyes.

In revenge, he began to sing again.

"Oh, the thought of a rope is most pleasant
    to me,
  Tho' for crimes I may swing on the three
    cornered tree,
  Singing rattin-a-roo!"

Rogers glanced from the melodious rascal to the brigantine.

He shook his head.

"They're no good, ship or hands," muttered he. "Let me see what this knave's fellows are come for."

He could have slain the sailor as he lay on his back, but the death would have been useless.

Frank had to mount the first eminence to see what had become of the three other strangers.

After a while, and after changing his place of observation, he not only descried them, but approached them as nearly as he could.

Unfortunately for the eavesdropper, the three

THE SCARLET CRUISER.

were on a level space, upon which the moon's rays poured.

He had to remain out of earshot, for that were the only bushes to cover him.

Under a clump of sand-plum trees, as they are called, but mere shrubs as they are, the youth ensconced himself to look, if he could not overhear.

One of the three men, a sailor like the boat-man, was a powerful fellow.

He was applying all his strength to digging a large hole in the soft earth.

The second, sitting on a rather large box, was smoking a cigar.

He was also a large man.

His dress, as well as his easy attitude while the other worked, bespoke an officer, perhaps the captain.

In his cap was a black gull's feather.

But all the watcher's attention was centred on one characteristic of his.

He wore his beard so long and large, that it seemed to cover his chest from shoulder to shoulder, and down to his belt, where it flowed over silver-hilted dagger and gold-damascened pistol-butt.

It was of a glossy black.

A moustache alone of hair like that, would have set up a lady-killer in profession. Such a beard was magnificent, splendid for any man who prided himself on looks.

Its deep blackness added to the effect of its profusion, and the man being so tall and large-boned, Frank himself felt a sensation of the nearest approach to fear that he had ever known.

And he dreaded to whisper the thought that came to him.

"It is Blackbeard, that renowned impover-isher of the wealthy on the sea. Captain Teach of the 'Just Revenger' brigantine!."

There could be no doubt now what manner of floating hell that anchored vessel was.

That hole that was being dug under the pirate's terrible eyes, ah! what was it to hold?

That third man was, where?

Bound hand and foot, prostrate on the sand, gagged as well.

Rogers felt his hand stealing to his pistols, and a wild desire seized him to rush out, and prove to Blackbeard that there was one man at least who feared not to tell him that the sea was angry, the land sick, for his fiendish crimes.

But a horrible fascination weighed on him, and compelled tho youth to continue to gaze.

His hand on his weapon still, he did look on.

The voices, only a murmur to Rogers, were important to him.

Blackbeard flung aside the end of his cigar.

"Nearly through, Hanger?" queried he.

The spademan rested a moment.

"Pretty near, captain. Only I wish one of the men were doing it instead of me, your first mate," returned he, bluntly.

"Pooh! I can trust you, Philip, but none of the rascals. A little more of this pleasant work, eh? and we can dig up the buried spoil here and elsewhere, and live like princes in any land, even in England."

"I was steward to a rich man once myself, captain," said Hanger.

"And you cheated him till you were worth more than he himself, and could hire better lawyers to get you off?"

"Not much, captain. I never have to do with land sharks or any of the same fry. The nobleman said I shared in his income, I said he lied, locked the room door, and when I left the chamber, a dying man, very much like my lord, breathed his last, pinned to the wainscot!"

"Ah! Philip! It was lucky I fell in with you, my boy," said the chief, playing with his beard.

"It didn't matter! If I had'nt met you at Panama, and become your first mate, I'd have scared up a ship of my own somewhere. They're easy got."

"Too easy," said Blackbeard, with an oath. "What's this Governor Pecador was telling me? That the seas hereabouts were being swept by a buccaneer—a child, 'sdeath!"

"A child, captain, that fought Loys de Goupille, and several more like a man of the right sort. I like the way he christened his 'Scarlet Cruiser,' I do!"

While he spoke, Hanger never ceased to throw up the earth in great masses.

He seemed to have reasoned that the sooner he got through the disagreeable task, the better for him.

He was knee-deep in the trench already.

"Peace, Philip!" growled the other. "I can't bear any one, boy or greybeard, to rove over these waters besides me. Didn't I blow Captain Kidd's first schooner to smithereens, because he came down into the Cuban seas?"

"You did, captain; there's no gainsaying that."

"I'll have no second Desperado of the Deep to dispute my sway of terror. Curse me! it would ruin the trade. Merchants shudder now to send a keel to the Indies —what would it be if they hear half-a-dozen sea-wipers are lurking for prey. With but one they have a chance."

"Not when the 'Just Revenger' is that one," said Hanger.

Blackbeard smiled grimly.

"Likely! I say, old partner of mine, there is little sight for a lumbering old gold galloon, when the 'Revenger' shoots over the brine with sail out alow and aloft, and the brass rings circling inside the portholes! Ha! ha!"

"The shot! and they won't bring to! The half-a-dozen balls, or the whole broadside! The boarding in the smoke! The flash and the slash! The groaning, screaming men!" said Philip, enthusiastically, brandishing his spade.

"And the weeping women!" added the captain, showing his teeth amid the black hair of moustache and beard.

Both laughed, as they exchanged a look.

Fiends would have envied such a glance.

The young captain heard that peal of demoniacal mirth, and so hateful was its accent, that again he felt the impulse to spring forth.

He even stirred to return to his comrades, and again the assistance requisite to overpower such evidently formidable men.

But he paused anew, for Hanger had leaped up out of the pit.

"There, captain," said he to Blackbeard, "is it deep enough?"

The other looked into the hole, and then let his eyes wander to the small box and the pinioned man.

"It 'll serve," rejoined he.

Thereupon the first mate of the 'Revenger' took up a piece of sailcloth and spread it, doubled up, at the bottom of the excavation.

This done, Blackbeard opened the small chest.

Philip stood in the gap, while his superior handed him in piece-meal, the contents of that box.

There were riches incalculable, and in all shapes.

First, a silver dish made trebly precious by its embossery by some great master; then a cup of rock crystal, with a stem of cornelian, and a stand of solid gold.

Here half-a-dozen jewelled dagger-hilts were wrapped up in a cloth of gold.

Next, the pirate tossed to his mate, a bunch of necklaces of all the precious stones.

A roll of lace let gems glint through its priceless meshes.

In a word there were ornaments of every kind among the plunder.

At the end of the mass, came the more solid ware.

Three or four little cases of silver coin, and some ingots, the gold of which had been rudely run into the bars.

"That's all?" inquired Hanger, tucking the tarpaulin around the layer of riches.

"That's all."

Philip scrambled out of the pit.

"Now then for the coverlet," said he, laughing grossly.

Blackbeard rolled the bound man to the brink of the chasm.

Rogers instantly cocked his pistol.

"Death or not to me!" muttered he. "They shan't bury the poor wretch under my eyes, without my lifting hand."

But the prisoner was let lay there.

The change of position allowed the moonbeams to fall on the captive's face.

Rogers strained his eyes.

"Where have I seen that face before?" thought he. "Oh! I recall it. It is Mannelo— the fellow who showed us how to enter the governor's palace. We wouldn't have escaped, only for that. How can he have come here?"

Simply enough, as Blackbeard could have told him.

That marauder of the main had freshly returned to that part of the ocean.

He went to visit his old friend the governor.

Pecador eagerly welcomed him, and introduced Loys de Goupille to him.

Moreover, he found Captain Teach quite ready to fall foul of the young commander of the "Scarlet Cruiser," which bid fair to eclipse the fame of his vessel.

In the meantime, Teach, who happened to be

in good humour with his own men, had mentioned that he "wanted a man."

Loys had smiled, fully understanding the villain's drift, and said that the governor would no doubt spare the traitor who had been of such service to our hero.

Pecador willingly released Mannelo from his dungeon, (for he had been seized in the town by spies), and turned him over to the freebooter.

These explanations over, let us return to the moonlit strand.

To the victim, the grave-diggers, and the lonely witness.

Blackbeard had stooped till his lips were close to the captive's ear.

"Never strain and try to speak, fool," said he. "The blood-vessels are ready to burst on your forehead, in your fear. Fear not this! that you are to be buried alive!"

What could the demi-demon mean, by hinting that the wretch's fate was to be worse than an entombment of the living!

The pirate chief stooped on the opposite side of the gap, to that on which Hanger had also bent beside Mannelo.

Then the pirate captain waved his arms as if he were beckoning invisibles to him, from all quarters of the atmosphere, where the silvery notes glittered softly in the moonbeams.

After that he bowed his head for a space.

Next, he saluted the four points of the compass.

In a deep, low tone he began, but it was loud enough for Mannelo to hear, and to quiver like a leaf as he heard.

"In the name of Satan, the first and king over all the angels that were thrown down from aloft to deceive mankind who dread them; Beelzebub, Astaroth, Baal, who knoweth all things past and present, who speaketh the voices of all living creatures, who detecteth treasures and mantleth with a cloak of darkness, I beseech thy power to call a band of thy spirits from every coast, to be diligent and obedient to me!"

"Amen!" said Philip Hanger, closing his eyes.

All was still as ever, except the harsh sound of Mannelo's breath forcing itself through the bandage over his pale lips.

The pirate continued:—

"Mighty, wicked, terrible, Prince of Darkness who hath plagued, who doth torment, and who shalt rack thy servants yet! By those and all thy cursed names, I do call upon thee, by thy own crimes, by thy impenitence, by thy hoofs and horns, by the anguish of thy soul when thou wert hurled from heaven by thy comrades in the ever burning sea, by thy devils and imps and fiends, I do beseech thee to accept the proposal I will use!"

Hanger moved his lips, but he could not speak.

But the pirate chief unfalteringly went on:—

"Oh, I beseech thee by that love of inhumanity, mercilessness, and dire cruelty, by which thou hast protected so far my floating hell, letting me and my comrades sink but in wickedness—give me ample number of thy familiars with power to draw them to this spot, to be and bind them, to gather them and to command, while they may not laugh at the words of my mouth.

"And I will devote my fellows to thee, and labour to bring others in to this same confederacy of vice, for this favour, those given, and those yet to come in riches and pleasures!

"So let the band of thy fell chosen, watch over the ghostly banner that I plant upon the guard of my treasure!"

Then he rose.

Philip continued stooping, but he bent over the form beside him, and clapping a long pistol, that he had already bended and primed, to] the ear of Mannelo, he let the heavy hammer descend.

Rogers, spell-bound during the impious ceremony that he had witnessed, but hardly understood, heard the loud report, and started.

Then the smoke that enveloped the trench for a moment, was lightly swept towards him.

When it was totally dispersed, he saw the chief and Philip vigourously shovelling the earth into the pit.

Mannelo's bleeding corpse was gone.

Soon the mound that heaved up above the level of the ground, betrayed that it had gone to overspread the nigots and the jewels.

And Blackbeard, stamping on the last spadefull of clay, ended the invocation.

"Lay the flesh brands the mark of the beast upon this spot for six whole months, oh, Satan! In half-a-year, I swear to come, and soul in body or stripped of flesh, I will relieve this guard!"

Even as he spoke, a cloud, the only one upon the sky, stole darkling over the moon.

And that sound of the water that is styled the "calling of the sea," echoed forth all around the edge of the shore, as if the whole island was encompassed by flying things, whose wings were fluttering.

In the darkness that the cloud sent down, the pirate chief and his comrade went away.

Furious at himself for having been held back by the horror of what he had beheld had given, Rogers sprang from his covert, and dashed to the spot.

But the cloud broke into rifts, and by the spars of light that gladly lanced downwards, Rogers saw the fresh earth, a pool of blood, and a stray jewel, half trampled into the sandy soil.

He wavered one moment.

His frantic impulse was to tear up the clods again with his fingers but cooler reasoning told him that such a patch of blood, mixed with the hair, could only be from a man dead already.

He turned to the thicket, and pushed on towards the pirate's boat.

Luckily for him, the thorns and matted undergrowth, prevented him falling directly into the hands of the buccaneers.

Besides his haste misled him.

Suddenly he found himself floundering up to his knees in water.

Another fragment of the cloud was obscuring the disc.

Rogers had blundered into a little creek, that ran into the land between rows of rushes.

But he did not turn back, and still eager to avenge the heartless assassination, he flung himself forward, and waded collar-bone deep to the other side.

As he reached the bank, caught at the reeds and held on, before scrambling out to recover breath, the moon once more appeared.

The moonlight showed him a form close to his own.

A rough hand was extended, and grasped his collar.

"By all the devils, what fellow have we here?" growled a deep voice, as its owner dragged Rogers upon the shore.

It was Hanger.

He had heard the noise of the young captain's falling into the creek, and had gone thither to see what it was.

Rogers had recovered breath.

He was in no mood for parley or delay.

Before Philip could utter a second speech, the youth had slipped his knife in hand, up under the other's arm.

With all the vigour of indignation at the fresh remembrance of the cold-blooded murder, he thrust the blade home.

Not once, but thrice, and even when Hanger's huge body dragged him into the water as it fell, the young commander repeated the stroke.

But Hanger had time to cry out :—

"Hillo! Captain! oh! death!"

Rogers heard a trampling of feet, bearing down the sand-plums and the cat-tail reeds.

Instinctively he dashed off the stiffening fingers on his arms and neck-cloth, and leaped into the shadowy side.

Under the mass of rushes, he buried himself.

At the next instant, Blackbeard, his cutlass drawn, appeared on the other side.

The second seaman followed him.

Hanger's body, face down in the stream, was sluggishly floating in the shadow, net ten feet from Frank's hiding-place.

"Fury and flames!" vociferated Blackbeard, "is that Phil's body? Death of a dozen lives, how came he dead?"

Then he turned wrathfully to his companion.

"You poor wretch; why stand you here staring, Quaymont! Get you in, and haul him ashore till we see!"

And not to let the fellow mistake the order, he caught hold of him by the neck and seat of his duck trousers, and heaved him towards the floating corpse.

As soon as Quaymont had recovered from the souse, which made him drop the cutlass that he had held in his fist, he waded down the stream after the body.

Blackbeard followed him along the bank.

The current had seized upon the body now, and Quaymont had to quicken his pace to over-reach it.

At almost the very minute that he prepared to dart upon it, Blackbeard saw the sailor stop, stagger, and fall forward.

"Help! Murder!" howled he.

The pirate chief saw his man, with a black mass seeming to strike against his breast.

Then a short but pointed snout, with beads of glittering eyes set either side, sparkled like a snake's at the end of the shield.

At the other extremity, a long lash, swishing the ripple for a second, whirled in the air like a waggoner's whip.

In vain the sailor sought to push it off.

The lash whistled in the air and over his arms; the point struck sharply into the wretch's eye.

Quaymont gave an awful yell.

He battled with the devil-fish, half-serpent as it was, in all the agonies of coming death.

Again the fish repeated its blow.

This time Quaymont fought weaker.

He missed his footing, and fell heavily upon the water.

The poisoned tail whisked above him as in triumph.

The pirate chief recoiled in affright.

"The sting-ray! He's past help!" cried he.

The tumult in the water, had stirred up the red mud and sand.

And the waves had turned over Hanger's body.

So, the pirate gazed upon the water seemingly changed to blood, the only relief to the dyed surface being the ghastly, swollen face of Quaymont, and the whiter, and as appalling one of Philip Hanger!

The pirate dared not utter the blasphemy on his lips.

He turned on his heel, and crashed into the thicket like a wild bull.

Rogers had levelled his pistol at him, and, as he fled, pulled trigger.

But he had not thought of the immersions.

The barrel was half filled with water, and every grain of powder was washed out of the pan.

He waded once more across the water, heedless if it contained more of such fatal demizens.

But he missed the track that the captain of the brigantine had made, and went wrong at every step.

When he did reach the shore, he saw that his pursuit was fruitless.

Captain Teach had long since jumped into his boat, and now, sculling like a madman, he was a quarter of the way to the 'Just Revenger' in the offing.

Rogers could do but one thing more.

He led his men down on the beach, and with their cutlasses and large sea-shells picked up on the sands, they disinterred Mannelo's body.

He was cold already.

They buried him in another place.

The treasure was also unearthed, and Rogers, concealing from his men the particulars of what he had beheld, let them take it, to be carried on board the "Cruiser."

When they had returned to the higher portion of the islet, they found that Captain Teach had lost no time in "sailing while the wind blew," as the proverb goes.

The yards, lifts, and braces were manned, and the skeleton of booms and cordage was soon clothed.

The breeze was off land, and so, even if the interval had been less, the "Cruiser's" men could not have heard the clink of the windlass catch, as the anchor-gang heaved and pauled.

Ere the iron hook was out of water, the brigantine had her sails sufficiently filled to begin to make way.

When it rose dripping and dropping fragments of coral and mire from flukes, arms, and shank, the 'Just Revenger' was taking a long stretch seaward, as if to outstrip the shadow that was formed by the now waning moon.

"Well-handled ship," remarked Bill Bowse, "tho' 'tis an arrant scatter of goods on her, with a crew of desperates, who have dived arm-deep into plunder, often and again."

"Aye, old mate," said Ned, "but don't you envy 'em, though they will be hanging up in chains in the sweet air, while were in the damp ground."

"Or under the wave is better," said Jack. "I'll take a swim to bottom any bell of the watch, to 'scape the night cap."

"Not much fear of that yet awhile, my hearties," said Bill; "d'ye mind that young commander of ours! He won't let one of us be harmed, hand or limb, if he can help it, and he'll see to them that do it, if they do!"

"Just think," coincided Nittle, "how he wouldn't take me along, and went down all alone to have a tussel with Phil Hanger, the scoundrel that was terror of Liverpool in the old days!"

"That boy—and I don't mean no disrespectfulness," said Bowse, solemnly, "that boy might stop my grog for all on a whole week, an' I'd grin and bear it, I would! That's my sentiments on his character!"

"Bill speaks like a book," said Jack, shaking his head profoundly.

"That's it," said Ned. "I mean to follow his fortunes while wind fills sails and men reefs 'em, and I'll do it without expecting a stiver of money."

As dawn broke, Ned, who was on the look-out, came down from the rock to his friends.

"Halloa, my mates," cried he, "here's old 'Scarlet' come again! Look alive, there's breakfast cooling."

Indeed the ruddy streak surmounted by a lacework of the same, was the "Wolf of the Wave," bearing down on the rendezvous.

The sailors hurried to launch the yawl that they had come to the islet in, and made to meet the brig.

Rogers steered her carefully, and incited the oarsmen.

"I would she had come hours sooner," muttered he. "But mayhap I'll have a brush yet with Blackbeard's ship!"

CHAPTER X.

THE DERELICT—THE REVELATION AFTER DEATH—THE CYCLONE—ST. ELINO'S FLAMES—FIGHTING THE FIRE-BALLS.

NED NITTLE was up at the mainmast head of the "Cruiser."

An aftermast had been stepped and fully rigged, so as to convert her into a barque.

Just beneath him, bestriding the royal-yard, Derrick was examining the timber, to decide whether it was too good yet to be condemned as an "expended" spar.

"Derrick," said Ned to the Dutchman, "you're got lungs like a bull! Just let 'em know below that I spy a hulk—a wreck on the sea to wind'ard."

"Een wrak op zee," said the Hollander, speaking his own sweet language.

"Yaw," replied Ned, laughing, "only say it in better English. Mein Gott, you've a cocoanut like a buoy—een kop als een boei—if you must hear it in Dutch."

The other laughed with a sound like a rumble in a schnapps keg, and, laying down the end of three or three and a half that he was splicing the lift with, he hung over the deck.

"Wreck ho! drifting down on us hand over fist!"

"What's she like?" was the reply from the deck.

"Two stumps standing!" rejoined Ned, singing out himself in a style to alarm the sleepers.

"If you sight the line about two points our side of the sun's glare, you'll see her, sir."

The officer brought his spy-glass to bear on the object.

He passed the word to the captain, and Rogers came up on deck.

"Certainly, Mr. Cambering," said he to the officer's remark, "we will see her nearer. My glass is better than yours, and I fancy there's a man or woman tied to the foremast heel."

"Yes, sir, it does look like something now."

"Will we fetch her in two tacks, think you?"

"Oh yes, sir, just about. Bo's'n, all hands to wear ship."

Pit—it—whit—tle—whit! went Bill Bowse's whistle.

"Tumble up here half a hundred of you! All hands to the braces! Slack away there, lee! Haul taut that foresheet! Edge away, wheelsman! Wide awake, you thick-fingers on the middle jib—jam it tight, man, till the forestaysail fills! Up, helm, now! and let her lay along—a point more, con closer—closer! Steady, steady!"

There was a creaking of the yards and boom, a jumping of the ropes in the blocks, and a thumping of the rudder, but immediately, the "Cruiser" sped away from the frothing spot, where she had half turned as on a pivot.

"The beauty!" said Rogers, looking up to see every stitch draw. "You on the foretop, shake out the royal again, and you may show the edge of the sky-sail, if it feels soft enough aloft."

"Aye, aye, sir!" said the two men up there, a couple of light lads who feared not to climb to the dizzy altitude where the fifth sail looked like a napkin from the gunnel line.

"The beauty!" said Rogers again, as the rushing of the barque came to his ears like melody.

"Ah, sir, where's the lovely woman that could go about, in or out of stays, like this little 'un, eh, sir?"

To any greenhand, it would have seemed a puzzle that the vessel was to reach the neighbourhood of the dismantled hulk, by speeding away from it.

But the wind compelled that, as to arrive at the destination directly, the barque would have had to sail into the wind's eye.

After taking a long stride, she fell off again, executed a second half-turn, and lay over, so as to cut between the quarter whence rose the breeze, and the object of her course.

As they drew nearer the latter, the colour of the sea lightening betrayed a bright bottom, and a certain shallowness.

"We must deaden headway," said Rogers, "ugly to run on a shoal for curiosity's sake."

He passed an order quickly, and the carpenter brought a new deep-sea line.

"Arm the lead," said Rogers.

They rubbed the plummet with fat out of the cook's kettle.

Bill Bowse took up the coil of stout line and the weight, and got over the bulwark into the forechains.

"Lay hold there. Stand bye to haul in. Hup, hup, hup!" cried Bill, swinging the lead.

It hurtled forward flying before the ship.

But she soon glided up to the spot where it had sunk, and presently the men manning the line, had their faces sternward as they pulled on the dripping cord, tight as wire.

The lead brought up sand.

Another cast, as well as the colour of the water, proved that they were near a sand bank, and perhaps a coral reef.

"Ready a-lee!" cried first officer Cambering.

"Aloft there, clue up sky-sails! In, r'yals! Let the t'-gallants rest! Now then, down flying jib! Let it drag in the spay! Haul up foresail, and get the f'catle clear! Bo's'n, rouse some of those d—— my eyes tars!"

This stripping of dress sensibly diminished the speed.

"Mainto'-bowline, there, slack away! Let go main-brace! Jack, does she mind the mizzen well?"

The man at the helm, revolving the wheel, responded that she'd do.

"Have the port chain clear," said Rogers. "You may have to anchor."

"Shall I go aboard, sir, or Mr. Atrip?" inquired the first mate.

"I will."

"Captain's cutter crew! In with the oars, clear away! Lower a bit now, steady, that will do."

The barque was under sufficient sail to bring her speedily as near the wreck as it was prudent to venture.

They brought her aback, and seizing that instant, Rogers leaped down into his boat.

Bill Bowse was coxswain, and Jack was the stroke oar.

Derrick and three more filled up the complement.

It was a short pull to the wreck.

She presented a most lamentable sight.

Not only had she long been the sport of the weather, but her ruin had mainly been caused by her having been a-fire.

The flames had despoiled her of most of the upperwork, and burnt away the decks.

She had been a dainty little boat in her day, it was evident.

As the cutter passed around her stern to accost her on the lee in the smooth water, Rogers uttered an exclamation.

Her cabin windows were encircled by a mass of once gilt carving, with the royal arms of Great Britain shining out, and her name was, though obscured by smoke, discernible.

"The White Swan."

The advice boat on which Lance Cavendish had been lieutenant.

With much emotion, Rogers bade the men make haste.

Derrick shipped his oar, as did the rest, and took up the boathook.

Bill ported the tiller, and the cutter ran against the charred and rotten side.

The Dutchman drove the pike-head deep into the worm-eaten timber, and laughed at the splinters he struck off.

"You can't damage a wrecked ship," said he.

They held the yawl close to the vessel's side, and the captain sprang up on deck.

The fire had burnt the inside almost completely out.

The hold was full of water, on which floated boxes, splinters, and casks.

Amid them, wrecks of mortality, were sundry bodies, but so swollen, so eaten by the fish that had thriven from minnows to large ones on that horrid food, that one could hardly credit that they had ever represented men.

The deck and the ragged bulwark was carpeted and tapestried with seaweed, green or black.

In and amid its tangles, clung, crawled, and crept, snails, sea-spiders, crabs, and some young eels.

The foremast, where most of the planks had been unconsumed, stood shattered some eight feet from the floor level.

To it, attached by ropes, still remained a man —the bleached, withered, shadow of a man.

One arm was free.

It was clear that he had lashed himself there, not to be swept away by the seas, that no doubt had so often washed over the drifted schooner from side to side, from fore to aft.

In some places the flesh had dropped away from the bones.

But the brine that had encrusted it, had preserved it from corruption.

Pale as a spectre, enveloped in a glaze of salt, it was sad to look upon; its one arm waving, held by the clothing, as if in mockery of life.

"Beg pardon, cap'en," said Bill, as his superior was gazing on this mute witness of the devastation. "Seems to me here's something!"

The captain looked down on the deck to which the old sailor pointed.

A sword, its gilt handle and steel blade tarnished with the sea air, was driven upright in the deck, as if to point out what was beneath it.

Rogers saw that he should require time now.

So he bade Bill make the signal agreed on to the "Cruiser."

Bowse ran forward on the heel of the bowsprit, and fired a pistol in the air.

The "Cruiser," in premonition at the ready about, wore round, stood for the wreck again, kept the lead going till she found a proper berth, and then let go her port anchor with some seventy fathoms of chain, a pretty good scope of cable in ten fathoms water.

After the iron had taken ground, they began to clew up sails, and make the ship comparatively snug, while hauling her up to anchor.

In the meantime, Rogers had examined the planks in between which the sword had been stuck.

A hand, vigorous at first, but growing weaker, had cut more or less deeply, many letters into the wood.

There was a date, and then followed:—

"H. M. dispatch-boat 'White Swan' left Antig. to bear letters to St. Christophe—Fell in with Blackbeard—Fight two hours—Heavier metal than we—Horrid fate to crew."

Then there was some indistinct lines, referring to certain men.

"Lieut. Lance Cavendish joined pirate! (traitorous coward)!—He said the French girl was his wife, he would be theirs—She safe."

"Oh!" exclaimed the youth, "this man did not guess the truth. Cavendish has enlisted with the scoundrels to be of service to Genifrede! Oh yes, it must be she!"

The rest said that the carver of the letters was the captain.

He had been left for dead, and when he re-covered, found the schooner on fire.

But it had burnt itself out, and then he escaped.

Escaped only to linger out his life.

With the mariner's habit, he had cut each day, the points that the winds prevailed from, and once or twice the sight of a sail.

At length a tempest compelled him to lash himself to the mast, and there he had been stifled or perished by famine.

By the young captain's orders, they cut the cords.

A scrap of sail was fished up out of the hold.

The body was wrapped up in it, with some bars and bolts of iron at the feet, and plunged over the side.

There was but one clue to the whereabouts of the destroyer.

The carved plank recorded.

"The 'Just Revenger' steered north-west on parting company."

But the rover had no certain destination like an honest ship.

Nevertheless, Rogers deemed that sufficient thread to he followed.

No doubt he would come across some fresher finger-post on the pirate's track.

So, self-constituted Redresser of the Seas, the "Scarlet Cruiser" was headed towards the American coast.

As she run out of the Gulf of Mexico, three days after, none would have recognized her.

False strips of canvas were nailed to her sides from stem to stern, and made her upperworks seem high.

Her rig was that of barque still, but her light sky-sail masts had been taken down.

Indeed the change in the weather kept the canvass well under hand.

There were unsteady north-easterly blows now and then, and fogs had several times imparted an ugly hue to the sunlight.

They had made the under circuit of Cuba, and had heard from a "molasses drogher," or treacle-carrying tub of a boat, that a disabled vessel had put into Havana some weeks before, having narrowly escaped Captain Teach.

The "Revenger" was reported in the Gulf stream.

They were doubtlessly on the right track.

On this afternoon, as they felt they were leaving the warmer latitudes, it came on to blow pretty fresh, with rain, from the north-east with a rising sea.

There was a warning that squalls were coming, one after another, by the flaws that made the reefed topsails quiver.

While the rattling of the wet and slackened ropes in the blocks, the creaking at the slings of the yards, and the junction of the topmasts and masts, were sufficiently ominous.

The young captain, pacing the quarter-deck, wrapped up in oilskin from head to foot, put his trumpet now and then to his lips.

Now the "Cruiser" was eased a trifle by the head; then a reef was shaken out of the topsails as the wind lulled.

As night drew on, the whole dome above was thick with black clouds.

They were in several layers, some massed and scarcely moving, the outer ones skurrying over the heavens like race-horses.

The young commander shook his head as he looked to the weather. After a short time. "Send down top-gallant and royal yards!" ordered he.

By nightfall the barque was plunging over a white cap sea, with fore-staysail, main storm-staysail, main and foresail, and mizzen, alone shown, and they were dreadfully curtail of their fair propositions.

Three men were put to the wheel, for the rollers so severely smote the rudder, that one would have been flung off at the critical moment.

The first watch was strengthened too.

"Rough night ahead, bo'," growled Jack, buttoning up his monkey-jacket to the throat.

" I don't care while the rain keeps off," re-turned Ned Nittle. "A dry blow's nothing."

Bill Bowse had ensconced himself forward under the bow-chaser, pulling the gun's tarpaulin over him.

He laughed as the bow would be poised a moment in the air, and then dart forward and downward, smashing the waves like a mighty hammer.

Bill only grinned when the spray of a green sea came in board, and drained off his tar-paulin.

"What a jolly old piece of oak he is," said Ned, walking up and down with Derrick and Jack, as they heard Bowse singing.

The sky all around was very black; the sea was dark blue except the white of the crests.

A lurid tinge was on the glistening ship.

There was no sound of man's waking, except the tramp, tramp, of the half-dozen on the watch, as they moved up and down the restless floor.

The wind whistled above and around, the seas bumped against the rudder and stern, or bounded along the sides.

There was the heavy splash as the rollers were overtaken by the barque and cleft in two, and the shower of spray deluging the prow.

It was pleasant, amid all this tumult, to hear the watch in a low, but cheery voice, singing to the time of their own footfalls:—

"Oh, jolly to be a sailor boy,
  The sea with plummet to sound ;
And find how many fathoms length,
  The barque is from the ground."

When the first watch prepared to turn in, there was rain falling, and so, as is traditional, the relieved guard invited their replacers to hurry up, as there was such a fine shower-bath waiting for them.

Contrary to expectation, the first part of the night passed thus smoothly.

But at the hours when it should have been dawn, but that no light revealed itself on the waste, there was a peculiar feeling in the ten-dency to a calm, that alarmed the old sailors.

They took unusual precautions against the enemy so awfully threatening.

The "Cruiser" seemed hardly to be a ship at all, so far as any spread of canvass went.

She rolled along now, rather than sailed.

But where another might have run away, the young captain kept on his course, almost in the teeth of the storm.

Finally the foreshadowed terror came.

The far-off line seemed to lift one moment, while a streak of lightning played on the edges of the dense masses of vapour.

Soon after, a rumble of thunder ran all around the vastness.

That was the signal for the unchaining of the cyclone.

There was seen a wall coming on, a wall of wave and spray, of ram-laden air and cloud-drifts.

One could not tell where the air joined the ocean.

"It's a rouser," said Bill Bowse, shaking his head, "but we've made all snug, and we'll do it."

"Yaw," said Derrick, "but I don't know. Hooge boomen vangen veel wind."

"What does that lingo mean to say?" queried Bowse.

Ned laughed.

"The Dutchman says big booms catch much wind. True enough, and we are heavily sparred."

They found presently that the Hollander was right.

That mountainous roller had already approached the vessel.

Frank sprang himself to the wheel.

"Meet her, meet her!" roared he, laying hold of the spokes with the three men. "It may stave her bow in, but passion of me! we shall go down facing it!"

"Hold on by your teeth!" yelled Ned Nittle, banging the forehatch down.

All seized some firm rope.

There was one terrifying space.

The ship, in a dead calm, rose on a wave and rested in the air.

It seemed that her head would never come around.

But it did, just in time.

The mountain towered, as high as her fore-cross-trees, lifted as she was herself.

Then, head and ears into it, the "Cruiser" boldly plunged.

A mass of water, snapping the jib-boom, tumbled on to the fore-deck, and rushed all the way along to the quarter-deck.

The barque heeled over till she shipped water at the lee gunnel.

On her side, thus, she continued, until the first blast had spent its force.

By a miracle, the shock had not shifted her ballast.

Two of the side guns were lifted from their runners by the wash, their cable-lashings was severed, and away to leeward they spun over the waves.

The violence of the gale prevented their weight sinking them, and they seemed but as footballs as they flew.

The "Cruiser" slowly was regaining tho upright.

The men below bumped against the bulkheads and stanchions at the lurch given their hammocks, tumbled out half dressed, and hastened to go on deck.

All thought that their last hour was now come.

Knee-deep in the water circling on the deck, unable to find room enough to leap out of the scuppers, Rogers, clinging to the weather bulwarks amidships, was giving out the orders to the men.

The broken jib-boom, pulled back to the ship on the sheltered side, by its tangle of stays and the flying jib, was thumping at the forechains and threatening to drive the larboard bower through the planks.

That done, the surge would have found the entrance that it coveted, and woe to each living soul, then!

One of the watch slid down the incline, leant over the bulwark, and sawed at the nearest rope.

But ere his knife could sever half the strands of that one line, a blast made the barque dip again.

A torrent of foam and spray blinded all eyes, and when they could see again, they peered in vain for the seaman who had been hurled into eternity.

"It's dragging her head round!" cried Rogers, in a lull of the wind. "She's falling off fast! Must I go to cut it away myself?"

"No, no, sir!" cried all those forward.

"Keep cool," said Ned, taking an axe from a neighbour's hand. "If I go where Tom's gone it'll be soon enough for the next man to have a turn."

He let go his hold of a spike, and glided over the slippery boards into the suds on the depressed lee side.

Dauntlessly he slung himself over the side, and vigourously they saw his axe plied.

Now in, now partly out of the breaking masses, in a cloud of spray all the while, the tar kept chopping at the tangled cordage.

The boom was less nearly chained to the bow now, and it yielded to the eddies whirling at the edge of the slack water.

Presently Ned gave a shout.

Bill slid down the incline, and helped him to climb in again.

He had dropped the hatchet in making a last cut.

It sufficed.

The spar gave into the pressure, and no longer towed, was speedily bobbing up and down in the trough of the sea abaft.

As if to stifle the joy that all felt as the "Cruiser" obeyed her helm, and pointed her cutwater nearer the tempest, a new terror alighted on the barque.

"Fire! fire! fire!"

It was a green hand who shouted.

Jack pushed him down off-handed.

But the alarm had been heard below.

The men under hatches, whom the captain would not let come up, as there was hardly room for the handful on the exposed upper-works, burst up the hatches, and swarmed on deck.

Fortunately, the fury of the elements had abated.

The ship rode steadily, though far from on an even keel.

"Fire! fire!"

The hardy faces grew ashy coloured.

A zigzag of lightning had fallen on the billows, and seemed to kindle them into tossing candles far and near.

The gale bore flames upon its wings, and as it sang through the rattlins, left fragments of the phosphorescence on the lines.

The patches of the green blaze fluttered towards one another, till they had rolled into balls.

The horrified seamen saw them roll upwards, sideways and tranversely, till they had quitted the stays, the lifts, and braces, the centres of

the yards and doubling of the masts, to perch themselves at the extremities.

Thus, at the earrings of each spar, at tip of the gaff, at the end of the splintered shaft of the jib-boom, a globe of the corpse-light burned brilliantly.

It did not consume the wood or hemp, as much from its peculiar nature as from the surface being drenched.

The huge heap of it at the mainyard weather earring, breaking into bits before the wind, began to melt and drop.

The sailors fled from the spot.

The Spaniards and Italians fell on their knees, and began to pray.

"St. Elino's fire!" moaned they.

"Silence, fore and aft!" roared the captain, through his trumpet.

"Quiet! don't you hear the captain; Mum, you whimperers!" cried Ned Nittle and Bowse, as they cuffed the cowards nearest them.

"Ten men to the powder-mag," said the commander.

A dozen men went down into the depths where, in the room lined with sheet iron, the powder was buried.

But a spark would have given it a mighty resurrection.

"Drag the tail of the foresheet over the bow chaser!" cried Frank, suddenly. "Spring you there!"

The lighted phosphorus was circling all over the deck.

One ball had rolled forward, and, climbing the bulwark, ran along till it dropped on the gun of which the young commander had spoken.

There, like an imp, the cinder sat on the hammer-cloth.

The two bow-chasers were always kept loaded, for signals and other emergencies.

But even as a seaman dashed his sou-wester on the touch-hole, the flame had burnt through the payed canvass, and ignited the damp grains.

The man was caught by the recoil after that loud report.

The kick of the gun was all the greater by the port having been closed, and its muzzle jammed chock up against it.

The piece was lifted from the floor altogether, and when it came down it was on its side.

The rings drew out.

The carriage and the cannon were detached, and man, gun, and block, rolled over and over down the steep, smote the bulwark, where the man was left smashed, and then all three were tossed like biscuits into the foam.

"Accursed fire! a thousand demons!" moaned the Spaniards, more especially.

"Good heaven's! they're coming on deck!" yelled the others.

The wind died away aloft, by one of those most unaccountable vagaries common to the cyclone.

The balls of pale green lustre were indeed descending.

Keeping pace, they slowly dropped downwards.

One would have thought them living things, to have seen them floating in such apparent order.

The sailors were seized with a panic, and crowded to the ladders.

But the young commander ran in amongst them.

"Are you greenhands on a store-ship, think ye?" sneered he. "Know that if Davy Jones comes aboard, we'll empty the shot locker, and break every cutlass, and sheath knife on his crew! Shame on you! Do you want to skulk to Fiddler's Green with a face like a fine lady's hands?"

He caught up a handspike, and met the oncoming of one of the fire-balls.

It seemed to waver to meet him.

He advanced and struck the body, not once but ten times, till he fairly drove it into the wind to leeward.

"Look at that!" cried he. "Three cheers every man, not a skulker! Stretch your throats like men of the 'Cruiser'! Once, twice, thrice, hooray!"

The men thought no longer of flight.

They sent up a shout that made their blood course again.

"Up, mops, spikes, bars, and bolts!" cried Rogers. "Overboard with the candles we never asked to burn! Laugh! it's sky-larking all hands. Lor' bless you!"

That was the way to talk to them.

The men snatched up brooms, handspikes, bars, and, where not them, used their hands.

Amid jeers at one another's former scare, laughter and jokes, they rushed at the flames, and beating them, whisking them, pushing them, left not a single fire-ball on the craft.

"The barque runs steadily," cried the young captain. "Set storm staysails, and clear the wreck away at the fore. Shake two reefs out of the mizzen, and send a lad to the main-topsail, bo's'n, who never sneezed!"

With this canvass shown, the "Cruiser" leaped over the briny hillocks.

"Have the waves that came in board left any of your coppers, cook?" inquired the commander of the "doctor."

The man laughed.

"Yes, sir, big kettle's all right, but the pots and pans hove gone to feed the turtles."

"Ask my steward to give you a keg of that particular French brandy."

The fellow hurried off, licking his lips.

The men were piped to extra grog.

The big kettle was filled with the cognac, and every man was passed a huge tot of the liquor.

Rogers held up a cup himself in one hand.

"There's the sun peeping out, d'ye see?" said he. "It's the red of the 'Cruiser' that it wears! Luck to it and the barque! it'll shine out ever after the storm we weather!"

"Hooray!"

And they drank fortune to old Sol, lancing his beams over the vexed ocean, and to the ship that had mastered the cyclone's buffets.

"My lads, you ought to know why I lead you from the southern seas up into such snorters as tha tjust blown itself inside out. I'll tell you. Puffed up with vain glory, Blackbeard does not spare to speak of himself as sole and only Commander of the Seas!"

"Bah!" groaned they all.

"We'll learn Captain Teach that his 'Revenger' ain't fit to be cock-boat to the 'Scarlet Cruiser'!"

"That we will."

"'Tention, lads!" shouted old Bowse.

At the twitter of his whistle, all grew silent.

The men were ranged amidships, except a few forward on the watch, a few more aloft, and the couple steering.

The 'Cruiser'!" said Bill.

They drank again.

"The song!" said Bowse. "Strike up, Ned, you've the voice! and the man that don't bawl in the chorus, goes to sing to the mermaids, by George!"

Nittle stepped out, and jumped up on the capstan.

There, though the vessel still rocked and plunged, he kept himself erect.

In his full deep voice he entoned :—

> " 'Scarlet Cruiser's' gone to sea,
>   Hey, boys! ho, boys!
>   With all the company,
>   'Scarlet Cruiser's' gone to sea,
>   Bound for v'y'ges fair and free!
>   Brave and jolly, oh!"

And "brave and jolly, oh!" rang out from the hundred throats.

It leaped from the prow ahead, to the froth under the cutwater.

It left a wake of melody far behind from the timoneers.

And up on the top sailpards, the men unfolding the tack, sent up the
            "Brave and jolly, oh!"

CHAPTER XI.

THE 'REVENGER' AFTER THE CYCLONE—BLACKBEARD'S SWEET TOOTH—THE MASK THROWN OFF—THE HUNDRED LIVES IN A SINGLE HAND—THE PROMISE OF THE PERJURER.

THE tempest that had visited the "Cruiser," had handled Blackbeard's brigantine much more roughly.

When the storm had passed over, the pirates relaxed into their usual bold and daring courses.

They repaired damages, and then, while the prow still pointed northerly, they were given a jollification.

They were crossing the Gulf Stream, to make the land about Cape Hatteras.

A light fog sat upon the water, and seemed to be thickening.

They shook out studding sails on this.

The wind was low and uneven, something in the nature of the flaws off shore.

There was a quantity of Jamaica rum on board, and the men did not stint themselves.

The officers were no less generous in their guzzling.

The deck presented a wild scene.

The rascals of all nations, and only alike in the villainous expression of their visages, were gradually getting stupid drunk.

Meanwhile they played at cards, three dice, tossed up golden coin, pulled strands of rope for " odd or even," and drank all the while.

One man engaged in none of these.

He sat amidships, under the shadow of the Long Tom.

With exceeding disgust he watched the revelry, and as he saw the man at the helm, no less intoxicated than the rest, he eagerly scanned the misty horizon.

But nothing appeared to him, or perhaps he would have risked all by taking a trick at the helm, and running the buccaneer's ship into the enemy's power.

This was Lance Cavendish.

He had joined the rascals, signed the articles, and drank the allegiance cup.

He had sworn over the liquor, the desperado's oath : that, if ever it came to pass that they should run into a danger, in coming out of which only capture awaited them, he would set foot to foot with a comrade, and so shoot one another.

The bad weather that the brigantine had met, and a disturbance that had occurred among the Spaniards, who could not bear the bleak winds readily, had compelled Captain Teach to keep the deck pretty much all the time.

This had prevented what Lance feared, any thoughts of Genifrede, whom Cavendish had so far saved by asserting her to be his wife.

The pirate's law ran that a shipmate's girl and his last dollar was shielded from captain and fellows, come what might.

Still Lance was uneasy.

So far they had had only to fight the elements, and he had *conned*, tucked in the bunt, tied a reef-point, unrove strained tackle, with any of the A B's.

But if they should come to blows with an honest craft, he would have to flinch from his gun, and dare the worst by saying that he would not act out the false part any longer.

Thus deep in thought, the naval officer lay on the planks.

Suddenly he started.

It was not the roaring song of the men near him.

" Strike fist on the board,
Hooray is the word !
Come into the fighting, my bully ! "

But a low sound of a voice.

The planks had conducted it from the cabin to his very ear.

" Come, come, no trifling, my fine minx ! I'll have your lover rolled in tar if you won't be my Dearjoy ! "

It was Blackbeard's voice.

The few girl's who did the washing and mending for the sailors, were forward, a set of mulattoes who drank rum like any man.

The woman to whom Teach alone could be speaking must be Genifrede in the between decks.

Lance lost not a second.

One glance told him that an elephant might have galloped over the deck without much startling the company.

He remained laying at full length, but he rolled towards the companion way.

On reaching the cabin-stairs, he noiselessly descended.

The captain's black steward was there, with his eye at a keyhole of the middle cabin.

Lance took him by the throat, choked him into senselessness with a turn of the hand, let him drop to the floor, and gagged and bound him with his own napkin, with a sailor's expertness.

He paused not to hear more of the ominous struggle going on behind the door.

He rushed at it, struck it with shoulder, hip, and knee, and hurled it from its bolt in the bulkheads.

His eyes, burning with emotion, saw but a hazy glimpse of disarranged garments, exposing a little foot and a luxuriant bosom.

He already had given such a blow with his fist to Blackbeard, that the burly ruffian released Genifrede, and staggered back.

Before he could recover, the young man had leaped at him, and pulled him down on to the ground.

In two minutes more he was tied like the negro steward.

Genifrede, her face and breast red as fire, her eyes full of tears of gratitude, thanked her deliverer.

" A second time you have saved my life," said Genifrede, gratefully; "how can I ever repay you."

" I don't know. It is no time to talk now. Hark ! "

There was a scuffle on deck.

" Avast there ! Mascarade, knock the knife out of the Portugese rascal's hand ! There let him lie, and throw some water on him."

" It's Ned Low, the first mate," said Lance. " He has woke up from a sleep, and now he'll rouse the men."

Indeed, they quickly heard him telling the idlers to take in the stu'nsails, as the fog collected on them, and weighed them down till they were useless.

" Lively there ! or I'll jump in among you ! ' cried Low. " Spring to it ! Why, that milk-and water young hand that we took out of the despatch-boat, is the best man in the barkey arter all ! Up aloft, and lay out on the foreyard, young 'un ; and show 'em how to pull up an armful ! "

" I'll be missed now," said Lance to the trembling girl.

" D'ye hear ? "

Of course the young lieutenant made no reply.

" Has he made a hog of himself on the Jamakey, too ? " thundered Ned Low, stamping about among the dead drunken ones.

" If you please, sir, I think he went down into the cabin," said a sailor.

" The deuce! he might as well have gone to Blue Fluegium at once," said Ned. " Come up here with you cheerily, if you don't want your neck broke."

With that he descended the cabin-stairs, surprised at such an atrocity in only a foremast hand.

To go into the captain's cabin, was like goin to Blue Fluegium in all officer's eyes.

You landsmen may guess what sort of place that queer name stands for, when tars assert that it is so cold there, that red-hot coals freeze into snowballs!

"We must be off," whispered Lance.

"Anywhere—yes, to death," said Genifrede, mournfully.

"Come on."

Cavendish shouldered the heavy body of Blackbeard, and dived into a narrow passage, that led forward into the mid-hold.

The young girl followed him.

Low had just found the steward rolling his eyes like a dying duck.

He cut him loose with his dagger, not over particular whether he pricked him in so doing or not.

"What in thunder does this mean?" roared he.

"Massy on me, Quimbo don't know, massa Low," faltered the negro. "Dar was somefin' like a big turcle (turtle) nipped me roun' de froat, an' den somefin' else fell on my cocoanut, an' felled me flat as a cheeseplate. Dat is all I know about it."

"Where's the captain?"

"'Spec' it was de debble, and he run off wid Massa Brackbeard," stammered the negro.

His heels knocked together in affright, and his nostrils opened and shut "like bellowses" as Ned Low said, as he snuffed for sulphur in the air.

The mate started up all hands, and they began searching for their leader.

All of a sudden, two pistol-shots, in rapid succession, brought all the searchers into the hold.

They held up their torches, and, when the gunpowder smoke had ascended, they saw a calm but deathly picture, which made the most daring of them recoil.

The door stood widely open, that had never before been other than carefully guarded.

The door of the magazine.

In the shadows of the powder-room, the pirates dimly beheld the crouching form of Genifrede.

Her hands were clasped, and she was earnestly praying.

In the doorway a heap of powder-barrels, the heads of some kicked in, and the glistening grains pouring out.

On them was extended Blackbeard's huge frame.

Above him towered the form of the young lieutenant.

At his feet, two corpses lay, while the useless pistols that had been dropped beside them, showed how their deaths had come.

They had been the sentinels over that awful depository.

One of their pikes the lieutenant had taken up, ran its head through a shot-plug (made of tallow and oakum), and set this alight.

The melted grease fell down every moment upon the deadly dust at his feet.

Horrid he seemed holding that grim candle up.

No wonder they who looked on, crowded back on one another.

"Bucket of water!" shouted the mate.

"Before you can get a drop of water, Ned Low," said Cavendish, "I'll wrap the whole ull in flames."

The mate cocked his pistol, but the young man laughed.

"Fool!" sneeringly exclaimed Cavendish. "Lower your weapon. I hold all your lives in this single hand! Shoot me! but the blaze falls none the less surely, and your shot would have sounded your own funeral knell!"

That was but too true

The fumes of the liquor they had drank, faded away before that stern reality.

"It is for me to command," said Lance.

He stuck the butt-end of the pike in a seam of the planks, so that a touch would topple it over on the spilt powder.

Then he leant over Captain Teach with his knife in his hand.

If he had meant to have slit the chief's throat before their very eyes, the men durst not have ventured a step forward.

But the lieutenant only meant to cut the leader's bonds.

This being done, he pushed the pirate captain away.

Sullenly, Captain Teach went across to his men.

"Now," said Lance, "there's a proof of how deep I feel you are all in my power. Listen, all of you."

There was a silence, except for the spluttering of the curious torch.

"I joined you villians," resumed the officer, "only for one thing. Not to save my life; but that of the young girl there."

He pointed to Genifrede, who was praying no less peacefully in that chamber of imprisoned devastation, than in a church of a crowded city.

It was a bright contrast to those rough and fierce-browed men, many of whom hardly knew what she was doing.

"That is all I steer for now," continued Cavendish. "I never would have eat biscuit or dipped into the grog with the least scoundrelly one among you, only for the sake of being her shield some day.

"Now here's the heart of the cable. Once asking: will you let her go into a boat and shove off, and swear by whatever can hold your stained souls, that she shall be left in the hand of heaven?

"Alone on the sea, no matter. She is safer I am sure alone on the ocean, with but the thin boat between her and the wave, than with all this ship under her feet."

The pirates consulted together.

"But you?" inquired Teach.

"Oh, I ask but this: when you touch land set me ashore, or if you sight a vessel first, put me aboard, and then come what may.

"The land may be but a bird's perch of rock, or a strip of sand, but I will stand on it contentedly.

"The vessel may be some poor ill-fated craft that you will capture the next hour, but I will die aboard it, before I visit your floating hell again!"

The buccaneers now entered into a new discussion.

There was some difference, but something that the leader imparted to them in a whisper made them all smile, and they nodded assent.

"All agreed," said Teach.

"You will let that girl leave the brigantine unmolested?" queried Lance.

"Not a man on board, from the weakest cabin boy to the strongest sheet-anchor-man, shall lift hand to stop her way or to draw her back," said Teach.

"Swear it over the steel like a rover," said Cavendish.

The other took the dagger that Low gave him, dipped it in the blood of one of the slain guards, and held the blade by the point before him in both hands.

"By the steel," said he.

He held it up over his head.

"Under the steel," proceeded he.

Then he let it fall to the ground, and set both feet on it.

"And over the steel," concluded he. "I swear that that girl shall be given a seaworthy boat and let go from this ship, not a man, young or old, fair or dark, to offer to stay her."

"Right. The vengeance of the steel be yours, Captain Teach, if you break the rover's oath," returned Cavendish. "And now, Genifrede, a word."

The young girl, who had been deep in her devotions, came up to the speaker's side.

Lance sighed as he thought what misery might be in the sole means of her escape.

"They are going to give you a boat," said he. "The weather seems settling down for a calm. You will be carried northerly by the current, and I trust, picked up by a Falmouth packet or some fishing boat. Pray for me."

"But you?" inquired she, looking up into the young man's eyes.

"Oh! I must stay here to be sure that they keep faith with me," responded he. Here, here's my pistol reloaded. I know it's peculiar ring among a hundred. When you are free of the brigantine, fire it in the air."

"Well," said she, taking the large barrel in her little hand. "But if——"

"If you have to use it on the way up, you mean. Fear not! he has sworn by the rover's oath, his own men would not let him break it. Go fearlessly, and heaven bless you."

They shook hands.

"Pass the word to clear away my cutter," said Teach.

In another moment they heard the piping of a whistle above.

"Cast off the boat-cover of the captain's cutter! Stand by, to lower her over the lee quarter! Steady! Jump into her one of you, and pull her along to the gangway! That 'll do! Hold her there. Take her aback, Tom, and let her shiver!" finished the boatswain to the steersman.

The brigantine yawed, and then came very slowly around into the wind again.

Genifrede turned from the lieutenant.

Tears sparkled in her eyes, and, in a faltering voice, she exclaimed:—

"God be with you."

"Good bye!" faintly answered Cavendish.

She drew her tall figure to its full height, cast her eyes imploringly to heaven, and then slowly left the hold, and went up the first ladder.

Then she went up the second steps on to the deck.

The men on the way stood still as statues as she passed.

She moved to the side, let the sailor in the boat assist her down, and then was left alone, by his climbing up on board.

The helmsman let the wet sails fill again, and the small boat with its lonely occupant drifted into the wake.

Alone!

Alone on the ocean!

What words can paint the harrowing thoughts that filled her young breast, as she felt herself drifting slowly away from all she held dear.

But death was better than dishonour, and the thought of Blackbeard's vile attempt, nerved her to face all the dangers that she might have to meet.

Before she had got out of earshot, she fired off the pistol, as she had been instructed.

Lance, who had calmly counted the minutes, walked with the impaled ball to the farthest corner, and lowering the fiery goblet to the floor, carefully stamped it out.

Blackbeard and the others looking on, drew the first long breath since they had discovered Cavendish.

Half-a-dozen men were left as sentinels over the powder-room, while the rest hastened on deck.

The fog had become so much the denser, tha the boat could hardly be descried.

Captain Teach lifted his powerful voice.

"Let's have half-a-dozen of those yellow gals sent aft," said he.

The Creoles came running from the bow.

"Who of you can row a boat?" inquired Teach.

"Ebery man Jack of us, massa," said one of the mulatresses. "Pull away like de debble. *Dieu-daunœ*! I row de stroke oar in de governor's galley at Saint Christophe"

"I'll make you coxswain! Choose six more strapping wenches like yourself, and clear away the long boat."

The seven women ran to the stern, and began to cast off the boat-tackle, and lower from the devits.

"All aboard," said Teach. "Now let's see you bring back that cutter of mine with its contents. Top your boom and cut."

The women feathered the oars right seamanly, and bid fair to overhaul Genifrede's drifting craft in a short time.

"Oh, perjurer! villain!" shouted Cavendish, when he perceived the design of the captain. "Disgrace to the name of man. Is this keeping your oath? But vengeance will overtake you. I——"

He had been seized by Ned Low and some others.

"What are you growling about?" said Blackbeard, stepping up to him. "I swore no man or boy of the ship's company should detain your Sweetlips! Have they? You don't call those saddle-coloured wenches men, do you? Where's your eyes? Any powder-monkey on board knows better than that."

There was a loud laugh.

They had forgotten already how promptly the young naval officer had fulfilled his part of the promise.

Lance set his teeth to cut short his indignation, which it would have been folly to have expended in words.

He had some hope still.

They misjudged his nature, and, instead of binding him, four men held him.

While the brigantine was checked by the skilful handling of the helm, they saw from her, the two shadows in the mist approach, melt into one, and that one come towards the ship.

In a short time the long-boat, towing the cutter, came alongside.

In a few instants more, the mulattresses, showing their teeth with grins of the utmost pleasure, pushed Genifrede towards the pirate captain.

"You see," said he sneeringly to Lance, "not a man has touched her till she is on the deck again."

Cavendish had already studied the position of affairs.

Granting he could wrench away, it was impossible for him to reach Genifrede's side.

The same space was between him and Captain Teach, besides the savage men.

But one more thing was left him.

First he had to have his arms free.

He pretended to be overcome by the change in affairs.

He let his head sink on his breast, let his muscles relax, and heaved a sigh like a child about to shed tears.

The men who had their hands on him, were deceived.

He felt their grasps much less tightly.

Then, collecting all his energies, determining not to make a slip of the foot, or a move without a aim, he drew a long breath.

With all the fury of which he was capable, he flung his whole weight against the two men on his right, while thrusting out his foot on that same side.

One was tripped up, the other let go his holfi to prevent himself falling.

The men on his left were pulled the opposite way.

Lance bent abruptly, making a back, and they fell over him, very much like leap-frog.

Shaking the hand still on his shirt off, the lieutenant bounded upon his prey.

This was a young man of slender form, whose resemblance to Captain Teach, and the latter's extreme partiality to him, made it be supposed that he was Blackbeard's son.

(The trial of Captain Teach some years after this, brought out that this youth William Teach was only a son of the captain's sister.)

Cavendish seized him like a lion grapples a gazelle.

He flung him under one arm, as a tar often carries a hammock, and took his flight.

The weather bulwarks were free of men.

As if unencumbered, Cavendish leaped up on a gun, thence on the inner-rim, and began to climb the main-shrouds.

Only then did the spectators awake from their surprise.

Twenty pistols were lifted up.

But Teach flung himself between.

"For your lives, forbear!" shouted he.

Lance had put the youth's body between him and the muzzles.

He reached the maintop before another move could be made.

There he paused to recover from his tremendous exertions.

One of the riggers had left a sheet-anchor axe on the top.

Lance took it up gladly.

Poising it over William Teach's breast, whom he held in a tight grip, he shouted down to the pirates :—

"Who has the game in his hand now, you wretches? bloody as you are faithless!"

The fog was closing slowly in, and the wind died away.

As through a cloud the pirates on deck looked up to see the gleaming axe over the favourite of their cheif!

CHAPTER XII.

IN THE FOG—BOWSE TELLS A STORY HARD TO BELIEVE—THE SEA SEPULCHRE—THE "CRUISER" OPENS FIRE.

THE "Cruiser" was skimming along, when the fog began to fall about her.

As she entered the cloud banks deeper and deeper her speed slackened as the breeze died away.

Finally, the barque limbered on, her wet canvass hanging straight down like boards.

It was rather dreary, as the drops coursed down the threads, and ran off the seams with a drip, drip, all the time.

Cambering, the first mate, was on deck, pacing the quarter slowly.

The men were huddled together on the forecastle, all wrapped in waterpl oof.

"Not enough wind alive to ruffle a midge's feathers," said Jack, who had come down from aloft.

"Ah," said Bill Bowse, for, boatswain as he was, the "Scarlet Cruiser" was such a free and easy going craft, that Frank himself could cut a slice of any mess's salt horse one moment, and at the next set them all to testing new rope, that most tiresome of work.

"Ah!" said the old boatswain, gruffly, "this is the still, calm, cutthroat weather that made Davy Jones give up sailing ship."

"What!" exclaimed Jack, "did Old Nick ever navigate?"

"Did he," said Derrick, shaking the water off his souwester. "I should tink so! He was der schkipper of der 'Flying Deutcher'!"

"No he wasn't cap'en of no 'Flying Dutchman,'" said Bill, indignantly. "A pretty mild devil it would be, that 'd wag his tail on a Holland-built oyster-boat."

"What was it then, bo's'n?" inquired Jack, offering Bill a square of tobacco to draw him out.

Bowse bit off about "seven-third's" of it, and did not think of returning the rest.

It appeased his irritation.

"If somebody 'll choke that Dutchman if he shoves in his oar, I don't mind telling on it," growled he.

"Do," said Jack.

"Once upon a time," began the old tar, "Davy Jones heard that the water covered the earth, and that Admiral Noah had it all to himself in his Ark.

"Well, that chafed him, and Davy had a temper of his own, one of them kind that can't bear unravelling."

"All the Joneses are that 'ere way," remarked Jack, "I knew one at Plymouth, who——"

"Who's telling this yarn—you or me?" burst out Bill, wrathfully.

Jack soothed Bill, who at length went on :—

"So Davy determined he'd have a ship that could outsail anything that ever carried canvas. So he mustered a set of his imps, rascally nimble chaps that could lash and carry sinners, just as man-o'-wars-men shoulder hammocks, and they made a clipper of a three-master."

"But look a' here, Bo's'n Bill, I don't want to interrupt you," said Derrick, "but how der duyvel does he find woodt when the deluge was cover the worldt, hein?"

"What a time it takes you to clue up a h'idee," said Bill. "In coorse Old Harry begun to build a-top of the mountains when it was low tide."

"In coorse," chorussed the others, led off by Jack. "Any fool but a Dutchman would know that! Clap on sail ag'in, bo's'n."

"Well, d'ye see, by the time Davy set his ship afloat and paid off the riggers, Noah had landed at a place in Azhee called Airy-hat, because of the people wearing covers to their heads, all rim and no crown, on account of the weather being always warm, and warmer in winter than in summer——"

"How do dey tell der summer from der winter," said Derrick, faintly.

"In coorse they has almanicks," said Jack. "Clap a seizing round your tongue."

"And better boy rum-eaters than us," continued Bowse. "Hows'ever, they put out for a virgin cruise, and baptized the vessel with a bottle of liquid flame from the Stromboli light, and they called her the 'Big Thunderbolt.'

"She was a goer! She allers carried the breeze with her, somehow or other.

"It was high old fun for a long while and more. Whenever the 'Thunderbolt' was 'made' by another craft, t'other craft would cut and run ashore if she could.

"Then Davy 'd play the deuce with the plunder.

"Afore long, the big hold was chock full up to the hatches with silks, laces, spices, cognac, gold, and silver, and Davy thought seriously one day of having satin sails with strings of dimuns for reef-lines, and painting her black sides with injigo: Injigo was worth sixty Mexican dollars a h'ounce them days."

Bill looked around in a way that implied that he'd like to see anybody that would dispute his settling of the price.

They all nodded, but said nothing.

"She could sail, too, the 'Thunderbolt'! If ever there'd come on a typhoon that Davy saw looked blacker than himself, he'd up helm, and scud away till the blow would lose breath, a-trying to get anywhere near him.

"So Old Jones had been careering on in this sort for a fleabite of some ninety years, when he found that he had swept the seas.

"The ships that he hadn't had the picking of, rotted at the wharves, or were pulled to pieces to build houses on, on shore. Only think on that!"

"No ships! Horrid! Scandangalous!"

"Davy grew sick! It was a sort of caniption fit—no cure for it.

"He couldn't make the people build a fleet, only for him to sail into, and blow out of water by a double broadside.

"He sailed to Etna because it smoked at him, and put a couple of balls through its mouth, and tumbled the old volcano's top in, till the smoke twisted into seventy shapes before it got out.

"'By the split in my hoofs!' thundered he one day when he sat on the taffrail, telescope in hand, 'my berge don't show me nothing for ten thousand miles around. Not even a fishing-boat that I can pepper. I know what!'

"Here he slapped his thigh, and the sea rocked.

"'I'll go fight the land!'

"And he cleared for action straightway.

"You can imagine how long ago this 'ere was, when you could cross from Britain to France dryshod."

"Oh!"

"Yes. It was land all the way.

"So Davy had the tiller lashed fore-and-aft, and all sail set except a little reef in the lower sheets, to give room for working the guns.

"With that he opened fire.

"First shot with the bowchasers! The port gun rolled the churches of Paris over like ninepins. The other landed slap in York, and so doubled up the swine, that York hams went up to a hawful price all through the kingdom!

"The 'Big Thunderbolt' made the land fast.

"'Stand to your guns, fore and aft, main deck, upper-deck, and swivels in the tops!' said Davy, through his trumpet. 'All ready, captains? Then let fly!'

"There were fourteen thousand guns on the 'Thunderbolt'!" said Bill, freshening his nip at a flask Ned Nittle offered him. "And the double broadsides went off so near together that the ship heeled over both ways, kept an even keel, and only shivered like a leaf.

"The King of France was so terrified at the uncountable balls that upset his dinner-table, that he said to his wife: 'Queen, I'm blowed if here aint't sich a sitivation for a r'yal family, as no one ever saw nowhere afore! Let's put the guineas in our pockets and cut and run.'"

"I thought they kept the guineas in the bank," said Jack, dubiously.

"But this was in France, you duff-maker! Let alone Johnny Crapaw for having the poor ignorant French people's money in his reach."

"Oh!"

"But as I was a-saying when you ran athwart hawse, the 'Big Thunderbolt' rushed on ag'in. She rose on the sea that she brought with her, and ran her figger head that rippersented old King Cole hisself smack into Dover Cliffs, with a swash that threw every man off his pins, and brought her up standing.

"Every line was a-taut-o, when she pounded once more, and then all—ahem!" coughed Bill, as a shred of tobacco went the wrong away, "couldn't save her.

"She began to go down, and bear the earth under her. There was an awful uproarious tumbling in of the rocks and ground, and pretty soon the cliffs stood up on either side of Sen' George's Channel, which was open as it stands now.

"The North Sea foamed down to meet the Atlantic Ocean, and there was a great hissing as they drowned the red-hot topmasts of the 'Thunderbolt'!"

"Line of reefs dead ahead!" cried the lookout of the "Cruiser."

The story-tellers jumped to their feet.

Frank was in the mizzen shrouds, prying through the fog.

"Stop that blind look-out's grog for three days!" cried he. "What traverse is he working, when it's plain from here that it's a ship, and no reef?"

The "Cruiser" hardly minded her helm, so scanty was the wind.

There was great danger of a collision, as the two vessels very slowly surged past one another.

"What ship is that?" hailed the stranger.

To each the other was but an indistinct shadow, known to be a ship but by the supposition that only a vessel would be moving on the ocean.

"What ship is that?" came the cry once more.

Frank had hesitated.

The stranger looked rather large, and prudence might be best.

So he rejoined :—

"The barque Anna, Maxwell—full laden, sugar and West Ingy produce—of London, for London! What ship's that?"

"The Sea Coffin! Blackbeard master! Of nowhere, bound for blazes! Cargo, double-refined flames! Heave to and let fall mizzen, or I'll send you a sample!"

This was a bullying return for the mild speech of the mock barque Anna.

"Soho!" said Frank, to himself. "Friend Blackbeard! Ned, you ought to have Long Tom always ready?"

"Aye, aye, sir! Jack, fetch a coal from the caboose."

"Sea Coffin, ahoy!" cried Rogers.

"Aye, aye!"

"You didn't catch my hail aright."

"What say?"

"This is the 'Scarlet Cruiser,' come to singe Blackbeard!"

Then turning to his own men, Frank commanded a change in the course.

The barque slowly wore round.

"Hull her, Ned! Fire!"

Nittle snatched the tongs from his mate, and clapped it to the breech of the big swivel.

A flash reddened the fog, and a loud report shook the vapour.

There was a pause of silence, and then a loud snapping told that some spar had been shot away, and was coming down by the run on board the 'Revenger.'

"Hooray, Ned," said the young captain. "By the queer row they are kicking up, you've hit 'em hard where they wore their hair short."

CHAPTER XIII.

THE CHANCE SHOT—A LEAP FROM THE TOP—A SPRING OVER THE GUNNEL.—THE ACTION—HOW THE PIRATE WAS SAVED.

THAT shot which, from the crash that had followed it, betokened something immense as the result to the "Cruiser's" company as she surged ahead, was really serious.

The large ball had embedded itself deeply in the brig's mainmast.

The first roll that she made caused an ominous splitting.

The damp had loaded all the top-hamper, so that it was very heavy.

Once, twice, and then, at the slings of the main yard, just under the top, the mast parted.

The "doubling" held well, and, each stay snapping, unstranding, or giving, the whole seat of spars pitched over into the sea.

Of course, with sailor's instinct grasping at the rattlins, Lance and his victim were carried down, and submerged in the water.

The topsail was partly unfurled, and it shrouded them for a moment.

Without hesitating, the after-guard cut away the wreck.

At that instant Lance appeared, as well as the other young man, struggling in the tangle.

The slack of a broken brace was hove to William Teach, and half-drowned, he was hauled on board.

With Cavendish standing on the mast-stump, the wreck floated away.

Blackbeard snatched a musket from the nearest hand, and fired at him, but with no effect.

He was furious.

"Sink you, timberheads," roared he to some men who were about to spring up the mizzen shrouds to secure the loose ends of the snapped stays, "let the wood break. Level the port stern-chaser on that fellow, and hand the slack of his lifetime in."

They rapidly trained the carronade.

At that moment, the "Cruiser" had loaded up the Long Tom once more.

It barked again.

Its missile, on account of the "Revenger's" disabled condition and change of position, danced along the line of the bulwarks, and at last smashing along the quarter, made match-wood of two side-ports, and smote the carronade so fiercely, that its carriage and the three men just reloading, were made to execute a dance, and a tumble over the stern.

One man alone caught at the steering-barrel, and did not follow his mates into the water.

There was great confusion at this.

As if to add to it, a sudden cry from Blackbeard startled them again.

"Stop her! Stop her on your lives!"

But Genifrede, who had been a little less tightly held when this last shot had had such a result, took advantage of it to wrest herself entirely loose.

This done, she boldly ran across the deck to the weather side, and leaped over the taffrail, crying :—

"Better to die with him, than perish in soul with ye!"

They saw her white dress buoyed up for an instant, and then she faded away in the fog, as had the other swimmers long since.

"Clear away the ——"

But then the pirate checked himself.

It was folly to think of lowering boats to pick up the girl, or the seamen, or Cavendish.

The mist would have only prevented the boat's crew from finding their way back, spite of the noise of the great guns.

"They're D. D. in the books," remarked an old pirate, who on such occasions ventured to speak even to the captain. "The only wind is a southerly puff, cap'en, and the wind south blows bait into fishes mouth! There's a black fin already."

A shark's dark dorsal wedge appeared above the water's surface, and the men saw his white belly plain, as he turned to snap at a block that had floated near him.

Blackbeard grinned.

"Aye, old teeth-in-rows will spoil the young fools marvellously," said he.

Notwithstanding the great loss of principal mast, the "Revenger's" gunners had replied to the "Scarlet Cruiser's" salute, by her whole broadside and bow-chaser, a few shots hulling the barque.

The concussion of the firing had imparted some movement to the fog bank, but immediately the cloud seemed to close in more thickly than before.

"We can't stand this, cap'en," said a boatswain to Blackbeard.

Ned Nittle had served his big gun so well, that a fourth or fifth pellet had splintered through the brigantine's side, by so large an orifice, that in rough water she would have been as bad as scuttled.

"The mate to that, cap'en," continued the old boatswain, "would send us under if the pumps were going a hundred strokes to the minute."

"Yes. We must drift right away—the fog thickens."

Suddenly he rushed forward like a wild beast more than a man.

Some of the men, not caring to be a target to the enemy, were taking an old salts advice, by going to show sail forward.

"Who bade you man the fore clue-garnets and f'tops'l clue-line?" cried Teach. "Shake a rag out, and I'll hang you up by the red rag in your throats."

A shot going clean through the little of the foresail exposed, after a bound from the waves, added to his rage.

"Oh, my soul to Satan if I could make that scoundrel cease firing!" growled he. "In guns, down port-lids, and dowse the glims fore and aft!"

They closed the ports, and the brigantine's side was of one black hue.

The slow-matches and red hot irons used to fire the guns, were extinguished.

"And now lie down on deck, all," continued the pirate. "And if you want to be blown out of water, and come down food for sharks, why, whistle for the wind that that accursed craft only wants to be down on us."

Silence the most profound reigned over the "Revenger."

On board the "Cruiser," the men were much jollier.

When the space between had increased, the firing had devolved on Ned's pivot gun.

"You're a lad that has good aim, and good luck besides," said Captain Rogers. "Let her spit fire again, Ned, and send in the rascal's head."

"Thank'ee, sir; but I must see her first," remarked Ned Nittle, peering over the lee gunnel.

"The fog is banked up thick," said Frank, looking. "She can't have sailed sharply with her main-mast overboard. "So let fly in the line of your last."

"Both of us drifted, sir. I don't know what allowance to make," replied the seaman. "I hate to lose a load on a rash venture."

"Wait a bit then."

Lifting his voice, Frank shouted to the man on the maintop.

"Look out, there! D'ye see him?"

"Not since his mast went, sir," was the reply. "His last fire was more for'ard, sir—'fraid the breeze has sprung up near him!"

"Is there a breeze?"

"Aye, aye, sir; leastways, its a bit colder every minute here."

That was true.

A chill, increasing in sharpness every moment, made the stripped men shiver at their guns, and so cutting did it become, that the hardiest began to pull on their guernseys.

"Ten dollars to the man who sights the brigantine!" cried Frank.

Up each mast to the royals, several men climbed.

Ned Nittle knocked the ashes off the lint-stock that he held.

In the midst of the cold and silence, the "Scarlet Cruiser" sullenly plunged through the waves.

All at once, the young sailor, who had climbed up to the top of the mainmast, raised his voice:—

"There she is! Crowding all sail on the one mast standing!"

"There she is!" shouted the others aloft in one voice.

"Seen from here!" cried several voices below.

Looming up through the mist like a shrouded giant, a white mass, running up to a point like a ship's mast with all canvass spread, was really surging slowly towards the barque.

"She's bringing the breeze with her!" said Ned Nittle. "That's how she's the weather gage so suddenly! Bear a hand, Jack!"

They rapidly whirled the pivot gun round.

"Out of the foreshrouds there—up or down," cried Ned.

They rapidly cleared out of the line of the piece.

"Elevate—depress—left, left! steady! Stand clear!"

Fizz—clap—boong!

The Long Tom recoiled powerfully as its heavy missile darted forth.

They heard a most deafening crash, and a splintering as if a thousand mirrors had been smashed.

"Dunder and blitzen!" roared Derrick. "There never was woodt of a schip make dat ise."

"Right, Dutchy," said Bill Bowse.

"Hark! Silence!" said Frank.

From the white tower which had been so severely hit, a shriek proceeded.

"In the name of all that's good, what is it?" said Rogers, rushing to the bulwarks and leaning over.

"Deck ahoy! An iceberg, not a ship!"

"Iceberg! Iceberg!" ran from stern to stern.

Did you ever throw two bits of stick into a pool, and find after a while that they were together?

On the ocean, in a calm, two vessels will insensibly draw so near, that collisions are inevitable.

The commotion in the air, caused by the thawing of the colossal block of ice, was not sufficient to belly out the smallest thread.

The "Cruiser's" only chance rested upon an accident.

From this irregular shape, the mountains of frost, much larger under water than above, sometimes have clear perpendicular faces.

If the barque was approaching it on such a side, she might escape.

But if this had a projection under the surface, the vessel would surely run upon it, and be very lucky if got off with only a leak.

The only means of avoiding the peril were adopted.

While the most of the crew began hauling the weather-braces to lay the yards transversely, two boats were lowered, and sent a-head and a-lee to tow the boat off.

All idea of the pirate brigantine was set aside now.

To overcome the great cold and the dull feeling, Bill the coxswain, set his men to singing as they rowed.

The others on deck caught up the strain, and it had quite a cheering effect to hear the pullers of oars and of braces, crying:—

"In hot battle,
When guns rattle,
He so boldly leads the van!
For he's a stout and valiant sailor,
All a-sailing on the main!
He will bring home gold and treasure,
For he's fighting France and Spain."

"Stash that!" said Bowse, suddenly. "Hark to that again."

A second time the scream resounded.

"It's on the berg!" cried Jack, at the stroke oar.

"A duyvel," said Derrick.

"A woman——"

"Der same ting," muttered the Dutchman.

They had given the barque so much impulse, that they were letting the tow-line slack.

On the ship, several of the men were holding out a long sweep in case the ice and the vessel should come closer.

"Bowse!" cried Rogers, running out on the bowsprit, "there's a woman on the ice. Cast off the line and take her in."

"I was agoin' to," muttered Bill.

They undid the rope, and with a turn of the tiller, the yawl went up to the berg.

On the edge was Genifrede.

"Save me! Save me!" cried she, wringing her hands.

She did not know that the boats cautious approach came from fear of the ice, not any unreadiness to help her.

"Why, it's the cap'en's lass ag'in!" said Jack.

At last bringing the boat as near the frozen edge as they durst, and holding on by a boathook, a couple of the oars were held out, the blade-end on the iceberg, the handles on the gunnel.

Genifrede ran up this frail and rather narrow bridge.

"Well done, miss! Like a sailor's girl!" said Bill, making room for her in the stern-sheets, and spreading out his jacket.

"You won't give me up to the pirates?" said she, hesitating.

Bill scratched his head, puzzled.

"Dip-ends on who is the pirates," returned he. "Pull away, lads!"

"Captain Teach."

"Oh, Blackbeard! Hain't we sunk him?"

"Oh, was it this ship that was fighting with him?"

"The 'Scarlet Cruiser'! I should think it were!"

"Oh! Then ——" but she stopped.

For Frank was standing at the side, bidding a couple of men sling the accomodation-ladder at the gangway.

The surprise of both was great.

However, the young captain could not do less than offer her his cabin again.

Then learning from her what little she could impart of the disabled "Revenger's" probable course, and the set of the current that had swept Lance Cavendish away, he returned to deck.

The fog continued to cloak the scene, but there was an alteration in the feel of the air that denoted a lifting of it soon.

CHAPTER XIV.

THE PORTUGUESE PINK—THE "CRUISER" CHEATED THE NEW HAND.

THE crippled brigantine had luckily fallen into a back-water line, which ran southerly alongside the Gulf Stream.

The mist had lessened around her by morning.

They had repaired damages, but had no time to put up a jury-mast.

Moreover they had discovered a serious leak, result of the strain when the mainmast had been carried away.

To add to their consternation, they descried a sail.

But quickly they regained their spirits.

Besides the new comer being northerly bound, she was a schooner and smaller than the "Cruiser."

"She sails well," remarked Blackbeard, to his second in command. "As our leak passes stopping, what say to changing ship?"

"She's a pretty set of sails, captain," returned the mate, eyeing the stranger.

"It's that or none. Let every man fill his bag with the plunder. We'll share aboard her."

The flag of Spain, upside down, was hoisted.

The stranger altered her course a point, and stood directly for them.

Meanwhile the pirates packed up the spoil and treasure in their bags.

"We must look more distressed," observed Teach. "After-guard and main-deckers, unlash the port guns, and run them starboard."

This accession of weight to one side, made the "Revenger" heel over sadly.

What with her broken mast and her nearly-capsized condition, she looked like a beggar of the seas.

"Call the men aft," said Blackbeard.

They clustered around him.

"Yourselves see," began the marauder chief, "we have a chap coming down on us, who's a Portuguese pink, I think. The 'Revenger's' getting down slowly; thanks to that cursed 'Cruiser.' We must have the pink to get to the islands again in.

"Keep you down under hatches, and let but four or five of you be seen above, so by scantiness of number, and by the wrecked look of our barkey, which you see he takes note of, he shall have no cause to suspect us."

"We can't lay him a board, but I'll go off in a boat to him, and then heaven perish me, body and soul, if I don't pistol with my own hand, him among my sea-ramblers who leaves both me and his own courage in the lurch!"

Half a dozen as the rascals lay down in the boat that was to be used, and pulled a tarpaulin over them.

The rest, except a hand, went below, as ordered.

The pink came slowly up.

She was a pretty little schooner.

Captain Teach was making ready to answer her hail with a doleful story of tempest and wreck, when the voice from the schooner startled him, as much by its familiar tone as by its unexpected words.

"'Revenger' ahoy! isn't it?"

"Aye, aye!" cried Captain Teach, surprised.

"Sinking?"

"No! Loys!"

The man occupying the quarter deck of the schooner was Loys de Goupille.

He had given the orders, and the pink's way was deadened.

While the two vessels remained together, Teach went aboard the pink.

He felt rather hurt at having no chance to butcher the crew and take the vessel.

"Sorry to find your gunnels under," said Goupille, shaking hands with the other. "I never expected to catch up to you, but thought to find you at New York!"

"Oh, I was going to see my old mate Captain Kidd, but I fell in with your friend of the 'Scarlet Cruiser'—"

"The boy commander? Burn him!"

"With all my heart! If it had not been for the fog he'd have blown me out of water. He has one terrible long gun, and his ship's a perfect rouser."

"I ought to know that, when I always intended to turn her into a rover. But to work now. I'm short-handed, your men will have plenty of room."

"Till we return to the Cuban seas," said Teach. "I'll give up Kidd this season."

As quickly as possible, the crew of the "Revenger," with their hammocks, were transferred to the pink.

The sea was smooth enough to allow the pivot gun being taken into the jolly boat, and then hoisted upon the schooner.

"Black-muzzled sons of lightning, yours," remarked Loys, laughing.

The last boat delayed only to scuttle the brigantine.

Being off her even keel, she went down very quickly after she began to fill.

For a few seconds her pirate flag of crimson fluttered above the waves.

"Poor Revenger!" muttered Blackbeard. "Down under the bloody colours anyhow! Well, well; an ounce of sorrow won't pay a penny debt."

"I yield the post to you, Teach," said Loys, politely. "How shall she head!"

"Anyhow out of the fog."

The schooner went about and took a stretch S. S. E., to entirely clear the cloud bank.

But that happened to be nearly the same course that the "Scarlet Cruiser" had taken in he same design.

On espying the schooner, Rogers ordered a crowding on of sail and chase.

She had been too near the scene of the fight not to be suspected of knowing something of the disappeared "Revenger."

At first, Loys had attempted flight, but half an hour's sail had proved that the pink was no match for the barque in speed.

So a Portuguese flag was run up, and sail shortened.

The "Cruiser" let one shot start the foam on the waves crests ahead of the chase, to let her know that she had acted very sensibly.

In a quarter of an hour, they were within earshot.

On the deck of the pink were half a dozen unmistakeable Portuguese and a negro who was lashed to a grating set up against the port side of the high quarter deck front.

The darkey was evidently in the course of being flogged.

"What ship's that?" challenged Frank.

The answer came in broken English:—

"The Saint Nicholas with a Crown! Cleared from Nueva 'Ork last, and bound for ——"

"That'll do! I'm coming aboard! Let fall your main-sheet, and take her aback!"

His cutter was quickly set afloat, and Frank leaped down into it, with its crew.

When they climbed up on the pink, the Portuguese was greatly alarmed.

The "Cruiser's" men bristled with weapons, carrying a brace of pistols, a knife, cutlass and axe by their sides and in their belts.

The trembling man who shuddered himself forward to Frank as the Portuguese captain, said he was Pedro de Busto, and that he had sold his cargo in New York, but that all the returns for his olives and wines were paid into a merchant's hands in that city.

Hence, there was nothing on board for the "great captain of the celebrated 'Scarlet Cruiser,' to see but empty wine-butts and some olive-oil jars that he was carrying merely as ballast."

His papers seemed correct.

Had he seen anything of the Revenger.

"No, nothing of a wrecked vessel. Oh, yes, he had seen a two-master bound south that very morning, hadn't he, Juan?"

So another red-capped seaman stepped forward, and in worse English than his captain, told Rogers that a vessel had been spied, but that they had been so frightened by the stories of Captain Kidd that they had not tried to speak the stranger.

Bill Bowse, who had gone down into the pinks hold with three more, came up to report that all seemed to corroborate the mock captain's story.

There was nothing worth seizing on board the craft, evidently.

Frank turned away.

Just then, the negro, who had remained triced up at ankles and wrist, gave a howl.

"Hold your tongue you black scoundrel!" cried Jack.

"Oh, no, gorramity! oh, 'ow! Oh, massa capitan ob de Scar'it Cruiser! leff me go out ob dis craf'!"

"What has the blackey done to be flogged!'" queried the young commander, carelessly.

"Stealing ——"

"Oh!" and Frank prepared to follow his men over the side.

"Oh, no, massa," cried the African, rolling his eyes. "That was a base calomel. I was berry hones' al'ays! I tol' Cap'en Busto dat dar was no use to run away from your splendificant Cruiser, but he would try it, spite of me, an' he had me triced up—on'y just for dat! Leff me go on your 'Cruiser! I al'ays liked to be a pirate—yah, yah!"

"Stash that!" cried a Portuguese, raising a handspike.

"Hold!" interposed Rogers. "I'll add the poor darkey to my complement! My men want something to torment for their fun."

"Oh, massa, I'se so dam glad! hee-e! You spec' to frighten dis chile by sayin' so—guess no, guess no."

"Cut him down, Jack," said Rogers.

Jack whipped out his knife, pushed aside the Portuguese captain, and severed the lashings.

The negro grinned.

"I likes you, massa Jack! Ki! Hopes all de Croo-croo-ser's crew is like you."

"Paws off!" said Jack, as the Ethiopian seemed about to shake his hand in his exuberance of spirits.

His ecstacy was such that he could not bring himself to go down into the boat until he had made a sign of great contempt for the Portuguese (the nature of which may be guessed when his face was directly from them in the act), and said—

"Good bye, Porkugeese! I'se guine aboard the 'Cruiser,' and gwine to be a pirate wid seven pair of pistols! I shoot you ebery one eber I comes on you ag'in'!"

"Keep still nigger," cried Jack, as the boat shoved off, "you'll upset the cutter!"

"Oh, no, massa, I won't capset the boat!"

They got the precious volunteer on the "Cruiser."

Sail was made, and the pink was hull down by nightfall.

The negro had made himself at home among the crew. They found he could dance, sing and play the fiddle.

The watch gathered around the windlass, and drank off their lots leisurely.

They were 30 N., 70 W., and on a bouline running south, the wind freshening.

"Golly! dis am sublime stuff!" said the negro, licking his lips over his grog.

"Toss it off, Sambo, and tune up the fiddle!" cried several.

"Yes, yes! he's l'arnt the 'Cruiser' song a'ready."

One of the men had a violin which Sambo had

mended and made fit to scrape a tune upon. So Sambo finished the liquor and commenced to extort the usual hideous sounds from the catgut, until the strings were tightened to his satisfaction.

"I got him now," said he.

"Massa Jack, you will lead off de chorus!"

And as the barque forged along, the air was resonant with the roaring voices.

"Sim Simpson was a trader,
    Who sending ships to sea:
By bringing home uncustomed goods,
    Grew rich right speedly.
He married of a bo's'n's wife,
    And a loo-tenancy got;
And then become a captain,
    By fighting very hot!"

"Chorus!" cried Jack, waving his hand in the air.

"So whirled the windlass,
    The well-whirled windlass;
The like whereof was never heard,
    The whirling of the windlass!"

CHAPTER XV.

THE KING'S SHIP—A MISTAKE AND A MISS FIRE ALL ROUND—THE TRAITOR—THE CHASE OPENS.

So far, by this cruise after the "Revenger," the "Scarlet Cruiser" had gained nothing except hard blows in the storm.

In heading for the West Indian seas once more, Frank meant to give his men a treat, by overhauling the first vessel of promise they should perceive.

So, on one morning, as they neared the Bahamas, with a light breeze, all were delighted to hear:—

"Sail ho! Two points on the weather-beam! Large ship, under full sail, stud'n's'l-booms out!"

"Very well."

The young captain examined the stranger with the glass.

"Good news," said he, to his men. "There can hardly be two of that size in these waters. I suspect that's the ship with the money to pay the garrisons of Cuba."

"Hooray!"

"Cash down, if we take her," said Rogers. "The men will go to breakfast, and then clear for action. At the helm, keep her as she is."

The other vessel betrayed no alarm, remaining on her course.

But her commander had made a better guess at the "Cruiser," than the latter's captain at the ship.

"Send Lieutenant Cavendish to me," said he.

It was the ship of war, "Royal Charles."

It had been beating up and down the Atlantic seaboard in search of Captain Kidd.

It had picked up Lance on his wreck, half dead with exposure and cold.

Learning from him the neighbourhood of the Revenger, and believing that the vessel that he reported as having opened fire on her was one of the British navy, the commander of the Royal Charles was eager to find one or the other of them.

But the fog had disappointed that hope.

Only this morning did the man-of-war encounter the "Cruiser"

"That answered your description, lieutenant?"

"Yes, Captain Sansom," replied Lance, surprised. "Would you oblige me with the glass?"

"Certainly she is not the 'Sir James Harley,' as I thought."

"Oh, no, sir. It's the 'Scarlet Cruiser!'"

"The Scarlet Cruiser! that notorious kite of the sea that has become as great a terror in a few months as Kidd in his many!"

Lance deeply regretted having let the secret out.

The gallant way in which Frank Rogers had rescued him in the castle of Governor Pecador, had not been without effect upon him.

Besides, Genifrede had even made him jealous by her warm praises of the brave young commander.

Lance felt all the more pain when he heard the orders given for the Royal Charles to continue the disguise which she had assumed to deceive Captain Kidd.

The trimness of a man-of-war was not perceptible on her now.

The utmost endeavours had been made to give the lumbering, sloven look of one of those great Spanish galleons, which had hardly began to alter their shape since the Armada days.

But her guns were made ready, and the portlids could be lifted in an instant.

The castles and lions of Spain floated out at the gaff, but a double set of halyards were at the peak, and on the second one the red cross was bent.

The barque came unsuspectingly on, and while saucily dancing before the heavier hull, the Long Tom tossed a bullet in front of the ship.

"He shall pay for this," muttered the greybeard commander, as he ordered the Royal Charles to be hove to.

The great bulk began to roll slowly as she became more stationary.

The Cruiser came up swiftly, but took her topsails aback once or twice when she drew nearer.

"What ship's that?"

"The Scarlet Cruiser," returned Rogers. "Send aboard your captain and two of your grandest Dons, or I'll strip you after a broadside!"

"What do you take us for?"

"The silver ship."

"Stand by your guns, fo'kesel, main, and 'tween decks!" cried the old commander, in his rage. "I'll silver ship the picaroon! Silver ship, eh? Down with the yellow and up with St. George's!"

The colours rose swiftly, and replaced the orange banner.

"Silver ship, the sea dragon," growled the old commander. "Hillo, there! This is the 'Royal Charles,' commissioned expressly to sweep the colonial seas of you piratical villains!"

The surprise was immense on board the barque.

The sides of the man-of-war began to yawn as the port-lids were drawn up, and the muzzles were exposed.

"Ready about, all hands!" shouted Cambering in fear.

"Avast!" cried Frank, in a yet louder voice. "We'll never go about soon enough that way, Fore-topmen, aloft! Fly!"

Breaking the spell at the surprise, a score of men swarmed up the foremast shrouds.

"Down haul foresheet, jib, and flying jib! For your lives! Furl r'yals, top-gallant, and top! Bravely done! Now, hug the spars like you do your gals! On deck, lie down, every soul!"

In good time.

"Fire!" had already echoed over the man-of-war.

The guns belched forth responsively.

A horrid rushing of shot tore through the Cruiser's upperworks, and mid-riggings.

After the broadside, the smoke circled around blindingly.

But the young commander's strange order, promptly obeyed, had saved the vessel considerably.

The abrupt stripping of the foremast, and the consequent redoubled pressure on the main and mizzen, had swung her stern round, and let her prow fall off inconceivably quick.

This had taken her out of her fore-and-aft position as regarded the royal ship.

Instead of being raked, she received the valley along her length.

But it was severe.

There were several ropes swinging in all directions.

Dead men and wounded tumbled out of the rigging into the water or on the deck.

"Top-gallants, to the r'yals! Topmen to the t'-gallant! Bo's'n, ten waisters to the fore-top!"

This recruiting filled up the vacancies of the corpses and disabled.

"Let fall all sail on the fore!" Shake out the oresail, lively! Now then haul on the fore-tack—steady! Up jib and foresheet!"

The "Cruiser" leaped into position almost, and surged on.

Her ports had been open long since.

"Give the big clumsy a warmer!" cried Frank.

The guns were ready trained.

"Depress!"

The muzzles gaped up at the high wooden wall, seeming so immense compared to the low Cruiser.

"All primed? Fire!"

The ten loggerheads and slow-matches were clapped to the breeches.

But instead of the stunning report to be expected, but one solitary explosion split the stillness which had followed the Royal Charles's broadside.

It was Ned Nittle's pet that had gone off.

It's single projectile splintered through the ship's side and dismounted a gun.

"What's that mean, captain of the gun?" cried Frank, boiling with rage, and laying his hands on his pistols.

"My gun's spiked, sir," exclaimed Jack.

"Undt mine, mein Gott!" said Derrick.

"And mine!"

"And all!"

"And are the starboard guns served the same?" queried Frank. "Clap a match to any one."

They did so.

But as on the other side the priming only burnt.

"Treachery!" said the youthful captain. "We'll see to this. And now, out studdingsails! I'll make matches of every beam beam before a traitor shall sell us this way."

They shook out every stitch of canvas, although the wind was freshening.

As the Cruiser showed the Royal Charles her heels, Nittle kept up a more or less effectual fire with the only serviceable gun.

The wind was quite strong enough to send the Royal Charles along, but, nevertheless, the barque kept her distance.

"All hands aft," said Boatswain Bill, as Frank hurried down into the cabin, to see that Genifrede had sustained no harm.

The crew, except a few aloft, who were busy splicing the cut cordage, were mustered on the mid-deck.

They were in a state of the goeatest excitement.

They had been so long together now, and had worked into one another's peculiarities to such a degree, that so flagrant an act of treachery was a marvel.

Each feared to speak to his neighbour, even though he had been his elbow mate in the reefing for weeks, or his messmate for as long.

Suddenly Ned Nittle dashed his cap down.

"Oh, thunder!" exclaimed he. "In course it is!"

And with those disjointed words he left the group and rushed down the mainhatch like mad.

It almost seemed as though he was guilty, and trying to hide.

But he presently appeared.

He had a tight grip of the shirt collar of the negro who had been so lately brought on board the Cruiser.

"Now, you scoundrel!" exclaimed he, holding him with his left hand, and drawing his knife with the other. "What made you crawl about the guns here in the morning watch?"

"Aha!" exclaimed all.

"Me, massa—me crawl about dem guns! Hope I neber stir if I did! I'se afraid of de cannonses, awful scared!" tremblingly replied the black.

"No slipping your cables that way," said Nittle. "I'll slit your lying tongue into spun yarn if you tell me them lies."

"I missed some nails the last time he was carrying my box from the sail loft," said the carpenter.

"Aha! Overboard with the villain!" cried all.

"What made you spike the guns, say?" cried Ned, shaking the African.

But suddenly the latter's suppliant and bending figure straightened.

He broke from the seaman's grasp by an effort of strength as vigorous as his, and though his stained face and hands remained the same, the flash in his eyes, and the look of pride in the lines of his fine-cut mouth, spoke of the dominant race.

"Why did I spike your guns," cried he, dauntlessly surveying the angry faces encom passing him, "Why? Because I am Loys de Goupille, once captain of this craft i and I mean to sink or swim with her!"

A roar of anger burst forth.

In each of fifty hands glistened a weapon, caught up here or there.

Pike, cutlass, fire-arm, marlinspike, gun-rammer, all threatened the audacious Frenchman.

Suddenly, as unarmed he was about to advance to meet them, the circle was forced in one point by a slight form, made strong by affection.

Genifrede, who had forced herself on deck in spite of Captain Rogers, had cleft the circle of passionate men to throw her arms around the Frenchman.

"Oh, my father!"

"Your father?" said one man, cocking his pistol. "It'll be a blessing to end the race of such traitors!"

And he pulled trigger.

But already a hand had encircled the barrel, and twisted it upwards.

The bullet spun up in the air harmlessly.

Frank thrust the man forcibly away.

"Oh, you will save my father!" screamed the girl.

Frank looked steadily at the defiant features of the once owner of the Cruiser, and recognized his foe under the dye.

Then he struck up a pikehead with his sword.

"Down arms!" cried he.

There was a murmur.

"Ned! Bill! Jack! Do you grumble at my orders. Don't think a dozen women could make me unjust to my comrades," said the youth. "But while that fellow is thundering in our wake, and may be on us any instant that a boom snaps, its no time to coil cable over one man's life. Take that man below and put him in irons."

They separated Genifrede and Loys.

The girl, too, was made to descend.

The night came on, but its darkness could not add to the gloom on Frank's troubled brow.

So the Cruiser glanced over the foam into the shadows, her red sails so blending with the shadows that the Royal Charles, plunging along after, like a bull in pursuit of an antelope, feared at every hour to lose the object of her chase.

CHAPTER XVI.

THE CRUISER LEADS HER PURSUER A PRETTY DANCE—THE FLYING LIGHT—WHAT BILL CALLS A "STARTLER"—LEFT IN A SINKING STATE.

ALL the night the two vessels kept on their way, the space between them remaining about the same.

At times the wind had freshened, and the heavier ship, gaining a trifle, prepared to experiment with her bow-chasers.

At such times, too, Ned Nittle, who cared nothing for sleep, and stood by his gun patiently all through the dark hours, would answer the one, by one as effectual as theirs.

As morning broke the young commander came up from below.

One glance showed him the far-off man-of-war.

"Not clapped a seizing on the Cruiser yet, eh Cambering?" remarked the young commander.

"Oh no, sir," replied the first mate, "that chap yonder will be dropped by noon if the wind lessens a bit."

"It'll hold, I'm afraid," said the captain. "There's a greasy look to wind'ard."

In an hour the breeze had freshened.

The Royal Charles was coming up much plainer in view.

The canvas of the barque was strained somewhat, and the masts leaned forward and bent like whip sticks.

She slid along with a "bone in her mouth," a curved jet of spray brilliant as a rainbow, when a sunbeam shines out between the flying clouds.

The frigate, bumping up and down on the billows, tumbled on in her course, and it seemed surprising that she could have kept so long and so near the low-masted free-trader.

"The royals will have to come in, sir," said Cambering. "The breeze is saying 'clew up' pretty plain."

"Yes. But they will stand the strain for a half hour yet—they must. Let the topmen stand by though. I've an idea, and to carry it out I don't want any spars carried away."

Then down into his cabin to look at his chart the young commander hurried.

In the course of a few minutes he was up again,

"Bos'n," said he, to Bill Bowse, "pass the word to 'Mujen Tommy."

"Tom, you are wanted by the cap'n," said they forward.

Presently a Spaniard, a Bermudian native, hastened aft to his superior.

The two drew aside to the taffrail, and they were soon deep in conversation.

"Good, I see you understand," said the captain at length. "Go you and take the wheel. I'll have the lead kept thrown. Bill, go forward and send word when the water pales."

The Bermudian went forward to handle the spokes, and the boatswain proceeded in the opposite direction to report the shoaling of the sea.

They were, as Frank's private maps indicated, in the neighbourhood of a large growing coral reef.

Meanwhile, the strength of the breeze seemed to indicate a storm before long, and had enabled the man-of-war to lumber up within short gunshot.

"They're busking, I fancy," remarked Cambering.

"My glass tells the same as yours," answered the young commander. "He may clear for action if he pleases. He will have plenty more to do than pull up port-lids on the slope. Ned, serve your pet, and try to dismount there bow chasers."

"Aye, aye, sir! My little brass girl has very long tongues, and they are abusive to the last degree!"

Most of the pivot gun's missils, however, skipped on the rollers.

Not one in a dozen touched the mark, and

flew wildly over the ocean in every possible direction.

The frigate's balls were harmless, and not one came in board the Cruiser, though a few leaped over her altogether in a cloud of spray.

Bill Bowse set up a cry.

It ran along aft till it was repeated to the young captain.

"Light green sea in patches," said a young sailor.

"Very well. Let Jack or someone step over into the chains, and keep the lead a-going."

A seaman obeyed, and was soon singing out for Bermudian Tom's benefit "by the mark."

Following other commands, tackle was rove out on the stay over the main-hatch.

They were not going to hoist any very weighty substance, so that there was no fear of harming the stay, on which the bending of the masts gave enough pressure already.

A gang of men manned the slack, and the wheel of the Bermudian was soon rapidly revolving.

They hoisted out of the mid-hold, all the stuff that will accumulate in a craft of the Scarlet Cruiser's profession.

The cases, boxes, bundles, bags of coffee, a few hogsheads of sugar, all things which they could easily ship again in a day at the first port, crowded the waist.

A hasty inspection was all they had to pass.

"Clear the leeward gangway!" then was said.

The carpenter had taken down part of the side.

The slope of the deck, (the Cruiser leaning over a little, spite of her square sails and her going before the wind) made it very easy to run the rubbish into the sea.

When it had been all shot over the barque seemed to lift herself up.

Her speed was greatly increased.

But the freshening of the impelling current enforced a reduction of sail.

The frigate, on the contrary, kept the same speed she had had for a long while; her stumpy masts were less liable to be broken than the frailer ones of theirs.

It was beautiful to behold her.

It was delightful to the heart to have her under one's feet.

There was a humming aloft on the weather-side, shroud, stay and rattlins even taut as a fiddle-string.

The rollers in vain were swept on to overtake the shooting star.

The hull appeared just to touch the surface of the water, and that slight brushing imparted a thrill to the whole mass, so that it seemed alive from keel to the streamer that was blown out straight on the course.

The discharging the useless cargo and ballast had puzzled the frigate commander.

"Lightening ship, the rascally pirate," said the old commander, in a rage. "He sees that we are coming up with him hand over fist, and he'd rather lose his stolen goods, than in any way endanger his rope-doomed neck."

Lance, dreadfully anxious about Genifrede, whom he had chanced to espy with the telescope in a window of the cabin, mechanically went through his duty.

He saw the man-of-war gain on the lawless letter of marque with pain.

Anyone of the shots, soon to be fired, might bear death to her that he loved.

They shook out the reefs in the fore and main sail of the Royal Charles.

The chase would be soon overhauled.

Every heave, there had been less and less of the dripping-line to haul in, and the leadsman had found his task easier.

"Steado, Tom," said Frank to the wheelsman, seeing he was nervous at the responsibility upon him. "Much as I love the barkey, I'd forgive you wrecking her, if she should be thrown away."

Suddenly, as the leadsman turned pale and stammered the call, Frank grasped his trumpet.

"Only a quarter-fathom to spare between her and bottom, and she so light," muttered he. "Bowse, hillo—"

"Hillo—a, sir," sang out Bill Bill Bowse from the quarter deck.

"Nothing above the waters edge?" queried Frank.

"Clear, but very yellow! Can almost see the rockweed at the bottom, sir," returned old Bill.

"Thunder! but we're in for it! No going about after telling the king's ship slip up to us."

He put the trumpet to his lips.

"Aloft! fore and main r'yals out; sheet home! Bowse taut the fore-tack! Fly!"

With his own hands he let out the mizzen-sheet-boom, so that it swung out to right angles with the mast.

"Luff, luff! Stepdy! She's straight at it! Hold the wheel firm, if she does touch. Now then, all hands, hold on for your lives!"

The men who had been gazing over the cat-heads or the sides, needed not that caution.

The roughness of the water did not prevent a cloudy view of something dark, amid the light sandy bottom.

The Cruiser was headed at a reef, nearly flush with the water.

With all the canvass spread that she could bear dead before the wind, and not a fold fluttering, she was skimming over that thin sheet of water, grazing the rocks.

There was a shock not so powerful as had been dreaded. It was followed by a long scraping, which seemed to have no end.

After a second, the speed not at all diminished, there was not a resumption of the same grating.

"We're over it," said the young captain. "Carn er, sound the pumps."

However badly the false keel may have been scraped, no leak was occasioned by the contact.

"All hands to reduce sail," said the captain. "Lay out there, foreyard and top! Clue up! We'll lay by, and see our friend get into a scrape too."

The Cruiser, her headway deadened, remained in view of the following scene.

"A star-tel-ler!" said Bill Bowse, turning his quid.

Urged on by her ample press of sail, the man-of-war ran down on the spot where the chase had so lately skipped over the unseen peril.

The shoal was so evident, that the look-out could not fail to espy it.

The helm was put up instantly, hard a-port.

But the impetus of the heavy craft, was too much.

The men, called suddenly away from the guns, blundered.

The Royal Charles fell off fast.

"Missed stays," cried Rogers. "Going, broadside on! Good bye, friend of the navy. You've had your look, my men. Ready to make sail."

And, resuming her plumage and her flight, that eagle of the billow flew rapidly away from the spot.

"We'll make for St. Thomas," said the young commander.

In the meantime, great was the dismay on board the Royal Charles.

She went side on the reef before a link could run out of the cable tier.

Before the anchor "bit" ground, she was thumping on the sharp hard rocks with all her weight.

Her sails catching the breeze, and unable to propel the hull, bowed right away from the wind.

Some of the guns of the port side broke loose at the rolling, and ran down to smash against the starboard bulwarks.

That increased the steepness of the slope.

Other guns snapped their recoil-ropes, both in gun-deck-room and on upper-deck.

The weather side rose fearfully out of the water.

Nearly capsized, and her bilge grinding on the reef, it was only a question of time when the leaks should extend, and she fill.

They got out the boats, and cut away the booms.

With them and the spare spars, they made a large raft to carry the officer's valuables.

Before night, while the triumphant Scarlet Cruiser was standing S. E., and her crew toasting her young commander in their jollification, the luckless company of the frigate were making for the Bahamas, the boats escorting the frail raft.

CHAPTER XVII.

ON THE OCEAN—THE MUTINY—THE REMORA CLEARS
THE FIELD FOR ITS OWN HORRID SPORT—DRIVEN
ASHORE.

THE wind increased to such a pitch by nigthfall, that the boats accompanying the raft, had to reef their sails.

The raft had a mast up in it, and a triangular sail, but made no great way.

About ten or so, as the moon rose amid the driving clouds, the boats were compelled to run before the wind.

The raft was left alone in its plight.

It was of an oblong shape, eighty feet by fifteen, mostly spars, but a few hogsheads lashed in the middle to form a higher deck than the rest.

The timber had been well joined at first, but the chopping sea compelled about a dozen of the forty men to keep at work with two-inch and three-inch stuff all the time, such was the chafing.

She was steered by a big oar.

Lance was commander.

An officer who had held the place before him, had been flung overboard with a couple of seamen in one of the plunges of the forepart under, he being at the bow then.

Soon after the boats had disappeared in the darkness, Cavendish noted the strange actions of the men.

They were nearly all in the middle of the raft drenched through every now and then by the flying scud.

But the conversation that had sprung up among them was so engaging, that they minded nothing of the wet.

They spoke in a subdued tone, which was blown forward, too, so that Lance, by the steering oar could hear nothing.

"I'll hoist my colours at once," said one sailor. "I'm for a dive into grog. There's three kegs aft, that the luff has for a seat. I'll strike hands with my mate to have a swig all round."

"Right you are, Corposant," said another bearded tar. "Our jackets are too wet for us not to deserve a warmer."

"S'pose we axes the luff, first," said one timid sailor.

"We'll axe him the right way," said Corposant. "It's my 'pinion, bo', and I don't edge away from it, that that Lance Cavendish is a Jonah ——"

"Ha!"

"Take a reckoning back a bit! He comes aboard in bad weather ——"

"Yes. Fog like the 'Flying Dutchman' sails in."

"The first thing we meets is a scud-away clipper that leads our ship plump on a break-up. And here—look at that! if so be this raft hadn't a curse, would it pitch and toss in this 'ere way——"

"It does dive some."

"Some ain't a word," said Corposant. "I've been rafting often and again, and I've seed worser floats than this ride rougher seas; may I never touch an entering-rope more, if I hain't."

"Good again, mate. And d'ye mind, fast as we lash one spar to its next, snap goes the stuff like a rotten buoy-rope. There's something onnateral in it."

"'Nough said! Who stands by me if I make a rush?"

"Me! and me!" said almost all.

The rest, some fifteen, had gradually separated from the conspirators and had given Lance warning of the plot.

Instead of waiting for the mutineers to open the palaver or the action, as the case might be, the young lieutenant went to the middle, boldly.

"Men," said he, "I hear you are grumbling for the liquor. Now, listen to reason. You should have it if it would only do you good. But you see that this unsteady flooring under us, is not to be trod by a man in drink ——"

"That'll do! you can down hammocks and turn in. Cushin, roll one of them 'ere kegs for'ard."

"If he takes one step ——" said Lance, clapping his hands to his pistol-butts. "All good seaman, rally round me. Your own lives will go, if the lawless wretches get the upper hand of us."

"Down with him! Down with the milksops all!" cried Corposant.

Weapons flashed on all sides.

The parties would have been nearly equal, but that Lance's force was lessened by three, who kept the steering oar in play.

"The last word! Will you down arms and return to duty?"

"No! Overboard with the Jonah!"

Bang! went several pistol shots.

The next moment, the two parties were mingled together in the centre of the craft.

It was a strange field for a battle.

Now and then a fighter would scream, as his foot slipping in the wet, was caught between two of the shifting spars, and jammed horribly.

The bodies that fell were trampled into these yawning joints, and served as awful wedges to widen the gaps.

There were some of the desperate ones, who, fallen half through the holes, fought waist deep in the water, half above, half below, the surface of the raft.

It looked like corpses animated, and trying to scramble out of graves.

Pistol-flash and a glint of the moon now and then lit up the scene.

Despite all that Cavendish and those who stood by him could do, the mutineers broke partly through their line.

Corposant and another got as far astern, as the so-much-coveted casks.

Corposant swung his hatchet high in the air, to dash in the head of one of the kegs.

But one of the three men at the oar, left his place, and grappled the seaman.

Corposant's mate laid hands on the keg to roll it away.

One of the remaining steersman had only to reach out one hand, with his knife in it to stab this fellow, and he did so.

With the knife-blade transfixing his spine, he fell forward on the small barrels.

"Bear a hand!" cried he who had grappled Corposant; "or the mutineering hound will have his axe on to me!"

Eager to help their comrade, the second steersman left the last to keep the oar, and sprang at the chief of the plotters.

Corposant was vigourous.

Notwithstanding the odds, he continued the struggle.

The fight among the survivors, was going on without intermission on the swaying timber.

There was suddenly a deepening of the gloom.

A soughing of the breeze followed.

There was a tone in it that startled even the hottest blooded.

"Oh, see! Men, men, down arms!" cried Lance. "It's a black squall! Cut away the sail for the sake——"

Too late.

Rushing over the water with a speed that was incredible, the gale came on.

Above, it hunted black clouds before it; below it chased a rank of white caps.

A few men, still in the grapple, continued to think only of throttling or stabbing one another.

The rest grasped at any rope whose other end was secured.

There was one sudden lull, a silence for a brief space, and then—

"Hold on! It's on us!" screamed many a voice.

Like a hammer swung by a giant, an immense volume of water was lifted high up over the float.

The latter tried to rise, but was not buoyant enough.

It might have shot forward, but the sail, collapsed and then filled out fearfully, had gone overboard with the mast itself.

The mighty mountain of brine curled over, so that the raft seemed to be in a cave of darkness.

Then down came the mass.

Flung flat on the spars, which were submerged, the men who were not dashed away were almost held down by the pressure.

As the after part sank under the weight, the front tilted up.

But the lines quickly parted, and two thirds almost remained, the rest was splintered and carried away, many fathoms in a second.

A score more of rollers broke of the half-sunken float, but each was less than the former, and they did little more harm.

For a time, the raft kept trembling.

The booms were struck together, completing the destruction of the human forms lying within their jaws.

The billows softened down into a long swell, and the raft rode on the undulations.

A desolate sight.

The moon, waning now, gave a sickly hue to the scene.

It showed that only break to the waste of froth and streakings of green and blue—the jumble of timber, keeping attached by a marvel.

There were ten bodies on it, lying here and there, their arms twisted around several rope ends.

It was impossible to tell which were the dead and which were the living, if any of them did possess existence.

The moon went down, and the breeze died away.

The darkness that precedes the dawn was upon the wave.

But the surface was not obscure.

All the wealth of tropical sea-life was afloat now in unparalleled brilliancy.

Little stars swam and sailed about the raft.

Jellies of irridescence were attracted to the spars and glued to it.

Shoals of angel-fish, chased by flying-fish, shot about the float, and tried to escape the pursuers by running under the beams.

A large space in the middle of the raft, had been left open by the timber that had been swept away.

In it floated a dead body, clinging still to the bight of a line.

Innumerable creatures seemed to find immense attraction in the corpse, for it was spangled over from head to foot by a ghastly phosphorescence.

Separate from the bearer of its companions, and yet encircled by the outer rim of wood, this shining horror seemed in some sort to guide the mass.

All at once there was a "sclup" in the water—the small fish were turning by schools, and swimming off in fear, with their peculiar quickness.

Yet no one on the water's edge could have suspected what had caused their dread.

The tiny globules of fire that made the surface lustrous, were too insignificant to be affected by the same terror.

But presently, with an abruptness that was awful in such loneliness, a sharp wedge rose here and there around the raft.

They were the back fins of sharks.

Out in the distance, there might be descried others of them, seeming to be engaged in a savage sport.

They were in groups each around one or more of the seaman's bodies, that had been swept away.

One of the monsters would hardly have seized a corpse and swam away, than half a dozen would chase it.

Thus would they tear the prey from one another until not a shred was left.

Thus clearing the surroundings of the dead, they seemed to come from all points of the compass to collect around the float.

Growing bolder as nothing occurred to startle them, they narrowed the circle more and more.

At length, one of the men upon the spars, quivered visibly.

Before long he moved his limbs.

In a few minutes more, he had recovered life sufficiently to lift his head.

His eyes, smarting with the salt, might well refuse to credit what he saw.

Darkness around, but that gleaming so unearthly on the water.

He sat up, collecting his thoughts.

The sharks glided up the very edge of the outer booms and snapped at the dragging ends of the stray ropes.

The clash of their triple rows of teeth the stealthy ripple that they made in their gliding, the pale yet vivid gleams from their glassy eyes, was appalling.

Lance shuddered, closed his eyes and almost went off into the slumber of exhaustion again.

But he was revived by a sound not far from him.

On looking, he saw that there was life remaining in others than him.

Three more of the bodies were struggling slowly back towards existence.

The chill of the approaching morning was bringing them to.

Lance shivered; he tried to restore the circulation to his arms, by moving them, as he sat up.

Suddenly there was a movement under the raft that startled him.

A dark blue mass, striped beneath with white rose in the pool inside the float, and half the corpse there rising and falling, disappeared in the shark's maw.

The rope still held the trunk.

The man had not been quite dead, for a tremor ran all over the sundered body as the logs were ripped away, and the upturned face was convulsed.

The eyes and mouth opened, one to emit a glance of agony, the other a faint but thrilling scream.

The phosphorescence was quenched by a gush of blood.

Taught where to go by this inroad, a number of these vultures of the sea bumped in under the spars and crowded their heads together in the space.

The remains of the sailor were pulled to bits in a second.

The sharks snapped at one another then.

One of them impaled himself in making a leap on the splintered end of a boom.

At the taste of his blood the rest fell upon him and a furious contest arose.

One small one leaped upon the raft itself, but floundered off into the deep.

The rest whipped the pool into froth and with the strokes of their powerful tails, broke loose from the fastenings.

Several of the seamen's bodies, rolling off the spars, were sent adrift.

Not far could they float, however, before they were pulled under and devoured.

The three men and Lance, the only ones who had shown signs of consciousness, had recovered sufficiently to witness all these repasts.

One of the men was Corposant.

He and the others lay near one another.

They were too much bruised to move yet, and then but slowly came round.

The sharks, the satiated ones having gone off, resumed their swimming around the edge of the raft, methodically as a policeman on his beat.

They continued to worry the rope ends and fragments of sailcloth, much as dogs tug at anything that displeases them.

"D'ye see, mates," said Corposant in a hoarse whisper, "there's Jonah alive yet! It's to get him that the sea-wolves have come around. We've lost all our messmates by him—ain't it plain."

"Aye, aye, bo', I think you are on the true tack," said another, rubbing his hands together. "Can you give him a hail so as to let him know we'll be at him as soon as we move a bit?"

"I can't speak yet, louder than this," replied the mutineer. "Keep quiet, we'll have him overboard before sunrise yet. What says Ben?"

"Oh, I'm numbered in, mates. My brother's gone, I notice."

"Poor fellows!" said Corposant, "I wonder if they're in the boats stood that squall out?"

"Likely; as they didn't have a Jonah aboard."

Lance saw the scowling looks of the three men.

He would have spoken to them, but he saw that their ill will was too deeply grounded for his words to root it out.

It was a match between them, who should be able to wield a weapon first.

Several times, Lance half rose, but his weakness was such that he had to sink down again

So with the others.

After they were able to move their arms, their lower limbs continued cramped.

Lance saw something glittering, not very far from him.

He dragged himself to it.

It was a knife, broken, but still of use.

It had been driven into one of the logs.

With this in his hand, he felt easier.

The sailors were weaponless.

The waves had washed away everything that could have been used for offence, even to the slivers of wood.

Morning dawned.

A red streak, like a line of rust on a sheet of black iron, appeared in the east.

If anything, the sharks grew more savage than ever, and, in more than one instance, seemed deliberately to charge the raft.

Striking against it, at all events, they dislodged one or two of the timbers.

The four men were upon a square, about twenty feet across.

To this shape and size had the great mass been reduced by the beating of the storm.

Lance saw the three men nerving themselves to come to his end of the float.

He was too proud to beg for mercy; knowing too that their superstition would probably render all his arguments worthless.

The three sailors rose, supporting each other.

"It won't do," said Lance to himself, "if I let the three together come at me. Now, to baffle them by superior exertions, even if not a jot of energy be left in me afterwards."

Making an effort that surprised him, he got upon his feet, and prepared to avoid those bent upon his destruction.

It was a strange thing to see upon that little stage, so frail and uneven, the three men bent upon executing a tragedy upon one innocent man.

None of the four could more than keep himself a-foot, and totter slowly.

Thus it came that keeping on the edge of the fragile structure, while the three remained in the centre and less rocking part, Lance could elude the sailors.

Seeing this, Corposant made his two comrades separate from him, and, spreading out, drive Cavendish to a corner.

If they could lay hands on him, the whole thing was to push him into the sea.

Into the sea, meant into the jaws of the sharks.

Twice he had the quickness enough to break through the line between them, and reaching the opposite side, compel them to begin their work over again.

The exercise gave them more and more power, but equally to all, and the young man kept his advantage.

Nettled by his escape, the hunters for his blood, believing more than ever that he was a supernatural being, grew more eager to seize him.

The young officer had paused for breath on the

weather side, when two of the seaman made a sudden leap, of which he had not fancied them capable.

One of them he eluded by a side spring, but that took him into the arms of the second.

The first, clutching only the air, fell forward, his foot catching in an iron band around the squaring of a topmast.

Hence it was head first that he shot straight upon the back of one of the sharks.

The frightened fish made a leap, and then plunged.

The man, only for an instant left on the waves, was attacked by a score of the ravenous creatures, and his frightful screams quickly cut short.

Meanwhile, Lance had hastened to rid himself of his antagonist, for Corposant was also about to seize him.

He struck at him with the broken knife.

Being pointless, the blade only inflicted a skin wound.

But the man, with the bleeding neck, started back in amaze.

"He has a knife!" said he.

"Of course," returned the young officer, delivering another thrust at him.

The man recoiled.

Lance followed up.

Then Corposant flung himself upon the latter.

In another instant the whole three, their arms around one another's bodies, or throats, were engaged in the most fiery of conflicts.

They had the loss of their messmates to avenge, they thought.

Lance had his life to preserve.

He also looked upon the mutineer as guilty of the recent deaths, not only in the fight but because the fight had taken off attention, and prevented any preparation against the terrible squall.

The knife left Lance's hand at last.

He had driven it so deep into the neck of the sailor that he could not pull it out at the moment.

The dying man dragged him to the level with him.

All three rolled over one another on the timbers.

Suddenly Corposant howled with pain and fright.

They had got to the edge of the raft without knowing it.

Three sharks had made an upward leap at them, their white bellies up.

Two had pushed the other aside, with their bulks and it fell heavily on the edge of the spar with a flourish of its tail.

One of the pair had pulled the sailor out of Lance's grasp with a powerful snatch like a giants.

The second, missing its bite at the same man closed its mouth on the right leg of Corposant.

With a spasm of anguish, the latter leaped in board from the fish, tearing—as it it sank—the tendons, muscles, and flesh of his severed limb.

Lance was almost suffocated by the embrace of inconceivable tightness which the wretched mutineer had given him in the convulsion of agony.

"If I must feed them, you shall go too!"

hissed Corposant, in the face of the young lieutenant.

In vain the latter strove to pry apart the clasping arms of the dying man.

Although the blood poured out by the main artery furiously, Corposant's strength seemed rather to increase by hate, than fail.

Fallen upon his knees, crawling on the one knee, and on the gory stump, his teeth grinding with the pangs that his thirst for vengeance scarcely could subdue, the malevolent sailor pulled Lance Cavendish back again to the edge, that both had receded from.

They formed a semicircle, ever moving, jostling one another aside, snapping at each other, but keeping their glaring orbs fastened on the expected offering.

"The whale let off t'other Jonah," said the dying sailor, in a faint voice, in which the whistling betokened death was near. "But t'warn't a shark, and these are, my man!"

With that, he squeezed his captive still tighter, and rose as well as he was capable.

The two bodies, bound together by the one man's revengeful embrace, fell into the water like one.

At the splash, all the fish drew back.

The next instant, their veracity overcoming their fright, they would rush at the victim and his sacrificer.

There was a quick beat of almost noiseless fins.

They were coming!

Lance could see all this, for Corposant was holding him there in that design.

Coming with open jaws, to whose hooked teeth yet clung patches of human flesh!

Coming with irresistible force, and turning for that bite which made their raven a grave!

Lance closed his eyes.

He could only hope that his death would be speedy.

Afloat or sinking, it was all the same to those ravagers of the billow.

Then came the rush of them all, making the water boil.

The surf they churned up, tasting of blood as well as of the brine, washed the swimmer's face.

The great fish seemed quite mad about him.

They were plunging, jostling one another, striking with their tails, all in some emotion that Lance could not set down only to their quarreling for him.

Just then one little sound pierced the splashing of the surge.

"A shadow-bird," muttered Cavendish.

His moist eyes recognised the large pair of black wings supporting a tiny jet body circling over his head and the sharks.

The latter seemed not to notice him at all, but breached around him, covering him with water, but happily not striking him.

Still the little bird kept calling "pee-we-whit!" overhead, now descending, now rising, seeming to be impatient at something not coming.

But it did come.

The sharks had appeared to quiet down for a moment and Lance almost believed they were going to attack him.

At that instant it was that he felt, for he could not see, or hear, that a strong but unearthly undulation under the surface was a tremor heralding some mighty advent

He shivered with dread.

He had time but for one glance.

The sharks crowded round him, like sheep pack together when the hounds follow the fox through a pasture, had fear dulling their glassy eyes.

Some leaped up, some dived, all were in motion.

Like a cork in a whirl pool, Lance was tossed this way and that.

A douse of spray was showering on his head, but through he could discern the on-comer.

A dark seagreen mass, with a sullen, savage head, but a beautifully and grandly tapering body, as large as a three-decker's jolly-boat, was ploughing the wave straight to the spot, as swiftly as a feather before a hurricane.

It leaped out of the water, as the whale does in sport, and its huge bulk fell into the thickest of the school of sharks.

Beneath it they sank, and it quickly followed them.

The water dashed up to a height, and Lance, overwhelmed in the eddy, was whirled round and round, his ears and mouth full of water, his senses nearly gone.

He confusedly heard more of the rushing swimming of the alarmed sharks, and the more ponderous assault of the monster fish.

As the lieutenant came up to the water-edge, his hands grasped a yielding body, that he bumped against.

It was warm, slippering with its own oil and blood, and his lingering consciousness prompted him to quit it.

But the desire of life clinched his hands in the rough skin over the yielding flesh, and the young lieutenant floated on the corpse of a fresh-slain shark.

Nor was that the only victim of the giant assailant.

The foam was reddened with gouts and strings of blood.

And, half-in, half-out of water, some painfully plying a broken fin or a shattered tail, a score of the sharks were to be seen.

And flying away from the sunlight, the rest of the pack of seawolves went, while the largest of their numbers, on whom the savage terror had fastened, having the life beaten out of him by the vast form of the tormentor.

Yes beaten out.

For the "Thrasher," disdaining whales for once, and no doubt in one of its "rusty fits," as old tars say, had fallen upon the sharks just to have the pleasure of hammering them.

Like a gigantic trip hammer the tireless thing raised and let fall its weighty form till the fish it rode upon, was but a shapeless pulp.

Then, eager as at the first, with the little "shadow-bird's" black pinions leading it in the air, the thrasher plunged on again to seize another victim.

Before its mighty power, the sea seemed swept clear.

All around Lance, his fingers deep in the shark's carcase, the surface softened down and was bereft of life.

A smooth expanse was what the sun beheld at noon; smooth except for the mangled fish, the bits of raft, and the single man, as listlessly riding on the swell, as the dead bodies around.

CHAPTER XVII.

LOYS IS JOLLY, CONSIDERING—WHAT HE GOT BY A SONG—A BIT OF TREACHERY, SOME TALK OF TREASURE, AND SOME MORE OF "MY CHEE-YILD!"—THE THRUST IN THE THROAT AGAIN.

"WELL, blow my timbers!" said Jack, "if ever I heerd a chap what expects a cord to be his only reward, a-singin' so gay like as him in there."

This he said as he pointed to a door.

Jack and another were on guard outside the little hole in the hold, where Loys de Goupille had been placed in irons.

"It's always the way with us Frenchmen," returned the other sailor, curling his moustache. "We are the gay nation, you know."

"Hark! what is he singing about?" asked Jack, as Goupille's voice came lightly through the oak panels.

"Wait till he finishes the verse, and I'll tell you," said the French sailor.

Loys was humming in French, some words, that ran to this effect:—

"Pretty young girls with the laughing eye, secure your lover. You may yet cry over the love that you've kept to yourself, like a miser keeps locked all his high-valued pelf. At nineteen you laugh, but at ninety you'll sigh; oh, what good my treasure now that I die! Ri-fla-fla-flon-taine!"

"Well, Pierre," said Jack, in a tone of intense disgust; "of all the blasted stuff that ever would make a middy sick, that's the worst that ever I knew a man to sing. What's he at now?"

The other had listened more attentively, and one could tell that Loys was singing with a deep emphasis on his words:—

"Pirate who's roved with the reddened sword, secure a comrade. Oh, that aboard this craft there were one to whom to confide where the sand covers gems and gold, side by side. In freedom, you laughed; in bilboes, you sigh; oh, what good my treasure now that I die! Ri-fla-fla-flon-taine"

"What's that, I say, Pierre?"

"Oh, Jack, more of the same stuff."

"Then don't give us any more," said Jack, taking a nipping bite of a chunk of niggerhead. "If the rascal must sing, why don't he rouse himself up with something cheerful like:—

"Come all you roaring boys,
　　That delight in roaring noise,
　　　It's the sailor boy that's master!
　When Jack he comes ashore,
　　With his gold and silver store,
　　　There is no other spends it faster!"

"There's truth in that, look ye! But what's the sense in 'fla-fla-flounting'—which is rubbish, and French rubbish, worse luck!"

"Come, come, Jack! Don't let us shut down on the poor devil ——"

"Devil enough! You warn't aboard the

'Scarlet' when that fiend was reducing the company with his thrusts in the throat. He's bound to hang, I tell ye, and all the singing this side of water and land can't save his precious throat."

So far Jack.

The French sailor said no more, and the two remained on guard in silence.

But the prisoner within seemed to be very fond of the second verse, for, varying it slightly, he repeated it several times, always in his own language.

A keener observer than Jack might have observed that Pierre's face lighted up with the glare of covetousness, in his eyes.

"Cursed down here so near the bilge-water," said Jack suddenly. "I won't be gone a minute—only for a pannikin of water in the sail loft they are working on a new sprit-sail for the launch."

"Keep good watch!"

"All right, bo'!"

And Pierre was left alone.

As soon as the other's feet ceased to sound on the ladder steps, Pierre changed his careless attitude.

Rapidly he put his lips to the large keyhole, and, in French, and in a loud whisper, said—

"Morning watch! I'll be with you. You hear??"

"Yes."

And Pierre fell back to the shadowy corner of the bulk-head and was apparently re-priming one of his pistols as Jack, wiping his mouth, came down the steps.

"Good, mate," said he. "They've got a bottle of glorious Jamaikey in the loft, and if you goes sharp, the palm-ers will have a drop left."

"Thank'ee."

"Oh, don't. One good turn desarves another, not that turns are ginerally good, 'specially in a cable," continued Jack, professionally.

The French seaman hastened up to the sail-room to have a liquidation.

Meanwhile, Jack, who had brought a flavour of rum with him, that quite overpowered the odour of the close air, now sat down by the door-jamb.

"Lucky!" muttered he, "no more of that 'ere moosic. Glad the French beggar has got his song stopped by sleep."

Was Loys asleep?

One glance inside his narrow prison-house, would tell a different story.

Let us take that glance.

The darkness is such that one can only make out vaguely that it is a low box of a room, scarcely large enough for the working of one gun.

Being on the lee side as the Cruiser was sailing, the sound of the water was very pleasant, having none of that abrupt tapping that the weather-side catches.

Being under the water line, there was no port open, and no lantern swung above.

In the corners were a lot of lumber, some junk of different thicknesses, a few lengths of rotten log-line, a heap of rubbish, such as a bundle of canes, a roll of tobacco not choice enough for the dainty Cruiser's tars, and other odds and ends.

Lying upon an oblong coil of ancient hawser comparatively soft from it being ragged and picked out, was Loys.

His ankles were banded with irons and his hands were tied.

Tied so seamanly that he had long before given up any hope of unloosing them.

No granny's knot in those, Bill Bowse had made them himself.

He could roll over by a great effort, but there was no use in changing his position.

Turning turtle would not bring him nearer a knife or anything to free him.

While he fretted as the Cruiser sped along so beautifully, cursing his luck that he should lie there while a mere boy trod the quarter-deck, he was not idle.

With his eyes accustomed to the gloom, he studied every bit of the place.

There was an old shackle in the bulkhead that made him writhe with pain at his being so powerless.

Its rust-eaten edge was sure to be capital to grind a rope quite through against.

But it was three feet from the flush of the floor, and it might have been fifty for all that mattered, as he could not raise his head, much less his body five inches from the ground.

For many hours he had expected each to be his last.

Every change of the guard over him, as the steps descended, might have been the signal for his being dragged up for execution.

He knew he richly deserved it.

One ray of hope had been his.

When he discovered by the fellow's accent that Pierre was a Frenchman, he had attempted to attract his greed or his pity, as we have seen.

He had not tried this with the Spaniards, for fear of not having that power over them, that he might have with one of his own race.

He did not dream of seducing the English seamen.

If he had tried it on with Jack or any of his mess, he would have got into a pretty mess himself.

His first breath drawn for many hours, was when he heard Pierre's short and rather rapid whisper.

He could not sleep with anxiety.

All night, upon his rough couch, he lay, his eyes open, his ears on the alert.

Such was the stillness, that the cry of "Watch there! watch!" re-echoing over the ship, the tread of the look-out's on the forecastle deck, came down to him.

Nearer were the scratching and scampering of the rats, only kept from him by the two new men on guard at his door, one of them being Derrick.

His sonourous Dutch oaths of "hagel und wetter," or "Scher-loppen," as if he was at a big oyster, would have frightened away an elephant, let alone so bold a thing as a down-right grey-whisker biscuit-grinder, who sticks to a ship like the steadiest old salt himself.

At length, as eight bells was sriking, there was a scuffling on deck.

Soon after the vessel's way was deadened.

There was a heavy plunge, and the grating of the chain-cable rushing after the anchor.

"It's making flood-tide!" Loys heard one of his sentries say to his comrades.

"Where was we, hein?" said Derrick, who was the latter.

"Oh, it's only one of the little keys—beautiful landlocked cave—Old Sir Henry Morgan used to lay his vessel up here. The Captain's going ashore—hark! Bowse is piping the captain's cutter now."

"They was lucky boys, eh? dem what was go ashore mit der poat, hein, I t'ink?"

"Not much to see. A few burton-trees and salt-grass. I wouldn't like to be marooned on it."

Loys shuddered,

What could the young captain be going at midnight on land, for? if water was needed, his presence was not necessary, and to careen the barque, any other officer could choose a butt just as well.

He dreaded that it was on some purpose connected with him.

He was right.

As he bewailed his folly in having let time pass while he hugged the delusion to himself that his countryman, Pierre, either would or could dare to help him, he started.

There was a scratching on the plank not far from a corner post that was too regular to be made by the vermin.

Loys whistled faintly through his teeth to show that he heard and that the coast was clear.

Immediately he saw a plank was started.

It required only a show to fall inward, but was caught by a ready hand to prevent it falling.

Pierre cautiously stepped into the black hole.

Replacing the board, he came to the prisoner and lay down beside him, behind the coil, bringing his face close to his.

"Now, old boy," said Pierre, "do you mean smooth-water sailing, by your talk of treasure buried? 'Cause if you're coming over-bottom sweeping seas, I'm not the man to be played with. It's death I run the risk of in coming here."

The prisoner replied in the same tone:—

"Fellow countryman," said he, "I've been a rover, and of the worst sort. I've pitted my gains here and there, after the regular chart fashion. I don't care a bit about trying to escape——"

"Oh, you don't?"

"Not I. I'm satisfied if my time is come," said Goupille, in a deep voice, calculated to draw tears.

The sailor was not effected more than the mainmast by a fly whizzing against it.

"That ain't the buccaneer talk," muttered he.

"You don't believe I've cried 'Haul your wind' to a silver ship, eh? Ask you the old men of this ship, and they'll tell you I'm the sort that sticks at nothing."

The old fierceness roughened the desperado's voice.

"Not so loud! The Dutchman has long ears, thick-headed as he is."

"I don't want to escape, but I do want to see my daughter."

"She in the cabin, eh? You'll miss it, for she is gone ashore."

"When?"

"Just now. Didn't you hear the captain's boat shove off."

"What's that for?"

"Nobody can make out. 'Spect she's to be left there to live on the tree-leaves and crab-shells."

"I must escape now, muttered Loys, wrestling with his bonds.

"I am agreeable since I have come so far. Let me have the particulars in this bill of lading."

"My countryman, I will speak to you fair," said Goupille," softly. "If I can get into the water, I can reach land, cramped as I now am."

"Humph! Nurses are after the ship—seen them this morning when cook upset the sweet 'tater peels."

"I am not afraid of sharks," said the prisoner, showing his teeth. "I am Matasiete."

"I don't know that—"

"Spanish my friend, the Seven-slayer!"

"What? you have killed seven men outright?"

"With my own hand. And that means deliberate death, not counting the fatality that will befal one's enemies in battle. Sharks let me swim by!"

The sailor had heard something of that superstition.

"That's out of the question, then," said he, quickly. "You want to reach the water?"

"That's all. I know the barque as I do my own pocket."

"Enough, now for the treasure."

"It is past summing up. I never counted it. Half was put in two months ago—all Spanish coin that I had to pay my men whom this young devil of the Cruiser slew, after firing my new ship—"

The speaker's eyes flashed brilliantly in the shadow.

"Calm yourself. There is time enough for all that. Where is it?"

"We will both go half-way," said Loys. "It's one one of the Alcrane Islets ——"

"Off Campeachy?"

"Aye, now undo my leg fetters."

"Steady. Lucky they are old, for the key could not find the way to the lock, so black is it here."

And Pierre pulled away at the rusty irons, till he ascertained the weak spot.

By using a pistol barrel as a crowbar, he prized off the bar at the junction, and soon left Loys only adorned with a metal ring round each ankle.

This would not interfere with walking.

"Which of the islands?"

The second from the northermost. It is a large white shining rock heaved up with pyramid of red and black ones."

"I have heard of that. They call it the Hogs Back."

"No mistake."

"Go on."

"I don't think I can tell you without marking out the lines.

"Ah!" said Pierre, doubtfully.

"A few scratches on a bit of wood will suffice."

"Seven-slayer! You must be innocent to think that I'll let you get steel in your hands?"

"Pooh! I harm such a friend as you! Oh, heaven!" said Goupille fervently.

"Not so loud!"

"I'll take any oath!"

"The rover's oath?"

"Yes! You shall be richer than King Louis! Oh, my friend and deliverer."

Pierre drew his dagger and severed the cords around Loy's thighs and a little around his body, so that he might kneel.

"As to a holystone," said he.

Then he placed the half of the knife in the prisoner's still bound hands.

It was impossible for him to do anything with them.

But he had dealings with a man who had a demon's cunning and never shrunk from injury to himself when a still greater should be given to an enemy.

Loys leaned his head over the knife so clumsily held, and, kneeling as he was, appeared to be about taking the oath.

But abruptly he lifted his hands as high as the line permitted and crowded his head forward and down on his breast.

This done he contrived to get the hilt of the poignard into his mouth, swiftly he drew it, till the butt end touched the back of the roof of his mouth.

Holding it thus by force of teeth, and of tongue, he flung himself sideways on the sailor beside him.

The blade, protruding like an unicorn's horn, pierced the throat of Pierre, and the prisoner's weight being behind it, it ran through altogether.

A flood of blood spurted up into the slayer's face, and the blood flowing from his lacerated mouth ran to meet the stream.

Spitting this out and lifting up his head, though bearing all his weight on the convulsed body of the seaman, Loys merrily sung, to drown the other's death cry.—

"Malbrook has gone out of this
And nobody knows when he'll come back!"

"Never heerd sich a man," growled one of the seamen outside the door. "He'd be singing when the gallows-grass is round his throttle he will."

Meanwhile Loys, having the knife thus firmly set in the stiffening spine of the fallen man, sawed across its edge the cords round his wrists.

In a long five minutes, he found himself free.

Free to escape, perhaps, to be revenged on one or more at any rate.

He gave up ten instants and over, to moving his arms and legs about briskly, but without any sound which might attract the watchers, so close that he heard their breathing.

As soon as he felt that he could move, he hurriedly plucked out the knife which had given its master his death-wound.

With its bloody blade he hastened to cut open the bundle of canes.

These he cut up into short lengths and wove them into a kind of cart wheel, lashing the free ends with the rope-yarn that lay in plenty all around.

Having done this in the dark, with a quickness that was amazing, he proceeded to another act.

With a handful of picked oakum he crept to the door, and, as carefully but more silently than a caulker working at a seam, he filled up the space at the bottom of the door.

Then returning to the middle of the room, he went on with another act that was very mysterious, conceived in that deep darkness.

As a few cracklings, sputterings, and hissings, sounded out, Loys rose from bending over a heap of rope and the reeds which covered a spar.

"It will serve," muttered he. "Let me go now!"

Squeezing himself through the narrow secret way (which he had already known of and which Pierre must have found out by accident) he left the place no longer a prison to him.

He was in the middle of the ship, under the water-line, only a few feet from the keel.

With that little knife that he held, he could have scraped such a hole in the planks as would have sent the vessel to the bottom.

But his great idea had ever been to recover possession of this craft.

The more he saw of her, converted into the rover that he had intended himself to turn her into, the greater that desire.

He scrambled in darkness over the ballast and the stowage.

Finding the notched post more by instinct than by espying it he climbed up out of the hold.

He was in the steerage.

Every foot-fall over his head was audible, and when the seaman stepped upon the bulls-eye that gave a dim light to the place, he was aware of their passing.

Climbing over more boxes and bundles he reached the port side.

By running his fingers over the side, he found the closed-up port-hole that he sought.

Actively he plied the knife at the edges of the square opening.

It took time, for the seam was tightly caulked up, this port being for the convenience of landing, and always fast as the solid side itself when on the seas.

At length, he was sure he could open the port-lid easily, for the water, slapped up against the side now and then by a ruffle on the surface, oozed in.

The bolts, one each side, were very rusty.

By an effort, he loosed them so as he could draw them back.

It was all strange to him, there resting.

Seated on a bale of plunder, the knife hung by its lanyard at his waist, he waited as patiently as if there were not all that crew determined to have his blood for that he had spilled so mercilessly.

He had on only his drawers and the red shirt of Pierre. He was bare-headed, bare-armed, and bare-footed.

So quiet sate he that the rats, great plump fellows, waddled out of holes scarcely large enough for them, gnawed away with terrible fangs at the objects of their fancy.

At last Loys started.

There was a movement on deck, the running about of many feet.

"It's the signal on shore," he heard one voice say. "Beware, send five men to bring up the prisoner. Ned, does the whip play free in the block?"

They were going to hang Loys de Goupille, although the young commander had not returned in his boat.

Nevertheless, Loys had settled down as calmly to listen as ever.

In a few seconds, he heard all that he had expected.

A sudden outcry of alarm and horror that found a hundred echoes all about the ship.

The deck resounded with the trampling of feet over Goupille's head.

Then he smiled such a smile as the devil must have worn when he thought for a space that he was winning the battle in heaven.

With a hand as eager now as it had been quiet for some time, he shot back the port-lid bolts.

A rush of air came in to fight the close atmosphere of the between-decks.

The surface of the water was not ten inches from the bottom of the opening.

Goupille forced through that wheel of cane which he had made, and then slipped out himself.

Putting the collar over his head and settling it under his armpits, he struck out into the open sea with a beautiful regular stroke of the hands.

Behind him, the Cruiser was alive with men, seeming to be wild with frenzy, but really acting energetically and in due discipline.

CHAPTER XIX.

WHY FRANK WENT ASHORE—THE PLEADING IN VAIN —THE SIGNAL FOR THE RUNNING UP OF THE MAN— THE EXECUTION OF THE CORPSE IN THE RED SKIN OF THE INCENDIARY.

"You must go ashore with me now," said Frank, as he stood by the doorway of the cabin given up to Genifrede.

"Yes, yes, but my father?"

"You must go ashore," repeated he, frowning.

"Oh, my father."

"Must I have you carried?"

Her eyes rambled indignantly, as they had only the moment before coming tears.

She rose from her suppliant position, and stepped forward, drawing a shawl over her head.

"Lead out! I will die with him!" said she.

The youth turned and conducted her up the stairs.

It was a lovely and clear night.

There was a sea-breeze fanning the ocean, so long heated by the tropical sun.

The captain's boat was at the starboard gangway, ready manned.

On seeing no signs of Loys de Goupille, Genifrede looked around searchingly, and then turned her large eyes on the boyish captain appealingly.

He diverted his gaze, and only motioned for her to descend the ladder slung over the side.

In another moment she was safely caught in a bowsman's stalwart arms and handed along to the stern sheets.

Frank was presently by her side.

He flung a boat cloak over her knees, and took the tiller ropes.

"Shove off!" said he.

The boat was pushed away and the men, bending to their oars, she was soon out of the dark shade that the vessel cast around her.

The shore, a small island, half of sand and rock, and then of a swampy and thickly wooded nature, was reached in a few minutes.

"Light the lantern," said Rogers, "one man can be boat-keeper. Follow me, you others."

With Genifrede in their midst, the party went over the beach to the first rise of ground, where a hut rose amid tangled grass.

The light of the lanterns showed the cabin, prettty strongly built, had been put up by some turtle-catchers, who had slept there and cooked at the door.

Fragments of skill, an old kettle, and some bent spoons and knives rusted on the stamped-mud floor.

"It will do," said Frank. "Tom, get you down to the boat again and bring up the spirits .in the jar and the hammock."

The articles of house-keeping were soon laid out in the hut, and the hanging bed rigged up.

The young girl had sat down on a stone mantled with weeds, and let her gaze wander from the barque gently riding at her mooring, to the several men who were obeying orders in the mild lamp-light.

Thanks to their skill and activity, the hut was made habitable.

Upon that Frank came to her.

The sailors withdrew a few yards, to light a pipe or two, or to scan the weather sky with a critical glance.

"My poor girl," said the youth, standing before her. "I am sorry to have you brought into contact with this moment. You know that the Frenchman, whom I dislike to believe kin of yours, murdered several of my men."

"Stay, I do not blame him for harm done me in fair fight. I could almost pardon him for his cruelty to old Captain Beekets, but I could not let him go, and yet retain the respect of my followers.

"They would obey me to more than that extent, but I do not want to play the tyrant over such brave and faithful hearts. I have done much for you. I would not have a hand in trying Loys de Goupille. I have left all that to the crew.

"Fear not, they will. be just, even in their revenge."

The girl had bowed her head, as if she could not find words to utter.

"Stand apart, you with the lights," said the captain, then, "and swing the lanterns half a dozen times."

That was the signal that the officers and company were to try the prisoner for his crimes against them.

Cambering ordered the boatswain to go for the captive, as we have heard.

Bill Bowse and his half-dozen acolytes descended.

They found Derrick and his companion half asleep.

"What's that?" cried Bill, snuffing with his capacious nose.

"What, bo's'n?"

"Smoke!"

"Smoke! or I'll drown for it."

"Oh! it must have been that Dutchman he had his pipe out," said the second sentinel.

"There were orders against smoking mind you! neither here nor there, but some of you will be setting the ship afire some of these days."

"Blastmy thumb!" cried Bill, abruptly, "why don't you open the door?"

"The padlock's free, but it catches at the bottom," replied the seaman who had the key.

"Taint the matter on that ere that can fetch us up standing. Put your shoulder to it. We can't have that Mounseer beggar playing us no tricks!"

A couple pushed the door.

"The panels, red hot!" cried they, as their hands pressed it.

"Have Davy Jones took him!" exclaimed Bill, as he added his weight.

The oak flew back.

The men receded, for a blast of flame, in a cloud of tar smoke, rushed forth and singed their beards.

"No smokers here!" said Bill. "There's the hound within! By blue blazes, I'll wig him out in a jiffy."

Like a salamander, the old salt plunged into the sheet of fire, and presently returned dragging a dead body with him. which was dressed in Loys de Goupille's clothes!

The first out-break of the conflagration had shrivelled up his features past recognition.

"Dead as a herring," said Bowse, dropping his burden. "Two of you up with this cold meat! Derrick and the rest into the room and stamp out the cables alight, or next thing 'twill be yellow bright amidships."

Most of the men hastened to pull the fiery fragments apart and trample them down, in spite of the smoke that half smothered them and the heat that would have fired any clothes except their rough canvas and woollen garb.

"Shoulder the carcase!" repeated the boatswain to the two remaining. "I know its no seaman's work to look arter corpses, but he must swing at the yardarm, cold or live! Up! while I pass the word for the baskets!"

The moment Bowse got up into the air he told the story.

Instantly all were at work, no idlers to be seen.

There's nothing in water to frighten a true blue, but fire is the startler.

The bars were slipped into the engine-sockets and the clank, clank resounded steadily.

The hose was let down the main hatch, up which smoke began to steam.

A dozen buckets were over each side and as rapidly replaced as their successors were filled.

Suddenly there was a rush up the forecastle

ladder of all the men who had been working below.

There needed no explanation of the desertion of their post, for right after the undermost of them (considerably quickened by the warm application to his breeches) darted a long flame of blue, quickly followed by many others.

These blended into one huge tongue that shot out of the fore hatch till it lit up the whole ship.

On shore, this sight made the boat's crew nervous.

"She's at me! the barkey's blazing!" cried they.

Frank suffered no less than they.

"Oars in!" shouted he, running down the beach. "All in! shove off! sharp's the word! pull away, pull!"

Genifrede was left alone on the strand.

Instinctively she kept her eyes on the vessel, so prominent now that the red and golden streamers floated over her.

A current that had set in after the slack water had fallen, and the tide had began to run out, carried the cutter out of the direct line, notwithstanding the vigorous rowing.

In spite of all, it was evident that they could not reach the barque in a very short time.

Genifrede gazed from the sands.

She saw the flames leap up or fall low, now changing the circle of water into a ring of crimson or letting the darkness fall all around again.

At last the ship seemed surely doomed by the conflagration.

The blaze reached the mainyard, and the canvass, had it been drier, would have been kindled; it was not furled but only caught up loosely.

Every line of the upper works stood out clearly in the light.

Genifrede could see the men, like black ants seeming to be running in and out amid the lurid glare.

A hoarse murmur had come already to her ears, but now the sea breeze bore a fierce shout to the land.

The figures appeared to her letting the fire do its worst, while all dropped down from aloft and gathered from other quarters to collect amidships.

Even at that distance, the brightness was such and her vision so strained, that the ropes were distinct from the starboard mainbrace, swinging slack.

One end was on board, the other, after running through a block, dangled at the earing-point, a noose.

The shouting was renewed more fiercely than before, and louder.

The slack of the line was payed away, and a man jumping up into the main shrouds, caught the lowered loop and pulled it on deck.

Genifrede could not prevent her attention being fixed on that cord.

Amid a continuance of the clamour, the figures were seen all in motion.

The line was tautened.

The loudest, most savage, most joyous of cheers, resounded.

Genifrede closed her eyes, or rather tried to shut them.

A mist crept over them.

When she saw clear, she beheld a mass hanging at the yardarm.

The cutter had run up alongside the Cruiser, and the looker-on watched the captain and crew assembling on board.

Trembling with excitement, Frank had leaped up the ladder.

He found the ship surrounded by hot smoke that the sea wind could not cool.

The crew, man and boy, were dotted amidships.

The oldest sailors were flocked amidships, the officers not being let penetrate their ranks.

The rope by which the pendent body had been elevated, was manned by these old sea dogs.

Bill Bowse was first belaying the line to a pin.

"What is all this? have you found him guilty already?" cried the young captain.

"They found him dead, sir," answered Cambering.

"Dead!" and he glanced up at the figure.

"Burnt up; look at his face—like the nigger he disfigured himself. In short, he set the ship afire, and must have done it out of pure deviltry, though he could not escape himself."

The young captain hastened to gain the particulars, but they only bore out that story.

"Let the carrion hang there!" said he. "It is a fit place for him, though I hate to see the Cruiser sailing under such colours."

The seamen seemed to be pleased that their punishment of the dead had excited no displeasure from their superior.

"To your stations!" cried the latter, "All hands to make sail! Alow and aloft, unfurl!"

The spars were quickly covered with men and as quickly spread with the canvass.

"What made the fire spread so?" inquired the captain, "when we are so full handed and you must have battened down the hatches?"

"Oh, sir, it was more smoke than blaze," answered the first mate. "But we found that the fire had blown out one of the side ports."

"Strange. Lucky it was discovered so early, or we might be without a plank under foot. Cheer boys! we have been under water, powder, and fire! There's nothing to harm the barkey, and the traitor swings in the air."

With that ghastly appendage to her tackle, the Scarlet Cruiser got under weigh and was far away by the morning light.

CHAPTER XX.

ON SHORE—THREE VICTORS—THE WAY—THE AMOROUS BUCCANEER—THE POOL OF GARFISH.

WHEN the young girl watched the barque disappearing with the black corpse distinctly outlined against the clouds of canvass, she fell upon her knees.

She could not but pray for the deeply wicked soul that she believed to have perished.

As her sight dwelt yet on the vanishing vessel she started.

There was something stirring near the late anchorage.

It was a small boat.

It tended shoreward.

Of the three men in it, two rowed single and the other pulled a pair.

What could these men, come from the Cruiser, be sent for ?

Only one mission could be theirs, after that sample of summary execution.

They had slain the father, why might they not mean to destroy her, the daughter ?

She was filled with a terror, as potent as the horror that the late scene had imbued her with.

At first she could hardly muster enough strength to rise.

But the boat had passed over the current sweeping around the island, and was rapidly nearing the beach.

There could be no doubt that where she had remained was their destination.

She rose to her feet and looked wildly about her.

Before her the open sea and the oncoming boat.

Behind her the thicket of beach, plums, burton trees and others.

She turned to fly.

The men were just shipping oars and crowding into the stern so that their conveyance might run the farther upon shore.

They saw that she was taking to flight and they shouted to her.

Her ears translated their words into such as spurred her on.

With all her might, she ran into the woods.

The three men left the boat beached.

The tide was going out now.

Genifrede heard a crashing, mingled with oaths.

There was a vigorous pursuit of her.

They called out after her all the time, but she was too frightened to catch more than the mere sound.

She did not know where she was going.

It was by a miracle only that her slight form was not torn to pieces by the interwoven boughs.

As it was, her dress was tattered by a hundred prickly palms or thorn bushes.

The hunters seemed to have missed her track.

It was in time none too soon.

She was all but entirely exhausted.

At last, being caught by the brambles that run on the ground, she missed her footing and fell.

Her head came in contact with a stone, and she sank into unconsciousness.

The last dread of being caught remained with still greater terrors in her senselessness.

Such was the torment of her mind that she awoke.

How long she must have been in the swoon, she did not know.

She was in the same place.

It was colder, and she judged morning to be near at hand.

There was no sound except the rustle of leaves, and the distant wash of the sea upon the strand.

The stars were sparkling brightly and that was the light.

But then star light in the tropics is very different to a night time elsewhere.

She could not remain there, and yet she was equally afraid to stir.

The men might be on the watch close to her, waiting for a misstep to point her out.

Still she could not bear inaction in her nervous state.

The darkness of the forest had shadows that made her shudder.

The creeping plants and Spanish moss that festooned from the boughs, took the shape of that hanged man which was ever present to her eyes.

Groping her way till her eyes were accustomed to the gloom under the trees, she went from the heart of the wood.

She had not chosen her path, but her wandering led her to the sea shore.

It grew lighter and lighter at every step, and ere long she was on the open sands.

Their glistening made each pebble lying on them plain to the view.

Genifrede, just stepping out of the covert, suddenly recoiled.

There was a man on the sand, high and dry.

But even her timid glance told her that she need fear nothing from him.

Such complete quiescence argued helplessness in the subject.

For some minutes she remained crouching close to the bushes.

But there was nothing like life around her, only the receding waters casting a ripple ashore regularly and mournfully.

Her fears had lessened.

Compassion sprang up in its place, and she blamed herself for having hesitated so long.

Cautiously leaving the shade, she went down the sands.

Two or three times she started, and prepared to turn back.

But it was only a terrapin on the water-side, or a conger caught in a pool and rolling in the shallows.

Even to one of her inexperience, when she stooped over the form, the closeness of death to so cold and pale a face and limp a figure was clear.

That sensation was sharpened to accurate pain by the feeling that followed.

The icy, white face and shoulders were scratched and cut by floating stuff that it had been dashed against.

The seaweed was tangled with the hair.

But the glimmer above was sufficient for her to recognize Lance Cavendish.

From him she had parted at one awful time when seeming to be in safety herself, he was surely doomed.

Now they came together.

He bloodless as a corpse, and she with a great fright hovering over her.

She found that a little warmth yet lingered in his breast.

Knowing that the spot was too exposed for her to care for him, both for fear of the sea returning and of being seen by the three sailors from the Cruiser, she seized the body by the shoulders and dragged it away.

Even after she had drawn it into the thicket she took it still farther.

She remembered that one place that she had shrunk into was a deep cave.

There could be nothing better for her to leave the lieutenant in.

It was hard for her to convey him there, but love gave her the strength.

Perhaps the being pulled over the more or less rough ground did the half drowned man no harm.

At least she found that his breathing was audible as she pushed him into the cavern.

Her alarm had greatly subsided since she was no longer alone and had something to engage her mind with.

She exerted herself to her utmost in bringing him to.

After a long, long while, full of many hopes suddenly quenched, the girl felt her heart leap.

Lance, his eyes still closed, made a babbling with his pale lips, which seemed to mean—

"Drink! drink!"

Tossed on the wave, scorched by the sun, smarting at every pore with the brine; thirst had been the fiend that had most tormented the castaway.

Genifrede started up.

The scarf about her neck would rock up enough water to give a drink.

But where was fresh water to be obtained on that sea-girt isle?

Could she dig deep in the sand she might find some strained sufficiently.

But that side of the island happened to be either stony or sandy, and shells were not to be seen, or were too small or too shattered to do for digging.

To look for a piece of a tree limb, or to collect the heavy dew from leaf and leaf, were both mere loss of precious time.

Again the sufferer immured his want, louder than before, although his eyes continued closed.

Above the low syllable he repeated, the girl fancied she caught another sound.

When she had stepped out of the cave, she heard it more clearly.

It was running water.

Not the wash of the thrown up ripple returning to the wave, but the gentle uninterrupted music of a tiny waterfall.

Half her scarf she hung up on a bush to guide her back, and she ran towards that point.

In another instant she found herself on the brink of a pool.

Its colour and its stillness proved its depth.

It was like a beautiful sheet of jet marble

Every now and then a line of bubbles would run along the level and break sluggishly: it was some tenant of the pond.

At one end a little brooklet rolled down a pile of stones and scarcely disturbed the mass it added to.

Dark as it looked, it was doubtlessly fresh and drinkable.

As she dabbled the scarf in it she was alarmed by it being pulled from her hand.

Something very strong had darted under water at the light hued web and carried it away.

As she caught her breath after the sudden start that this had given her, she was aware that she was no longer alone.

It could not be Lance recovered magically, that was beside her.

That red shirt marked with an "S.C.," the belt garnished with weapons, the rough face—she had seen many such on board the Scarlet Cruiser.

The man gazed at her at first with surprise and then altogether with rapture.

"Well, my charmer!" said he, in a husky voice, balancing himself on both legs wide apart, as if he were on deck in a cross sea. "Well, little love, here you are! I've only been half-an-hour s'archin the iselet for you and didn't 'spect to find you afore mornin'. Hows'ever, since you are so soon within hail, let's have a buss, lassie, to open the action like?"

On one side the thicket of prickly pear, on the other and at her back the pond; before her the drunken sailor blocked up the way.

She tried to run by him as he leaned one side unsteadily, but he was too quick for her.

In the very act her wrist was seized in the powerful hand and she was swung back roughly on the grass.

On her knees she remained, and clasped her hands.

"Oh, kill me!" moaned she, "kill me at once as you were sent to do!"

"Who was? Kill you? Ha, ha! Me and my mates were sent by the cap'an to look arter you till we hears in three days from him——"

"No!"

"I say yes. Lor' bless them sweet lips on yourn, I'll be at 'em in next minute. Think all on us aboard the ship didn't see why he was so much in the cabin along of you? It's all right! If its money's the bar, I can count down more shiners than that boy of a capin, I'll warrant."

"Don't lay hands on me then!"

"Pooh! But I likes the gals what fires up! they're more enjoyable."

"If you touch me he shall know, and he is prompt to avenge if he is young in years."

"That lad? ha, ha! Hold your noise! Come, stow it, or I'll knife you! Avast heaving! By thunder, you're a fool! My mates are t'other side, to leeward, of the island! There's no one to hear."

"Help! help!"

Yet she could not hope that Lance, so feeble, so far from ability to help, would be raised by a miracle to her assistance.

Fruitless her struggle in such powerful hands.

Each time that she sought to run, she was dragged back.

Twice beat down to her knee, she rose as many times and fluttered in the brutal embrace like a petrel in a seagull's claws.

All at once, as she breathless with striking the hard-headed ruffian, feared she was about to swoon in the wretches grasp, both of them started.

Both glanced into the thicket.

They saw the shadow, catching a little glimmer of the starlight, defined upon the mass of thorny chapparals.

But at a second glance her lightened heart was loaded down again.

The seaman laughed gladly, relieved from dread of an interference.

The new-comer wore the red shirt that was the principal item of the uniform of the Scarlet Cruiser's crew.

"Aint it you, Pete?" cried the sailor, holding the girl down. "Thought so, bo'!" added he, as the stranger advanced, apparently in pain. "You al'ays was a most for'ad man, and you've parted cable too soon. Arter me is manners!"

He stooped over the trembling shrinking girl.

"Come, that kiss, my light-of-love!"

"Oh, no, no, no! Oh, help! help! for the sake of the woman who bore you!"

The rascal clapped one broad hand over her mouth.

With the other he made a threatening gesture.

"Play me fair, Pete, or I'll make a clencher nail of my knife, mind you!"

The stranger had not spoken yet.

He moved, dragging himself along like one paralyzed, but forcing himself onward by energy of mind.

Had his face been turned upward, its deathly pallor would have been plain.

But the sailor who had overpowered the poor girl, was too excited, and his eyes too much affected by passion and drink, did not notice him.

Content in the belief that his threat would leave the field to himself, he took away his palm from Genifrede's face and pressed his foul mouth to her lips.

At this sight, the stranger uttered a hoarse cry of frenzy.

One could see the blood rushing into every vein so that his white face was instantly suffused with vermillion.

Getting the better hand of his lassitude, he reached the brink of the pool in three long leaps.

More like a rock hurled from a hill-top than a man, he fell upon the seamen,

He himself was so stunned by the shock that he fell back senseless.

The other dashed forward went rolling into the pond.

It was about mid-deep where he fell.

On finding bottom, he turned furious and began to wade to shore.

Genifrede could have fled now, exhausted as she was, but she had not the heart to leave him who had saved her, to the ruffian's revenge.

Catching up a fragment of wood that had been broken under their feet in the assault, she prepared to combat him.

If she could keep him from climbing the bank, her superior station might gain her the victory.

But, as she nerved herself for the encounter, she beheld the seaman stop.

The next instant, he gave a howl of pain, and seemed to miss his footing.

Dancing wildly in the water, now throwing up his arms in agony, now plunging them frantically beneath the surface, he seemed to have gone mad.

His struggles grew weaker and weaker.

He sought to reach the bank, but still the invisible power drew him back.

Plunging from side to side, rocking to and fro, up to his neck one moment and then again half out of water, the man changed his position every moment.

In one of his wild leaps, Genifrede thought she saw something like broad silver swords stabbing with the quickness of lightning at the wretch's limbs.

But the bubbles and splashing covered all that immediately.

With a horrid oath, screamed out in his torment, the man's arms and body rose upward from one deep plunge, in which he had almost gone under.

The trunk and arms were all that were there.

For they fell over on the surface, bereft of limbs.

And upon that half a man, some fifty long thin fish, half their length being a lengthy head, like a great pike's, were feasting.

As the gush of blood that painted the white sides of the savage garfish, at the devouring of the man so lately full of life, beside her, Genifrede was seized with such horror that her senses fled her.

And as the dawn broke, the early light penetrated the forest and flickered over the man's and the woman's motionless figures, beside the black pool still ensanguined, upon whose ruddy mirror streaking of bloody bubbles were stoutly bursting.

———

CHAPTER XXI.

BLACKBEARD SPENDS HIS TIME PLEASANTLY—THE ATTEMPT AT ESCAPE—HOW THE PIRATE CLEARED THE DECKS—THE LAST OF THIRTY—RANSACKING THE NEWS IN THE PAPERS.

THE Spanish coaster the "Two Hands and a Sword," as her long title ran, had cleared from Cardenas with a light but fair wind for her northern course.

She had about thirty men aboard her, some of these being English seamen who were going to the American colonies.

Soon after they had bowled out of the port, they saw that a small foreign craft, a two-master "junk," came along the coast.

Instead of entering the harbour this new vessel fell off before the wind, and shifting her sails wing and wing, she took the same line that the Spanish coaster had sailed over.

All day long the two vessels were in sight of one another.

There could hardly be a doubt of the real character of the junk. For, trimming her sails just as her leader did, all her efforts seemed to be directed to keeping in view.

Probably, seeing the proximity of the port, she did not care to enter into an engagement during which some coastguard cutter might appear.

Towards dark, at the time when the land wind dies away and the sea breeze flies into shore, the air softened into a calm.

At intervals a cat's-paw ruffled the glassy undulations.

Otherwise, they might have taken in the sails at once.

The junk got her long oars out and began to loom up large.

"Their sweeps are out, Ralph," said one of the English sailors to a neighbour leaning over the bulwarks.

"Aye, and he's coming up hand over fist. A bad egg, she, or she wouldn't be so strong manned for a little 'un of her tonnage.

"Right there, mate. Ah! there's the Spaniard a distributing arms."

The captain of the Two Hands, sure that the dogger of his vessel was bent on making fight, was indeed giving out the weapons.

There was a cutlass or pistol for every man.

Ralph and his friend chose axes as the handiest thing for them.

The two bow chasers were old three-pounders, but were serviceable at short range.

There was a gun on board, an article of cargo, a six-pounder.

The captain did not hesitate about breaking bulk for it.

They opened the main hatch, upset the packages that were in the way, and soon unearthed the desired box.

A blow or two of Ralph's axe knocked the boards asunder.

As many hands as could lay hold did, and in half an hour the piece was mounted on the carriage.

They chopped the starboard gunnel though to widen a port, and ran the new gun out at this embrasure.

By this time the stranger had come up under the impulse of the sweeps.

They could guess how numerous a crew the junk contained, as they had four men to each sweep, rowing three aside.

Besides, there were more crowding the decks.

The Spaniards expected, as the junk forged ahead, her sails laying flat as a board, that they would receive a broadside first thing.

But, hauling in the sweeps, and passing within easy hail, the crew of the stranger remained in their stations.

But the chief man on the quarter-deck, putting his hand to his mouth, and smothing away his heavy black moustache and beard halloa'd—

"Schooner ahoy? Name and master?"

"I'll answer him fair," said the Spaniard.

He lifted his voice!

"The Hand and a Sword! I'm Anibal Gogliso. What are you?"

"Blackbeard's longboat! old Goodeyes! Depress that barker, or you'll have something hot heaved on to some of you!"

"You be hanged!" it was Ralph who shouted that.

He was one of the bluff sort, who cared nothing for arguing when he had his shirt sleeves rolled up.

As he spoke, he and his three friends working the six-pounder, did depress it a little.

But not so much as Blackbeard had desired. Only so much as to bring it to bear on the pirate.

The gun exploded with a deafening discharge and recoiled with such force as to upset it from the carriage, which it had been too weakly attached to.

"If that bit of good advice don't suit the ocean theives, it's a pity but we can't sarve 'em out more!" said Ralph, looking down ruefully at the dismounted cannon.

The shot had lodged in the cheek of the pirate shaking it tremendously.

The Spaniards and English raised a cheer, but the more numerous marauders drowned it with a yell of rage and menace.

"Isn't that a puff of wind, there aloft," cried Gogliso, holding up his moistened hand.

"On'y a breath! died away! But the seabreeze is a coming!" cried a man on the maintop who was reloading the musket that he had fired.

"My men," said Captain Gogliso. "It'll be hot work, but if we can keep it up, we can run before them when the breeze comes."

"There's nothing like trying," returned Ralph for the crew.

Now Teach had only pursued the Two Hands because he wanted to perform the neat little transaction of changing ships.

He had found his little vessel very inconvenient for so large and noisy a flock of villains.

Hence he did not reply to the shot with so murderous a volley as was in his power to do.

The two were in a current, and if that impulse continued they might be drifted unpleasantly close to shore.

"Those proud and lofty Spaniards," said Teach to his pets, "are standing on their resolute points. But we're not river-boatmen to be scorched by their pestilent fire. Cut sweeps, four a-side and we'll run 'em aboard! to the tune of—

"Hey, boys, up go we!
Hooray!'"

The set of the current had swept the light junk around to the stern of the heavier laden schooner.

"They're down on us" said Ralph. "Mate of mine, if I'm ever to be took by them bloody minded scurf of the sea, won't you act a friend's part, and send a bullet spinning through my gizzard and I thank you afore the v'y'ge!"

"I'm there, Ralph! But I hopes we're a sight, if we can only meet 'em like a channel blow and not milky like a sheep's-head wind!"

The small arms were re echoing in the tops and below.

The coaster's defenders were greatly protected by their smallness of numbers, as they fired into a mass and had to be aimed at separately.

Only sheering off a point as her jibboom grazed the schooner's stern, the pirate came forcibly against the after windows.

Through them and over the taffrail, the marauders entered the prize.

"I'll break you of your cursed reserve!" cried Ralph, chopping at William Teach, and breaking his cutlass.

Old Teach fired his long pistol at the bold seaman.

The shot missed him and killed the Spanish captain.

The defenders of the Two Hands, fell back.

More of the robbers were swarming up.

"My mind misgived me," said Ralph taking breath. "We're gone, now that we ever let them stand on the level with us."

"Holy Virgin!" said the first mate, "shall we give in, Senor Englishman?"

"Give up! and be tied back to back and rolled, like pudding balls into the sea?" sneered Ralph. "Not me! I'm for holding out as long as there's a flash of powder in a pistol pan!"

"We'd sooner die, eh?" said the Spaniard.

"By a long shot."

Spaniards and English, they determined not to let the notorious miscreant have them to torment.

They had beaten a retreat down into the waist.

They would have been slaughtered there as in a pen.

But Captain Teach was too eager to finish.

"Fight closed!" cried he, drawing his cutlass after having emptied his pistols.

"Haint you the pith of a reed, that you can't kick up more of a rumpus!"

THE SCARLET CRUISER

He drove his own men before him.

There were half a dozen of the Spaniards who were cut off from thier comrades.

They took to the main shrouds.

One or two were ran through with boarding-pikes.

The rest offered targets to the marksmen below.

It was pitiful to behold them, dropping blood at every rattling that they drew themselves up.

Growing weaker each minute, their climbing was slower and slower, until they scarcely moved, but remained flattened in against the cordage.

One or two stiffened there in death.

The others were too heavy to be upheld by their bloodless hands, and soon pitched over into the greedy waves.

The pirates began to mount the rigging to get at the fellows in the tops, who were galling their companions with shots, blocks, and cannon balls.

"Don't let one give you the go-by!" cried Teach. "Run down after that fellow in the forecastle. Fling the bread-cask over on that knave towing by that line! Don't you see him there? Look sharp to spare not one, or I'll make some of your peepers as big as a bung-hole!"

The scoundrels had swept forward to the windlass, bearing a red carpet covered with a score of dead and dying under foot.

Blackbeard stood by the starboard cat-head, leaning on his cutlass.

"Ha, ha!" laughed he, "It's as lively an hour as ever I saw."

"It's the deadliest hour that ever you saw!" shouted a voice close to him.

One of the men fallen, covered with wounds, on the forecastle, had got upon his feet.

It was Ralph.

One glance showed him that, during his being struck down, every one of his friends and allies had been cast into everlasting sleep.

With all the power of which he was capable, he struck at the rover chief with the first thing that met his hand.

It was half a rammer, one of the bow-chaser's set.

Under such a stroke, Blackbeard fell, like the oak upon which a thunderbolt had spent its force.

The pirates who had been unable to prevent so unexpected a reprisal, now awoke to revenge.

But Ralph, hurling the club full in their faces, threw himself over the bows.

As he did so, a stray shot glanced off the fore-bits and entered his shoulder.

At the same moment, there was a call from the handful left on the junk.

"There's the breeze rising!" said they.

There was a fresh ruffle on the surface, and the sails began to wrinkle.

Both vessels began to move. The lesser one worked free of the coaster's stern, and fell off.

"Don't let that scoundrel die!" screamed Captain Teach.

A flask of brandy had been applied to his lips and some of it getting spilt, he had been returned to consciousness by the smarting.

"Don't let him die, the villain! I want to torture him, to cut his heart out, a thousand flame's seize him!"

"He's over the bow, sir! on an end of the flying-jib down haul."

"Have him up!"

Here lay the puzzle.

It was all very well to say "have him up!" but a grater man than the gentle hearted Blackbeard could not compel a man to cling to a rope.

The schooner was going through the water at a very slight pace.

Ralph could keep his grip, nevertheless, if that had been all.

"Here's a rope's end, old fellow" said one pirate. "Shall I heave the slack to you!"

"Thank you! I'm considering. I'm ready to die!"

"Die? we ain't thinking, of a chap that fought so stout. Come up, and sign the articles for a jolly cruise."

"Oh, don't you wish you could tempt me! No such boat for me!"

"He's let go the line, sir!" said they all.

Ralph had let himself float free.

The ship slowly passed him.

At the stern he caught the end of another rope cut in the action, and trailing.

"Make it fast round you!" said one of the rovers again.

"You needn't be afeard, you didn't kill the cap'en!"

"Didn't I? worse luck! Wish I'd stayed aboard and below, and given him a wrapper of flame for a watch coat!"

"There's another for that!" cried a voice.

The speaker popped his head out of one of the cabin windows.

"What you, Steve? said Ralph, hardly believing his eyes.

Their heads were not ten feet from one another, but then Steve was high up from the surface.

"What cheer?"

"My life line's veered out," answered Ralph. "All above slain by the picaroon's mate."

"I've pinned two that come below arter me. There's the table and a locker ag'in the door, and I can hold out till I lay the train."

"Lay the train!" echoed Ralph, in the same low voice that the other used.

"Aye. I've a bag of powder here, and mean to have one flare-up afore the rascals shall sail her!"

"Good!"

It was impossible for the swimmer to get into the window even had he been stronger.

The reason of his being left to himself so long was clear.

The pirates had cleared away a boat over the side, unseen by him, and now it appeared close to him.

"Luck to you, Steve! Remember? duty's duty! and there's a way aloft for even us rough souls!"

The boat rounded the stern and was nearly upon him.

The stroke oar and the second seat man rose, shipping their oars, and held themselves in readiness at the bow to lift the sailor in.

But, even as their eager hands were outstretched, the stout old tar let go the rope, threw up his arms straight over his head, and sunk.

They touched his very hair, but already the water had closed over him with an ominous sound.

When he came up he was twenty feet off.

Before the boat could overtake him, he had gone under again.

He rose no more.

Disappointed, the boat made for the junk, which lay nearer them than the vessel they had quitted.

In the meantime, the pirate chief had been filled with vexation at the resolute way in which the brave salt who had left him with a bleeding head, had gone to his death.

He turned his attention now to the interior of his prize.

Since the seaman in the cabin had killed the couple of pirates who had gone below after him, and blocked up the door, there were but two ways of getting at him.

One was to lower one's self to the cabin windows, and break through in.

But it was rather risky to travel by that route.

And the fellows held back.

So, while one watched to hinder any escape by that way, there was a party set hammering at the door.

Only a few at most could be supposed to have taken refuge under hatches, so that Captain Teach was easy as regards that.

Had he been aware that these was only the last of the thirty left, he would have been still more delighted at his conquest.

Of his better-armed men the defenders of the schooner had only slain eight, but three more were so badly wounded, that in that hot weather they were not likely to recover.

The pirates were handling the sails, and the little pink had been hailed to follow in the wake.

Midnight was near at hand, and still the door had resisted the axes.

It bid fair to be down presently if only in chips.

By lantern light the hold and forecastle had been searched and the goods were brought up on deck.

To the music of that fierce pounding on the cabin-door, for the dozen ruffians to be in at the death of the one survivor, the plunderers overhauled the booty.

"I'll have to jump down in among ye, and flatten in your jib," cried Teach angrily.

He was standing at the doorway of the cabin entrance, looking down on his men.

"It's giving, sir" answered one of the axe-men.

At the very instant that the door, completely cut away from its fastenings, yielded altogether with a crash, a broad sheet of flame, upheaving the floor of the cabin found egress in two places.

Out of the cabin windows with a fierce gush, through the shattered door, into the faces of the ten or twelve men.

Blinded, their hair, whiskers, clothes, and flesh singed as if a furnace had been opened, they fell in a heap on the boards.

Along with the blaze, the heated air brought a chorus of execrations in all languages into the captain's face.

"Santissima! Maldito! Diable! damnation!" howled the sufferers.

The first flash was instantly fellowed by a dull explosion.

The stern rose a little out of water.

When she settled down on an even keel, she quickly took a heel to one side.

The powder that Steve had spoken of had done its work.

"There, you cowardly beggars!" said he.

He ran up from the cabin, trampling over the writhing men.

Blackbeard struck at him with his fist.

But the vessel lurched still more fearfully.

There was the sinister in-rushing of water.

The explosion had started three or four planks clean from the pins on the starboard side fully under the water-line.

The deck was on such an incline now that every time a-port went sliding down the steep, carrying the surprised sailors with them.

Teach was flung headforemost down the stairs, accelerated by a kick that Steve had just time to give him.

"To show the love I bear him!" muttered he, catching at a belaying-pin and holding on.

"Cut him to pieces," roared Blackbeard picking himself up and climbing up the stairs. "He's scuttled the ship!"

"He has!" shouted Steve fiercely, as he faced the men that were proceeding towards him. "And she'll go down, aye, if she were the biggest of the big and had ten tier of ports! Oh, you can't have me to pelt with wine bottles, no, ye scum of a stagnant pool!"

The steady sinking of the schooner and her pitching as the sails began to fill, made progress on the deck covered with the bales and boxes no easy matter.

Steve got up on the bulwark and steadied himself by a twist of the hand in the foretopsail brace which had not yet been spliced after being shot loose in the action.

Blackbeard had come up now. He was previously stepping over the packages to get a cut at the hardy mariner.

Had the studdingsail booms been out on the square foresail that the coaster carried, the starboard one would have been in the water, so far over did she lean.

Steve cast one glance around and above. Close to him were the ring of cut throats in a few minutes sure to have him at arms reach.

Luckily the plunging prevented their firing pistols at him.

One fellow was coming down from the maintop. As he had the shrouds to cling to, he could take that aim at the exposed seamen which his comrades were debarred from.

There was no hope of salvation.

By leaping backwards, he could drown. The only other vessel in sight was the pirate, and, of course no mercy was to be expected from her.

Still the sailor would not kill himself.

"Down with him!" cried Teach.

The man in the rattlins extended his right arm and fired.

They saw Steve sway wildly, but he kept his footing.

A trickle of blood ran down his shirt and proved that he had not escaped the bullet.

At that same point of time, there was a peculiar sound.

The sighing of the air confined in the hold, and, while boxed in by the timbers, was pressed up by the in-coming water.

The crash was sure to come.

And nothing could withstand the power of the entering sea.

The deck was started, and the destruction of the Two Hands was sure.

The air blew out the port-side ports, like so many guns discharged.

The hull righted itself for one instant.

Then into the port-holes, through breaches that it made for itself, and leaping up over the bulwarks, the brine came surging in.

Everything was afloat in a second, and all the men, dropping weapons, seized on something to bear them up.

Amid a mingling of unearthly shrieks, groans, cries, for the ship did not break to pieces without its lament, the hull went beneath the wave in a whirlpool of its own creation.

There were a number of the pirates swimming out of the eddy.

A few remained in the tops, climbing up as they sank, and some were drowned by being entangled in the rigging.

In the middle of all the swimmers, weakened by the pistol wound, Steve was descried.

He lifted himself breast high out of the eddy, and shouted in a voice full of the force that a dying man may have under strong emotions.

"Some of you dead discharged, you accursed sea-rats!"

"But I see acted up, to my rating! Ay you scoundrel, its true blue, and he was sinking, it's true blue won't stain!"

And with that sublime sentence not to be washed from his soul though dashed from his lips by the foam, the gallant heart saw his last of the skies, and was buried in the seaman's grave.

* * * * *

"What's that you have, William?" asked old Teach of his young namesake.

"Ship's manifest and clearance," was the ready reply, as the young man opened the book that he had, and searched for more papers.

Except half a dozen men sucked down in the eddy the buccaneers had succeeded in keeping above water until the pink's boats had picked them up.

"Yes, but what book is it?"

"Oh, the log book!"

"Let's have a look."

Blackbeard took the volume.

At first opening he saw nothing more interesting than the trafficking in sugar that the sunken Spaniard had entered in his previous voyage.

But after skipping a few leaves, the pirate uttered an exclamation of surprise.

"What now, old man," said William Teach in his usual affectionate way. "Have you a fit from that soak in the water?"

"Curse you and the water! Here's an entry, see! "Saw a fire off the Caymandillos. They lined so that the light could not be made out on which one, for sure. Would have altered course and borne down, but feared it to be a pirate's decoy. The saints will that it was, and not a shipwrecked sailor."

"No reason you should turn pale over that, old man."

"Aint there, William? You don't know the treasure I have buried there, from the old days before you could talk up saucy to me. Kyd knew it—and Captain Kyd's there nuearthing it!"

He flung down the book in anger, and ripped out an oath or two.

"He promised me fair play and I've been fool enough to expect his performance to the utmost. This is why I couldn't find him up nort'ard! Oh, mik him, the traitor! And hang those Spaniards for scuttling that craft when I want her so much just now."

"Out of luck that time, old man," said William placidly. "It was a cake of ice for sunshine!"

"Get below or out of my path now! cried Blackbeard. "Or I'll veer away the fall of your heart's clue-line! D'ye hear, at helm, there? Keep her full! If you lift a cloth, you'll never more show your nose above deck!"

The steersman took it all quietly.

But when the Captain and William had gone down into the cabin, he leisurely rolled his quid, and observed to a comrade repairing the broken taffrail.

"The old man's as pleasant as a crocodile when her eggs is took away. I'd rather be in an old waggon on a bad road than at sea along of him!"

CHAPTER XXII.

A BIT OF SUPPER—THE DESERTER—A SLEEP THAT KNEW NO WAKING—AVENGER'S ALLY.

"I'm 'spicious of that fish! Sam, it smells to me as if it was on the go!"

"It was only caught yesterday."

"Then it must have been spiled in the cooking. Now look here, we needn't think of anything but a jolly blow out on the pork and the yams—we've got lots to last until the cap'en sends the boat for us in three days."

"Lashings. Let's have the pork."

So the three men, who were those landed from the Cruiser, set to work building a fire and scraping the sweet potatoes for the meal.

We have gone back to the evening which had nearly resulted in being a fatal one to Genifrede.

The three men had been sent ashore by Frank with these orders.

To guard the young girl and let her have a peaceful dwelling in the hut.

In three days, by which time the Cruiser would have reached the island where they meant to carry her, a boat would be sent to take the men and Genifrede off.

Her future could be arranged for afterwards.

Unluckily the girl had fancied that only harm could be intended her.

The three men found that the more they hallooed to her the more wings they lent to her flight.

So, having run against one another in the wood, they came to the conclusion that they had better give up the chase.

They were pretty sharp set, for the fire on board and the exercise it had compelled, had ground their appetite to extreme keenness.

Sam and another of the name of Sloper were average looking able bodied seamen.

The third had a phiz not a bit too promising, and was the same that had met his fate in the pool by the teeth of the gar-fish.

They called him Neap.

Before a great while, the old fryingpan was set upon the coals, and the pork cut up into slice, sputtered and hissed like a pack of enraged cats.

But the aroma of the hot fat, mingling with the sharpness of the sea breeze, would have made a less relishable repast go down.

After indulging in the sweet potatoes and the fry till they could not even touch the few crisp pieces left, tempting as they were, the men lit their pipes, and, their feet to the fire, gave themselves up to conversation.

At first, it turned on only common topics, and the late fire.

Naturally, after a complete blowing up of Loys de Goupille, the talk reverted to Genifrede.

"Of course she's innocent looking," said Sloper. "I never seed a more sweeter face on any woman! She's no painted creature that bowses up her jib at the smell of tar, neither. I've watched her the few times that we saw her above hatches."

"She's no better than the rest," said Neaps. "Do you mean to tell me that our young captain is cold as an Esquimaux, and that I did'nt see him kissing her hand, one time when I had my turn at the wheel and looked down through the bullseye that was broken there."

"Mebbe you did, and then again, mebbe you did'nt," said Sloper, letting a long whiff of smoke issue slowly from his mouth.

"What do you mean by that?" cried Neap fiercely.

"Never you lay your hand on your knife, my lad," said Sloper calmly. "I only made a general observation. If I had 'tended to say you lied, I would have said it short, so "You lie, Neap!""

This was hardly the way to smooth over the rupture.

But Neap, it would seem, had something else in view at this moment.

"Well, I did see it, as I says," went on he. "Not that I would blame the young commander——"

"Don't you! I never had such a fondness as I have for him," said Sloper.

"He's fit to be a hadmiral, as I've heerd old Bill Bowse say time and ag'in," said Sam, tapping his thigh emphatically.

"Come, come, what's the use an old pull-together a quarreling over nothing in this way. What I was going to prop—hose is a bit of pinketing for us."

"Did you bring a bottle of brandy ashore."

"Or some guava jelly! it eats tremendoes between a biscuit," said Sam, smacking his lips.

"Oh, no! it's a grey goose of another colour. Look a-here."

"Aye."

"This here's an island, and not so large that a woman on't is like the needle dropped in the sail-room never found, not nohow."

"Well?"

"Well, seeing that she can't get away she must be here. So, we three waits a bit till to'ards morning, when the stars are brighter, and goes on the hunt."

"For her?"

"For her, rather. We'll be safe to find her. I never knew that woman yet that could conceal herself. They're like the horsetrige which, mebbe you've been in the Guinea trade, and have seen a hiding its head in the sand."

"Not me," said Sam "I've been about on the rough, and had my little slish slash to fill the locker, but I never was in the blackbird catching line."

"It don't matter. So we comes across the girl somewhere in the bush, and—and—Well, when the cap'en sends for us, we har to tell him that the poor thing must have been caught in the undertow, leastways, we ha'int seen her from the first——"

"You scoundrelly thief of the world."

"Wait a bit——wait a bit, Sam."

"Well, you speak to him, seeing you're older, Sloper; but if you don't talk to him correctly, curse me through and through but I'll knock both of you down and kick you into the sea!"

The two seamen had started to their feet in their indignation.

Neap had kept his seat, but his hand had stolen to his knife, and he looked rather uneasy.

Sloper worked his hand as if he was pumping emotion up.

When he did burst forth, the outflow was overpowering.

"You double-boiled cowardly son of an unsarvicable, never fit to be about a cuttle barge cook. I've a mind to sew you up in a bag full of the biggest kind of sharpest sort of p'ison thorns! I'll let you know——"

Here he laid hold of Neap, who had his knife out, and shook him violently.

"I'll let you know that that man never came of woman that would a woman harm."

With an irresistable force, he implanted a kick at about the middle of a patch of duck that adorned the rascal's trousers.

Neap gave a prolonged howl, and his knife still in his hand, was propelled into the bushes of prickly palm and scrub palmetto, as fast as if he was running a race.

After crashing through half a dozen bushes, one stopped his way, and bending quite sufficiently to let him settle nicely into the midst of their points, the branches closed in over his head.

Out of breath as he was, yet the innumerable prickings made him utter an unearthly howl, full of such queerly strong notes that the sound was laughable.

At all events, Sam and Sloper were ready to split their sides with merriment.

After a time, the yells and groans of the sufferer ceased.

He had struggled out of the tangle.

The two men, their heated passions faded, called out for him to come back.

They were ready to shake hands and make it up.

No answer came.

"He's sulky, he is," said Sam. "Let him go hang! He'll turn up for breakfast in the morning."

"Not a doubt of it, but I'm going to sleep on my arms for fear he might be revengeful. And I rather suppose we'll be all the better for taking it watch and watch."

So, while Sam lay down, the other sat by the fire, quietly smoking and letting his eyes wander over the strip of sand and the dark underwood.

Neap had worked himself out of the thorns, at the expense of his clothing and skin.

He felt a tingling all over him as if he had been scourged with nettles.

Burning quite as hot with thirst for revenge as he was with pain, Neap felt overjoyed when he found that a shining object near him was his knife.

He heard his comrades calling him with a laughable voice, and he muttered a round dozen of oaths, not much for their benefit.

Then crawling into the bushes out of the thorn clump, he pulled up some wild sage and rubbed the most severe of his lacerations.

More relieved by his rage from feeling pain than by the plant having been of much benefit, he proceeded to meditate as he lay under a tree.

His running was rendered far from amusing by the pangs that made him twist and jump every second minute.

The voice of his companions had faded away.

He crept stealthily to the outskirts of the wood, avoiding the prickly peals much as the burnt child of the proverb dreads the fire.

To his high disgust, he saw that one of the seamen was awake, and guarding the other in slumber.

In the day time he would soon be hunted up by them and secured if he intended any underhanded measures.

He did not dare to go out of cover and attack the watcher.

However sudden his onset, the other could not fail to be aroused, and then woe to the miscreant.

So he waited, with that restless patience of the tiger and wolf.

Sloper dit not quite suspect that such eyes were on him, hungry for his blood.

For a long while the silence reigned over all, though the breeze rustled the palmetto and sand palm leaves over head.

Neap caught himself dropping off to sleep.

At length he sank into a broken sort of a nap.

It was ended in a startling manner.

Something cold like a trail of liquid glass, was shinily dragging over his hand and face.

He awoke on the instant.

The starlight was reflected from the glittering scales of a moving animal.

A snake.

Almost sure to be venomous in that latitude.

Neap shook like a leaf in his horror and affright.

Luckily he had gone to rest, knife in hand, and

as he lifted up the blade, the serpent darted out its coil.

Out by the edge, it twisted under the very knees of the half risen seaman.

His very efforts to escape led him to crush the reptile under his feet.

Convinced that it was really dead, he bent down as much to regain his coolness as to examine the thing.

"The barber's pole!" exclaimed he, in almost as much terror as if the snake had life.

The serpent, was one of the species whose dark stripes along a liver colored body had earned it that very expressive name among the common people of the West Indies.

It's bite is past cure, and dreadful speedy of bearing death in the heartiest body.

"It's a female. The skin is awful loose. Thunder!"

He started to his feet and stared at the ground, equally afraid to stir and to remain.

"She's young some where around. By heaven, inside a rope would be safer than here!"

At a glance, he saw that Sloper had been overcome by sleepiness like himself.

But unlike him, he had not had so unenviable a rouser.

A fiendish suggestion seemed to enter by his many wounds, even as he had prepared to run.

It suited his low mind to a T.

Snapping off a twig, he sharpened one end into a point.

Sticking this firmly in the reptile's still agitated remains, he cautiously left the undergrowth.

Behind him he dragged the snake.

It left a trail of blood from its cuts and bruises, and of venom from its crushed poison bag.

Neap noiselessly appoached the two slumberers.

A smile of hideous triumph lighted up his scratched face.

"Ho, ho!" said he to himself. "So you wouldn't chime in with my little love tune, eh? and would kick me into a bramble bush! Ho, ho! you'll have visitors, before the sun looks at you!"

He left the serpent in the firelight, between the two men.

"Good bye mess-mates mine," said he. "I'm off to find the pretty one."

So saying, he returned as noiselessly as he had come.

It is unnecessary to follow him to the forest.

It was evil that he left behind him, and to the evil-doer's sudden cruel end he went.

*   *   *   *   *

The stars had lost their brilliancy, and it was as dark as if there had been clouds in the sky.

Any one who might have been watching the circle of light around the half burnt-out fire and the sleepers, would have been startled by the abrupt appearance of several variegated lines on the yellow sands.

Moving slowly; but after they had, to the number of six or seven, come together, all collected around the dead snake.

One of the new comers was very large, and he was adorned with a kind of ruffled scale on his head that was like a crown.

The rest were small, very small compared to this chief of his malignant race.

By a hiss, varying in modulation, he directed the others.

His eyes, glittering like rubies in the chance rays of the fire, were fastened on the seamen with a deadly glare.

Hazard willed it that a twinge of cold, or some slight cause, led Sloper to move.

As he lifted his arm and rolled his head to one side, the king-snake gave a hiss.

So long was it that Sloper awoke fully.

"What's it, mate?" began he.

But already the fangs of the large serpent were fastened on his throat and the long coil lashing his face and shoulders.

He cried out with pain at the bite.

Sam sprang up.

But the young snakes had enfolded themselves upon him.

The two sailors, their limbs wound about by the coils, missed their footing and fell.

The snakes never let go their hold.

The poison began to mix with the blood and drive the poor wretches wild by the unnatural action of the heart, resisting so potent an attack on the life stream.

Upon the embers of the fire the two dropped in convulsions, pressing the death quiver down into the scorching ashes.

Upon the bed of cinders, their deep inroads of the fiery coals hardly felt amid the agony of the serpents stings, the two sufferers writhed out a last spasm of anguish, a last breath of exquisite pangs.

One or two of the singed snakes dragged their burnt length away, to die in the bushes.

The sun rose on the corpses smouldering on the charred brads of the fire.

Of the fire; its light extinguished just as the light of the two souls had gone out for evermore!

CHAPTER XXIII.

NED NITTLE FINDS THE COAST NOT QUITE CLEAR—A LITTLE DODGING—THE PIRATES CRY "NO QUARTER" A TRIFLE TOO SOON—NED'S HOSTAGE GOES TO GET RANSOM!

IN the evening, the third day after the Scarlet Cruiser had left the Caymandillos, the sea had fallen calm.

Over the long smooth swell, a row-boat was steadily progressing.

Its prow was pointed to the islet which had been so suddenly tenanted the half week before.

In the stern sat Ned Nittle, acting as coxswain over the six men at the oars.

"Steady!" said he, all at once, as he gave the port tiller-rope a pull, and the yawl changed her course. "Hang me high and dry if there ain't spars, or something ship-like above the rocks."

The other sailors turned their heads and saw plainly that a vessel was on the other side of the islet.

Only the top-gallant mast was visible, as the trees intervened and hid all the hull and upper works.

"Anchored," said Ned, after a long scrutiny, during which the men lay on their oars. "It's a risk, but we'll land. See to your fire-arms, every man."

Making sure of their pistols, and seeing that their cutlasses played freely, they fitted their oars in the thwarts once more.

As noiselessly as they could row without making more noise than any oars except muffled ones are guilty of, the sailors pulled in shore.

They made the landing without exciting any alarm to such persons as might be on the island.

They drew the boat up into a little cove where it lay covered by the low-lying boughs of a tree.

Two were left to watch the yawl.

Ned and the other four, scattering a little, made their way through the trees.

Ere long, they heard such sounds as bespoke the neighbourhood of the vessel, but still these were indistinct.

They went ahead but slowly.

Partly from fear of stumbling upon somebody, and partly from the hindrances of thorn and thicket in the way.

At length, the seaside was reached.

They had gone nearly straight across the island at its narrowest end.

Ned had the lead.

When he had parted the bushes and peered out, those next to him saw and felt him start and turn aghast.

All crowded around and gazed upon that which had affected him.

"Our men!"

"Sam!"

"Neap——"

"No, it's Sloper! Neap's a smaller man."

So exclaimed they, in an under tone of horror.

For there lay, most dreadfully contorted, and with the limp serpent now still intertwined with their limbs, the victims of the striped snake and their false comrade's malice.

"Quite dead!" said Ned, shaking his head.

All felt there was no doubt about that.

It was impossible to go down the beach, even those few steps, without being discovered, for within easy hail of shore, rode at anchor the pink which had come thither as speedily as wind would waft her, after the Spaniard had gone under the billows.

"By George!" exclaimed Ned, "Yon's the two-master that we got that precious nigger Frenchman out of. She's here for no good. I wish we had sent her to the bottom with all her rascally swabbers."

"A nice stroke of work they've done here," remarked a sailor, pointing.

"I can't make it out. It's either them or the snakes, and either way they're dead—poison or treachery of man killed them, for they're not the lads to have given up the ghost with their pistols in their belts, unless they were stolen upon from behind."

"Right, Ned; I know Sam too well not to agree with you there."

"I'm afeared that our young captain will never see more of that girl we came to bring. If they treats men so, Lor'! what chance for a woman?"

"Right, Ned," said the same seaman, again. "Not much use looking for her. 'Spect we'll never find her 'less it's on Cape Flyaway."

"We'll look about for her, anyhow. Perhaps if she don't turn up, we'll have a chance, after dark, to let our mates have the last ship in Mother Ocean. That'll be something."

Still keeping together, but scattered sufficiently to beat a good space of ground, the four seamen explored the islet.

They found broken twigs here and there, indicating that something living had passed in different directions.

Some of the paths were made by Genifrede in her race of terror, some by Neap in his route to death, some again by Loys de Goupille.

The latter swimming to land, which he had attained in a spent condition, had been seeking a hiding in the shrubbery when the outcries had brought him to the spot where aid was so much needed.

Following these tracks, the four seamen reached the cave in which Lance Cavendish had been left.

Ned lifted his hand to signal to his comrades that something new had transpired.

On stopping and listening, a murmur of hushed voices was audible.

Ned stole forward, taking advantage of the leafy screen.

On coming to one point he could look into the hole in the rocks.

The scarlet shirt of one of the two men within, was the first thing that caught his eye.

But he soon recognized the but too well-known features of the relentless Loys de Goupille.

He could not credit his eyes for a space.

He beckoned one of his companions to come nearer him.

"Look there!" whispered he. "Who's that in one of our red shirts?"

"Oh, heaven!"

"Who is it, say you?"

"The double of the man who swings at the Cruiser's yardarm," replied the sailor, full of alarm.

"The double? It's some new trick of the Frenchman! I'm ready to believe him Old Davy Jones himself!"

This opinion was pretty generally entertained by all.

"I think I see into it," said Ned. "Look here! it was a man we strung up!"

"Every bit of a man, Ned. I felt the weight as I hauled on the ropes."

"And I."

"And then again," went on Ned, "yonder is the Frenchman in flesh and blood!"

"Rather. Look at that girl with her hand in his."

"It wasn't him that was hung."

They shook their heads dubiously.

"Look you, mates, when we called the roll after the fire, next day, it was Pierre that was reported dead, s'posed to have tumbled over in the running about. It's not an unlikely thing that this juggling son of a gun substituted Pierre for himself!"

"So that we stretched a rope with the wrong man."

"And a messmate?"

"Let's settle him for good this time!"

"Easy!" said Ned, as the others were flourishing their weapons. "No burning powder. A pistol would be heard on his ship."

From the connection that Loys had had with the two-master, Nittle naturally supposed he was her captain.

Back to their belts went the pistols, and they drew their hangers.

Nettle was about to whisper: "Rush at 'em and overpower them at once."

But at that very juncture, a pistol-shot rang out and by his very side, one of his comrades was laid dying in his own footprints.

Instinctively, all turned that side.

A boat's crew of Blackbeard's, roaming through the woods, had fallen upon the Cruiser's men, and had been the first to recover from the surprise.

It was William Teach who acted as leader to the party, and who had discharged the firearm.

Nittle's reply shot brought Teach to the ground, his arm hanging broken by his side.

Loys rushed out of the cavern.

"You'll go wring and wring no more!" cried Nittle, to Teach, who was groaning with pain. "Up helm, lads, and bear away! they're too many for us!"

Under cover of the pistol smoke from both parties, the Cruiser's men took to their heels.

In the undergrowth and canebrake, they could hope to scatter their pursuers and pick them off one by one.

In a few seconds, Ned called all around him, and the first two of the dozen pirates who came jumping over the bushes in hot haste, were made to measure the ground by their length.

"Wish 't had been the Mounseer," growled Ned, flourishing his cutlass. "On again! Stretch to it, lads!"

But the buccaneers had blundered into a clearing, and a few more a little ahead of the fugitive.

"It's buckle to is the word!" said Ned charging. "We mustn't let them take old Scarlet's boat!"

"Not a thole-pin!" cried the rest.

A hatchet flashed under the tamarind boughs above Nittle's head.

It was Loys de Goupille who wielded.

He was given new life by the sight of his foemen, as if their scarlet shirts were as the red rag to the bull.

"Strike in!" shouted a big pirate, swinging his blade.

Ned let Loys go for the present, leaped sideways from the axe, and ran his steel half up its length into the last speaker's body.

On withdrawing the weapon, a stream of heart's blood ran down the groove in the metal.

The fellow reeled back and poured out his breath and blood on the bushes.

Ned only had time to lift up his wet cutlass.

Such was the chop that Goupille let descend that the sword was bent to the hilt.

Had it been harder metal, it would have been shivered.

Ned sprang at the Frenchman, who had been carried forward by the force of the blow.

"I'll seize you up this time, ghost or no ghost!" cried he, tightening his grasp.

Two or three pistol shots added their smoke to the shadows that played under the forest trees even in noonday.

Nittle and his struggling antagonists were suddenly upset together by a rush of all the interlocked fighters.

"Hoorah!" shouted a pirate. "Will Teach has halload for the old man and he's coming! Knock 'em over, black flags! Hoorah! and hark!"

There was a distant cheer.

"It's Blackbeard, my fine fellows," continued the pirate, to encourage his comrades and frighten their opponente.

But the Cruiser men had not been brought up at sea to be frightened at a gull's scream.

"Is he coming?" sneered Ned Nittle, rising to his feet, "You needn't be so noisy! Here—hold a bit—let this stop your mouth!"

And with the words, he hurled Loys' body, whom he had strangled, at the marauder.

It made him kiss the trampled sod in a twinkling.

"Scarlets, away!" cried Ned, picking up a cutlass and dashing madly forward.

The cheer of on-coming men was near at hand.

"Only you, Johnson?" exclaimed Ned, in surprise.

"Aye," said the only seaman by his side "They're all down 'cept me, and I'm near off the hooks!"

"What say?"

"Bullet struck bo' slap into my wind-store-room!"

In fact, there was a bubble of blood on the man's lips at each breath he drew.

"You can't run?"

"No farther. Go on, Ned!"

"Go on! Damme, Johnson, but I've a mind to rate you soundly for that. I leave a mate of mine—not if he'd robbed me of my last hounce of bacca on'y the hour afore!"

"They're coming, go!" gasped the poor fellow, leaning against a burton tree.

Ned coolly planted his feet firm, and felt the weight of his cutlass.

All around him the wood was alive with the clamour of the hunters, at fault as to what had become of the two momentarily escaped.

"Down with them! No quarter! There they are! Not this way! Here's the skipper—hoorah! Away, you go!" and a pistol shot now and then, fired at random.

"Can't I carry you, lad?" said Ned.

"To the boat? Lor', mate, an elephant couldn't go far in this thicket! Curse the land! There never was good luck to a man on it!"

"They're near us!" said Ned, hoarsely, and setting his teeth and swinging his sword,

Johnson had slowly let himself sink to the foot of the tree.

His life-tide was ebbing fast.

"Ned, you must go and get the boat off. Tell Captain Frank how we all went down, every inch like his men! And, true heart Ned, scatter my kit 'mong the sheet-anchor-men, eh? There's my palm and needle, take it you, or give 't to Bill Bowse. I'm off soundings, mate. Where, where's your hand!"

Ned passed one arm around him and grasped the placid hand of the dying one.

"Here it is!"

"I know the feel! Ned, mate, there's my little boy at Havanna! Little Jack! He may grow up into my station! Ah!"

"All right, lad! is the woman gone?"

"Long ago, Ned! She was honest, and followed me out to Cuba! Ne'er mind that! Don't open old seams!"

"The lad's as my own, Johnson."

They shook hands.

The mariner'se yes were glazing fast.

All at once he started.

THE YOUNG CAPTAIN SPRUNG AT HIM WITH THE BLOOD-DRIPPING BLADE HIGH IN AIR!

"Lor'! I thought you and me were leaning 'gainst the waist-beltings again, Ned, in the old Free Trader! Good-bye!"

"Good-bye!"

"I took my part, seamanly, Ned?" said the sailor, wanderingly.

"Yes, like a king of the topmen!"

"Ah!" A pause—his breath issued noisily.

"Oh, Ned! it's opening, it's opening!"

"Yes, yes!" said Nittle, eagerly, to humour him.

"The entering port thrown up! The entering port!"

And with that vision of the passage into the new and endless life to soften his final moments, the jack tar yielded for the first time in his life!

"And now for those treacherous roaring buccaneers!" muttered Ned, rising from his knees.

A pistol left in Johnson's belt had only to be loaded and primed.

He had scarcely dashed the powder into the pan, than a crackling of the brush advertised him of the danger.

Two men came blundering through, and saw him at the same time that he beheld them.

"Oh, here he is!" cried one.

"The first truth ever you spoke, and the last!" retorted Nittle.

He had but to extend his arm and the pistol almost touched the buccaneer.

The explosion resounded.

The man, a hole literally torn in his side, fell dying, with a howl of agony.

Ned had already started at the other man, who was calling out.

It was William Teach.

His arm had been hastily bound up, and he had been so full of rage and revenge as to have joined the pursuit.

"Ha ha," said Nittle, "the chap with my mark on! 'Spent your'e second luff, or master's mate! Something! Silence, or I'll stave your head in!"

He lifted up the young man and flung him upon his shoulder after the fashion of carrying bread bags.

"He'll come useful to the captain, I've a notion," muttered he.

Refreshed by his short rest, and but little embarrassed with his burden, the sailor crashed through the thorns, as if they were as brittle and and harmless as the frosting on a wedding cake.

Behind him, a score of men were pushing,

with many an oath and fierce halloa!

Guessing his way by the glimpses of the sunlit sky that he caught through gaps in the foliage, he came out on the seashore within a few yards of the boat.

The two men, who had been set on the alert by the firing and clamor, no sooner saw their comrade than they forestalled his wish by clearing the boat from the boughs.

Ned then flung Teach's body into the middle of the yawl like a bag of biscuits.

"Jump in and shove off!" cried he, stepping in himself and taking up an oar.

The two obeyed.

"The rest are coming?" queried one of these, as the noise of the breaking twigs echoed out.

"They will never come!" said Ned, gloomily.

"Never?"

"Never! never more haul the maintack inboard! never more clap thumb on cannon touch-hole!" answered Ned. "You're well off! Keep her steady while I step the mast."

He went forward and hastily ran the lower end of the mast through the hole in the port stroke-oar seat and lodged the square point in the socket firmly.

The pirates, with blackbeard in their van, swarmed down on the beach.

Ned camly shook out the sail and filled the sprit.

Then he passed aft to take the helm.

"Ship oars," said he. "They can't take us, for they'll have to go clear across the island to get their boat. And lets hear what the beggars are a-saying of."

At first, the buccaneers had recharged their pistols and levelled them.

But their captain had ordered them to uncock them, for the volley could scarcely fail to have some bullet in its number for William Teach.

"Hallo, the boat!" shouted Blackbeard.

"Hallo yourselves, you black-wiskered hairy looking cutthroat!" returned Ned, full of the consciousness of his power.

It was no moment to stand upon trifles.

"Give up that young man," said the pirate captain in a voice of some emotion. "Give him up, and I'll reward you—my word on it!"

"You go hang! You shan't see this specimint of the scum you command never again, as its in the watch bill keeping a lookout at a yard-arm end."

Bitter talk this for the ferocious depradator to be compelled to hear.

Ned's comrades enjoyed it all.

"I'll give you a ransom! What you will!" called out the chief from the shore, wading in, in his anxiety.

"O, no,! not for a neck'an'kercher full of guineas, old swab round your jaws! Take the short turn in that, and belay!"

"Oh, man! You are in our own trade, you Cruiser men! what do you want to make prisoners for?"

"I knows my duty, you impudent waking slush-bucket! We've rats aboard the Cruiser that are fat on picking buccaneer's bones!"

He gave the tiller ropes a touch, and the shivering sail began th take the wind.

When Blackbeard saw the boat about to sweep away, he was ready to burst with rage and grief.

The latter passion gained the upperhand.

William had been as a son to him.

They quarrelled daily, yet he could place that confidence in him which he durst not give to any other of his myrmidons.

"Oh, my boy! my boy!" exclaimed he, in really touching accents.

"Hold hard!" cried Nittle. "Your boy'l die soon! Who'd 'a thought he ever had a child. Take the helm, you!"

He jumped up.

"Your boy, is he?" shouted he, for the shore people to hear. "I woulden't let one of such a Jonah breed sail with me."

Blackbeard's spirits revived at the words.

"Aye! put about and land him! And ask your price!" cried he, eagerly.

Ned had lifted up the young man.

He had in being tossed into the boat, struck his skull against the headsheats and been stunned.

"Price?" repeated Ned, scornfully. I'd sell a cargo of such for a farthing, and chuck a penny in!

"Here's your hopeful!"

He grasped the still unconscious form, his hands apart, like one about to heave at a capstan bar.

"He's born to the hemp for mourning-ribbon!" said he, in the same taunting tone. "Water won't hurt him!"

As he spoke, with a powerful swing, he launched young Teach's body off the boat.

It splashed into the water, half disappeared, but floated.

There was a movement of the limbs as if the touch of cold water had restored him partly.

"I hear oars!" exclaimed one of the sailors.

Ned stepped over the seats to his place at the steering.

"Some of the rascals have got away all this time and passed the word. You'd better out oars."

The boat began to make way under sail and the pair of rowers.

In good time, for shots dipped into the ripple around it.

William Teach was moving his arms, but he was far from complete consciousness as yet.

Blackbeard waded still farther in, and, though he had on sea boots and three heavy pistols and a heavy hanger at his waist, resolutely let bottom to swim out to the floating man.

The boat had begun to feel the full force of the wind, lessened in shore by the intercepting forest.

A longboat, manned by six men pulling powerfully, was rounding the islet easily.

It went to pick up the captain, however, instead of attending to the fugitives.

Ned Nittle watched them draw Blackbeard and William Teach over the gunnel.

"They'll dance in the air yet, I'll warrant," muttered he. "Hallo! Pooh! those fellows can't dream of catching this yawl with their six oared tub! Pooh! grunted he, contemptuously.

It was Blackbeard's passion, not at all cooled by the water, that made his men begin to chase.

But the folly was evident.

The yawl bounced along under her sail faster than the oar's motion.

The pirates turned round before long.

"There! they've their eyes open," said Ned.

" Give 'em something cheering, lads ! I hope the breeze will let them hear it. Now ! with a will !"

And the three bawled out a little bit of personal scandal upon the illustrious Captain Teach, to the effect.

" I never was born for to be took by the blackbeard renegade who's only a green hand at the best, for one in the rowing trade !"

CHAPTER XXIV.

RETURNING WITH THE PIRATES TO LANCE—TEACH IN A SWEET HUMOUR—THE CHANCE FOR LIFE— THE FATAL PATH—THE LAND-EDDY.

If diabolical language would have dried wet clothes, Captain Teach would not have had to sit by the fire so long in the damp of his soaked apparel.

Discovering now that the Scarlet Cruiser touching at the islet had had nothing to do with his buried treasure, Teach determined to stay over the coming night on shore.

His men pretty well scoured the forests, and killed a few bags-full of birds and fat lizards that stewed up into tempting messes with the fruit.

Blackbeard hailed Loys as a fellow of his own kidney, that he rejoiced to feast.

But his hate to Lance made him clap the latter into such a prison as the cave afforded.

Genifrede would not share in the revelry, but kept company with the prisoner, whom she had revived on the beach apparently merely to let the sea skimmer wreak vengeance upon.

The pirates landed, except a handful to keep ship.

They brought ashore plenty of liquors, and broached the casks with so free a hand that that alone would have convinced honest men that they had never bought them.

After midnight, they were still at it.

The large fires, plentifully heaped up with resinous wood, showered a light upon the wild demons' forms and ferocious faces, clearer than noonday sun.

The savages were too drunk to dice or play cards, and were getting into the fighting mood fast.

Blackbeard was no exception.

His features were flushed, and his eyes shone with a savage glare, as on those days when he let his men pelt captives with broken bottles, or send them on the narrow way by a plank tilted on the bulwarks.

" Oh, I forgot that prisoner," said he, suddenly. " I'm so glad you saved him for me, old mate Loys."

Goupille grinned.

" He was fished up out of the surge by no hand of mine. My girl saw him stranded, and brought him to."

" What shall I do to have my spite out of him, Loys," queried Teach, snatching a horn goblet from the nearest man, and drinking the brandy brimming it. " I'm tired of wasting the wretches fingers at the binnacle lamp, of making them walk the plank, and as for hanging the rascals, I'm e'en a'most sick of looking on the living bunting going aloft."

Loys dipped his can into a cask of Hollans that had had its head most conveniently stove in.

" Come, come," said he, " he's not so bad a chap for a king's officer. If I was caterer to his mess, I'd give him a chance for his life if I should have to serve up his soup hot."

" Scalding hot," said Blackbeard, getting up on his feet with an effort, and steadying himself by the table. " He's got to pay the piper and no mistake for the tune he made William dance to."

William Teach, who drank to deaden the pain in his injured arm, grinned in accordance with the ' old man.'

" Baptist John, some of you who have your mouths full, hurry and lug that spy out of the burrow and drag him here," cried Blackbeard.

In a few minutes the three or four men were hauling Lance to the fires.

Behind the prisoner came Genifrede, her hair flowing loose, her hands clasped in appeal, and eyes full of terror.

" Sling him down on the boards, and be hanged to him !" snarled Teach, drinking again.

The men let go of Cavendish, who fell, bound as he was, on the hot sands near the fire.

The young man looked up firmly into the shining faces of the villains round about him.

Teach, trying to sober himself, was puzzling over some refinement of torture.

Meanwhile Genifrede had entreated Loys, enlarging on all that Cavendish had done for her.

Gradually she saw Loys' face brightening up.

" Keep quiet," said he to her, " I'll let him have something like fair play."

So, rising, he went a few steps from the canvas spread on the sand for a table, to where Blackbeard stood.

" Haven't you an idea," said the latter, " there's something in the brandy, for I cant couple two thoughts together."

" My idea is this," returned the Frenchman, " The poor wretch is a gallant heart, and he must have a chance to retain life."

" Avast heaving, mate," growled the chief of the vagrants of the sea, " there's no must where Blackbeard stands."

" You needn't fire up," said Loys, his own eyes flashing. " What I say is this. Let the swab-shouldered officer race for life, run the gauntlet, any thing but—black or whitebeard— he shall have a loophole open."

He looked at the ravager steadily.

" I mean it, added he."

Both carried their right hands to their belts.

Teach thought better of resistance, however.

A good many of the ruffains before him had belonged to Goupille's enrollment, and some of his own men were French or Spanish, who would sooner obey Loys than himself if it came to a conflict of commanders.

" No offence," said he, thereupon, as he let go the pistol-butt he had grasped, and offered his hand to the other.

" Not the least bit in the world," answered Loys, smiling.

The two tigers of the ocean knew very well what a hollow peace they were mutually agreeing to.

But one man's life was too petty a thing to bar their sailing along for a while yet.

Teach returned to the banqueters.

"Empty cups, and fill no more," cried he, in a thundering voice, "Dash them down, I say."

The ocean robbers grumblingly drained their drinking vessels.

"Now, get sober as much as you can. Babtist, cut loose this man, and watch him well."

They severed the cords around Cavendish, and let him recover from the cramps and stoppage of the circulation·

Genifrede dared not rejoice at this seeming lenience, for the savage smile of Blackbeard portended nothing very merciful.

"Hark ye, prisoner, traitor and spy, you merit browning over a slow fire," began Teach, " but my friend Loys here has interceded, and I'm going to behave like a lamb to ye."

The pirates showed their teeth in broad grins at the notion.

"You're a young man, but a bit benumbed by being tied up. Now my pets here a'int on an even keel, seeing how they've been at liquor. That makes the game even."

Blackbeard pointed to the forest, whose edge was a score of yards away.

"You shall have so much start. Make for the salt water. My men shall use nothing but steel upon you. If they overtake you before you dip foot in the brine, why—why—there's an end on ye, and good riddence !"

"But if you so much as damp a finger tip in a shallow on the beach, the raven of my flock that fleshes his beak on you, shall taste of red pepper lanted with a score of gashes in his hide !"

"All hear ?"

"Ay, that we do!"

The pirates nodded assent, and showed their impatience to begin the hunt for the human prey.

They put aside their firearms.

They lightened their dress to run better, and drew their belts tighter.

Lance made his preparations, too.

"It will only be anguish to her, if I die here under her eyes," thought he. "It will be best for me to fall in the dark thicket, in the death-grapple of some of these scoundrels !"

He could not believe he, so weak, could reach the haven through the mass of briars.

As no opposition was made to his doing what he could to aid himself in the flight for his life he had hastily bound up his feet in rude sandals of strips of canvass that was tough enough to keep out the thorns.

He had little to carry, as all his apparel was his shirt and trousers.

There was no use in delay.

So he drew himself up, boldly, and confronted the pirate chief.

"I am ready," said he.

"Stay!" said Loys.

The Frenchman took up a horn from the ground, and half filled it with spirits·

"No! no !" shouted the pirates. "As he is, let him run !"

"Peace, you young hounds," cried Goupille, haughtily. "If you clamor again I'll lend him sword and dagger—by this hand, I will !"

He turned to the prisoner.

"Take this stuff," said he, "when you get to the woods, toss it off and fly ! I've a liking for so brave a lad !"

Lance clutched the vessel.

"Good-bye," said he to Genifrede, who was held back by Loys.

One look he gave upwards, to see by what star he should be guided, and he began the task.

On reaching the forest trees he lifted up the horn to his lips.

"Long life to true hearts, and eternal death to the black-souled servants of the fiend !"

So he shouted, and poured the liqued fire into him.

Hurling the horn far from him towards the bloodhounds, he whirled round on his heels and plunged into the gloomy tangle.

With a loud whoop at his defiance, the hunters darted over the sand to pursue him.

The drink did wonders.

In an instant it had coursed to Lance's heart, and then was dispersed over all his exhausted system.

Every nerve burning, every vein leaping, he seemed to be lifted up on wings.

He was well nigh driven mad, that was the truth.

Straight on he went, only swerving for trees and rocks.

He never felt it at all as he crashed through the undergrowth where the twigs and thorns lashed and pierced him.

The pirates had spread out, so as to be sure not to let him escape, one side of them.

Lance could hear their calls to one another, and the screams of the birds fluttering up into the nightwind at such a noise as they made.

Lance had tried to keep straight on his way, but a small brook that ran down to the seaside, compelled him to take a turn.

That brought him back for some yards, and he ran nearly into the arms of a pirate.

Both came together so roughly that they were naturally stunned and surprised.

Cavendish recovered himself first.

Springing forward from the tree against which he had been dashed, he fell upon the still staggering ruffian.

Bringing him to the ground, the two, inter-locked in deadliest grapple, rolled over and over.

Lance saw, even in the shadow, that the fellow was opening his saucer mouth to call for help, and he summarily prevented that.

He had got hold of the sea-ravager's pistol, and he jammed its butt right into the man's jaws.

The next instant the lieutenant had the mastery.

In only a minute more, he left the man sense-less, and was flying away.

He had the pirate's cutlass in his hand.

It afforded him means to sell his life for a higher price.

Meanwhile, it came in handy for cutting away among the brush.

The pursuers were collecting together, and from stray words that came from them to the fugitive's ear, he believed they were in fear that they had overshot him.

As they "tried" back, Lance was worming on through a very thick clump of prickly pear.

He did not dare endeavour to go around it, as on both sides of him he heard the trampling of feet and the clatter of weapons.

At last, bleeding by a hundred gashes, he scrambled out of the thorns.

The aroma of the seaweed told him that he was near his goal.

He paused to take breath and listen.

He heard, not twenty yards from him, some three or four men who were stealing ahead of the line he was on.

There was no resource except to bear away a little to the right hand and plunge into the briars.

Unluckily, he had hardly thrust himself into the brambles a few steps than one of the twigs hooked on the hammer of the pistol that he had taken from the pirate, pulled it back, and let it fall.

The explosion scorched his side a little, but the bullet went down into the dead leaves on the ground.

"Here he is! there goes the swab!" shouted a dozen voices.

All were turned to that quarter instantly.

Lance uttered a yell of defiace, tossed the smoking pistol from him, and, steel in hand, struck away at the bushes.

The men after him, clothed thickly, or wearing leather breeches, could stamp through the prickles better than he.

They gained on him.

Five or six shots resounded, and the flash lit up the forest.

"Stop firing!" roared Blackbeard all at once. "He'll have a chance the more under cover of the smoke."

That was true enough.

Still Lance had crashed on.

Better a lacerated skin than the torments the sea-demons might devise.

The pursuers and the chased man were so close now that he heard their every motion.

The noise they made drowned his steps.

Finding some easy way, three of the pirates had darted on, and were now in advance of Cavendish.

The sea-shore was inside a biscuit toss.

But this trio were between the strand and the the young lieutenant.

"It's a scrimmage alone can clear the way," muttered Cavendish, grasping the cutlass convulsively, "Somebody's got to be beaten, and sink me! it shan't be me!"

So saying, he jumped out of cover.

He found himself on the grass of a small glade.

The three men were so surprised by his bold and unexpected appearance, that, only one of them had his hanger drawn.

Lance cut down one of the others at the very instant that he laid his hand on a weapon in his belt.

The birds overhead shrieked dismally as the man howled forth his last breath in agony.

Cavendish did not look to see the effects of that stroke.

Whirling his sword upward again, he let it fall a second time, and it only ceased to cut after having cleft another of the ocean rascals clean through the collar-bone.

He missed his footing, and fell to the sod, his neck and breast being instantly deluged with blood.

His sudden fall nearly wrenched the entangled blade out of the young lieutenant's hand.

The latter held firm nevertheless, and the metal being poor stuff, the cutlass broke a few inches from the loosened hilt.

The last of the three, who had his sword out, had been too much astonished and horrified to intervene yet.

It was not until Lance lifted the fragment of blood-dripping iron upon him that he remembered himself.

The lieutenant, full of desperation at being so near the promised safety and yet in danger of failing to attain it, did not see with his passion, filled eyes that so little of a weapon had been left to him.

So, when he delivered a cut, he struck much too short.

That helped him.

For the force of his attack threw him forward under the arm of the pirate.

Up came the whole mass of pursuers.

It was "do or die!" now.

Their hands were already extended, armed with firearms or pointed steel.

Take him alive—take him alive! or I'll be the death of some of you!" cried Blackbeard, trampling over some cactus plants.

Lance did not wait for that.

Taking advantage of the pirates changing their pikes and hangers from right to left hand to grasp him, he wrenched himself from the embrace of the one who had clutched him.

Fierce as a hungry tiger, he struck out right and left, and cleared a space around him.

They formed a ring enclosing him.

He flung himself at the weakest point, but two men were there.

They might as well have tried to stop a shark in its career as to check Lance Cavendish, who heard the wash of the sea just before him.

Bruised and maimed he left them both, as he flew between them.

"Hurrah" shouted he. "Oh, you driftwood of the sea that you sicken, no ten of you can beat an honest tar."

Recovering from the defeat, all followed.

But the sailor, knee deep in the water stood breathless but undaunted bleeding but defiant, on the promised place of salvation.

He in the water, stood calmly waiting.

They, hot with the flush of shame as well as the exertion, glared at him, and threatened him with pike, pistol, and axe.

"Remember your pledge," said Lance, steadily, to Blackbeard.

"Remember your oath," said Loys de Goupille, leaning on his long rapier.

"Ay, remember the oath!" said a third voice, so low that none noticed it if they heard it.

Blackbeard, still frowning, lowered his hand reluctantly.

"I s'pose I must," muttered he. "Well, the match is off till next time. Can't be helped my sea-dogs," continued he, to his men.

They were scowling, not a bit less pleasantly than he.

"Put up the toad stickers and carvers," resumed the chief of marauders, "and uncock the barkers!"

"Not afore I have my shot for his spiling my messmate!" growled one of the gang.

With that he stepped forward down the beach, pistol primed.

"No you don't!" said Loys de Goupille, pressing forward.

He pushed ahead of the man and snatched the pistol from him.

The fellow made a snatch at his cutlass, but Loys, with his hand like iron, tore belt and weapon from his waist and hurled all far off into the sea.

"Then blast my eyes!" cried the ruffian, in rage. "I'll see what flesh hammers can do!"

He lifted his clenched fist, and sprang away from Loys towards Lance.

Lance, to wary to let the furious scoundrel charge him while he was so deep in the sand and water, moved in shore to meet him.

Blackbeard smiled to himself.

The pirate who was so bent on engaging Cavendish was a powerful bully, who seemed sure to win.

Teach would most liked to have been the death of the lieutenant himself, but the presence of Goupille restrained him.

"Captain," cried the Frenchman to him, "You swore you'd strike the life out of anyone who harmed that noble young fellow after he had won the race!"

"If I shoot now, it might be said I tried to kill the prisoner," returned the chief, playing with his pistol. "See, they have caught hold of one another."

So they had.

Lance had been sufficiently rested by that short space to make him no mean antagonist.

The salt water made his wounds smart so that that alone nigh drove him wild.

Then again, he knew too well the cruel spirits of the ocean thieves to believe that Loys de Goupille would care to risk all to save him.

It was clear that Captain Teach was in no hurry to redeem his pledge, and hoped that he would be slain in the strife.

At least he would leave his mark on more than one of the merciless band before they should stain their feet in the blood of his corpse.

All these thoughts flitted through his brain in half a breath.

He caught the wrists of the pirate rushing at him, to prevent him striking him down.

Then, the two, Lance having underhold, went at it in the wrestle.

The lieutenant had never so thirsted for the blood of a fellow being.

It was such an extremity of cowardice, for the wretch to set upon him, when he had been hunted so cruelly through the forest.

He tightened his grasp till the bloop spirted out through the many scratches on his fingers.

The pirate felt, where the pressure came, as if vices were screwed shut upon him.

In vain he writhed—in vain his only thought now was to escape from the fate that he had sought to inflict.

He tried to bite the hands that held him so firmly.

Lance bore him downwards, spite of the digs of his teeth into his arm.

He bent back to work one hand loose.

Lance took advantage of the movement, by throwing himself on him with all his power.

The footing was shifting in the sand.

The two staggered, and seemed ready to fall.

They heard a groan come from the pirate's suddenly whitened lips, as he was bent double so abruptly.

Cavendish heard a faint snap as the spine was dislocated, and felt the strong man's powerful frame settle into a limp mass.

In horror he let go his hold.

A spasm swept over the pirate's body, as it measured its length on the strand.

Life had departed.

But the last tremor in the broken spine-cord gave a twitch to every perishing nerve, and, while the eyes of the still warm corpse leered awfully, the jaws moved into a ghastly grin.

Cavendish leaped away from the horrid sight.

The pirates had beheld all, for, ager to view the contest, several had flashed powder in the pans of their pistols, and lighted branches of dwarf pine.

On seeing the lieutenant recoil towards them, triumphant from the conflict with their brother in crime, they ground their teeth in rage.

"He brought it on himself," said Loys. "He's more than earned peace from you!"

The crew looked to Blackbeard, who said nothing.

The men were undecided upon that, and the first outburst of their anger might have passed harmlessly,

But Cavendish was too excited to wait for them to decide.

He lifted up his voice in coldly cutting tones.

"You dastardly beach-combers," stormed he, "you fresh water rowboatmen! you pack of sea spiders! you castaway deadeyes! you scum that a seaman wouldn't spoil a bucket of slush by flinging it over ye—come on, and do the bravest act of your crawling lives—cut me to pieces!"

The sneer was so vehement that the vilest of them felt some shame in assailing the weak and unarmed man.

But the torrent of abuse that he poured out on them stirred up the dregs of their brutal nature.

Lance rejoiced to see their faces covered with fury once more, for he only wished for death.

One took the lead, and advanced.

Calmly the lieutenant awaited his approach.

He might, or he might not, be able to wrest the cutlass away, and begin a struggle, fruitless as it might be. "Stand!" shouted Goupille, waving his long sword.

The ruffians hesitated, and looked towards their leader.

But Blackbeard turned away.

"I'll make him a useless man that stirs a foot after I speak!" cried Loys, fiercely.

"Hold your noise!" said William Teach. "We want no soft hearts within hail of we rovers, eh lads!"

"Not we!"

"Seize him!" said William, then.

Half a dozen flung themselves on Loys and disarmed him.

"And upon the long-tongued scamp, that talks so bold to our faces!" continued the pirate. "Down with him!"

The cry found a mighty echo and all seemed over with the lieutenant, the centre for so many deadly points and muzzles to be bent upon.

"Fly!" cried Loys, who was struggling to get free. "Out on the spit of sand, my boy!"

There was a long strip, scarcely broad enough for a van to run along, that jutted out for about thirty feet, and ended among a few rocks.

Part of it was sand and part of it was shingle, and at high tide it was always covered.

Inspired with a sudden desire for the existence that he had been ready to lay down, the lieutenant bounded away, splashed though the few inches of water, and ran out along the edge of the sand.

The pirates turned, and proceeded on his track.

They had to go in single file.

That was one thing in favour of the fugitive.

If he could reach the end of the point, the high rocks there would shield him from pistol shots.

He strained every nerve to do so, giving all his energies to that, and not glancing behind.

He had all but attained the rocks when he heard a strange series of cries behind him.

So singular were they, that he could not help looking back.

To his amazement, the most of his hunters, still moving, seemed cut in halves!

Only their bodies were above the level of the moist path.

Then only their waists, and, still sinking, they bid fair to going down to their armpits.

The ground had been shaky to Lance's light tread. The heavy boots of the pirates had churned the sand into motion, and mixed up the water with it.

There was a circling movement in the quicksand, and the whirl so increased in force that the engulphed men were spun round faster and faster, proclaiming that they had fallen into the power of a land-eddy.

The ones thus entrapped dropped their weapons and tried to scramble out.

But there was no foothold in the yielding stuff, and nothing to grasp to pull themselves out with.

The more they sought to tread water or wade out of the snare, the deeper and faster they settled in the slough.

It was folly to seize hold of a neighbour, for if they lifted themselves an inch by that means, it was at the cost of burying themselves deeper in the next moment.

This grappling one another caused angry words, and blows very quickly after them.

So the wretches were to be seen perishing in the quick sand, their hands on one another's throats.

Three out of ten escaped.

Two were near enough in shore to get upon less shifting ground, and then on dry sand.

The other had been the foremost, and had been so close upon Cavendish's heels as to have passed over the danger almost as happily as he.

Only hindered by the edge of the eddy catching him, this fellow would have been able to have arrested Lance, but that the scene behind him had enchained his steps.

There was indeed an awful fascination in seeing those companions in crime dragged under, as though by some unseen but irresistible hand.

They had disappeared to their necks, but their arms waved desperately for a time.

But the seaset force never ceased its work.

They had to descend slowly, but surely.

At length, only the heads, with swollen eyeballs and mouths, blue with discolouration, and open from the effects of strangulation, remained above the mire of sand and brine, broken with bubbles that contained the last grasps of the wretches!

A pause, but not a silence, for sobs and smothered groans formed a last appeal to the inevitable.

The next instant, all that was human was vanished.

Not a lock of hair floated on the whirl, while the sweeping motion ceased, and the disturbed grains floated back to form again that straight and narrow way which had been a path of death to so many.

Blackbeard had viewed the absorption of his Hectors with affright.

When his amazed eyes could see no more of the strugglers, he uttered a howl of rage.

"Seize that scoundrel, Baptist!" screamed he to the pirate who had reached the rocks, and stood beside Lance. "Cut him to pieces for being the bait to the desert's trap!"

That shout startled the man to whom it was addressed.

It made him eager to avenge the wicked spirits drawn from the surface of the earth as though destined for the abodes below.

Cavendish was too much spent now to offer much resistance, and that would have been less than nothing towards Baptist, who was comparatively fresh, and had his cutlass poised over him.

Shapeless he gathered himself together to finish this too long and too unequal a contest.

Loys was wrestling with those who held him.

Blackbeard was applauding his man's readiness to obey.

At that juncture, during the silence that fell around, a shot resounded.

And all beheld the would-be executioner forget his intended stroke as the bullet overtook him.

It needed but a slight push from Cavendish for him to hurl the wounded Baptist back into the quicksand.

The eddy was no more loth to swallow the corpse than it had been to gulp down the animated.

"Who fired that shot?" cried Captain Teach, looking around.

"I!"

So replied a voice, soft and feeble, but steady of tone.

And Genifrede stepped out of the brake, the smoking pistol in her slight hand.

She was breathless with running through the mazes of the wood, and pale with the exertion, but not a jot abashed by the fierceness of the pirate chieftain's gaze.

"I did it!" repeated she, firmly. "And that is but little to what I would do for the man that I love!"

CHAPTER XXV.

THE BUCCANEERS IN PORT—THE JOLLY BOS'N TAVERN—THE LEAGUE AGAINST THE CRUISER—THE EAVESDROPPER'S REVENGE ON THE BETRAYER.

THE English buccaneers in these days so favoured Matanzas, among other places, that one broad place near the Long Jetty, was commonly known as the Plaza de los Ingleses. (The Englishman's Square).

The chief feature among its sides of huts and frail houses, was one stone building, standing near a canal.

It had been an old powder magazine some years before.

But Patsy Maclarrup had bought the place with some money that he had made by some little rioting on the ocean, and turned it into a house of carousel.

He called it the "Jolly Bos'n," and painted the sign himself, with three or four roaring drinkers, who were only to be known as boatswains by their whistles of silver, which he had suspended around the painted necks with real chains.

This combination of art and reality had drawn great praise upon the Irishman.

The governor of Matanzas and the chief inhabitants had been rather uneasy of late.

For four or five fast vessels, of different tonnage but equally wicked looking, had entered the harbour and moored there.

Their men, regular whiskerandoes, used to come ashore of nights and startle all honest folk (few enough in the town) with songs about

"With Teach, and Kyd, and Lolonnais,
    We may yet go to hang;
But they are the blades we hail,
    As leaders of the gang!"

Pretty soon the different rovers found their chums, and made certain of the taverns their regular haunts.

The crew of the "Mortal Arrow," the brig belonging to the noted Philippe Lolonnais, selected Mr. Maclarrup's hostelry to get drunk in.

This night, about eleven, the whole band were holding their orgie in the large room.

In the back parlour, if one may call a little box of a chamber so, there was their captain and four other men.

Loys de Goupille and Teach, who had made up their quarrel; Teach having been content to leave Lance Cavendish on the desolate island.

The remaining two were the bluff visaged Captain Kyd, an old chum of Blackbeard's, and Brasilano (a mysterious Portuguese, whose name was never known).

They formed a new circle of faces, faces browned and heavily moustachioed mouths.

They were armed to the teeth, and wore the usual holiday attire of successful marauders.

That is, plenty of the precious metals and stones glittered on their coats and hats, in lace, in buttons, in clasps and plumeagraffes.

There were two seamen at the door who watched that their officers should not be interrupted.

The latter kept their heads close together and spoke in under tones.

So earnest became their colloquy that they neglected their wines and insensibly raised their voices.

"Enough," said Captain Kyd, "I've come down to the Mexican Gulf to elude some of the king's ships. If you mean business, I'm ready to steer my little 'Venom-cup' at the enemy!"

"By the candles burnt before all the saints!" swore Brasilano, rattling his sword in its gilt sheath. "I can't bear the idea that any but myself and my friends should skim over these seas and snatch the game out of our claws! By the ever living flames below, I cry war against the Scarlet Cruiser!"

Loys nodded.

"I shan't rest!" said he, "till I stand on her deck a victor."

A laugh, suppressed so that none of the ocean terrors heard it, seemed to be given under their very feet,

"Or she lies fathom deep in the main," went on the Frenchman.

Blackbeard and Lolonnais moved their heads in assent.

The former had his personal spite against the Cruiser for having sunk his brig.

As for Lolonnais, he wanted no rivals to interfere with his greed for treasure, Kyd and his allies being quite enough.

"Agreed!" said Loys, "It's a bargain then?"

"Yes. We'll hunt the interloper to death!"

Again that laugh might have been heard, if they had been less intent on themselves.

"Right," went on Goupille. "What pleasure can a bold son of the steel and torch have on the broad ocean when we don't know at what moment the Cruiser may be clearing away her long gun to drive a red hot shot into one's vitals?"

"Oh, to be sure, we must make the audacious young cub knock under," observed Captain Kyd, between two gulps of Amontillado wine.

"We can sail to-morrow night, eh?" queried Loys.

"My ship's ready," said one.

"And mine! and mine!" echoed the rest.

"One of the crew of the Wolf of the Wave is in town. He came with a boat's crew, but the rest went back to their barque. She is high and dry on the Lesser Cat Island, about fifty hours sail from here if the right wind prevails."

There came a knock at the door.

"Our man," observed Loys. "Come in," said he in a louder voice.

The man who entered was a rough looking chap, in sailor's trousers and the Scarlet Cruiser red shirt, only that he had buttoned up a large freize dreadnought over it.

He doffed his Dunkirk cap, and scraped his foot to the party.

The buccaneer leaders merely glanced at him.

"Any thing fresh?" enquired Loys.

"No, captain," returned the new comer. "The barkie is banked in on the sand, and, 'less there comes a hard blow, the water won't lift her off."

"Good. Here is your reward for the intelligence."

"Now, mind't'll be a bad thing for you if you play us false."

"I have given you the true bearing, captain," rejoined the man, meeting the Frenchman's eye without turning.

"All the better for you. For I and Blackbeard and Brasilano, and Lolonnais and Kyd, are just the men to follow a double-betrayer to the confines of the earth, and jump after him into Davy Jones's locker, but that he should reap his reward!"

"Very well captain, I speak to you fair, I can't do any more, and what's the use of me taking Bible oaths."

"You can go. You had better make yourself scarce, in case we leave any of your old friends to go hunting after you."

"Thank 'ee kindly, master," returned the fellow, grinning. "I've a berth on the molasses drogher, bound to Havanna, for my skin would be bored like a wormeaten hulk, if any of the Scarlets should light on me arter this."

"That's your lookout."

"Wish you success, my noble skippers!" said the man, edging away to the door.

As he was going forth, he was muttering:

"Forty doubloons made by that! Ah, who says a little treachery won't sell well!"

And a voice, as if issuing from the ground, seemed to respond to his terrified ears—

"Digger of a pitfall for another, beware thyself!"

Loys and his friends started.

"What's that, man?" they cried, for they had caught the words indistinctly. "What are you mouthing over, you knave?"

"Nothing!" answered the trembling man. "I——I thought somebody spoke!"

"Get out! you're drunk——go! I say go!"

The sailor left the chamber hastily.

"It must have been fancy," muttered he; "for how could those strange words come from Captain Frank, when all the men went back to the island with him?"

While he hugged this idea to himself, to lull a growing apprehension of that judgment befalling him which his faithlessness richly merited, the pirate leaders had resumed their conversation.

Loys showed them a paper that he had received from the traitor, being a chart of the place where the Cruiser was.

"Good!" said Brasilano, pulling down his shaggy forelock over a large scar on his brow. "It's a bit of smooth sailing. We've only to land and drive the red shirted knaves off the island into the sea."

"Wish 'twere as easily done as said," muttered Blackbeard, the late fight with Ned Nittle and his handful being fresh in his mind.

"I'll go aboard," said Kyd, "and get ready to call off my men; they can get sober between decks all to-morrow."

"I'll go with you, Loys," said Lolonnais; "I want to see the pair of pistols you spoke of, that Sir Henry Morgan shot down the Governor of Chagres with."

"Come on," said Goupille, "I'll make you a present of them if they should take your fancy."

13

Teach, Loys, and Lolonnais, swaggered off in company.

Kyd and Brasilano went their way out of the tavern.

The sentries at the door of the chamber, gladly left guard and joined their mates, halloaing over the liquor in the big room.

Soon after they had gone, a man entered the little room.

He struck his heel on the floor four times.

Then he moved away the table and lifted up a square in the floor.

The head of a youth appeared in the trap, and Frank Rogers leaped up from under the flooring, where he had overheard (underheard?) the pirate commanders' plot.

"Not so very roomy a lodging, Patrick," remarked the young captain, stretching his legs and throwing up his arms.

"No, surr, for I've throyed it moisilf, sure," returned Maclarrup.

For it was no less a dignitary than the sovereign master of the Jolly Boatswains, the speaker.

He was a shortish compactly built Irishman, with a good humoured face, very brilliantly illuminated by the reflections from his hair.

This crop was not auburn, or chestnut, or any fancy colour, but downright flaring, scorching red.

When he had been aboard ship, his companions used often to propose that they should discharge the cannon by letting Patsy lay his head on the guns, or station him in the shrouds as a signal lantern, or forbid him ever going near the powder room.

"It's not a large place," went on he, "but I thrust it served your designs, surr?"

"Quite. I heard all they were up to. You have had that traitor secured?"

"Ned Nittle was lying in wait for him at the door, and he s'cured him under their very eyes, widout lettin' him give the laste taste of a squale to warrn thim at all at all."

"He shall be attended to, all in good time," said Frank, frowning. "I came near ruining all ——"

"Now did you, surr?"

"Yes. My feelings made me speak so loudly that they heard me——"

"Oh, jabers!"

"I had made up my mind to pistol the first that should open the trap, but luckily they thought it was that faithless rogue of mine, and turned him out."

"That was foin," said Maclarrup, wagging his head.

"Now, to business; I have enough men to make a rush in upon those half drunden swaggerwells——"

"Whole-drunken," corrected the landlord; "they were half-drunken an hour ago. But they made me and my John roll in a cask of Jamaikey, and sorra a won in thim can walk two steps on any chalked line but a cruked wan."

"All the easier, then, to tie them hand and foot!"

"Oh, you needn'n go to try to do that, surr. There's no thrusting thim wild cats; they're so cute at pulling the thrigger that two or more would rise the divil's own rumpus if they was let have a chance, drunk as they are. No, surr, you l'ave it to me."

"How can you alone master some forty such?"

"It's a little saycret," returned the Irishman, mysteriously, "but I don't mind lettin' the sillybrated captain of the Scarlet Cruiser into the puzzle. Would you be plazed to come wid me?"

Frank nodded and prepared to follow the innkeeper.

The latter took one of the candles off the table and blew the others out.

"Sure I hate to be wasting foin wax candles on thim piratical spalpeens," said Patsy, "It's mutton-fat rushlights that would be too *sheep* for the likes o' thim!"

He laughed at his own wretched joke, for the young captain was too intent on his thoughts to smile, even from courtesy.

Maclarrup opened a side door in the wall, and led the way through a very narrow passage for about twenty yards, making one turn.

"This intry goes half around the big chamber," said he, in a whisper, "ye se's them imps of the ocean inj'ying thimselves, the saints between us and sich enj'yments, say I! On'y luk, surr, at their divilment!"

He had slipped back a small slide in the wall, and they could see into the large hall.

A long table of solid slabs of mahogany ran up the middle, flanked by benches.

On these lay sprawled and sate, nearly half a hundred of rude fellows, their faces garnished with untrimmed beards, and their belts on, strung with weapons.

They were principally engaged in drinking, pouring down hot punch, and liquors equally as fiery, into them as if they were proof against the compounds.

Some had had their quantums, and had been tenderly kicked into the corners and had had their boots, the empty flaggons, and bottles heaped up over them.

Some more had the whim seize them to eat, and, with their knives (the same that had often and again flashed in the heat of battle) were making laughable attempts to carve wild turkies and rounds of beef, set in wooden trenchers before them.

Two couples were trying to dance in a limited space on the floor, little caring if they stamped on some of the insensible drunkards strewn here and there.

They had no music to their dancing, unless the songs that were roared out in snatches every now and then by some sailor who wanted to clear his throat before applying to the rummers again.

"Oi'll be back soon," said Maclarrup, to the young commander; "in half a minute. I must get my man John out of harm's way, before I begin my operations."

"Very well."

Frank was left alone to gaze on the scene of tumult.

Presently he beheld Patsy, staggering under a huge bowl of reeking aguardiente, on the top of which was a rich and luscious froth of cinnamon, lemon peel slicings, spice, nutmeg, and still undissolved sugar.

The pirates managed to clear their eyes at this crowning temptation.

"Hooray!" cried one at the head of the board. "By the long nine-pounder of the

Mortal Arrow! the Mick is an Irishman that the whole world of merry red-noses should be proud of!"

Patsy set the bowl on the table.

" Be gar! Patrice," said a one-eyed French-man, smiting the board with his hand, " fill me out one gallon, and I will drink him down widout taking one breat', morbleu!"

" Donner!" cried a Hollander, as Patsy gave a stir with the ladle and made the steam rise and spread till it condensed and fell in aromatic and appetising drops. " Thunder and flashes of forked lightening, come aboard mit our ship, und ve veel keep you makin' de grog from mornin' till night und gif you more a tree t'ousand guadruples a week. Yaw!"

All made a snatch for the cups of hot liquor, and but that the bowl was somewhat of the largest, its hot contents would have failed to go around.

Even the sleepers stirred as if eager to partake.

While the greedy guzzlers were quarrelling, Patsy and his servant left the room and carefully closed the door behind them.

In another minute, the landlord was beside Frank in the narrow passage again.

" Hope to hiven I've not kep' you waitin' too long, cap'en," said he; " I've had to soother down thim vill'ins, that was all."

" I saw you serve up some glorious looking punch. I can scent it here."

" Thrue for you. It's a foin tickle-palate for a Toby Tosspot, on'y I've added a swatener of sand-berries unbeknown to 'em——"

" Poison them?"

" Is it p'isen guests of moin under moy own roof—under the Jolly Bosins! Sure, I've ruffled the feathers of many a party burrd, but I never wud go so far as to sind men to sleep altogether. Oh, no, it's only to make them slumber for some hours. Look now into the room while I set the machinery to worrk."

So saying, he laid hands on a large iron lever and pulled its upper end out of the wall towards him.

" This was a prison wanst, cap'en," remarked he, " and there's more tricks in it than this that I'm a showing of you, surr."

The bar worked on a hinge, or a ball and socket-joints, at its other end.

When it had been depressed sufficiently, it seemed to release something heavy, for which a loud sound was audible.

" It runs rusty, cap'en," said Patsy, by way of explanation. " I niver used it but twice, to get some drunken sailors under hatches whin there was on'y me and some wimen in the house."

" The ceiling's falling in!" exclaimed Frank, suddenly.

" Oh, no! look quietly, surr, look quietly!"

A grating sound, like the grinding of an endless chain over wheels, was continuous.

The pirates, intent on the liquor alone, were clamouring out, when one of them silenced the mass with a powerful shout, and volunteered a song.

At that moment, Frank had seen the ceiling of the large room move, and move downwards.

But a glance assured him that it was not falling in.

The floor and the roof kept the same distance apart, but were descending together.

Patsy chuckled.

" That's a blyssid sort of a tune they are hammering at," said he, " when they're expe-riencing such tratement!"

For, while they were unconscious of the chamber bearing them all below the ground level, they were bellowing this evil song :

" Down in the depths the dead folks dwell,
As far from the earth as they're near to hell.
The air above fans their corpses no more,
But they boil in the heat that flows from Satan's
　　door.
How did they come to the depths below?
It is the rover's grim labour of woe!
It is the rover's grim labour of woe!
　　　By fire and lead,
　　　By gaps in the head,
　　　By thrusts to the heart,
　　　By poisonous dart
That's how they sank to the depths below."

And while the demoniac chant issued from their blasphemous lips, the fiendish crew were being lowered.

To Frank's amazement, as the ceiling came to the level of his eyes, he perceived that its upper surface was a floor, just like the room beneath it.

The resemblance even went so far as to have this second apartment furnished with a similar long table and benches.

Still singing, the large timbers had enclosed the vanished pirates.

Their voices, smothered by the intervening mass, sounded like a hollow groan.

" Shall I bear on still more, cap'en," asked Patsy. " In five minutes, that whole box will be in the canal, and they will be choked, ivery mother's son o' thim (if sich blaguards of the sea iver had mothers) choked like kittens in a bag!"

" No! I am not the one to wish the vilest of mankind to be cut off from existence wantonly."

" All right, surr; on'y it's little the rest of mankind wud notice their loss, surr; but it's jist as you plaze, surr, jist as you plaze!"

So saying, the Irishman let the bar rise into its former position.

They went around the passage and stepped into the newly produced room.

It required but a little activity on the part of Patsy and his men to scatter bottles and dishes around so as to complete the likeness to the disappeared halls.

When lighted up as profusely as the one under foot now, had been, the keenest eyed would have had to inspect it closely to understand the clever operation so magically performed.

" Call in all my men," ordered Frank. " And have the disguises brought in here."

Ned Nittle, Bill Bowse and others, making up the number of thirty well-armed men, tramped into the hall, and saluted their youthful leader.

In their midst, carefully guarded, was their late comrade, he who had so villanously sold the secret of the Scarlet Cruiser's whereabouts.

" Report, Nittle?" said Frank.

The seaman stepped forward, his tarpaulin in hand.

" I kept watch by the door, captain. Out comes Mayrick, and me and Jack brings him to. We finds this bag of shiners stowed away under his pistol-jacket."

With that he banged the leather pouch of coins down on the table.

"What's all this for?" said the prisoner, determined to brazen it out. "Can't a man come ashore to have a swig of a flowing can and see a girl but his own mates grab him like a wrecker seizing a box of goods. Come now, I've only desarted, make the most of it!"

"Mayrick," said the young captain, sternly, "you should have remembered that the diggers of pitfalls should take heed that they do not fall into them themselves!"

At these so solemnly spoken words, the wretched fellow turned pale.

"I——I confess!" howled he. "Mercy! Mercy!"

And he dropped upon his knees.

"It was the lives of a hundred men which depended on you," replied Captain Rogers. "The messmates who too long have been kind to you are the ones to pronounce your rightful doom."

All looked savagely on Mayrick.

"In favour of letting the self convicted traitor free, to end his miserable life elsewhere, hold up their hands!" said the captain.

The captain ran his eyes eagerly along the rows, but not a hand was shown in his favour.

"All who say death!"

"Death! death to the betrayer!" shouted the thirty, like one man.

Mayrick felt that he was as certainly lost as if the halter was around his throat.

"Since I am to suffer!" thundered he in desperation, "I shall drag one soul down to blazes with me!"

And he flung himself forward, to the head of the table where the leader stood.

Frank lifted a pistol, cocking it at the same time.

"Doan't foire," shouted Patsy. "You'll murther some of us. There! he's settled widout any n'ise or smoke!"

Sure enough, for Maclarrup, hurling a three-legged stool at Mayrick, had been so skilful as to send the man to the floor like a poleaxed bull.

They lifted the seaman up, but he breathed but a few seconds longer.

"He's gone to his account," said the captain. "Move him away. We have important business to dispatch now."

*   *   *   *   *

Towards the twilight in the morning, Captain Lolonnais came ashore and proceeded to the Jolly Bos'ins to see in what state his crew were.

He was a good deal surprized to find the windows of the tavern all alight, and loudly resounding a seaman's ditty to this effect:—

"We never did flinch,
Nor give back an inch,
For sweet Revenge was all the cry!
We scorn for to run
From a son of a gun,
But with sword in our fist, we will conquer or die!"

"They sing the right stuff," observed Lolonnias, entering the door, "but the wine has roughened their voices so that I would not have known them."

He pushed open the large room door, but started back on the threshold.

He never was more astonished in his life.

There were a parcel of fellows at the board, sure enough.

They were wrapped up in jackets, Guernsey shirts, and oilskins coats, and many wore their sowwesters and tarpaulins, all as if they had been used to cold climates and had not seen fit yet to conform to West Indian weather.

At the head of the table sat a large Dutchman, who had a big schiedam before him, to which he paid his devotions very regularly.

As Lolonnias stood at the door, spellbound at the strangers peopling the scene, Patsy Maclarrup crossed the room to him.

"What the deuce does this mean?" demanded the pirate captain. "Where are all my men?"

"Don't you know? oh, worra!" said Patsy lugubriously, and rubbing one eye with his knuckles.

"Don't I know, what? Where are my men?"

"Gone!"

"Gone?"

"Ivery man of them, with all their young cannons in their belts, and their rib-ticklers," blurted out the Irishman mournfully. "Soon after you had gone away, noble captain, there was a pack of yellow girls, thim flaunting ribboned mulattresses that never comes for good, and they wint arrm and arrm, a man and a girl, and they tould me to till Old Scaramouchlby, which they mint your honor if you plaze! that they were off to Old Mother Quasha's house in the Mountains."

"Levanted, by thunder!" ejaculated the pirate chieftain. "I thought they were too drunk to stand!"

"The girls brought unripe guavas with them, and after making the poor lads as sick as dogs, bedad, they were sober enough all of a suddint."

"I tould thim that the master (maining your noble self) wud be angered at their laving the ship in the lurch; but wan iv the lot, him in a big hairy cap, gave me a skelp on the side of the head, and whin I waked out of the senselessness, they was gone, like the snow of last winter, and laving not one to the fore."

Lolonnias uttered a long string of curses.

"The govenor wud sind the sogers afther thim, av your honor was to salve his palm," suggested Patsy.

"Oh, I know. He would get all the money he could out of me, and say he had ordered all the garrison to go hunting for the runaways, and he would stick to his story till either my purse, or my patience ran short. I've cruised too many years in these latitudes to let the hungry Spaniards feed fat on me!"

Lolonnias curled his mustachio ends fiercely.

"Well," broke in Patsy consolingly, "its good that its no worse. In a week you can collict a much finer crew of nenerdowells to man your purty craft."

"In a week!" roared the pirate, so fiercly that Pat gave a great jump. "I must be in the offing to morrow night."

"Is it to morrow night you say? oh! now, if you only could talk to him—But may be you would'nt like—But then again, they're such rollicking boys—"

"What's all that disjointed talk about?"

"Oh," returned Pat, "all that I'm afther aiming is, you can aisy fill up your vessel. Here's a mynheer with his men. Their clumsy sea-tub is that wreck you must have seen on the rocks under the fort. They ran on the reef, and bilged their craft. Since then, they've been spending their coin all about the town, and now the're running short, they come to my poor place. Oh, weirasthru! it's my luck! it's a big score ag'in 'em already with what they've had, an' they're calling for more!"

In fact, the drinkers were swearing at the man John for his delay in supplying their wants.

"Oh! Captain darlint," said Patsy mournfully, "if you could but take thim off my hands. I'm ruined entirely wid them!"

"They seem a sturdy set of rascals," remarked Lolonnais, examining the revellers.

"Oh, they are all that! rare divils, ivery man jack of thim! and none too honest, not they! Sure it's not gone long since I heard them tillin stories of smuggelin—and, piracy are twin-brothers, or pretty close in the same family!"

"I must have men," muttered Lolonnais.

"And there they are, forenens you master. They'll go for the axin, I'll warrant. And I'll inrol mesilf, too, bedad, an' I will!"

"You!"

"For why not? I've been a rover on the main, did you niver hear of Vernon and Ogle? I sailed before the masts of the two of thim! An I'm sick of land. Oh, captin,' this is a chance I delight in, to cruise under such an Admiral of Iniquity as your noble self!"

The pirate chief appeared to listen to the Irishman, but he was really studying the figures before him.

"Is it a bargain, surr?" inquired Pat. "It is? Thin, good bye to dry land, and welcome the rocking cradle of the foretop in a five hundred and fifty knot snazer! Hoorooh!"

And Pat cut a caper and struck off several extravagant steps in the sailor's hornpipe.

"It's pack up my kit I will, at once, and where's the strake of lightening to aiquil the way I'll laeve my man John to manage the Bos'ns? Oh, but youve a diamond of sea desperadoes, me jewel, Captain Lolonnais!"

"Ill go to the side room. Send in that Dutchman who seems head of the rollickers."

"I will, surr. He's the captain. By name, Nicolhas Schweibreechen. It's no wonder, muttered Pat as he let Lolonnais into the little room where the pirate chief had sate at council, and returned to the carousing seamen, it's no wonder at all that the worrld should be a hard one whin thim Dutchmen with such names prospers, and the rispictable families of Maclarrup of Bolobally, Slambocklish, niver rises to avin a dacent fortin!"

Although he had expressly stated the apparent head of the jolly crew was Mynheer Nicolhas, he saw fit to address him——

"It's done, Derrick!"

He winked to a youth who was in a sea-boy's rough dress, but winked in a very respectful manner.

"It's all right, captin," said he. "If Derrick can spake to him fairly, we'll be the crew of the Mortal Arrow before morning."

"We will?"

"Aye, we, surr. I've taken a notion to go to sea again, especially as I consayve that there's some fun in the prospect."

"More likely hard knocks, and no end of them," rejoined the sailor-boy in the young captain's voice. "Well, Derrick, finish your can, and go confer with the rascal. If your stupid tongue blunders, I'll have you drowned in a cask of schnapps!"

"I tink not," said the Hollander rising. "I can speak mit any man and pull the wool over his eyes like one lawyer, mein Gott!"

Off turned the big sailor to settle the terms with Lolonnais.

The latter said nothing about the real character of his vessel, but engaged Derrick and his thirty followers as seamen, relying upon the inducements he should offer when the occasion came, to seduce them from whatever honest principles they might chance to possess.

Having paid them "hand-money," he insisted on, their accompanying him to the vessel.

They wanted to linger, and made various excuses.

"Pshaw!" grumbled Lolonnais, "let that boy stay ashore, and one man to settle your tavern bills and collect your pawned pistols and clothes. I'll let a boat land to take to take them off first thing in the morning, but now I am in haste to get on deck myself.

So Frank and Ned Nittle remained in the Jolly Bosins, while their comrades marched off with Lolonnais to make themselves at home on the Mortal Arrow, and top off their drinking bout, for Patsy Maclarrup took some liquor with him, as he said, to celebrate his return to the sea.

Frank watched them wind their way across the plaza, and over the dock, until they were to be seen crowding three boats and pulling off for the Arrow.

"All has fallen pat," observed he. "Loys de Goupille will hardly come aboard the Arrow, and only he is likely to recognize Derrick and the rest of us."

"Just that way I look upon it, captain," said Nittle. "I'm ready to laugh when I thinks what a startler, as old Bill Bowse is so fond of calling 'em, we shall give friend Blackbeard and his chummies."

"Meanwhile, I'll take a stroll through the town. I believe the buccaneers are all under hatches, but to be fully assured that all goes well, I'll see that it is so. You may as well make up a bundle of anything useful to go aboard with us in the morning, Ned."

"Very well, sir. There's a hammock here, and I'll cram it chock-a-block with articles."

For his saunter along the water side, Frank disguised himself again, by donning vest, long skirted coat, a huge "fore -and-aft," or cocked, hat. He added a sword to the equipment, and went forth.

It was at a most timely moment that he did so.

He had just stepped out of the door when he saw two figures rise, as it were, out of the ground.

Disbelieving in ghosts, he hastened to check his steps, and see who they were.

One of them was helping the other to climb up out of the cellar windows of Maclarrap's house.

They were not robbers, but two of the pirates of Lolonnais.

They had happened to be less intoxicated than their comrades, and when they had puzzled out the mysterious sinking of the moveable chamber, they had the cunning to keep quiet.

Chance aided them in finding a panel which let them through into the cellar of the tavern.

After blundering over the casks, they had found the window opening on the street, and had just clambered through when Frank had come out and nearly stepped in between them.

If they should escape, the whole scheme would be blown to the winds.

There was no time to open the door behind him and call Nittle.

The only course was to dash at them, and disable them by surprise.

Luckily one of the two, pressing his hand to his feverish forehead to collect his thoughts, and gazing round to see where he was, had his back to the young commander.

The latter bounded forward, and delivered a blow with the flat of his sword on the top of the second fellow's skull.

Frank had never been in favour of shedding blood purposelessly.

The stricken pirate dropped to the earth as though the house had fallen upon him.

At the sound the other turned, insinctively clapping his hand to his hanger-hilt.

The young captain sprang at him with the blood-dripping blade high in air.

In vain he swung his cutlass into position.

There was too much at stake for the leader of the Cruiser to fail now.

After a few passes, in attempting to parry a cut at his head, the buccaneer's blade was hurled far from him.

Then he was compelled to stand fast, while the victor whistled for Ned Nittle.

The two men were bound securely and bundled back into the cellar.

In all ease of mind, now, Frank could resume his interrupted promenade.

The bankside was comparitively quiet now that the buccaneers had been called off to their several ships.

The taverns were but half tenanted.

The young captain went along the bankside until he had reached the governor's castle.

It was lonely there.

All was darkness around and about him, except a lantern or two on the castle ramparts or the sparkle of the sentinel's cigarettes, for the Spaniards were smoking even as they paced over the powder room.

The town lay on his right hand, gloomy except for a little light on the great square before the Church, and silent except for the howling of the mongrel dogs that were scavengering in the narrow streets, and frightening the watchmen.

Frank was looking out on the bay.

The four piratical vessels had warped themselves well up to their anchors, ready to slip out, and lay weathermost all the moored craft.

The lights on them, saving that lantern dangling in the foreshrouds to prevent collision in case of cables parting, went out one by one.

The pirates had wearied themselves by their orgies, and were probably fast asleep.

The distance was too great for Frank to see the watch moving on the decks.

Suddenly he started, and rose from the stone that he had made his seat.

A flash of a lantern had momentarily shot out in the waist of Blackbeard's pink.

Soon after, the watcher discerned a boat pushing off from the ship's side.

As it progressed towards the shore, he could make out that the something white in the stern sheets was, in all likelihood, a female.

"If it should be her I suppose—if it should be Genifrede," murmured Frank, "what can it be of horror that menaces her! I feel a shadow stealing over me as though the next few minutes contained wierd and affrighting mystery, full of dreadful import to her and to me—and perhaps to others !"

This he added as he felt for his sword, and watched the boat come to the sands.

There was much in his strange foreboding.

The lives of more than one person were renewed or cut short for evermore in the few coming moments !

CHAPTER XXVI.

IN THE DEPTHS OF THE NIGHT—WILLIAM TEACH ASTONISHES BLACKBEARD, AND BLACKBEARD AMAZES LOYS—THROWN TO THE DOGS—THE CAPTAIN OF THE CRUISER TO THE RESCUE !

THE water scooped into the beach under the stone where Frank had been stationed, and into this little cove, the boat from the pink proceeded.

On running upon the strand, the men jumped out of it, and came to the drier land.

All the young captain had to do was to crouch down and listen.

For the three men, to be out of ear shot of their boat's crew, drew all the nearer to the hidden youth.

The latter did not need the hearing of their voices to recognize Loys, and the two worthies of the name of Teach.

Glancing from them to the boat, he noticed that what he had mistaken for a female's dress was a figure wrapped from head to foot in a spare royal sail.

A corpse, or a living being? thought he.

By listening to the pirates, he would probably learn.

He had no difficulty in this, for the silence and the clearness of the midnight air offered no hindrance to his eavesdropping.

"I hope now," said Loys, in no pleasant tone, to William Teach, "I hope you'll tell me why you would not let me bring the girl ashore instead of this bundele of old bones or rags, or whatever you have done up in that piece of duck."

"Don't you fret," said William, "there's that in the canvass worth many a girl, to men like us who think more of a solid feeling like hate, than of the flimsy thing the fouls call love."

"You think I went to all the trouble for a bag of old bones, ha, ha ! They are bones, but there's human flesh around 'em."

"What say !" exclaimed old Teach and the Frenchman.

"A man. You won't blame me for giving him precedence over the girl, who can be put ashore to-morrow."

"That's true," said Goupille.

William lifted up his voice.

"Feldese get one of the others to bear a hand,

and bring me that roll of old sail!" ordered he.

Two of the oarsmen jumped up from their seats, lifted up the bundle, and carried it up the sands to the feet of their leaders.

"It's dangerous to strike a light," said young Teach, "when the fort is so near. Stoop down, you'll know the face."

As he spoke, he whipped out his knife, cut the stitches of twine that secured the folds of duck, and opened the upper end of the long package.

Frank saw Blackbeard and Loys bend over the form, and start erect in immense surprise.

"Blue death!" swore Goupille. "It's the Englsh lieutenant!"

"Lance Cavendish here!" cried old Teach. "How the devil—when I left him on the island?"

William laughed.

"Dont you remember I came off in the last boat with a load of bananas under the boatcloak! Ha, ha! it was this chap! By the blood I have shed!" said the young man fiercely "do you think I'll let oaths bar my vengeance on the man who ever held steel in triumph over my heart!"

It was clear that the promising juvenile pirate was not like to forget the time when Lance had swung the axe above him, in the top of the Just Revenger brig.

Blackbeard smiled grimly at the emphatic utterance of the cub.

"Well, let's waste nothing over his carcase. I suppose I have half smothered him, for 1 bundled him up and stowed him away like any dogs' meat, for fear that our fellows would snatch him away from me. For they are growling that he ever was let off, as they think, after having led so many of their comrades to give up the ghost!"

"Say on."

"We three have all a spite against him!"

"We have!" returned Loys, and the other, looking down malignantly on the shrouded figure.

"I propose tying him up in the woods for the gallimppers to sting him to death—it's an agony of about eight and forty hours, that kind of death," said William, nursing his wounded arm as he spoke thus fiendishly. "If either of you know of anything worse, out with it! I want the curse to suffer!"

And he kicked the helpless body at his feet.

"There's better than that," said Loys. "Carry him aboard again. Rig up a spare windlass barrel, and I'll guarantee to furnish ye with a rack that'll twist more torture into the wretch stretched on it than any machinery of the Inquisition!"

"No," interupted William. "It's giving him a chance for life, this deferring his doom. Besides, the men would mutiny with such a Jonah on the same planks as them."

"I'll tell ye what," said Blackbeard grimly. "You made mention of dogs' meat but a while ago, William. That's the idea, right up and down. Think of the dogs of this place, hungry as shipwrecked mariners, savage as Indians, and their teeth poisoned with their graveyard food!"

The younger pirate shook his head.

"They're mongrels, but they tell me the crop's out. They won't touch a live white man

on no account, ready as they are to fall on the niggers, and reds and yellows."

"Won't they?" replied Blackbeard, contemptiously. "That's all you know. You've seen cats climb a high wall, to eat valerian?"

"Rather. I used to bait traps with it to catch the mousers when I was a boy."

"There's a thing that dogs get just as wild over."

"So there is!" cried Loys. "I never thought, I remember the *raceme agave*—the voilet agave of the Antilles! Dogs love it, say you? That's nowhere near it! When I was a prisoner in the Castle of Cha—ah, but that's no matter—Any way, a dog will race ofter a drop of it's juice till his legs are worn off to the shoulder socket!"

"I see you know," said Blackbeard. "Enough. The Jew on St. Gabriel's Wharf, who buys our silver plate, has some of the plants exact, as I know——"

"Aha!" muttered Goupille, cunningly.

"Between ourselves, he distils it to export the tincture to Spain—there's a deal of fine ladies about the throne of Madrid who are too eager to be maids of honor to wait till nature remove the dames who have the posts."

"It's poison, then," said William.

"Deadly as methylide of quicksilver, and that slays while the breath is on the turn," answered Blackbeard.

He waved his hand for the two sailors to approach.

"Call hither a couple more. Make a litter of two oars lashed end and end, and carry this carrion where William bids you."

He turned to his precious relative and Loys.

"You know the churchyard? We were there in old time, eh, Loys? chuckled he. There is no better spot for revenge to be consummated. I will speedily rejoin you there, for it won't take me many minutes to procure the drug from Aaron Medicaments."

He turned towards the city, and his long powerful strides bore him rapidly from sight.

Loys and William, followed by the four men, made the circuit of the town to arrive at the burial place.

Two of the seaman bore the burden, while the other pair marched some paces in the rear and front, respectively, as scouts and rearguard.

Frank would have much liked to have gone to the tavern, and called Ned to assist him.

But he had to keep close on the track of the mysterions train, for there were three cemeteries in the outskirts of Matanzas, and he knew not which was the particular one.

He had to be very cautious in dogging the party, as they were on the alert.

However, the ground outside the wall of the town was low, uneven, and hid in deep shadow.

There was no moon, and it was a trifle cloudy that night.

The heavy dew and the thick rank grass deadened the footsteps of the party to that extent that any watchmen who might have espied them from the walls would have set them down as unholy spirits bearing a phantom prisoner to some unheard of receptacle of horror.

In about half an hour Frank saw that William and Loys, who led the rest, had stopped.

He instantly slank behind behind a clump of old man cactus.

It was well he did so, for presently Blackbeard came quickly up behind him and passed on, nearly running over him as he lay on the ground.

When he rose, he saw that the seven men were standing together under the old walls of an enclosure, over the crumbling top of which a cross on a roof denoted the site of a chapel, or charnel house.

As the pirates made an attack on the gate with their cutlasses, and with a small tree that they cut down to make a crow bar of, proving they meant to enter this burying ground, Frank took his course.

He made a circuit, and getting close up to the wall in a different part of it, found a spot where a sapling grew up like a ladder.

To a seaman, it was like child's play to climb up and swing himself on to the coping of the wall.

It was dark beneath, but he did not hesitate to drop down inside.

He landed on the grass of the graves safely.

"That poor fellow shant die so fiendishly, if they were a hundred and I alone!" said he, resolutely.

There was something of a crash at the gates.

The fastenings had been shaken and the pirates were putting their shoulders to it.

Frank, concealed behind a tall urn of basalt, set up to the memory of Donna Angelica Somebody, saw the buccaneers tramp into the church yard.

It was so far away from the town, and so sure to be shunned by the superstitious, that the rascals began to talk aloud and tread noisily on the flat gravestones.

They felt no awe whatever in this city of the dead.

It was very large, being the one first consecrated by the Jesuits when the Spanish settlements were established.

In daytime it was not easy to see one wall if one stood at the foot of another.

At night the boundaries were not visible at all.

All at once, as the party were striding by the back of the charnel house, Blackbeard held up his hand to enjoin silence.

━"There's somebody in the house," said he, in surprise.

The men started and grasped their drawn hangers, in readiness for action.

There was a light at the window of the motuary building.

Not a light to excite any ideas of corpse-candles, though.

It was a matter-of-fact horn lantern.

The pirates saw it lifted up by a hand, and that was probably as real as the lantern.

They were convinced of this presently.

For, after a rattling of bolts pushed back, and chains let down, the door opened.

An old man, holding up the lantern before mentioned, peered out before.

In his other hand he carried a blunderbuss of a truly gigantic description.

It seems that the street-dogs having become furious, had burrowed under the cemetery walls, unearthing, the entombed.

So the authorities had determined to set a guard over the field of mortality, and, with that brilliancy of intelligence that distinguishes them to this very day of ours, had chosen, instead of a file of soldiers, one poor old man.

The decrepit venerable confronted the pirates.

When his aged eyes made out the strangers, he was alarmed at first.

But seeing the enshrouded form that they bore in their midst, he presumed that, despite the unusal hour, it was merely a funeral party.

So he saluted Blackbeard and Loys, who were richly dressed, and wished them good night in Spanish.

"Good even," repeated Loys.

"Who is the poor soul dead?" inquired the old watchman, coming out to hold the lantern up over the shrouded man.

"What does the old mumble jaw say?" queried William Teach. "Who is dead? Why, you are you blundering old fool, for being where you are not wanted!"

And without further ado, he ran his drawn cutlass into the watchman's side.

Shocked at the wanton and cold blooded act, none of the by standers interfered.

The poor old man died even as he dropped, and lantern and blunderbuss rolled from his unnerved hands.

After a pause, one of the men picked up the lantern, and all moved on.

The quicker they turned their backs on the victim of such atrocity the better.

"I hope there is no more of them," remarked Loys. "No. All's still inside the house. Come on."

A few yards from the chapel was an open space, chancing to have no tombs upon it, except one tall column of lignum vitæ which had been set up over the grave of the wife of the captain of the governor's guard, until a more fitting memorial of stone should replace it.

"Capital," said Blackbeard. "Rip open the sail and revive the man."

They cut up the seams of the sailcloth, and pulled Lance out.

He was half dead with cramp and suffocation.

They prized his jaws apart, and poured some raw spirits down his parched throat.

That brought him to, and the cool night air finished his restoration.

He looked about him like one aroused from a dream.

It was strange to behold the burying ground profaned by the rude buccaneers.

They gave him no rest, but bound him to the pillar of wood.

"Not so taut, not so tightly, I say," said William, "I want him to struggle a little and prolong the agony when the hounds are tearing the flesh off him!"

It was evident that the drinking which the speaker had indulged in, had enormously increased the fever of his broken arm, and goaded his evil nature into an attempt to outdo itself.

Blackbeard was amazed at the young fellow's malignant spirit; it had never shone out so luridly before.

The sailors completed their work.

Lance, his back to the column, was affixed to it immovable.

He was too weak to cry out, even if he had not been too proud to give his tormentors the satisfaction.

The suspense and anguish crowded into the last month had been more than any one could bear.

He was all in a whirl, and was fain to believe that he was still in a vision, too frightful to be anything but a dream.

"He's going mad," muttered Loys, shaking his head, as he viewed the prisoner.

"Well he's going off soundings, any how. That's as broad a sea as any other. Come, old man, let's fiddle no more over the affair," concluded young Teach, to his elder.

"I'm not delaying."

He had taken a large phial from his pocket, and was carefully wetting a strip of canvas with the liquid that it contained.

Even at the distance that Frank had to keep from the group to spy and not be discovered, the pungent emanation of the fluid was wafted.

It was of a strong but agreeable quality.

"Feldese and Molock, stay here, and Blackbeard, handed them the bottle. "William and Loys return to the ship, with the other brace of gallows birds! I will undertake to carry out the rest!"

"What will you do?" said William. "If I can't have the fun, I want to enjoy it in fancy, at anyrate."

"Well, here it is in words. I will go straight to town, dragging after me this naked rag to make a trail leading up to this point. The dogs will

desert the gnawed bones, and pickings of kitchens, to follow up this scent. When the first of the ravenous pack shall have raced in by that open gate, Feldese and his mate break that bottle they hold over the head of that poor fool who has crossed the Arch-pirates' course too often, and in a woeful hour for him!"

"And then?"

"Then what?" cried Goupille. "Can't you think of that form saturated with the fluid, and a hundred famishing, frantic, wild dogs tearing each shred of flesh from his very bone, and then rending bone from bone till a crumb of the eaten man will only be found entombed in the mad beast's bowels!"

All shuddered.

Blackbeard nodded.

"Friend Goupille has told you what will happen much clearer than I could. Go!"

William, the Frenchman, and the two sailors left the cemetery on their road to the seaside.

Soon after, Blackbeard issued his last instructions, and went out of the walled grounds trailing on the dewy earth behind him the perfumed sailcloth, whose odour scattered around widely.

The guards over the extract of agave, sat down on a stone near the column of which Lance seemed a sculptured ornament, and chatted as merrily as their hideous task and the nature of the scene permitted.

All of a sudden, Molock, a large strapping brute, slapped his thigh as a thought struck him.

"It'ud be a shame to leave that undergrown cannon here to rust," said he, rising.

"What cannon?" queried Feldese.

"That everlasting monstrous blunderbuss that that old whitehead had, who was so cleverly laid toes up by Masser William."

"Oh, yes, Mo'. Go to it! It may be useful——"

"To sell for old brass, by weight," laughed the other. "Lor' love your sinful soul, Feldese it would be worth the purchase of a man's life to undertake to discharge it! But I'll go after it n'atheless!"

It was only a few steps to where the watchman had been butchered.

Molock was looking for the firearm, his companion examining the jar of agave essence, which was furnished with rather a complicated lid.

"I'll have to smash it with a pistol butt, after all," thought he.

He started.

An unaccountable noise had reached him.

On the spot where Molock was stooping over the watchman, two figures were seen!

Something glittered.

Was the dead alive?

Yes, for Molock was drawing his sword.

The two figures like shadows, intermingled.

They fell.

One rose.

But one!

"In the name of flames, what's it mean?" stammered Feldese, his trembling hand rattling his cutlass in its sheath.

He strained his eyes.

The upright figure came straight towards him.

"What's your steel out for, Molock?" said Feldese, trying to laugh. "You scared me—I thought you were fighting with the cold meat!"

But the next instant he saw how great was his error.

The man was not the pirate, but a stranger.

He did not await his attack, but over come by the fears that this mysterious new comer inspired, he turned his back and fled from the spot as if all the fiends were leagued to chase him.

The person who he believed to be supernatural did not pursue him, but hastened to cut loose Lance Cavendish.

The latter opened his eyes in as much astonishment as relief.

"The Captain of the Scarlet Cruiser!" said he. "Oh, heaven reward you! You don't know what they would do!"

The excess of joy at deliverance so unexpected, made the lieutenant swoon.

It was Frank, who had stolen around to secure the blunderbuss himself, when he had run against Molock, whom he had killed at the first pass.

Feldese had fled in the opposite direction to the gate, and hence was not likely to give warning to his chief.

The young captain tried to revive the insensible lieutenant.

Suddenly he looked around.

The faint yaffle of a dog on a trail came to his ears.

"Oh! the hounds! the hounds are racing along the trail that Blackbeard has made!" muttered he.

He caught up Lance in his arms, and took the lantern.

"The house! the charnel house! it may shelter the living as it does the dead," he cried.

And, desperate, he shouldered Cavendish, and carried him into the chapel.

And still louder sounded the greedy sniffing, whining, yelping of dogs.

Not on the side towards the town, but in that direction in which the surviving buccaneer had fled!

And as the barking crescendoed into ear coplitting chorus of canine melody, the shriek of a human being in acute agony.

This scream ran along among the tombs, and the echoes that the gravestones sent up seemed a peal of mocking laughs, issuing from appalling throats of beings not of earth, too evil to be named!

CHAPTER XXVII.

FELDESE RUNS INTO THE RELENTLESS JAWS—HUNTED DOWN—TORN OUT OF THE BOOK OF LIFE—THE HOUNDS BESIEGE THE CHARNEL HOUSE—A DESPERATE MEASURE BEATS THEM OFF!

WHEN Frank had carried the lieutenant into the chapel, he went to the window, to see what the infernal uproar portended.

His curiosity was speedily gratified.

Feldese, flying away frantically tumbling over the gravestones, and picking up himself with unwearied perseverance, was only brought to a full stop by coming against the eastern wall of the burial place.

There was no pursuer at his heels.

But the darkness was full of phantoms to his feverish fancy.

The wall was too high, and its face too smooth, for escalading.

The monks of old, who made the Indian converts labor for them, were to skilful to have the work ill done.

Feldese made the attempt in a couple of places, by sticking his knife in between two of the slabs.

But the mortar was of such good quality that it was really easier to cut away the solid stone itself.

Feldese, with broken nails, dropped to the ground again, and pulled out his knife.

He was in a puzzle what to do, when a scratching sound alarmed him.

He was on the eve of taking to his heels, when he made out that the sound was on the outside of the stones.

He paused and listened.

The scratching was interspersed with snuffing and sneezing.

It was clear that it was some animal that was digging out the earth, and stopping ever and anon to apply its nose to the hole.

Every moment the sound redoubled, until it was quite plain that more than a score of the animals were seeking to burrow under the enclosure.

It was something more than the appetite for the interred remains that incited them.

Feldese shuddered as he became aware that his custody of the phial had imparted a powerful tinge of the extract to his hands and clothes.

"Oh, curses on Blackbeard and all his fine tricks! If these yelpers get in, they'll be the death of me!"

He had barely got the word out of his mouth, then he saw the ground fall in at his very feet.

Struggling in the aperture was the head, and shoulders of a dog, his paws plying frantically to clear the earth away that entangled him.

Feldese up foot, and delivered a kick on the animal's nose, with all the force of which his terror made him capable.

The recipient of the blow uttered a loud yelp and sank back stunned into the gap.

As it strove to scramble through, the comrades of it, savage to get in likewise, tore at it with their claws to remove the obstacle.

Meanwhile Feldese, prefered to hurry back on his steps, even at the risk of meeting the phantom (as he supposed the Cruiser's Captain to be).

At least, that had a human shape, and those dogs, starved almost to skeletons, with mangy hides from their foul feeding, were far from earthly working.

As he turned, the howling behind him betokened that the hounds had enlarged the hole and were crawling though.

Feldese cast one glance backwards.

But one.

It sufficed to make the hair bristle up on all his frame and ice the blood in his veins as if he been plunged into a Nova Zemblan snow drift.

Long and gaunt, their jowls skinned and drawn back from their long fangs stained purple, and sickly yellow by their inroads on the garbage heaps, their sides so tight from thinness as to show every rib's outline.

The animals bounded on in his track, more like the hideous griffins of the fables than "man's brute companion."

The agave that had been spilt over the pirate, drew all their attention on him, so that they forgot entirely their purpose of entering to upturn the graves.

They had so little flesh upon them, that they moved with inconceivable swiftness.

Nothing but the wings that intense terror lent to the hunted buccaneer enabled him to keep any advance whatever.

He had a fair start, but the space was diminished momentarily.

Ere he had reached the lignum vitæ column before mentioned, he could plainly hear, above the beating of his terror-stricken heart, the breathing of the rushing pack, and the yet more horrid sound of their clattering jaws and their tongues licking their ragged lips in anticipation.

By this time, the man and his fore footed chasers were visible from the window of the chapel where Frank had stationed himself.

He had been called to it by the infernal hubbub that the hounds kept up as they tore on at the heels of the doomed wretch.

As they drew near the spot where Blackbeard had had Lance Cavendish bound fast, the emanations from the jar of agave increased in power.

The nostrils of the dogs opened greatly, and they drank in the perfumed air greedily.

They seemed to have identified the man as the cause of it all, for they never let their outstretched muzzles be diverted from him.

Feldese felt that his tremendous efforts to avoid his fate had but broken him down.

He never could reach the gates, it was plain.

He was even so greatly exhausted then, he could not dream of resistance.

The ferocious beasts were so excited by this time that they would have pulled down a Bull of Bashaw, and a man was less than a mouse to a cat to them.

The pillar of wood stood some twelve feet high, and on somethinglike a fair elevation.

It was carved and ridged, so that it was rougher than many trees.

A desperate idea shot across the fellow's mind.

If he could climb up the column, it might afford a respite.

In fact, he was driven to that resource.

For one of the hounds, and more powerful, fleeter than the rest, had suddenly shot ahead with so much impetus that had not the sea-bandit swerved aside, he would have been caught by the ankle.

As it was, the brute tumbled tail over head after missing its snap at him.

However, when it rolled and gathered itself up, there it was in front of the fugitive.

The latter had nothing to hesitate at.

He collected the energy remaining to him, broke away from the half dozen snarlers at his heels, and leaped at the column.

By grasping the entablatuse high up on the post and scrambling vigorously with his feet, he contrived to make a ball of himself on the very top of the wood.

This summit was bevelled off, so that it was only by a powerful setting of his muscles that he could retain the place.

This sudden exaltation of their prey deeply amazed the hunters, as well it might.

For a moment they ran against one another and tossed their snouts in air like foxhdunds at fault.

But their old leader, the one that had the tumble, uttered a loud yelp, and leaped up as high as it could, towards the apex of the monument.

The example was imitated instantly by a score of them.

It was but temporary, as we have said, and it had been dislodged by the volient climbing of the man.

These blows of the dogs jumping short and tilting the post continued to losen it.

Feldese was afraid to change his awkard posture, curved on all fours, as his being on the upper end made the whole timber like a lever, and his motion might pry out the buried end.

To add to his fears, his eyes, compelled to be down-cast, saw that some of the animals, fatigued, or unthinking to reach him by leaps, were running their muzzles into the earth to root the drops of the extract of agave.

Frenzy of the beasts, persevering in attenpts

at seizing the man, unaccountably to overlook the large phial of that potent potion.

But several, less furious for flesh, after a few instants, lighten upon that prize.

Luckily the bottle was hermetically sealed.

All their pawing and gnawing was without avail in removing the well secured stopper.

The jar, upset by their struggles, for they jolted one another in a way that would have been laughable if they had not been so terribly in earnest, got rolling on its side.

Feldese's wicked heart, worried by its anxiety; received a little relief on beholding this, for he fancied that the jar would draw off their attention altogether from him.

The largest number did at first throng around the new object of their greed; but, as many could not pierce the outer ring around it of their fellows, these ones kept aloof, returning to the perched-up man.

If possible, they had their passion quickened by the brief pause.

Again the wretched man saw the beasts, some times singly, and oftener by twos and threes, spring up to clutch him, snapping at him as they rolled over after contact with the post only a few feet from him.

One long, gaunt, wolfish creature, very bony but very powerful, a living embodiment of those lean horrors that the old painters set about the car of Death, seemed headmost of the canine terrors.

It had come to take the lead, vaulting higher than the others and never a bit daunted by the failures that it had.

With a grim air of business, that was appalling at the same time as fascinating, to the target of all these self propelled bullets, this hound would draw off a few paces, run at the pillar, and spring up with immense energy.

Though it either missed the wood and shot on by its side, thereupon to roll on the mould, or struck the slab and was flung back bruised, yet it never whimpered or showed any signs of weariness.

Feldese began to have eyes only for this one, till his onwrapt gaze saw in it a devil incarnate.

The example fired the rest.

The column shook from the violence of the blows, and threatened a speedy downfall.

Feldese, so long in suspense over the bristling jaws and eyes rabid to devour him, had almost so exhausted nature that it needed but little to make him relax his cramped grasp and drop headlong into the clamorous medley.

A distant sound happened to rise during a lull in the chorus of growls beneath him.

The dogs themselves pricked up their eyes, and turned to look westward, towards Matanzas Town.

Ere many minutes the sound was audible again, and very much louder, to prove that it was drawing nigh and at no very slow pace.

It was the cry of many dogs on a trail, the "*clamore del rastreadors* (the bloodhounds' call)," as the West Indians say.

Blackbeard, on reaching the town, had carried out his part of the plan of torture, by setting a band of the mongrels on the path he had so ingeniously devised.

So, had any one been on the graveyard wall, looking westerly, he would have seen a strag-

gling mass rushing along straight for the burying ground.

In five minutes, the dogs collected around the pillared man, were themselves surrounded by two hundred at least of as ugly quadrupeds as themselves.

There was a deal of growling, snapping, and snashing, and several fights.

But the agave did not cease to pervade the air, and while that taunted their appetite they could forego the bites sure to be received in combat.

It was like gazing down on a sea of ferocious Besberuses to sea that heaving mass, of which the pirate formed the centre.

The man grew dizzy by being the object of so many savage eyes.

The end was not far, now.

The column, almost completely undermined by the scratching of the animals, tottered, and only appeared not to fall because it was yet undecided which way it should lean.

The hounds had ceased to clamor, and with half open jaws, over which glistened a disgusting slaver of anticipated enjoyment, they kept their expectant gaze on the prey.

The post shook, and twice already, the wretched man had fancied he was lain low in the enemies' midst.

Meanwhite, the Captain of the Cruiser had not been idle.

A drain from a spirit flask that he carried, had brought Lance Cavendish to his senses.

The horrible uproar kept up out of doors led them both to station themselves at the window.

As soon as their eyes became more accustomed to the darkness, they could watch the dogs baiting the wretched myrmidon of Captain Teach's.

Perhaps, the pity they could not help but feel for that miserable being in torture, would have led them to rush out, and seek to relieve him.

But at the moment when the two young men prepared so to do, the hounds received that great increase of their force, in the pack of canine savages come from the town.

To leave the inside of the four walls, unless they had been coated in complete steel, would have been madness.

They stood at the casement, gazing.

They beheld the dogs mostly surrounding their prisoner, while a few roamed restlessly about.

These latter scooped up the earth of the freshest graves until wearied by their exertions, and then would rove about again.

They came across the two bodies, that of the old churchyard keeper, and the pirate whom Frank had slain.

At first they had only smelt at them, and snapped at them.

But presently, the impulse that had restrained them, be it what it might, lost its influence.

One, boldly bit at the pirate, and another at the other.

Instantly as many pair of jaws as could find room to close upon the flesh, did so.

On seeing this, many more of the dogs came to share in the banquet.

In a trice, the bones bid fair to be picked clean.

Then the flesh feasters severed the skeletons.

The lookers on saw the gouls' fighting over the remains.

So soon as one blood-besmeared mouth contained a fragment of the human flesh, that moment half a dozen set upon him, and hunted him whereever he went.

The cemetery seemed alive with pandemonium's troop.

Over the gravestones leaping, on the mound rowling, barking, howling, mumbling over thigh and arm bone, the dogs were in the most active motion.

Throughtout it all, albeit some of the pack gallopped past their noses with the horrid meat in their fang, a number of forty or fifty old hounds kept around Feldese.

No escape!

No, not a shadow of it.

The excitement was soon caught by the old carrion-mongers.

They redoubled their exertions.

Where there had been but half a dozen springing up before, there were ten or fifteen now.

Where only two or three had been digging at the base of the column, eight or more of claws were at work.

The pillar rocked like a topmast in a storm.

It leaned as a ship gunnels under beneath the hurricane.

Feldese drowned the racket of the dogs with the superhuman scream that pealed from his bloodless lips.

It was returned to his ears like a laugh of fiendish mockery.

He and the column fell to the ground.

The fall made the dogs draw back a space.

Feldese jumped up in desperation the most absolute.

At the same instant five dogs sprang at his head, and breast.

Two clung to his collar bone, getting a grip of his shirt.

One missed his bound, and rolled past him.

His right, and his left hand were severally grappling the second pair.

He could not shake them off, and so he wrestled with them.

"Oh, heaven! by all my sins against you, pardon! help! help!" shouted he, madly.

Clinging to him the bony hounds, around him the multitude of similarly ravenous visages.

All came flocking to share in the new meal, except a few who had stolen off to suck the marrow under the caves of some tombstone.

He beat off the dog hampering his right arm and laid hands on the huge old king of the pack at his throat.

"Then—as heaven renounces me!" groaned he, trampling down one young brute under foot, "I call for aid from below!"

But there was no answer to his appeals other than three other of the animals set their teeth in his legs and tore each away its morsel.

The exquisite agony as the blood rushed from all parts of his body to pour forth like red hot metal by those jagged wounds, give him a power that appeared impossible.

He uttered a howl, so loud, so unearthly, so dreadfully piercing, that the hungry pack recoiled.

He broke his left arm loose from the teeth that confined it.

With both hands he caught the king of the savages by the throat, and squeezed and squeezed, till the fury of the animal was pressed out with its life, and it remained dead and flaccid in his gripe.

With that carcass for club, he belabored the brutes clinging to him, and bearing him down.

For a moment he stood, centre of the rings of his enemies.

That was the minute that Frank and his friend had been waiting for.

They could not strike in while the dogs were twined around the man unless at the risk of robbing the pirate of life instead of aiding him.

Now they took quick aim, and fired off a pistol apiece.

Two of the foremost of the graveyard feasters emitted a yelp, and tumbled down on the rough ground, dying at the feet of the pirate.

The letter was astonished.

The pack too, terrified by the shots from the window, which seemed so loud in the loneliness of the place, huddled together.

Feldese cleared away the mist over his eyes, and espied the light, and two shadows in the charnel house embrasure.

There was help!

Sure help, for they had already sent aid to him.

The dogs were, for the time being, distracted.

Feldese hurled the carcass at their heads, and jumped in amongst those between him, and the house.

He kicked several from his path, who rolled on the rank grass with broken ribs.

His movement broke the spell.

The whole set were immediately after him.

Once again Frank, and Cavendish pulled trigger.

But though a couple more of the brutes fell lifeless, the rest were too hot in the chase to be checked.

It was not impossible, such were the efforts of the fugitive, that he might reach the friendly doorway unscathed by another tooth or claw.

But the doom had been pronounced against him.

Even as he grew exultant, and thoughts of evil pleasures in the future revived within him, he set his foot on something that rolled treacherously away.

It was the jar of agave.

He fell forward, and with all the impetus of his running, upon the phial.

What the dogs could not do by dint of clawing that shock performed.

The otter case, and the inner glass, shivered to atoms.

The man rolled on the splinters, and, while they peirced him, the fluid poured over his body.

Uuged on by their race, the headmost of the hunters came up, and rolled over the fallen pirate.

He, and they scrambled together in the pool of aromatic liquor.

The scent attached itself to them, and dogs, and man, who had been saturated with it, shrieked in pain as the fiery stuff ate into them!

They were put out of their misery soon!

For, as that perfume pervaded the air, the numberless quadrupeds were made rabid.

One cry of immense joy they sent up.

Then they fell upon the pirate, and such of their fellows as had been immersed in the spirit.

And such was the appetite that the liquid provoked, that the dogs that had been soaked in it, greedily were licking up the luscious drops from their own flanks, even while their fellows devoured them!

Frank and his comrade shot again, but the time for pistol or sword had gone by.

The receivers of the leaden missiles, were instantly set upon and rent to pieces.

Before they had fired, Feldese had been leaped over by a host of his tormentors.

When the smoke cleared away, its sulphurous stench, reduced to nothing by the overwhelming agave, the place where *had been the man* was covered with the pack, with bloody mouths, and fangs between which dangled threads of flesh.

In ecstasy the hounds rolled themselves in the spilt liquor.

They ate the earth that drank it up.

They swallowed the shives of glass.

Then those whose skins reeked with the fluid, were eaten up by the rest.

They presented an ever moving pile of gnashing teeth, now gleaming white, or yellow, now streaming with red, rending claws; their lean sides swelling and the hair bristling with the extreme intoxication.

All at once Lance gave a shout.

"Good God! see! they are coming this way!" cried he.

Even as he spoke, his words were verified.

One of the hounds frantic with the mighty juice that it had imbibed, and flying from its mates, ran straight ahead, as if blind with passion.

With one prodigious vault, it left the ground, and smashed through the lattis right in between Frank and Cavendish.

"Bang to the shutters!" cried the former. "I'll settle this howler!"

He promptly clapped his recharged pistol to the side of the dog which had alighted on the floor of the room rather suprised.

A touch of the trigger let the hammer kiss the nipple, and the flame burst forth.

The vitals of the brute were plastered against the opposite wall.

Meanwhile, Lance had obeyed the command and swung the shutters into place.

In good time, for, amid an outburst of yells, two heavy bodies broke in the lattice, and were only repelled by the just closed panels.

Luckily they were of solid live-oak and the bolt held firm.

Through a split in the panels, the two young men could peer and see the herd of frenzied animals outside.

Again, and again, they flung themselves up at the casement, though they only bruised themselves, and were thrown back.

They scratched, bit, and tore at the wall, at the window, and at the door.

"It is only a question of time," said captain Frank, "as to how soon they will get in, by dint of their frantic action.

We must get out of this chamber, and into some stronger one, whose entrance we can hold against the pack."

"What is below, I wonder?"

"A vault, I suppose. There ought to be a trap somewhere."

As he said so, the young captain held the lantern down to the floor.

Suddenly Cavendish uttered an exclamation,

"There's the trapdoor now," said he, pointing.

In one corner, a ring was attached to a square in the thick flooring.

The door had not been used for a considerable space of time, which was clear from Lance being unable to lift it up alone.

But after the rust and mould had been shaken off by sundry stamps, and kicks, and the two young men had united their efforts, they made out to lift the square a very little.

At the instant that they raised it an inch or so, there arose thrugh that space a stench so noisome that even that faint whiff of it made the men let go their hold, and tread the trap into place again.

"Horrible!" ejaculated the lieutenant.

"Detestable above anything that ever poisoned the air," said Frank, coughing.

Whence comes it. There must be bodies stowed away under us."

"No doubt. Well, we are blocked off from escape in a downward direction."

"And the dogs wont permit any levanting on the ground level." continued Lance.

"And so we must try, and get a little nearer to the cherub who, unlike other cherubs, manage to sit up aloft to watch over poor Jacks."

The upper story of the charnel-house was very high, and divided by an openwork floor into two lofty rooms.

The lower was empty, as the two perceived as they viewed it by the lantern light.

"There is absolutely nothing to barricade the stairs we came up by with," observed Lance.

"Then, down go the stairs!" said the youthful commander, drawing his sword.

Cavendish pulled up a board in the floor so that he could look down and fire through into the chamber that they had just quitted on the ground floor.

Frank chopped at the top of the steps with his blade, and made the splinters fly in a manner likely to make many a woodcutter stare.

All this time the besiegers had not been idle.

Though their claws were bleeding and their teeth broken, yet they persevered in assailing the wood and stone.

Finally, louder even than had arisen before, resounded a deafening diapason of furious barks.

The dogs had found a part of the outer wall crumbling and rotted away, and thus they had entered.

They had to come in one by one, on account of the narrowness of the opening.

Lance shot the five first in succession, loading up and firing in all haste through the gap in the ceiling.

Frank, working with all his power, hacked away at the stairs, till his stout sword was bent and jagged.

At length a vigorous kick started the planks, and the stairs split up and went down by the run.

"Cease firing, friend Lance," said the young captain. "We can't see for the smoke, the stairs have merrily rattled in their ears!"

The dogs, their number added to every moment, roared with rage when they found the two young men above them, and all communication cut off.

Still their number increased, and they began to be crowded so that they could hardly turn.

"Don't let us fire any more," observed Frank. "They mind their puppy comrades being drilled through by bullets no more than if 'twere balls of paper we pelted them with. Let us consider what is to be done."

"I wish they would cease their yelping and growling!"

"And I. But, spite of them all, must be at the harbour by daybreak."

He told Lance in briefest terms of the contemplated attack on the Cruiser.

When Cavendish heard all, he offered his services.

He had to avenge so much on Blackbeard that he rejoiced at this opportunity of "making all straight" between them.

But how escape?

If all the hounds had entered the lower room, something might have been attempted in the way of blocking up the hole that had served them as entrance, and thus secure them in a trap.

But the pack outside prevented a descent for that or any other purpose.

The candle had been removed from the lantern and stuck into a sconce in the wall by Frank, and it was out of reach of the animals.

Everything else in the chamber below they savagely attacked.

They gnawed at the stools and the watchman's bed, till the floor was covered with the splinters.

This they did in sheer rage at being unable to reach the two men looking down on them.

"I wonder if a large flash of powder in their faces would not disgust them?" proposed the lieutenant.

"I was thinking of that myself," rejoined the other, "but all the powder I have is in these five cartridges and this horn. See! only a few grains. Not more than will suffice to prime for a couple of shots.

"We are in for it! Or, can we smoke them out?"

"I don't see how to fire the building, and not scorch ourselves."

"That's true."

For a time the two were silent, not to listen to the row made by the restless animals fretting beneath, but to frighten out what was to be done.

Even if they had not been desirous to get away from the place by morning, the prospect would not have been been very brilliant.

No one came near the cemetery except on occasions like funerals.

The old watchman kept provisions for a week by him, and did not care about going to town.

No doubt the dogs, with the unlessened patience of their race, even when the effects of the essence of agave should be gone, would persist in waiting until the men should fall into their power.

The watchman's food, locked up in a cupboard had been already found and destroyed by the brutes.

If the young men did not take some course speedily, there was but a dismal seige to look forward to.

Suddenly Frank uttered a loud exclamation.

Lance looked up, and saw that his companion's features were lit up with something like hope.

"What have you imagined?" he asked.

"Oh, a way of settling most of those hungry devils! Think you their bones would'nt grind to powder if the bells fell on them, crowded together as they are?"

"The bells? the bells?"

"The bells! Look aloft!"

Till then, neither had given more than a glance upward to examine the room above.

There were no planks on the joists, so that one could look upright through the spaces.

It was a belfrey, and not only was there one large bell, the one used to toll over the dead, but several others, in the loft.

"Let's go up and have a look at 'em," remarked Frank.

So, letting the pack keep up their useless uproar, the two men ascended by a ladder.

On surveying the place they saw—

First, the bell that was in order, hung on its swinging-beam.

This was about six feet high, and four or five across the mouth.

The reason of its being so large was that it was necessary to have its note heard in the town, because (when any person of eminence was interred) the cathedral bell "took its time" by this one at the charnel-house.

Besides the pendant bell, were three more, small, coated with rust, cracked, half covered with cobwebs, in the corners.

They belonged to the cathedral chimes, but, having been broken, and replaced had been bundled off here as in a species of lumber room.

"Capital!" cried the young captain. "They're just light enough for handling and heavy enough to hurt!"

The two took hold of one of the chains and rolled it to the gap in the floor where the ladder came up.

The metal cup was too broad to fall through between the joists.

Cracked already, the bell had no sooner been pushed over to fall on the floor beneath than it fell into two pieces.

A second broke likewise, on being similarly treated.

The last one landed entire.

All three had sent up a doleful sound at the shock, as if in warning of the fatality to come.

Though the heavy falls had shaken the old building, the rabid animals, after a pause in wonder at the noise, had redoubled their barkings and growls.

"I can roll them through the staircase head myself," said Frank, "I'll go down and do it, while I am at that, suppose you take ny cutlass here, and see if you can't sever the supports of this big bell so that a touch will loosen it."

"Very well, it's a heavy old bit of metal, it would cast half a dozen small guns. Go on down, and I hope you will well ring the knell of those hairy crops, flesh and blood cannot longer stand such a racket as they keep up."

The young captain nodded, and descended.

When he went to the opening, from which he had cut away the stairs, the impatient hounds descried him in the shadow.

They began to leap up, crowded as they were,

and set up a howling that outdid all their previous efforts in that line.

This continuous hubbub of theirs had a very irritating effect.

Especially as to men who were thus imprisoned by the yelpers.

"Peace you cursed mongrels!" shouted Frank, rolling one of the pieces of bell metal to the aperture. "If you are hungry, here's something to blunt your appetite upon, and be hanged to you!"

As he spoke, he flung the missile through the opening.

It was heavy, jagged, and sharp at the edge.

The dogs were massed many deep under that very place.

The projectile fell on four or five, it severed the heads and limbs of them as if they had been under a guilotaine chopper·

The outcries changed to one of pain, but, almost instantly, the unhurt dogs drowned the yelps and groans in one vehement outburst of rage.

Frank pushed a second, and heavier fragment down into their midst.

It laid half a dozen low, maimed and crushed, bounced up from the floor, and falling again upon another or two of the brutes, caught them by the leg, and held them down under its weight.

These trapped 'beasts wrenched to get away, all the time vociferating their agony as their fruitless leaps tore the flesh from the imprisoned bones.

Their blood, and the others, had spurted on every side, and besprinkled the rest of the pack.

Its warm drops, tasted eagerly by them, if possible added to the fervor which the racema agave had imbued them with.

Spite of the havoc that had already visited them, they would not quit the space under the stairway.

They mounted up on the hill of dead, and sought to leap up from that gory elevation.

"Howl away, my beauties," said Frank, rolling the bell which had come down unbroken, "here's something more that I hope will stop your mouths!"

This whole bell required all the youth's power to move it, for he and Lance together had enough to do with it already.

By stooping down and putting his shoulder to it, he got it to the edge of the orifice, and only one vigorous push was needed now.

"I'll play old gooseberry with 'em, muttered Frank, resting a second. "Well, its either they or we that must give up the ghost, and I prefer the two legged creatures should be saved."

He laid both hands on the brazen rim.

The hounds were gathered thickly together, and he could see the gleaming of their teeth.

"It's one, two, and away!" cried Frank, heaving at the huge bowl.

Once launched into the air, in less than no time it was upon the pack.

It literally cut through the layer of living bodies, and smote the floor.

The percussion was so immense that the house shook from the foul air in the vault to the cross on the belfry top.

A long, doleful tremor of sound rang out from the fallen mass, as the blood of the slain streamed from its fatal edges.

But far above the moans, the shrieks of the canines that had been cleft in twain by the bronze edge, rose a warning shout.

"Stand from under, dear friend!"

It was Lance Cavendish who called.

Such was the fright in his voice, that Frank instinctively sprung aside and pressed himself closely to the shuddering wall.

There was a creaking, a swaying overhead corresponding with the shiver throughout the pile. Again Lance shouted out.

At very nearly the same moment, a crash was audible, followed by a dragging sound.

The bell, whose stops had been severed by Cavendish, had broken away the rest of its holdfasts when that shock had set it in motion.

And Frank hugging the wall, saw the ponderous circle smash through the rafters as though the floor had been pipe stems, and break through the floor that he stood upon no less easily than if it had been an egg shell.

Nor was its might descent checked by the ground floor.

With a hum emanating from its sides as it hurried though the air, it crushed down the planks as like many to those it had shot though above.

And, carrying down with it one awful mass of splintered wood, or mangled dogs glued together by the pressure and their own blood, the big bell entered the vault.

The house shook as if an earthquake was raging beneath it.

On the large gap being made, the great body of mephitic vopour collected since many a day in the underground chamber, sprang into freedom with a fierce and awful rush upwards.

In the briefest space, it had diffused itself all through the house.

Lance and Frank flung themselves down on their faces to avoid inhaling so sickening, and noxious an air.

Even as they feared that they would be poisoned, they were surprised by a peculiar hissing, as if a myriad of flying serpents were fighting all around about them.

It was a mystery to them, and they could see nothing.

It was a combat.

The aroma of the agave was in contact with this carbonic acid gas, and the conjunction of the two had evolved a new exaltation harmless to breathe, but deadly in another way.

For the carbonic acid gas being neutralised by the agave and both combined into the protochloride of oxy-ammoniacal gas, an alarming hiss, a hundred times louder than that evolved while the chemical change had been operating, sounded out.

The flame of the candle had fired the transformed air.

A blaze burst out down below and spread upwards and downwards as swift as light!

In each chamber there was an explosion.

But by far the heaviest, was the detonation in the vaults.

For the fire damp, sluggish for years, was fearful when in action.

The walls cracked from top to bottom.

The casements were blown out as if a cannon had been shot at them point blank.

THE SCARLET CRUISER

THE DESTRUCTION OF THE FREEBOOTERS' FLEET

Frank and Lance tried to rise and fly.

But already the broken building was coming down.

And besides, the flame had found food among the splinters, and its steadily increasing radiance betokened that the woodwork was afire.

With a crash almost equal to the thunder of the explosion, the upper stories fell in, and, in a few minutes, the ground it had stood, was covered with a misshapen heap of discolored stones, burning wood, whitened with time, blackened with smoke.

And out of this entanglement of destruction, scrambling over the half-buried, but yet living bodies of the dogs, roasting, wounded, in agony, **Lance Cavendish was stumbling in his way.**

His face and clothes were scorched, his eyes full of dust, and smoke; but, when he had got upon the firm ground, he did not fly from the scene, where conflagration was finishing the ruin, but searched as best he might for his young friend.

"It can't be that he only saved my life, that I should be left to mourn for him?" murmured he. sorrowfully. "At least, he shan't perish among those curs, and I'll turn over every stone,

and stick so that I shall have his body to weep over!"

He was unmolested, for those of the canines that had escaped the explosion, had scampered off at full speed.

While Lance was searching the heap of fired fragments, he heard the cathedral bell peal forth in the town.

The watchmen there had spied the fire, and no doubt people would be hurrying out to the cemetery.

Lance redoubled his exertions.

With a large club in his hand, he walked amid the smoke as if a salamander, and never ceased to call out the young captain's name.

But no answer came.

For a sound and good reason.

Accident made Cavendish turn over a number of the dogs' carcases.

To his joy, under them lay the form of the youth.

Dead or alive, he could not tell yet, but he quickly bore him out of the circle of fire.

With a strength that was wondrous, seeing how weak he was, and how much he had labored within the last few hours, the lieutenant carried his comrade's body away.

Soon after a number of people on horseback,

or on foot, hastened up to the spot.

Immense was their surprise on seeing the broken gate, the trampled tombs, the picked bones strewn here, and there, and the number of dogs roasting on the embers.

As they busied themselves entirely in striving to extinguish the fire.

Lance Cavendish was not noticed, as he stole cautiously away.

CHAPTER XXVIII.

THE SAILING OF THE PIRATE FLEET.—GENIFREDE LEARNS THE TRUTH ON LANCE CAVENDISH'S FATE —WILLIAM TEACH, SPITE OF HIS ONE ARM, SEEKS TO GRASP A GREAT DEAL—SOME STARTLING SIG-NALS FLYING.

THE mysterous affair of the profaned church-yard gave a quantity of excitement to the whole town of Matanzas.

A good many were not slow to say that if any human being had been at work there, as ally or otherwise of the dogs, they were the pirates of whom so many crowded the port.

This idea was in some degree supported, by many watchmen asserting that, soon after the fire had alarmed the town, a young man covered with dust, smoke, and blood, and on whose arm leant another youth, had been seen going to the waterside.

There, on one of them burning powder three times in a pistol as a signal, a boat had been put off from the Mortal Arrow, and taken them aboard that craft.

So, having pretty well settled that the buc-caneers had been up to some diabolical labour at the cemetery, the inhabitants were mightily pleased to see preparations on all the suspicions vessels for a departure that night.

Indeed, about eleven o'clock, as the night wind was in force, and the tide was running out, Blackbeard's pink got under way, and took the lead of the desperadoes' fleet.

When morning broke, they had all made the offing.

The day passed drearily on board all the crafts.

For the men were only just recovered from the debauch on shore, and were now miserable beings.

Their blood-shot eyes, cracked lips, languid movements, lack of life, in fact, made the crews resemble those of a plague-ship.

Some few had smuggled a little liquor on board, and were taking it off, what they called " tapering off the drunk."

Luckily there was little to do on board, after the sails had been set, and the officers humored the men's sulleness, knowing that the seabreeze would soon drift the lingering fumes of intoxica-tion out of them.

Now that the expedition had fairly started, the captains themselves took their ease.

The sun was hot, and an awning had been rigged up over the quarter deck of Blackbeard's vessel.

Under it, in the shade, lounged or reclined on soft carpets, spoil from some trader, Captains Loys, Teach, Brasilano and Kyd.

Lolonnais stayed on his own deck, as he had a young Spanish girl there, whose attractions made him often keep his cabin.

The rest of the rovers rarely embarrassed them-selves with putting such an article in the cargo list, as they said.

It was a pretty sight.

The sea all a-glitter in the sunbeams, the fading land in the far off, the half dozen vessels, under nearly all sail, careening as they bounded along.

The buccaneer chiefs, while regaling them-selves with pipe, cigarette, and wine-cup, chatted of future deviltries.

They looked upon the destruction of the Scarlet Cruiser as already completed, so confident were they.

Now that they were banded all together, what a fine chance to repeat the assaults on the towns of the rich Spaniards, in the same way as Drake, Morgan, and their compeers had stormed Panama, and Chagres.

"Belize has come rich planters near it," re-marked Brasilano, fingering his sword-hilt, "Old silver miners, who feed their bloodhounds on silver plate, and cover their horses with dollars."

"Aye," chimed in Kyd. "There is a man aboard my craft who told me how many thou-sand crowns they made Don Somebody pay down to ransom his daughters and house, and this Don lived near Belize. They found him obstinate at first——"

"They all are," observed Loys.

"They spoke of putting his wife head first into a rain-water butt, but he persisted in declaring he had no money or metal. But a threat to cut the ears off, his very beautiful daughters woke him up——"

"Ah!"

"Yes. And he disclosed where half his treasure was, under ground."

"Only half ?"

"Yes. But a little idea of the victors made him communicative."

"What was it ?"

"Simple thing; but ingenious. They tied his hand and his youngest daughter's together, and bound up a slow match between their united fingers. A touch of a cigar set the fusee fizzing——"

"I see !"

"Fine !"

"Original—as far as doubling the torture goes !"

So exclaimed the pirates, with faces lighted with their unfeigned agreeable astonishment.

"You see," went on Kyd, "you understand. When the match burnt down and the young girl's, and the old man's fingers began to scorch and melt together under the heat, the two set up a screaming, and the old senor yelled that he'd say anything thay had a mind to dictate from cursing the Virgin to telling where was the plate !"

"It's as devilish a trick as ever I heard," chorused all the chiefs.

And so the ball of conversation rolled between them, only that more horrifying than Captain Kyd's narrative were the atrocities that the rest recounted.

William Teach had been among the leaders for a time.

But his broken arm gave him great pain, and

the surgeon, or the rascal who acted as such to the ship, insisted in telling him that he could never heal the fracture if he persisted in carousing, and going without rest.

So, feeling no relief by drinking, and imagining that there might be some truth after all in what the surgeon said William went below to his berth

His state room was directly under the centre of the quarterdeck, and next the steward's pantry.

He could easily hear the voices of the captains close to him over his head.

He fell off into a doze, and yet the feverish state of his blood kept him sufficiently awake for him to understand what was being said.

For a time, the leaders had been chatting wickedly of one thing, and another, of their desperate deeds.

Kyd had led off the chorus in the noted song, made upon his own self, of—

"Oh, my name is Captain Kyd,
    And so wickedly I did!
As I sailed!"

And Brasilano had rhymed on his manner of treating the rightful owners of such unfortunate ships as crossed his course—

"We laid them aboard on the larboard side,
And we pitched the crew in the sea so wide,
And those of their number we left remain
We hung, cut down, and then hung again!"

Loys de Goupille, happening to be in a gentler mood than these other ocean tigers, warbled something mild in this style—

"I am thy true lover,
    Thou art my true dear!
I will never be false;
    That thou need'st not fear!"

Captain Teach uttered a long syllabled oath.

"Pooh! friend Loys! those mild as milk women are useless as a fair weather boat, used up in a storm. If we must have the soft sex, I cry out for the terific minxes, the girls like her in the old song—

"She took a musket then,
    And charged it up to the brim!
And says she, resign that other of mine,
    Or fire I will at him!"

While the verses were being roared out, Loys de Goupille left the group, and walked forward to fan his forehead in the spray-filled breeze swelling out the jib.

"Ah!" said Blackbeard, "you never saw this girl below in my cabin, she's Loys's daughter, he always says."

"Ho! some such a daughter as that bright eyed that keeps Lolonnais so much in his own state room," remarked Brasilano, with a sneer.

"Oh, no! she's some relation. He behaves very strangely with her—some days being very fond, and at others, not having half a dozen words to throw at her."

"Is she good looking?"

"A look from her would make a coward bold and tempt a saint to sin," returned Captain Teach.

"Here's her health then," said Brasilano, emptying a large partial-gilt goblet.

From thence they branched off into similar topics, and William Teach had to listen to glowing stories of beauties, Indian, Spanish, English, French, as each of the old corsairs took his turn at narrating.

Now, Master William had previously regarded Genefrede in no cold manner.

He had even gone so far of taste as to imagine some evil deed might be perpetrated if Loys should be ashore while he was on the ship.

The state of mind that he was in made him fit for any thing that would divert his thoughts.

Thus having a turn given to them, to linger longer was impossible to one of his unstable character.

He rolled over the edge of his bunk, uttering a curse as his broken arm began to ache poignantly at this change of posture.

"I've got a key to all the doors in the craft," said he, meaning that his dagger would pick any lock. "And if I once catch the girl with her eyes shut, she'll see may loving face close to her when she opens them, by George, she will!"

The cabin of the junk was not a large one.

William was quickly at its door.

On trying the handle stealthily, he found it locked inside.

He was about to make an essay at burglary, when, to his surprize, he heard voices within.

By clapping his ear to the keyhole he could distinguish that one was the girl's, and the other a man's, and that of a man known to him.

It was the steward.

"In the name of all that's hot," muttered the pirate, "what is that Spaniard hatching, I wonder, 'ware hawks, my lad, for I'm coming, and if I catch ye at any treachery, I'll make you sleep uncomfortable, by the living flames I will!"

Not to interrupt the colloquy, whatever it might be, the young man cautiously stole into the larboard spare room, next to Blackbeard's own.

He had to cut loose the gunport; but he easily did so, and lifted the lid.

It was a risky thing, this feat of his, for a one armed man to perform.

But he got out, clung to the main chains, keeping his figure bent to prevent those on the quarter-deck from seeing him, and worked his way aft on the out side streak of the vessel.

So doing, he reached the cabin windows

The stern of the junk was a mass of carving, fluting, scolloping, and in a word, as rough as the face of a rock.

He had but to twist his legs around a bar of iron, supporting a statuette, and a nosegay of flowers, each rose as big as a cabbage, and to wreathe his sound arm around another.

Then, peering carefully into the open window, he saw all he had expected to behold.

Genifrede was seated on the cushions of the after locker.

She had been reading for there was a book near her hand.

On a stool near her, was the steward.

This was a young Spaniard, who had a face that was at first sight honest and good natured.

But there was a lambent flame at present quiescent in his eyes that was kindling as he slily surveyed the young girl, who received his asseverations of fidelity as truth.

"Yes, lady," said Migel, as he was named, "I have long waited for a chance to aid some poor captive who might be on board such a nest of villains as this ship. I did my best to free the Englishman your friend, but that cub of the seahound William Teach guarded him too well!"

"Hallo!" muttered the listener outside, "is this the chap that made the nice cup of chocolate, senor, because you are ill with your arm!' I'll murder him!"

"I can hardly believe that Lieutenant Cavendish was on board," replied the girl. "Captain Teach said that he should be left on the island to die by the desertion."

"So he did, but his young hopeful stuffed him into a canvas bag, and they lugged him on board in the last boat like a sack of biscuit. I assure you he was brought here, for he is here at this present speaking——"

"The deuce he is!" muttered William a little amazed. "Then the dogs didn't eat him after all? Now, how in blazes does this Spanish traitor know this?"

But he saw at the next moment that Migel was only weaving his little story to gain his own ends.

For the steward continued:

"You, and he, and me, might manage an escape."

Genifrede's eyes lighted up.

"I can provision the boat hanging half here," went on the man, "and any night—this evening we could lower away and pull off. The crew are nearly all ill after their drunk."

"Oh, if you realey mean to lend us help, may heaven reward you!"

Migel said "Ahem!" to imply that he preferred some other recompense than any that might drop from the skies.

"It aint that," said he, "that will content me——"

"It's a kiss or two, dear one of my heart," said he, in a deep voice.

He saw the disgust only too plainly exposed in her convulsed face.

He hastened to lift his hand warningly.

"A breath," said he, "and the Englishman shall die! I'll tell old Teach he is here, and good bye to life with him! Did you ever dream of how Blackbeard can torture men he hates!"

"Oh, away!"

"Loved one, don't be tempted. Mind, a cry, and he will have the dagger at his heart! An hour's dalliance, and then we shall escape!"

"No! no! I shall call."

"Fool!"

"I shall call, come what may!"

"Will you? I'd like to see you!"

The Spaniard dexterously swung a heavy shawl forward, and with the art that his country women have in flirting a mantilla, completely muffled the head of Genifrede.

Her cry was utterly smothered beneath the thick woollen folds

As she tried to pull away the cloth, her horror was increased by the Spaniard seizing her arms.

He was holding her down, when it seemed to her (for she could not see) that something fell upon him and threw her, and him down on the cabin floor.

Then a flood of something almost scalding hot rushed over her bosom which had all its treasures laid bare by the rude hand of the ruffian. And next the latter's grasp relaxed.

There were the sounds, and the action of two men scuffling over her body.

By hearing alone did she follow the events of the struggle between the two men.

For, at the moment when Migel had had everything in his own way, and was already gloating over the innocent beauty at his mercy.

William Teach had scrambled through the port, and run him through with his knife.

The blade had missed the backbone narrowly, and the pain of so ghastly a wound had made Migel writhe like a bruised serpent.

Nevertheless, though his blood poured out as from a dolphin in a death-flurry, the steward turned round, and grappled the intruder fiercely.

For the latter's steel had been too deeply buried in the back of the Spaniard to be drawn out.

Then the fellow (burning with rage, and the smart of his wound) wrestled with the pirate, and, failing to twist his arm out of the socket, attempted to bite him.

"Cospeto! Maldito! puerco that you are!" he gasped, in intervals of the deadly conflict, "I will tear you as the tiger rends the flesh!"

"I'll be burned if you will!" returned William, bull-doggedly. "Come, come, none of that! you won't, eh! then put this—and this—in your cigar and smoke it!"

As he uttered this speech, he shook the steward so violently that the latter could not get a chance to bite, and had as much as he could do to keep his head on his shoulders.

William did not let the game rest there.

Following up the advantage in having quite confounded his opponent, he got his right hand free, and letting it fall with the speed, and force of the thunderbolt, he drove the steward's own knife up to the very haft into the body of the hapless villain. He fell, dead

William quickly turned from gazing at him.

Genifrede was endeavoring to tear off the shawl, and draw free respiration.

William threw his unhurt arm around her, and lifted her up, and put her upon the cushions of the after locker.

She had unloosed the knots of the shawl, and she stared like one before whom was a spectre at the sight of her rescuer.

Strange rescuer he, for he did the act of liberation to execute the contemplated crime himself.

Pale from his wound, yet flushed with passion, and the excitement of the strife, young Teach was no agreeable vision.

He was dabbled in blood from the Spaniard's death-gashes, and streaks of red on his broken arm told that the bandages had slipped, and the shot-cuts broken out the twists received in the combat.

He did not pause to indulge in any long oration about his love, but rattled off a score of words about "better give in or I'll serve you as I have that beggar," or "nouse whimpering! there's nobody dare to gainsay me when I speak up for a girl on this craft!" or "your man is food for the dogs hours ago, my lass!"

She uttered shriek upon shriek.

The men on deck could not help hearing, and their heavy, and hurried steps were to be heard decending the booby-hatch ladder.

William let go the girl for a space, emitting a frantic oath.

Leaping to the door he shot the inside bolt into its socket, and hastily dragged a chest up against it besides.

The voices of Loys de Goupille, and the other captains rose in wonderment on the threshold, and they began to push vainly at the barred panely.

William made no reply to their outcries ; but proceeded to carry out his vile design.

Genefrede had shrunk breathless into one corner.

She cowered down to the floor as the young villian came towards her, betraying that he had no mercy by the fiendish expression of his heated countenance.

The pounding continued at the door.

"No help for you, if they do break it down," hissed William Teach, lifting up the poor girl, who was all in a tremor of excessive fear.

"Father! Father!" Genifrede exclaimed, as she heard Loys calling out.

"An axe! an axe, I'll have the door down! I've broken my sword on it, death to it!"

Indead there was the end of a sword-blade bristling through a splintered cut in the lower panels, showing with what force the infuriated Frenchman had struck.

"Father! Father!" screamed she, as the the young pirate flung her down on the cushions once more, and strove to silence her.

"Peace! hush, I say, or I'll smother you!"

Fainter, and fainter grew her appeals under the pressure of the ruthless fingers on her delicate throat, weaker, and less availing became her resistance as the miscreant rushed on to his dastardly triumph.

Once only he paused.

A gunshot on the sea had startled all on board the pink.

During the pause, the lookout had shouted :

"Deck ahoy! something wrong with the Mortal Arrow! She's run up signals 'Mutiny!' and now the flag for 'Master overboard' is flying!"

Blackbeard left his compeers, and ran up on deck at that alarm.

The rest headed by Loys de Goupille, who had obtained a heavy battle-hatchet at last, continued to endeavor to force the disputed entrance.

Hope might well fly from pitiful Genefrede now. Aye well!

Totally at the mercy of that vagabond of the seas, the dark demon of despair could join in the horrible laugh of victory that William Teach set up as he bowed his fervid, polluting lips to profane the virgin cherries upon the young beauty's face!

CHAPTER XXIX.

LOLONNAIS IS AMAZED—"MY LIFE BUYS THESE SIXTY SOULS!"—HOW GALLANTLY PERISHED!—THE SHOT THAT ACHIERES SO MUCH RUIN!—THE NAVAL FIGHT.

THE piratical fleet had so far progressed as to be nearly within sight of Lesser Cat Island, where the Scarlet Cruiser was said to be beached.

Lolonnais judged it well to call all hands aft. They swarmed around him as he stood on the quarterdeck.

Rapidly he painted to them the delights of the life of ocean ravages.

"Won't you take oath, and be brave, daring, dashy, pirates, eh ?"

"We is agreeable," said Derrick, speaking for all, and winking slowly, "it was very fine thing to be pirates, mein frien's, eh ?"

"Oh, yes !"

"Good," said Lolonnais, in raptures. "I tell 'ee what : I'll prove to you what manner of man I am. In the first place we are all rovers, free as the breeze——"

"Oh, yew, free," said the Dutchman.

"We'll elect our own captain, and I'll only have the one voice like the rest of you."

All nodded.

"Have you made up your minds?" queried Lollonnais, after a while.

"All settled," returned the seamen.

Lolonnais rubbed his hands, they would surely choose him.

"Well, who shall be your leader ?"

"Frank! Hoorah !"

"Eh ?" and the master of the Mortal Arrow fairly staggered under his surprise. "Frank! who in the fiend's name is Frank ?"

At his question, the boy who had till then mixed in with the seaman like one of themselves, leaped upon the capstan, and flinging off his jacket, evposed a red velvet shirt on which were silver letters worked.

Lolonnais's amazement was immense at this sight. "Who are you gasped he.

The youth smiled, and waved his hand to all the sailors.

They flung off their caps, and like their young commander, pulled off their jackets, and overcoats, exposing the red shirts that were the uniform of the wolves of the waves.

"Who am I ?" said the youth, looking down on the astonished Lolonnais. "Who am I, men ?"

With one mighty voice, like the roar of a breaker on the shingle, the men cried :

"Hooray for the Captain of the Scarlet Cruiser !"

Lolonnais saw that he had been trapped. He must warn his comrades in crime at any hazards.

He rushed to the binnacle locker, smashed in the door with a kick, pulled out a roll of flags, unrolled them, and chose one, the signal-halyards off the clat, and bent on the green and yellow flag.

This he did with a seamanlike skill, and celerity that was truly admirable.

Before the Scarlets or their leader could well make out, the streamer was fluttering in the air far over head in its ascent to the vaneball.

As it spread out the other vessels read as aforesaid.

"Mutiny !" and they tacked, and stood for the Mortal Arrow on the instant.

"By George, that's let the cat out of the bag too soon !" cried Frank. "Down with him !"

Half a dozen men jumped up on the bulwarks, ran along aft, and climed the poop to sieze Lolonnais.

He stabbed one, but Derrick got a giant grip

of him with one of his leg-of-mutton fists.

Then Lolonnais yelled out in Spanish, to be heard by his mistress who was below,

"Mutiny, Coradon! Up, my love, and fire the train! There, you dogs, the fire will rob you of your capture!"

Half the crew, headed by Frank and Lance, ran below hatches.

But Coradon, with great quickness (for Lolonnais had so often expected a mutiny among his ugly crews that she was always in training for the event) had sprung off her seat, caught up a lighted candle, and lit a long slow match that ran from the cabin to the powder magazine.

When Lance, and the Cruiser's Captain reached the cabin level, they found themselves in the sulphur smoke curling up from the slow match, which was like a fiery serpent spitting flame. They would have passed on to trample it out, but they were confronted by Coradon.

The beautiful Spanish girl had taken up a pair of pistols, and levelled them at the oncomers.

Jack did not retrace his steps; but darted on.

One of the pistols went off and the sailor fell dead in his tracks. The rest, recoiled even Frank himself. The men on deck called for the Captain.

"The other ships are wearing round, and are making for us, sir!" said Cambering the mate. "Do come on deck, sir!"

Frank ran up the stairs, and seeing that a fight was imminent, ordered the signal to be hauled down and another bent on. This was run up off hand, and the shake was given to the halyards to unroll its ball.

The streamer was the signal for "Master overboard!"

"It won't do to tell a lie!" said Frank. "Derrick, roll that rascal into the sea!"

The Dutchman lifted up Lolonnais in his sturdy embrace, and hurled him over the counter.

"Now!" said the young commander "Clear for action! double shot the guns! and hoist at the main the Scarlet Cruiser ensign, and at the foreold Rawhead, and Bloody-bones!"

So at the mainmast head flaunted defiantly the Scarlet banner, and at the fore the black flag on which glistened the red skull, and the bleached bones! In the meantime, Lance Cavendish had been urging on the seaman to dare all that the woman could do. She could only kill one more; but who would be that one?

The match was fizzing in a sinister manner, and in five seconds the powder would be reached, and all would be crushed amid the sundered timbers, amid the flames, amid the devastation!

Then Lance stepped forward one stride.

"Sixty souls shall not perish because one man seeks to save his breast from being a bullet's cave!"

"Messmates, I go to my death!"

He sprang forward. The pistol exploded, and the ball pierced the lieutenant through and through. The life stream spurted out fearfully copiously both over his breast, and down his back. But he never winced nor omitted a sound. Resolutely he had set about his task of devotion. He flung himself on the blazing powdertrain and let his blood pour upon it. On that fiery track he died as on the bed of honor! The Spanish girl was bound hand, and foot, and

bundled into a corner. All went upon deck. The Mortal Arrow was surrounded by the freebooter's fleet. Her guns were run out both sides.

Ned Nittle was at the long Toms.

"What d'ye wait for?" inquired the captain of him.

"A ginger pill," answered he.

He meant a red hot chain shot, which was brought from the galley fire to be rammed into the pivot gun. He aimed at Blackbeards pink, which was nearest, and let fly. It struck her in the cabin windows. That was the juncture when William Teach had stood over Genefrede's prosate form. The two cannon balls fastened to one another by the bolt, knocked the two stern windows into one like cardboard, cut William Teach in two pieces, and tore onward through the door at which Loys, Kyd, Brasilano, and others were hammering. The redhot missile ploughed through their thick ranks and still continued its destructive flight. Smash through solid bulkheads till into the magazine it whanged. The powder room had just been opened to serve out ammunition for the action.

The twin ball ran swiftly over the iron floor, and stove in several kegs. There was one hiss, a flash that spread far, and wide, and an explosion that sounded in those wretches' ears as if hell had burst up, and overwhelming the earth. On the Arrow they saw a dense cloud of orange, and whiteblue vapor covered over the pink. When it blew aside the vessel had been transformed into splinters which floated on the stained, and bubbling waters, with horrifying scorched shreds of human flesh attached! This was the end. The Arrow beat off the other vessels, whose men were bereft of their usual leaders. Among the few survivers, Blackbeard was picked up. The young captain took him to Matanzas, and landed him, leaving him a bag of doubloons, and bidding him live honestly. But old Teach took to the old path, and closed his sinful days on the gibbet that stands at the end that broad road of crime. Frank took the Arrow to Cat Island, where the Cruiser lay. A fair division was made of the rich spoils. When the young captain summoned all around him

"My real name is William Lovell," said he, "and I am of Bristol, England, If ever you are distressed, all or one, come find me, and be sure my last coin, and last biscuit will be shared with those gallant hearts who made so famous the Scarlet Cruiser."

"Good luck with you Captain!" cried all.

"Aye," said Ned Nittle dolefully, "all the good luck goes with you. We'll never know such deeds of daring, and adventure again."

"No one knows" answered Lovell (as we may call him), "we are young yet, and perhaps in the future there are incidents still more startling mysteries of the sea, and its wonders yet more awful, actions of villany, and heroism far more enthralling, for you or I to pass through!"

[To see that the young captain spoke true one has but to regale himself with the splendid pages (gilded with magnificent romance, and vivid facts) which form the "CRIMSON CORSAIR; or, the Queen of the Pirates!"]

THE END.